Ma

H

Also by Marian Murphy

Take 2

Millions

Making *it* Home

MARIAN MURPHY

POOLBEG

This novel is entirely a work of fiction. The names, characters and incidents portrayed in it are the work of the author's imagination. Any resemblance to actual persons, living or dead, events or localities is entirely coincidental.

Published 2003
by Poolbeg Press Ltd
123 Grange Hill, Baldoyle
Dublin 13, Ireland
E-mail: poolbeg@poolbeg.com

1 3 5 7 9 10 8 6 4 2

A catalogue record for this book is available from the British Library.

ISBN 1-84223-077-8

Typeset by Patricia Hope in Palatino 10/14.5
Printed by
Litografia Rosés S.A., Spain

www.poolbeg.com

About the Author

Marian Murphy lives in Wicklow with her husband and two sons. She has been writing for five years since attending a creative writing class whose tutor, poet Eileen Casey, has been an ongoing source of support and encouragement to her.

Making It Home is Marian's third novel. The first two, *Take* 2 and *Millions*! were also published by Poolbeg, and *Millions*! has recently been published in German.

Acknowledgements

This story has been a long time in the telling.

And it's a love story.

Actually, two love stories.

It began as the story of Michelle, who is searching for a house, and it grew to include the story of Charles, a fictional character who went to fight in the First World War with his brother Hugh and never made it home.

My first, and most heartfelt, acknowledgement goes to my grandfather, Jack Merner, RIP, who survived the First World War trenches, lived well into his eighties, and gave me the idea for the 'story within a story' in this book.

His two brothers fought in the war with him and one of them, Daniel, died in battle at the age of twenty-two.

And what my grandfather remembered – or at least what he talked about – all those years later was his sergeant-major's instruction that *"if your brother falls in front of you, jump over him and keep on going"*.

I wondered how that must have felt, for a man with his two young brothers there, to be told such a thing.

And so, before ever I thought of writing a novel, the spark was there.

Suppose two brothers went off together to the First World War? Suppose one of them never came home? Suppose the other . . .

So, my thanks to Granda Jack, as we called him. And to Daniel, whom we never knew but whose memory was with us as I wrote.

I'll keep the other acknowledgements very brief!

So – thank you, everyone! –

– Liam, Luke and Michael, who know that I couldn't do it – *any* of it – without them . . .

– All the rest of the family who – among so many other things – bought *loads* of my books (Hint to Aspiring Authors – marry into a big family. And have a Dad with a gift for telling stories and organising book launches) . . .

– My friends in SJH, who supported me from the beginning, and in Naas, who spurred me on to the finish – especially Suzanne and Fran, who told me all about wood-turning (of which I only used a tiny bit – but hadn't we a great day!) . . .

– Mary, John and Emily, who took us (and the manuscript!) sailing in West Cork for a few perfect summer days, when that was *exactly* what we needed . . .

– Bernadette and Thomas, who were standing by with champagne for the finish (and who helped us drink it with two chapters still to go) . . .

– Eileen Casey, who came to the rescue with her

usual generosity of spirit and sound advice when I hit writer's block and stalled for a week, two chapters from the end (Other Hint to Aspiring Authors – save the champagne until the book is actually *finished*) . . .

– Bernie, who did a lot of listening, and all our friends who were generous with their dinner invitations (maybe *too* generous – my next novel's about losing weight!) and who will now, finally, get an invite back as the dining-room re-emerges from under the manuscript . . .

– My neighbours, friends, and 'support team' in the local shops who reminded me, whenever I needed reminding, that I should be at home writing. You kept me going! . . .

– Sean Connolly of the Royal Dublin Fusiliers Association who was quick and generous with the information I needed at the very last minute . . .

– All at Poolbeg, especially Paula and Kieran, who were patient and understanding when an unfortunate encounter on a twisty road (long story – for another time) put a stop to my gallop for months and months . . .

– Gaye Shortland, editor and friend. Here I run out of words – but she knows them all . . .

– And you, the reader, without whom we writers are only half the story. Hope you enjoy this one!

Marian

For Liam, Luke and Michael.
Again!

Chapter One

There wasn't a sound as the auctioneer's gaze swept the room one more time. Michelle Larkin tightened her grip on her husband's hand, hardly daring to breathe as she glanced over her shoulder in an attempt to see who had just upped the bidding to four hundred and ninety thousand euro.

She caught a glimpse of him at the back of the room – the horrible little man with the wispy beard and scuffed shoes who had barged past her on her first visit to the house, grabbing the last brochure from the auctioneer and acting as if he already owned the place. And now he had made what looked like the final bid for the house. *Her* house. She couldn't bear it. She took a deep breath and shot her hand up as the auctioneer raised his gavel. He paused, nodding slightly in her direction to acknowledge the new bid.

"For God's sake, Michelle!" Rory whispered urgently to her. "We can't –"

"*Shhh!*" she said, eyes fixed on the auctioneer whose calm, assured tones were echoing round the room.

"Five hundred thousand. I have five hundred thousand euro on my right."

The gavel was raised again. Michelle thought she'd explode with tension. Any second now –

"Five hundred and thirty thousand!"

There was a stir towards the back of the room as people craned to look at the bidder.

Him again! Michelle thought, her heart lurching as she began to raise her hand once more in response to the auctioneer's inquiring look. *Way* over budget, but –

"Stop!" Rory said, loudly enough this time for several heads to turn in *his* direction. "It's gone, Michelle."

"But –" One look at Rory's expression brought her to her senses. Reluctantly she looked back towards the auctioneer, shook her head slightly, tried not to cry as the house was knocked down to the man with the wispy beard.

"Let's go," Rory said, leading her firmly from the room as people began making their way towards the door.

"But maybe –"

"Maybe nothing, Michelle." They reached the footpath, walked the few yards to where the car was parked. "We knew it was out of our league," he added as they got in. "I was mad to let you talk me into coming in the first place!"

They were silent as he manoeuvred out into the Saturday-morning traffic, silent for most of the short journey home.

The house still filled her thoughts. She had fallen in love with it the minute she saw it. A double-fronted redbrick close to the South Circular Road with plenty of space and, best of all, a good-sized back garden for Katie. Exactly what she was looking for. And she had been so sure it would be theirs . . .

"We couldn't have managed it, you know," Rory said quietly, breaking into her thoughts. "Not with the way the business is going –"

"Yes, we could!" Michelle's voice was sharper than she intended. She had visited the house several times, walked past it every day for the last two weeks. She had wanted it so much. She knew what colour she'd paint the front door, where she'd put every single stick of furniture . . .

Counting her chickens, her mother had warned her. But this time, after nearly six months of searching, Michelle had finally found a house she wanted. And they had a serious and substantial offer on their own. Their auctioneer would be pressing them for a decision any day now.

Their house was fine, a little two-up two-down in Harold's Cross, and even with the slight downturn in the market, worth far more than they could ever have imagined. A fortune, Michelle had thought – until she realised that the kind of house they were looking for would cost way more than they could afford.

Maybe they needed to re-think their budget again . . .

"We could just stay here, you know," Rory said as he turned into their road, searching for a space to park.

She glanced at their house as they drove past, seeing Katie's little face at the window. She waved, and her daughter smiled and started tapping the window. Any minute now she'd be crying to go outside.

And that was part of the trouble, of course. There was nowhere outside that was safe for a three-year-old to play. The 'back garden' was barely large enough for the clothes-line and the dustbins, while the narrow little footpath to the front of the house was no protection against the increasing volumes of traffic that used their road as a rat-run morning and evening and, it seemed recently, every minute in between.

There was nothing else for it, she thought.

Whether Rory wanted to or not, they just *had* to move.

Chapter Two

Michelle sat cross-legged on a heap of cushions, running her hand distractedly through her hair as she looked at the pile of property details spread around her on the polished floorboards.

"This one?" she asked without much hope, lifting an A4 sheet with its glossy picture of a thirties-style semi-detached house.

"You've seen it, remember?" her sister Sarah said, taking the sheet and adding it to one of two piles on the floor in front of her. "Week before last. It was that place with the dry rot, wet rot or whatever it was. And a north-facing back garden."

Michelle sighed and continued sifting through the pages. "It wasn't the worst."

"No," Sarah agreed. "These were." She reached across to take several pages from the floor in front of Michelle.

They bent over the brochures together for a moment, dark brown heads almost touching, two pairs of brown eyes focused in concentration, looking like the twins they were often assumed to be. "Remember this one?"

Michelle had to laugh in spite of herself as she looked at the picture Sarah was holding up. Remember it? She'd probably have nightmares about it for the rest of her life . . .

"Can you trust one word an auctioneer says?" she asked, still laughing. "Fabulous views, my granny! The back of the local supermarket!"

"He did say it was convenient for the shops," Sarah reminded her.

"Okay, so that bit was true. Just about. What he *didn't* mention was that great big hole in the kitchen floor and the wires sticking out of the walls and the ceiling that nearly collapsed on us!"

"*'In need of some slight renovation'*," Sarah quoted from the brochure. "Obviously an optimist, whoever wrote it!"

"God, optimism! They should send all the optimists out looking for a place of their own and see how *they* feel after six months!"

"So the fun's finally gone out of it?" Sarah asked, gathering up the remaining leaflets into one neat pile.

"*Fun?*" Michelle exploded. "You think this is *fun*?" The phone rang and she jumped to her feet to answer it.

"You told me you loved it," Sarah said.

Michelle pulled a face, reaching for the phone. "A

few months back, maybe. *Definitely* not now!" She leaned against the old writing-desk, the phone to her ear. "Hello?"

It was Jim Farrell, their auctioneer. By the time she finished the brief conversation Sarah was standing by the table at the far end of the room, re-sorting the leaflets into several piles.

"Throw them all out, I'm sick of looking at them," Michelle said crossly, coming across to stand beside her, arms folded, glaring down at the glossy pages.

"All of them? But –"

"All of them," Michelle repeated firmly. "I couldn't live in any of them – this place is small, but at least it's not falling down around our ears!"

"You could always stay," Sarah suggested, making a final sweep of the sheets and dumping them in the wastepaper basket by the desk.

"I *could,*" Michelle said. "But I've my heart set on moving now. Besides, Rory's finally come round to the idea. If I tell him it's off he'll hit the roof! It's all we've talked about for months . . ."

Sarah laughed. "Don't I know! Talk about being obsessed! Still, you shouldn't back yourself into a corner."

Michelle sighed. "I feel I already am. Farrell says the buyers are pushing and if we don't let them know today, they're not interested."

"But where would you go, if you sell now?" Sarah asked, startled.

"That's the problem, isn't it?" Michelle stretched, yawned. "Come on, we've been stuck in here too long. Mam will be back with Katie in an hour or so. Feel like a walk?"

"Where to? The auctioneer in Rathmines?" Sarah asked with a grin, already reaching for the jacket she'd tossed on the chair.

"A *real* walk!" Michelle insisted, heading for the front door, collecting her own jacket from the hallstand and keys from the little table as she passed. She buttoned the jacket, pulled a hat from the pocket, waited as Sarah slammed the door behind them. "But if we *happen* to pass any interesting places . . ."

"We'll ignore them and keep going!" Sarah added, laughing. "Come on, let's head for the canal. Should be safe enough there!"

It was a gorgeous day, unusually warm for early April. The sisters walked briskly along the canal bank, stride matching stride. Sarah, at 5'6", was taller by an inch, but otherwise there was little to distinguish them. Narrow faces, dark intelligent eyes and rich brown hair tucked up under soft hats. They had the same slim bodies, the same habit of moving their hands as they spoke.

"Any word from Helen?" Sarah asked as they neared the top of the Rathmines Road. Michelle, resisting the temptation to turn towards the village and the auctioneers' windows, grimaced. Their elder sister had never been her favourite person, but she was particularly irritating at the moment.

"Only the usual tarantara on the phone about how I should stay at home with my child instead of thinking about going back to work. As if I had a choice!"

Sarah hesitated for a moment before answering. She didn't often agree with Helen, but in this case . . .

"But you do, don't you?" she said finally. "Have a choice? I mean, you could stay at home with Katie and give up the idea of taking on a bigger mortgage . . ."

Her voice trailed off as she saw Michelle's expression.

"And then what?" Michelle asked. "Sit at home like I've been doing, stuck in that little box of a place, while Katie starts playschool and then school and I'm left climbing the walls?"

"You could –" Sarah began.

"Don't even go there, Sarah," she warned. "Just don't! You're as bad as Helen, you know that?"

She regretted it the minute she said it. She knew she had a lot to be grateful for, and it was no secret that that's exactly what Sarah wanted, to stay at home with a child of her own. So far, it just hadn't happened for her. "Sorry," she muttered. "Don't know what's up with me at the moment."

Sarah was quick to forgive. "The house, that's what's up," she said, slipping an arm round Michelle's shoulders. "It's really getting to you, isn't it?"

Michelle nodded, sighed. "I don't think I'd have bothered looking in the first place if I'd known how hard it would be. It *seemed* like a good idea – a bit of space for Katie, nice big rooms I could do something with, a room for Rory to use as an office, somewhere to park the car. Not much to ask, is it?"

"Depends how much you're willing to spend! That's the other thing – you know I think it's mad to be putting yourself under that kind of pressure. You're looking at a mortgage of, what? A hundred and fifty thousand?"

"Rates have gone down again," Michelle said brightly. "And I'll get an extra bit off. Working in a bank has its advantages!"

The career break Michelle had taken following her maternity leave was due to finish in just over four months, and part of her couldn't wait to get back to work. She missed the buzz, lunch with the girls, having money of her own to spend.

Not that there'd be much of that, she reminded herself, if they went ahead with this house idea.

"It's still a lot to take on . . ." Sarah said.

"As Rory keeps telling me! The thing is – counting my chickens again! – Jan said the other day that personnel finally got their act together and those promotions will be coming up at the end of the summer. I'm in with a good chance, but only if I'm back at work. It would mean a good bit more money."

"And a lot less time to yourself!" Sarah reminded her. "Taking on a new house, maybe one that needs fixing up – you won't have a minute if you're working."

"I'll manage!" Michelle said, her face taking on the

set expression that warned Sarah there was no arguing with her. "Besides –" she stopped in mid-stride, turned to face Sarah. "I kind of have to, don't I? I started this. And you know what I'm like."

Only too well, Sarah thought, but knew better than to say it out loud. Once Michelle got an idea into her head it took a lot to change her mind. 'Determined', Sarah called her. 'Stubborn', Helen insisted, loudly and often.

"And Rory is still going along with it?"

Michelle smiled, her whole expression lifting. "Just about. He's getting a bit fed up with the searching and stuff at this stage, but he says he'll hang in there for another while. He's great, really. And I'm lucky to have him. Anyone else would've packed my bags for me long ago!"

"Too sure," Sarah laughed, thinking it was probably true. Her brother-in-law had a lot going for him, but best of all was his ability to see through Michelle's stubbornness – *determination*, she corrected herself – to her warmth and energy, her enthusiasm for new ideas. Without that energy they'd probably still be living in the cold top-floor flat they'd had for several years in Rathmines, instead of that gorgeous little house of theirs. And Rory was the first to recognise it.

They walked along chatting, Michelle keeping an eye on the auctioneers' signs outside several of the houses along the canal. She had seen most of them advertised already, but there was always something – too big, too small, too expensive, too totally horrible – to put her off looking at them seriously. And yet the time had come to *be* serious, or she'd lose these buyers and have to wait God-knows-how-long for the next lot . . .

"I'd better talk to Rory tonight. I mean, really talk."

"You mean you don't?" Sarah teased.

Michelle gave an impatient 'tut'. "About the house, you know what I meant! Farrell said they want to move in by the end of June."

"That's a bit tight, isn't it?" Sarah asked, alarmed. "Ten or eleven weeks? You'll never find somewhere else by then!"

"We could rent," Michelle said, a bit defensively. She had always told Sarah she was mad to be paying out rent until Sarah finally gave in and bought her own little apartment, just over a year ago.

"Or move in with Mam and Dad," Sarah suggested. "Better than paying out dead money."

"Not much!" Michelle said, and was immediately sorry. Her parents were the best going. They'd be happy to have herself and Rory, and as for Katie – Michelle sometimes felt she could disappear off the face of the planet and her mother and daughter wouldn't notice, they were so caught up in each other . . .

Is that what's wrong? she wondered. *Am I jealous?*

But it wasn't in her nature to be jealous. Most of the time she was delighted to see the close relationship between them.

No, she decided. *I just don't want to go back to living at home again, no matter how good they are.*

"It wouldn't work," she said, in response to Sarah's quizzical look. "I don't want to go back to feeling like a kid again. And it wouldn't be fair to Rory. Anyway, I just want to get this sorted and get on with my life!"

"So, should we go and have a look at those auctioneers?" Sarah suggested.

"Thought you'd never ask!" Michelle laughed, as they left the canal and turned back along the road to Rathmines. "Let's see what's new since – when was it? – two days ago!"

It was the usual story at the auctioneers. Vague talk of a fluctuating market, promises to keep in touch – and nothing with four walls still standing for less than three hundred and fifty thousand euros.

* * *

"Monopoly money," she said crossly to Rory that evening. "Where do they get off, asking that kind of money for that kind of rubbish?"

"We're asking a fair bit ourselves," he said reasonably. "If we're still going ahead, that is. And you have to admit most of them aren't rubbish – they're just too expensive for us."

"What do you mean, if we're still going ahead?" Michelle asked. He looked exhausted, she noticed, and this probably wasn't the best time to be getting into it, but they hadn't had a chance to talk until Katie was tucked up in bed. First thing in the morning she was going to have to ring Farrell, one way or the other.

Rory looked uncomfortable for a moment and then took the plunge. "We said we'd give it six months, right? And if we hadn't found somewhere by then, we'd leave it for a year or two?"

"I know," she said, getting up and crossing to sit beside him on the sofa, her fingers reaching to caress the back of his neck. "But it's not six months for another two weeks. And we *did* find that great place in McMahon Street – we just didn't have a buyer for our own then. So at least if we sell here . . ."

"We'll be sleeping in the back of the van for the summer," he said lazily, smiling at her. "You're distracting me, you devil, and you know it! You know my weak points . . ."

"And I know what's good for you!" she laughed. "Come on, Rory, think about it! Imagine having space at home for an office, no more hacking your way through traffic –"

"I take great exception to your description of my driving!" he said, raising an eyebrow, the corner of his mouth twitching as he suppressed a smile. He began slowly to caress her shoulder, looking as if the last thing on his mind was taking exception to anything. "Want to continue the discussion upstairs? It's more comfortable . . ."

"No – wait – " She pushed him back a little, resisting the temptation to snuggle in against him. "We have to let him know tomorrow . . ."

"So go for it. Tell him we'll sell. I'll move in with my

mother-in-law – she's not that bad! Or with that sister of yours, Hellish Helen. Whatever. Now, come on, let's go to –"

"Rory, be serious! Please! Just for a minute –"

"I *am* serious," he said, reaching for her hand and looking intently at her. "I was thinking about it today, and you're right. If we sell we'll have ready money when something comes up. So go for it. You really want this move, right? We'll sell, and I'll manage a few days off and we'll hit every auctioneer in town. *Someone's* got to have what you're looking for."

"You're the best, you know that?" she said.

"So show me." He stood up, reaching out his hand to take hers.

She laughed. "Save your energy for slogging round the auctioneers!"

"Oh, you can do that bit! Me, I'll use the Internet . . ."

"Whatever," she said. "Now, we'll need to – "

"Shush," he said, bending to kiss her. Tomorrow they'd accept the offer and begin their search in earnest. But right now, tomorrow was a long way off . . .

Chapter Three

The pub in Rathmines was bursting at the seams, and Michelle almost suggested giving it a miss and going back to her place. But Jan was already grabbing a tray and taking her place in the queue, looking enthusiastically along the counter to see what was on offer.

"The stroganoff looks good," she mused, as Michelle picked up her own tray and tried to find something that might tempt her flagging appetite.

"Still no luck?" Jan asked sympathetically as she staked a claim to one of the little round tables as the occupants were reaching for their coats.

"Nothing." Michelle grimaced.

They sat down gratefully and Michelle began toying with her stir-fried chicken as Jan tucked into the stroganoff.

"Something wrong with it?" Jan asked, noticing

after a minute or two that Michelle wasn't eating much. "It looks good – I was sorry I didn't go for it myself."

Most weeks Jan said the same thing. It was the one thing that still annoyed Michelle after ten years of friendship – Jan's inclination to want whatever Michelle had chosen. Still, it was hardly a big deal, she told herself. Jan was great most of the time. She gave Michelle loads of support and encouragement, and right now that counted for a lot.

"It's okay," Michelle answered. "I just don't have much of an appetite these days. I'm too distracted."

Jan laughed. "Wish that happened me!" It was a standing joke that Jan needed to watch her weight like a hawk while Michelle could eat whatever she wanted and not show a bit of it.

"Trust me, you don't!" Michelle took a small mouthful, then another. It actually wasn't bad, she thought, but eating seemed like a real effort at the moment. Everything did.

"How long now before you've got to move?" Jan asked.

"Thanks, Jan! I was trying to forget it for a while!"

"No, come on – if there's a deadline you're better off facing it and planning for it."

Trust Jan to take that approach, Michelle thought. Jan was speaking in her best business voice, the one she used when making all those high-flying presentations at work. And at work it was perfect – crisp, professional, efficient. But right now Michelle could have done without it when all she really wanted was to enjoy their weekly chat before she had to spend the afternoon, yet again, going through the newspapers, or on the phone to auctioneers.

"Let's just have lunch and not talk about houses," Michelle suggested. "Come on, fill me in on all the gossip!" Normally that's how they spent these lunch hours, with Jan bringing Michelle up to date on the happenings at the bank where they both worked.

"Nothing much going on," Jan said dismissively. "Besides, you really *do* need to think about this. No point trying to avoid it."

As if she could think about anything else, Michelle thought, suppressing a sigh. She could have done without Jan pushing her right now. She was brilliant at dishing out encouragement, but there were times . . .

Jan was looking at her expectantly and Michelle abandoned any thoughts of avoiding the topic.

"Closing's in eight weeks," she said quietly. "And I'm beginning to wish I'd never started this!"

"But since you have, you've no choice but to keep going. Although," she paused reflectively, "I suppose you could always back out, couldn't you? Leave it until there was a bit more on the market?"

"No," Michelle said, shaking her head firmly. "There's plenty on the market at the moment, so if we wait any longer we might find it harder to sell our own. Besides, I couldn't do that to them. They're a young couple with a small baby and she's expecting another, and they've been let down twice already."

Jan's expression said clearly that Michelle was mad, but she only shrugged. "Are you finished with this?" she asked after a minute, beginning to pick at Michelle's abandoned meal, hardly waiting for a 'yes'. "What about the place you saw the other day?" she asked, between mouthfuls.

Michelle sighed, pushing her plate across towards Jan. "Smaller than our own and you'd want to see the state of the kitchen! Nothing like it said in the brochure. Some of those auctioneers should be shot!"

"They're not all bad!" Jan said a bit defensively. Her cousin Andrew was an auctioneer in County Laois.

"I didn't say they were," Michelle said hastily. "I've met a few lovely guys, but it's a house I'm looking for, not a man! I just wish they'd tell the truth a bit more often."

"Like, *'Ordinary, very boring little house in run-down area, three poky bedrooms and tiny back yard, ridiculous asking price, but we know you're desperate'?* Jan suggested. "Something like that?"

Michelle laughed in spite of herself. The description was a bit too close for comfort to some of the places she'd seen recently.

"So what are you *really* looking for?" Jan asked for the umpteenth time, taking the last mouthful of chicken.

"Anything, at this stage!" Michelle pushed her hair back impatiently. She'd spent the past two weeks in a panicky search for somewhere, *anywhere*, even remotely suitable as the deadline drew closer. "I'm trying to be a bit realistic about what I want. Forget about original fittings and a parking space now – I just want something big enough with a little garden, that doesn't cost a fortune! And not too far from town."

"Beggars can't be choosers!" Jan said lightly. "I still don't understand why you have to live in the middle of everything. If it's space you're looking for, what about somewhere *outside* Dublin? Loads of people commute these days, and Andrew says –"

"Jan, Andrew's in *Laois*, for God's sake! There's no way we're driving up from Laois!"

Jan laughed. "I don't mean Laois, idiot! But you don't want the suburbs, and there's nothing much around here you can afford. You've looked at masses of houses and still you haven't found anything. So maybe it's time to think of something different. Close to Dublin, but without Dublin prices. Somewhere like Meath or Wicklow or Kildare . . ."

"Jan, get real! Can you see Rory's face if I suggested that? Besides, there's no way I'm leaving Dublin! Damien might talk night and day about going back down home, but believe me, it's not everyone's idea of –"

"He's given up the idea," Jan interrupted, clearly uncomfortable. She and Damien had had yet another row on the subject just last night. "*He* wanted to do it the hard way, moving sixty miles from Dublin, for God's sake, to the back end of nowhere. I told him he could go, but he'd be going on his own!"

"But it's okay for me and Rory?"

Jan shrugged, grinning. "Suit yourself! It was just a thought, that's all. You were the one drooling over that picture in *The Independent* last week –"

"The farm in Kilkenny?" Michelle asked. "It *was* gorgeous, wasn't it? All that space outside, and four bedrooms, and we'd have money left over from our own! Pity it wasn't a bit closer to Dublin . . ."

"Like, right beside Bewley's in Grafton Street?" Jan asked, laughing. "Okay, I give in! So you're a city girl at heart. You wouldn't just ask them to sell you that gate-lodge place in Stephen's Green, would you? I've always fancied it myself!"

"Now, *there's* an idea!" Michelle said, standing up to get their coffee. "Wonder how much that would cost?"

Jan laughed again. "You could always talk Rory into doing whatever it is you have to do to be let live there!"

"Mmm. Might be easier than getting him to move to Kildare . . ."

"Don't close off any options! You might be glad of a place in Kildare in eight weeks' time."

She might be glad of anywhere at all by then, no matter *what* it was like, Michelle thought glumly as she queued for their coffee. It was starting to look like her worst nightmare, with the house sold and nowhere to go. How long now before they would have to start looking for a place to rent or, worse still, think about going back home?

She wasn't sure exactly why that felt like the very

last thing she wanted. Something to do with trying to live as an adult in her childhood home, she thought. To her parents she'd probably always be a child. Fine, ten or fifteen years ago – but hard to take now, at almost thirty-four. And it wouldn't be fair to Rory at all, even though he got on well enough with them. No, she'd really have to find somewhere of their own, at least to rent.

As for Jan's idea of moving to the country, forget it. They had never even considered that before, and there was no good reason for doing it now. Except the prices, of course. Jan was right about that. This morning's post had included an updated brochure from a Terenure auctioneer who also handled country property, and she found herself thinking again of a house on his list, near Roundwood in County Wicklow, that had been on the market for a while, so the price was reasonable and the sellers were open to offers. Not that she and Rory would even think about living there, of course – but they might just go and have a look. It would do them good to get out of the city for a few hours at the weekend . . .

"I might go down to Wicklow with Rory tomorrow," she said to Jan as she came back with the coffee. "Just to have a look around. I always loved the mountains . . ."

"Sure, for Sunday walks," Jan said. "Living there's a different matter."

Michelle laughed. "I thought *you* were the one raving about the country! Anyway, we've no intention of living there, I'm just going to have a look. I'll go mad if I stay in the house any longer, going over and over those brochures from the auctioneers."

"Mind you don't fall in love with a place in the back of beyond," Jan laughed. "It's hard enough getting to work in the mornings without being stuck in a traffic jam halfway up the Dublin mountains!"

Michelle grimaced. "God, I'd forgotten the hassle of getting to work. I won't know what's hit me once I go back!" Even she had to admit that punctuality had never been her strong point.

"So stay where you are," Jan suggested again. "It's as close as you'll get to town, and it's gorgeous, even if you think it's a bit small. You don't know how lucky you are, getting it before property prices went through the roof."

It was a constant refrain of Jan's, how she wished she and Damien had bought somewhere when they had the chance. But they were still renting, because Damien had said time and again that he'd never settle in Dublin, and Jan had never found a house that appealed to her anyway. Except Michelle's. She'd always loved it, and often joked that it should have been hers, if only she'd seen it before Michelle did.

Before putting the house on the market Michelle had asked Jan if she was interested – but Damien was still dead against Dublin and anyway, Jan said, the price was now way out of their reach. But she said it cheerfully, to Michelle's relief, with no hint of ill-feeling.

Michelle shook her head now as she reached for her bag. "We're committed now, so we can't stay even if we wanted to," she said. "Which I don't. I just hope to God we find somewhere decent in the next couple of weeks!"

Chapter Four

"No way!" Rory said. "Are you out of your *mind*? No bloody *way*!"

He was looking at her as if she had completely lost it, dragging his fingers through his hair in consternation. "*Wicklow*, for God's sake! *Roundwood*! Isn't that the highest village in Ireland, the place that gets snowed in for three months every winter –"

"A week or two," she said mildly. "And I'm sure it's not every year. Rory, let's at least have a look. It sounds fantastic and it doesn't need a single thing done to it. Come on, let's just go and see what it looks like!"

Rory tossed the newspaper onto the floor and sat down.

"Michelle," he said slowly and carefully, looking across at her. She sat down on the cushions facing him, surrounded as usual by a pile of auctioneers' leaflets.

"Michelle, let me get this straight. When I left this morning you were talking about looking at houses in Terenure. You never said *anything* about Roundwood. I'm not even sure I know where the bloody place *is*. And now, out of nowhere, you want us to go and *live* there? You haven't by any chance lost it? I mean, *Roundwood* – "

"I want us to go and look, that's all. Just to see what the place is like. The auctioneer's brochure makes it sound brilliant –"

"They all do that," he interrupted. "Even for kips no-one in their right mind would want. Besides, what's the point? We're not going to live there, Michelle, so you're wasting your time. And mine. And right now I'm up to my neck in this job over in Inchicore – I'd be better off spending tomorrow there than on a wild-goose chase up the mountains."

Michelle sighed. Since Rory set up Dundarra Computer Installations he often had to work at weekends, but she suspected that he was using it as an excuse this time.

"Fine, I'll go with Sarah," she said. "Or Jan!"

"As long as you know you're wasting your time. There's no way I'm moving out there – I want that clear."

"Don't worry, it's clear!" Michelle said, going through to the hall, grabbing her coat and closing the door quietly behind her. With Katie in bed and Rory staying in for the evening, she was free to go out for a while. A walk into Rathmines was just what she needed.

She set off at a brisk pace, making for Leinster Road.

As she passed the handsome redbrick houses, most of them in flats, but many now reverting back to family homes, her mind was filled with thoughts of what she could do with such a house, how she would furnish it . . .

Forget it, she told herself crossly. She'd never have a house like that, not on their income. And she knew she was lucky to have a house at all – some people would never get that chance.

But still . . .

She turned off Leinster Road and down a side street, heading roughly in the direction of Sarah's apartment. She needed to get her head round this sudden urge to move out of Dublin.

I'm fed up, she realised. Immediately she felt guilty. Her three years at home with Katie had been wonderful but, she finally admitted to herself, there was a part of her that couldn't wait to get back to work, now that Katie had started playschool. She just didn't have enough to fill her days, and couldn't wait for the challenge of work again.

"Challenge, my granny!" Sarah said a few minutes later when she and Michelle were sitting in front of the fire and Michelle told her what she'd been thinking. "You were totally fed up when you were working, don't forget! The same thing day in, day out, you said, and no end to it for the next thirty years! I think you're mad, myself. If it's a challenge you're looking for, why not try something completely different? You could join me for a while, set up a customer base like you've done for Rory, maybe do a few of the easier bits and pieces until you get used to it . . ."

Sarah ran her own small graphic design company and had suggested several times that Michelle join her. And once or twice Michelle had been tempted – but she had a strong streak of realism and reminded herself that, though she had loved sketching in school, she'd hardly lifted a pencil or sketchpad since the day she finished her Leaving Cert.

"It wouldn't work, Sare," she said reluctantly.

"You could at least *try*," Sarah said, exasperated. "Extend your career break for a while, tell them you'll go back next year – "

"No. It's just not for me, Sarah. You know that – not definite enough. I need to know how much money I have coming in every week – I couldn't live like you do, not knowing from one week to the next. Besides, *that* kind of challenge isn't what I have in mind –"

"And trying to get promoted is?"

"Yes! Because then at least I'll be in a better position to pay a higher mortgage . . ."

Her voice trailed off uneasily as she watched Sarah's expression change.

"Do you hear yourself?" Sarah asked, her eyebrows raised. "Talking about promotions and mortgages as if nothing else mattered in the world?"

"There's nothing wrong with talking about mortgages," Michelle said defensively.

"No," Sarah agreed. "Just not all the time, Chelle, okay? To be honest, you're beginning to sound a bit obsessed. Whatever happened to having fun?"

Michelle made an exasperated noise. "I need to get this sorted before I can think about fun, or anything else. It doesn't seem a lot to ask, just a nice house somewhere close by, that we can settle into and get on with our lives."

"You don't think you'll be bored? I mean, after the excitement of searching?"

"No, I won't," Michelle said. "You said yourself I won't have a minute once I get back to work, between that and looking after Katie and doing up a house – it'll be fine once I find the right place."

"Maybe you need to change your ideas a bit," Sarah suggested tentatively. "It's all very well holding on for your ideal place, but if you just broadened things out a bit . . ."

"That's exactly what I'm doing. And that's why I'm going down to Roundwood tomorrow –"

"*Round*wood! Are you *mad*!"

"Thanks, Sarah. Just what I needed, when Rory's saying the same thing –"

"I don't blame him! What in God's name would you go to Roundwood for? I know it's a lovely place, but get real! It would take, what, an hour and a half to get in – and that's on a *good* day!"

"Nothing like that! It's really not as far as you think." She stopped as she noticed her sister's expression.

"Sarah, I'm just going to see it, I've no intention of buying it. Rory wouldn't live outside Dublin in a fit, even if *I* wanted to. But this place sounds amazing. And I've looked at damn near everything else on the lists so I might as well see this. And I could do with a drive to the mountains tomorrow . . ."

Sarah smiled. "You think getting Rory up into the hills will make him remember your misspent youth, and he'll agree to anything!"

"Misspent, my eye!" Michelle laughed. "Oh, I know you think we spent every Sunday curled up under a pine tree somewhere, but believe me, after walking fifteen miles you wouldn't have the energy to get up to much!" Her expression changed. "Besides, I don't think he's coming. I'll have to go on my own."

"Well, there's not much point in that," Sarah said. "I still think you're mad – but if you're that keen on going, then I'll come with you. I suppose you're right – no harm in having a look."

Chapter Five

It took them well over an hour to get to Roundwood, and half an hour more to find the place. By no stretch of the imagination was it 'a short ten minutes from the village', but in every other detail the description was absolutely accurate.

The house, a dormer bungalow, was stunning. Michelle tried to mute her reactions as the auctioneer, Gerry Quinn, showed them round. But it was difficult. There was so much to love about the place; a huge living-room with windows on three sides giving views out over the mountains, a smaller room that would be perfect as an office for Rory, a kitchen that didn't need a thing done to it, four big bedrooms . . . the list went on, and Michelle had to struggle hard to remind herself that it was nothing like what she was looking for. But it was beautiful – and, best of all, they could afford it.

"Well?" Quinn asked finally, as they went back into the kitchen a second time. "What do you think?"

He was a quiet man in his mid-forties, experienced enough to know when not to push it, letting the client sell the house to herself. And Michelle had done just that.

"I'll have to come back with my husband," she answered. "It's not really what we were looking for. Actually, it's nothing at all like what we were looking for . . ."

The man waited.

"But it's lovely, isn't it? Though it's a bit off the beaten track . . ."

"You get used to that," he said encouragingly. "Distances are different in the country."

"You can say that again," Sarah muttered.

"You probably came the long way from the village," he said. "After a while you'd get to know all the little back roads."

"You're not from here yourself," Sarah suggested. The accent was definitely Dublin.

"No," he admitted with a slight shrug. "Rathfarnham, as near to the mountains as I could get. I couldn't afford a house like this when I was buying," he added quickly.

"It's very remote," Sarah said.

"Not at all. There are neighbours all round – you'd be surprised the way these hills are lit up at night."

Michelle, meanwhile, wasn't saying a word. She was busy looking around the kitchen, taking in details of the tiling and finely crafted kitchen units and the freshly painted walls, exactly the shade of green she'd have chosen herself . . .

"Is there anyone else interested?" she asked.

The auctioneer hesitated. *No,* was the short answer, not since the last viewer broke his car's axle on the way back down the hill. But no need to mention that, it was nothing to do with the house itself . . .

"A house like this would never be on the market long," he answered instead.

"How long so far?" Sarah asked.

"Not that long. Hard to say exactly. They've come down in price in the hope of a quick sale, so I'm expecting that any day now I'll –"

"What have they come down to?" Michelle asked quickly. "It says four hundred and ninety thousand in the brochure –"

"And it's four hundred and eighty thousand now," Quinn broke in, smiling broadly. "Bargain of the year, if you ask me –"

"So why does no-one else want it?" Sarah asked, raising an eyebrow. Michelle wanted to flatten her. If there was one thing she'd learned from her dealings with auctioneers it was the importance of keeping them on-side. Buying a house was difficult enough – she didn't need to get the auctioneer's back up . . .

For a second she remembered that sleaze-ball – there was no other word for him – who showed her round the first house she was interested in, a lovely place in

Terenure. He'd accepted her offer, told her it was hers and then – in the next breath, it seemed – sold it to someone else who'd been waiting in the wings. She still felt stung when she thought of how he'd just used her to raise the price a bit.

This man, on the other hand, seemed like someone you could trust. That's if you could trust any of them. They were, after all, acting for the seller, not the buyer, as Rory kept reminding her . . .

She flashed Sarah a warning glance, but there was no need. Quinn was already answering the question, still smiling. "Oh, believe me, plenty of people want it. But not everyone can afford it. And living in the country isn't for everyone – though a lot of Dublin people have moved into Wicklow in the last few years . . ."

Nice and vague, Sarah thought. *A politician's answer, saying nothing at all . . .*

"I'll have to come back with my husband," Michelle said again as Quinn locked up and they began walking towards the cars parked in the long, gravelled driveway outside.

"Any time you like," Quinn answered. "You just give me a ring. I'm always glad of an excuse to get up into the hills and get a bit of fresh air, away from all that muck down below – I often think if the kids were younger I'd definitely have to live out here, no matter how I'd manage it – have you kids yourself?" he finished smoothly.

And who d'you think the baby seat is for? Sarah wanted

to ask. It wasn't six inches from him, in the back of Michelle's car. He *must* have seen it.

"A little girl," Michelle said.

Quinn inclined his head slightly and smiled. "I have boys myself, four young tear-aways they were, and growing up hasn't changed them! Right, you have the number, Mrs Larkin. Ring me any time at all."

"I'll ring Monday, one way or the other," Michelle said, as she and Sarah got into the Fiat. Quinn's big Volvo was already pulling away as she started the engine.

They both started talking at once.

"Well, you were no help at all – "

"You're not serious, are you, Michelle? It's the middle of nowhere –"

"Asking him all those questions –"

"What d'you mean, no help? You're supposed to be the sensible one, and there you were, drooling –"

"Shush a minute, will you? I think we've gone the wrong way." Michelle pulled into the grass verge at the roadside as she tried to remember what direction they had taken as they approached the house.

"Well, what do you expect? Chelle, it's *miles* from anywhere. There're no signposts. Imagine breaking down here in the middle of the night – you'd never be heard of again . . ."

"Come on, Sarah, don't be such a sourpuss! It's *gorgeous*, you have to admit that! All that space, and the views – I never thought I'd find somewhere like that, after all the disappointments. It's at least worth thinking about, isn't it? Now, left or right?"

"Right, I think," Sarah said as they pulled out again onto the narrow road. "I think I remember that beat-up shed down there at the corner."

They drove in silence for a few minutes, relying more on instinct than on the one or two signposts giving names of unfamiliar little places, but no indication as to where Dublin might be.

They guessed well. A few minutes more and they were into the village of Roundwood and back on the road home.

"I suppose you know yourself," Sarah said finally, as they passed through Enniskerry. "The place *is* lovely, you're right about that – but it'll take you all day to get into work. And what about Rory? He has to go all over the place . . ."

"In his own time," Michelle pointed out. "He can easily work it so he avoids traffic jams – and we won't hit those anyway until we get to Dundrum." She would have crossed her fingers behind her back if she hadn't been driving.

"You've it all worked out, haven't you? What about Katie when you go back to work?"

"I'll bring her with me, drop her off with Mam on my way in – that's what the plan was anyway, no matter where I'll be living."

"You're seriously considering this place, aren't you?"

"Yes."

"So what changed? You never even *mentioned* living in the country before! Within a mile of the canal, that's where you said you wanted to live!"

"But I can't afford it, can I? Not for the kind of place I want. And God knows I looked at every single thing that's on offer around there!"

"You'd want to be very sure, Michelle. What'll it be like in the winter? And what about Katie? She'll need other kids around before long –"

"I'm willing to bet they have kids in Wicklow, Sarah! Just like in Dublin!"

"Further away, though. You'd be living your life in the car."

"But it'd be worth it, for Katie's sake. You heard what Mr Quinn said – the country's great for kids –"

"You didn't expect him to say anything else, did you? It's his job, for God's sake – he'll say whatever it takes –"

"I happen to believe he's right."

"Maybe," Sarah said glumly. "I just hope for your sake that Rory feels the same."

* * *

What Rory felt wasn't immediately clear – at least, not until he started speaking to her again. And then she almost wished he hadn't.

"If that's how you feel," she said when he finally drew breath, "then you're right, there's no point discussing it. I just don't know what else we're going to do, that's all. So you'd better start going through the paper and find somewhere to rent – because I'm not going back home, and that's final!"

"And I'm not going living halfway up a mountain! Michelle, be reasonable! We never even *talked* about this. I *never* agreed to move out of Dublin – I don't know where this stupid idea came from. Come on, you've got to look at other options. I've marked a few new places in the paper – we can take a drive past them tomorrow, see what you think and ring the auctioneers on Monday –"

"I'm getting tired of all this, Rory," she said quietly. "Exhausted. I really am. D'you know how many houses we've looked at now? Forty-three! I counted them last night. And not one of them right, or if it was, then we couldn't afford it. But the place in Roundwood –"

"Is in *Roundwood*. Michelle, you said yourself: walking-distance from the canal. That's the main thing you wanted. It's a long bloody walk from –"

"Let's leave it, Rory. Let's just leave it. Talk about something else."

They made the evening meal, and ate, and put Katie to bed, all the while chatting away as if there was no tension between them. But there was, and they both felt it. And there wasn't a minute when Michelle wasn't thinking about the house in Roundwood and how she had fallen for it, and how great it would be to be settled there. Or almost anywhere else, she thought ruefully. Just so she could stop thinking about houses, and looking at houses, and get on with her life.

Chapter Six

The following day was not a success. Katie was fractious, Michelle tense and even the normally good-humoured Rory was feeling the strain. They had set off just after eleven in the morning to drive past the three houses Rory had seen advertised, and it was immediately obvious that two of them weren't worth the effort of going inside.

"No wonder they're so cheap," Michelle said bitterly as they pulled away from outside the second one. "You'd spend the rest of your life filling skips – and that's just for the front garden. How can anyone think it's okay to dump a fridge –"

"That was the least of it," Rory agreed. "The windows are about to fall out, from the look of them. But if it was going cheap enough –"

"I still wouldn't want it," Michelle interrupted.

"*'Quiet road'*, my eye! It's got 'rat-run' written all over it! I want a place where we can let Katie out –"

"Michelle." He said it quietly, ominously. "Look, I don't have much hope for the next house – I've a feeling it'll be over our budget if it's as good as they say –"

"Huh! When have we *ever* seen one that's as good as they say?"

"Right," he agreed. "So I think, once we have a look at this, it might be back to the drawing-board."

"Meaning?" She could do ominous too.

"Forty-three houses, you said it yourself. And those two make forty-five, and the next one forty-six. If this one doesn't work out, it's time for a re-think about what we want – and what we can afford."

"We know how much we can afford," she said quietly.

"To the cent," he answered. "But you have to admit, you've been getting a bit carried away. Remember, if we spend everything we have on *buying* the place, there'll be nothing left to do it up."

"I'm not looking for a place that needs doing up. I mean, I'd enjoy doing it, but really I don't mind if it's all finished."

"That's just the problem." They were pulling into Kenilworth Park and he slowed down, looking for the 'for sale' sign. "If the work's done, we can't afford to buy, and if we *can* afford a place it's because it's in bits – and we'll have no cash left to fix it. Face it, Michelle, we're kidding ourselves. I mean, just look at that!"

He nodded towards a handsome redbricked house with bay windows and an auctioneer's sign in the little front garden. Quickly he pulled into a space just across the road from it and they sat looking at it.

"They got it wrong," he announced finally. "We should've known, from the address – nothing in this road would go for less than six hundred thousand. I'm sure of that."

"What does it say again?" Michelle asked as he pulled out the paper with the advertisement. "Hush, sweetheart, not long now," she added to Katie who was beginning to grizzle in the back seat. "Just a few minutes more, and then we'll go to Granny's for a while. You'd like that, wouldn't you?"

Katie, pacified, smiled and started to chat to her doll.

"Here we are," Rory said, turning to the relevant page. Quickly he skimmed through the details. "Three hundred and twenty thousand."

They stared at each other.

He broke the silence. "Can't be right. Impossible."

"But what if –"

"Michelle, that's what we're getting for ours! Come on, it *has* to be a mistake!"

"Shouldn't we just go and ask? I mean, what if – well, what if –"

He waited, half exasperated, half amused.

"If what? They're living in the Dark Ages and don't know about inflation? They've decided to join a monastery and are donating their worldly goods to the poor – like, us? I don't think so!"

"Oh, *you!* At least let me go and ask!"

"Tomorrow," he said. "I'll ring the auctioneer first thing."

Michelle didn't answer for a moment, then, "No," she said decisively. "Tomorrow might be too late. I'm going to knock on the door."

"You can't do that!"

"Of course I can. We're offering to buy their house."

"I still don't think –"

"Wait here," she said, getting quickly out of the car and going up the short tiled pathway.

She knocked, the door opened and he could see her talking to someone.

It didn't take long.

"Let's go," she said quickly as she got back in. "Let's get out of here." Her head was down, her hair falling forward slightly to screen her face. She brushed her hair back and shot him a look. "Come on, Rory, move!" Her face was slightly flushed and she was blinking back tears.

He pulled out, knowing better than to argue, and drove slowly along until they reached the junction at the end of the road. As he stopped to let traffic pass on the main road he glanced across at her.

"Love?"

No answer.

"Michelle, are you okay? What happened?"

Silence for another moment. "He *laughed* at me!" she burst out then. "Laughed, and asked me was I a fool, or was I living in the real world at all, not to realise it was a misprint! And then this woman came out and he told her what I'd said and she laid into me, asking what I was doing knocking on their door on a Sunday, and anyway how *dare* I think I could have their house for *three* hundred and twenty thousand, when any fool would know it was worth at least *six* hundred and twenty, which was the asking price except the stupid newspaper got it wrong! Well, they're welcome to it! I wouldn't take the bloody place at *any* price, now!"

He almost laughed himself, but thought better of it. She was raging, but also on the verge of tears. He turned left, drove for a few minutes until he found a place to park, then put his arm around her.

"Let it go, love! It's not worth it. Come on, let's get to your folks . . ."

She was leaning in against his shoulder and he could feel her tension, the struggle to keep the tears at bay. *Three months ago we'd have been making a joke of this, laughing at ourselves,* he thought. *Three weeks ago, even . . .*

"I'm fine now," she said after a minute or two. "I'm okay. Let's go." She turned to look at Katie who was sitting quietly in the back seat, knowing that there was something wrong but not quite sure what.

"Lunch at Gran's, Katie. That'll be nice, won't it?"

Especially if Helen's not there, she thought. She didn't feel able for her right now.

She was out of luck. Her sister's dark blue Renault was sitting in the drive when they pulled up outside her parents' home in Dundrum, and Helen was in the kitchen, taking charge as usual.

You'd think she owned the place, Michelle thought resentfully. No use saying anything, of course – that would only start a row, and that was the last thing her parents needed. Better just to go along with her, like always, and hope that she wasn't too bad *this* time.

She was bad enough. She had her three children organised around the kitchen table eating their lunch – she didn't believe in letting children into the dining-room – and was already giving Sarah instructions on how to carve the leg of lamb.

"Good job you're here, Helen. We'd never manage otherwise, would we?" Sarah said cheerfully, grinning across the kitchen at Michelle as she spoke. Helen shot her a venomous look and quickly re-directed her attention to their mother. Una Keogh had swept Katie up into her arms in a big hug, and Helen wasn't pleased. It was obvious that she was wondering why Una never hugged *her* three children like that.

The answer, as Michelle and Sarah could have told her if she'd bothered to ask, was that long years of *'Don't crease her new frock'* and *'Remember, he doesn't like people kissing him'* whenever Una or Maurice, her husband, so much as *looked* at one of Helen's children had taught them to keep their distance. Recently, though they loved Helen's daughter and sons every bit as much as they did Katie, they had adopted a strictly 'hands-off' policy unless the children came to them first, which they usually didn't.

She can stop glaring, Michelle thought as she saw Helen's expression. *She has only herself to blame.*

Her mother put Katie down and came across to kiss Michelle's cheek just as Maurice came into the kitchen.

"And how's my best girl?" he asked, lifting Katie, oblivious to the look Helen was giving him behind his back. Helen's daughter had exactly the same expression, Michelle noticed, and her lip was beginning to tremble. Joanne, at seven, was her mother all over again, and quite capable of making a scene if she felt she was being ignored.

Rory was quick to spot potential trouble, and moved to deflect it by taking some sweets from his pocket and putting them on the table in front of the children.

"For after your lunch," he told them.

"I don't like them having too many sweets," Helen said, while looking slightly mollified.

You don't like it either if we don't bring any, Michelle thought. She gave a small sigh.

"Are you all right, love?" her mother asked quietly.

"Fine," Michelle said. "Just a bit fed up, that's all."

"No luck?" Una asked. Michelle had told her how they were spending the morning.

"Not a bit. And wait 'til you hear . . ." Halfway through the story of the house in Kenilworth Park she started to laugh, to Rory's great relief, and the atmosphere lightened as they carried the food through to the dining-room and served it up and began eating – Katie included, in spite of Helen's usual hints about how she was *sure* Katie would prefer to be in the kitchen with her cousins.

"So what next?" Maurice asked finally as Michelle brought them up to date on all the houses she had seen in the previous week. "What about that place up in the mountains? You're not seriously thinking about it, are you? Sarah was saying –"

"Forget about that one," Michelle said quickly, feeling Rory tense beside her. "It was just an idea, something a bit different."

"I still can't understand why you don't do the sensible thing and move to the suburbs, like us," Helen said. "I mean, it's not as if you'd be off the face of the earth, is it? And, my God, if you're considering *Roundwood* –"

"I told you, we're not," Michelle said stiffly. "And I've nothing against the suburbs. It's just that I don't want to face the motorway every day –"

"You'd rather drive down sheep-tracks?" Helen said acidly. "And it's not a question of motorway driving – there are *plenty* of nice places that – "

"Let's just leave it, okay?" Michelle said. Rory, she noticed, was busy concentrating on the food on his plate, pretending the conversation had nothing to do with him. "Give us a break for a few days!"

"All the same, love, you've no time to waste,"

Maurice said as he lifted his napkin and began dabbing at his lips. "What is it now, only six weeks or so before –"

"Dad," Sarah said in a warning tone. "Leave her alone."

"I was only saying –" he began, but stopped quickly when he saw the looks Una and Sarah gave him.

Rory still hadn't said a word. Now, as Helen began clearing the table and Sarah went to make a pot of tea, he said quietly, "I don't mind just going to have a look."

"What?" she asked. From the corner of her eye she could see her parents listening intently while busying themselves stacking more dishes.

"Michelle, I know you won't rest until I look at this place in Roundwood. Only look at it, that's all, and then we'll add it to list of rejects and you can put it out of your mind."

"Well, that's a hell of an attitude! What's the point, if that's how you feel about it before you even see it?"

"I didn't mean it like that. I mean – God, I don't know what I mean! Just that we're running out of options fast, and so far this is the only place you like that we can come anywhere near affording. Look, we'll go and have a gander, and then we'll sit down and work out what the next step is."

"It really does sound lovely," Una ventured.

"Now, don't *you* start!" he said, but he was smiling. "If you wouldn't mind baby-sitting for a while, I'll take your daughter for a drive up into the mountains. Remember how you never used to let me do that?"

"Get out of here, you divil!" Una laughed. "And don't come back here until you've bought a house!"

Chapter Seven

The day was perfect for driving along the twisting roads under the furze-covered mountains. Michelle found her thoughts drifting as the Sugarloaf came into view. She loved that mountain, always had since she first climbed it with a gang of friends when she was about seventeen.

"Nearly there," she said when she thought Rory was beginning to look a bit impatient.

"To be honest, I'm enjoying the drive," he said. "Nice to be on our own for a bit."

He slowed as a few sheep straggled on to the road, giving him a chance to admire the view.

"Remember that place?" he asked after a few minutes as they passed a small track sloping down to the left towards a stand of pine trees. She caught the flash of water through the trees.

"Sure." She smiled at him, reaching to touch his hand. "Seems like yesterday."

She knew that if she closed her eyes she'd see every detail of it, hear the sounds, almost taste the musky scent of the fern-covered ground under the pines where they'd made love for the first time.

"It's – what? Eleven years?" Rory said. "Hard to believe." He pulled in under the trees at the far side of the road. "Want to stop for a while?"

She pulled a jokey face. "And there you were, telling my mother you only wanted to go and look at a house."

He laughed. "I don't think she'd care now. We're safely married."

"I don't think she cared then," Michelle said, smiling. "She just said the things she felt she should – but you know Mam, she believes in letting people live their own lives."

"So, how about it?"

"Maybe on the way back?"

"You're a tough lady." He lifted her hand and kissed it, laughing again.

"Rory . . ."

"Hmm?" He was still holding her hand.

"We don't have to look at this place, you know. I'll let it go and never even mention it again."

"But I know you. You'd always feel we should at least have looked at it together."

"No. Promise. It *is* a bit further than I thought. The journey seemed quicker last time."

"Meaning you talked non-stop when you dragged poor Sarah up here," he teased. "Look, we're nearly there. Might as well keep going and let me see what it is you've been raving about!"

"I'm not sure –"

"What's wrong?"

She hesitated, trying to work out what she was feeling.

"I'm afraid that if I see it again I'll *really* fall for it . . ."

"If that's how you feel, then there's no question – we have to go and have a look. No promises, mind . . ."

He started the car again and followed the signposts into Roundwood and then Michelle's directions out the other side.

"There it is – see, just past the gate, there."

He pulled into the side of the road again, opposite the green gate leading to farmland, looking towards the next gateway through which he could see a short, gravelled driveway with a cut-stone dormer bungalow sitting comfortably at the end of it.

"I have to admit, it looks interesting," he said after a few minutes.

Michelle had been sitting quietly, giving him a chance to take it in.

"It's even better inside," she said.

"As long as you don't suggest knocking at the door," he teased.

She felt herself relaxing. "So, what do you think?" He liked it, that was obvious. Otherwise they'd have been halfway back down the mountains by now. "Is it worth ringing the auctioneer tomorrow?"

He hesitated, spread his hands out on the steering wheel, still looking at the house. Finally he turned to her.

"It *is* a hell of a long way up, Chelle. Imagine trying to get down from here on an icy morning, with Katie crying in the back seat and traffic all the way in from beyond Enniskerry . . ."

"But there are back roads!" she said.

"That would take even longer! What's so special about this house, miles from anywhere? If it's space you want, why not the one at the KCR –"

"The neighbours kept pigeons!"

"Michelle, here they probably keep sheep and God knows what else!"

"Well, at least *they* won't drop stuff all over my clean sheets!"

They were still laughing when a knock on the window startled them.

"Sorry, but would you mind pulling up a bit?" The man was cheerful, mid-fifties or so, dressed in a light grey suit. He indicated the car that had stopped just behind them, the driver's door half-open. "I need to swing round to get through the gate – it's a bit tricky."

"No problem," Rory said. "We were just –"

"Having a look at the house," Michelle said quickly, cutting across any suggestion Rory might make about leaving.

"Ah, right," the man said. "Well, if you want to come in and have a look around, you're more than welcome. Just give me a chance to get the glad-rags off and I'll be happy to show you."

"No need," Rory said. "We can always ring the auctioneer tomorrow."

The man hesitated. "Maybe that'd be better. He's always telling me to leave it to him, not to be showing people round myself. Still, it seems a shame, seeing as you're up here . . ."

He paused, gave a slight shrug and Michelle gave Rory a pleading look.

"Look, I might as well be honest with you," Rory said to the man. "I only came up here because Michelle really wanted to. I think it's too far from town myself."

"Whatever you think," the man said.

"Rory –"

"What about a drop of something anyway before you head back down?" the man suggested. "I've just come from a christening on my wife's side of the family and talk about a gang of Holy Joes! I can't wait to get rid of the suit and get something decent into me instead of that bloody sherry they were pushing at us."

"Thanks, but we don't usually drink during the day," Rory said. "You know, Guards and everything."

"Whatever you think," the man said again.

"But we'd love a cup of tea," Michelle said quickly.

"Michelle!" Rory hissed.

The man at the car window burst out laughing.

"That's what I like to see, a woman who speaks her mind!"

"Don't they all!" said Rory.

The laughter stopped abruptly. "Indeed they do not, boy!" The man's face took on a thoughtful look. "Count yourself lucky if you've never come across one who says one thing but means half-a-dozen others, until a man doesn't know where he is . . ." He paused, seemed to shake himself mentally. "Will you listen to me! Come on, I'll make that tea. If you just pull up a little bit, I can –"

"We wouldn't want to put you to any trouble," Rory said. He shot Michelle a look that said *'Get me out of here!'*.

"No trouble. But suit yourself. You can think about it while I'm pulling in to the drive."

"Rory, *please*," Michelle said as he drove forward slightly to let the other man swing round and in through the gate. "It'll only take a few minutes."

"Michelle, he's a weirdo! All cheerful one minute, and then look at him! I'm not going in there!"

"Oh, for God's sake, Rory, all he's doing is offering us a drink, and a chance to see the house!"

"He doesn't even know us."

"He doesn't have to – he knows we want to look at his house. It's not like he dragged us in off the street!"

"I know I'm going to regret this . . ."

"Not as much as you'll regret not doing it!" she teased. "And you know what Sarah says: better to regret what you do than what you *don't* do! Come *on*, Rory! Just for a few minutes. Look, he's there at the door watching us."

"*Definitely* a weirdo," Rory muttered, but he opened the car door all the same.

The man was back in cheerful mode again as he ushered them inside.

"Bill Gallagher's the name, by the way," he said, holding out his hand.

Rory, after the slightest hesitation, shook it. "I'm Rory, and this is Michelle."

Bill Gallagher nodded, turned to shake Michelle's hand. "Fine. Fine. Make yourselves comfortable in there while I run up and change my clothes. Won't be a minute." He gestured to the living-room to the right of the hallway, left them to it and went upstairs.

"Relax, Rory, he's all right." She sat down beside him on one of the blue sofas that flanked the stone fireplace.

Rory grinned. "Maybe. Just don't get him talking about women again!"

They lapsed into silence then, taking in every detail of the room. It was big and bright, painted a soft, warm yellow. The ceiling was timbered, giving it a cosy feel, and the floor was timber also, with muted rugs here and there. A happy room, a welcoming room.

Best of all were the windows, on three sides, giving views down over the sloping back garden towards the mountains and, away to the side, to a little stream that

Gerry Quinn, the auctioneer, had told Michelle bordered the one-acre site.

She stood up, unable to just sit there any longer, and moved to the tallest window, looking out over the back garden.

"Come on, Rory, have a look at this!"

He was just moving across to join her when Bill Gallagher came back into the room. He was dressed now in a pair of faded brown cords and a check shirt, and was visibly easier in himself.

"Well, what do you think? Some view, isn't it? That's one of the things I'll miss about this place."

"Where do you plan on moving to?" Rory asked.

Gallagher's face clouded slightly. "Don't talk to me. Back into the bloody city, would you believe! Last thing I want to do, but the wife won't have it any other way, says it's too –" He caught himself in time, leaving them to guess at what he might have been about to say. "It's a young person's place, that's what she says," he added brightly. "I mean, look at that garden, it'd take you all your time to look after it . . ."

Rory did just that, and frowned.

"Of course, you could just leave it a bit on the wild side, like we've done. See that fence over there? We normally have a couple of sheep down past that – the buggers will eat anything and you've no worries then about keeping the grass down!"

"Sheep?" Rory looked alarmed now.

"You don't have to, of course," Gallagher added

hastily. "It's only an arrangement I set up with Shemmy Byrne – a great neighbour. He farms all around here and he puts in a few sheep whenever I want to tidy the place up. Now, what about that drink?" he asked, sensing that he was digging himself into a hole. "Or, it was tea you wanted, wasn't it? Come into the kitchen with me – you might as well have a look at it while I make the tea."

The kitchen was exactly as Michelle remembered it.

"Look, Rory," she said quietly, nodding towards the kitchen cupboards as Gallagher busied himself with the kettle and put cups out on the worktop beside a bottle of whiskey and some glasses. "Handcrafted, the auctioneer said."

Gallagher had good ears. "Indeed they are. I did them myself, put a lot of work into them."

"You made them?" Rory asked, interested now. His father had been a master joiner, and from time to time he lamented not going into the business like his brother Matt. For the past couple of years now he had been taking lessons from Matt in the evenings and had put them to good use at home.

"I did indeed," Gallagher said, turning with a pleased expression. "The best bit is the stairs, though – come on, I'll show you –"

And the two men went off into the hall, tea and whiskey forgotten, leaving Michelle to wander round the kitchen and into the adjoining utility room. All that space, that's what she couldn't get over. The kitchen was big enough to live in, never mind the rest of the house. She could just imagine them, Katie at the big table there – well, something like it, anyway – and Rory sitting by the warm range working on a piece of wood while she . . .

She laughed quietly at herself. *Getting carried away there, Michelle!* The reality was likely to be a bit different, with the two of them dashing in the door in the evening, late already and exhausted after the long drive up, trying to get the meal going and spend time with Katie and organise themselves for the following day . . .

She was mad to even consider it. This house was too far away from town, from work, from their families and friends. It was isolated. They might never get to know the neighbours. They might hate them when they did get to know them. They might be stuck here for three weeks solid their first winter, if it snowed and they couldn't get out onto the road . . .

But none of that mattered, and the voice of reason was wasting its time. She wasn't sure why, exactly, but she loved this house. And one look at Rory's face as he returned from a quick look around upstairs made her hope that maybe he could love it, too.

Chapter Eight

Rory worked hard at talking himself out of it as they drove back home.

"It's too isolated, for starters," he said, concentrating on the narrow, twisting road.

"Private," Michelle corrected. "I counted six houses from the back garden. Two of them are only about a hundred yards away."

"It's still a long way out, Michelle."

"We'd get used to it after a while. You heard what Gallagher said, you can cover the first ten miles in ten minutes or so."

Rory raised an eyebrow. "You can, but would you want to? On these roads?"

"Well, maybe twenty minutes then," Michelle said quickly. "But once you're past Enniskerry you'd be hitting the traffic anyway and be no worse off than anyone else."

"But the idea was supposed to be to avoid traffic,

wasn't it? To live close to where we are now, and be able to walk into town?"

"Yes, but we never do, do we? Except in the evenings. During the day I'm in the car half the time anyway, bringing Katie to see Mam and to the park and wherever else we're going, and you spend your day driving around from one company to another. So it doesn't matter where we're living – we'll still be in traffic, especially once I go back to work and I'm dropping Katie over to Mam every day."

"And that's another thing – what about Katie?" he asked. "What if she doesn't settle in the new place?"

"Of course she will. She won't care where she is as long as she's got her toys and her teddies, and we're with her and she still sees her granny and grandad – she'll love it!"

"So what about us? What about our social lives?"

She laughed. "What social lives? Face it, Rory, we haven't exactly been setting the world on fire since Katie arrived, have we? All we do is go to a film occasionally, or for a drink in the Bridge Inn –"

"Come on, Michelle! What about concerts, nights out with the lads –"

"When does that happen?" she demanded. "Once in a blue moon, maybe! We can still do all of that, and stay overnight with Sarah, or Mam and Dad, or Eoin and Ally . . ."

"We'd better, it's the only way we'd get to see them – or any of our other friends!"

"Are you kidding?" she laughed. "They'll be beating

a path to the door, coming in their droves for a weekend in the country!"

"Maybe," he agreed. "But – I don't know. It's a hell of a decision, Michelle, moving out of Dublin."

"I suppose," she said.

They fell silent for a while.

"What is it you like about the house?" he asked abruptly.

She thought for a moment.

"Everything. There's not a thing to be done to it – we could just move right in and not have to worry about builders and stuff like that. The rooms are all a good size, the views are magic . . . It's what I've been looking for, Rory. Okay, so it's not in the right place, but it's the right house. I have a good feeling about it. All that space . . ."

"I'm still not sure, Chelle –"

"Is there anything *you* like about it?" she prompted. She'd seen how he'd run his hands over the carved banisters and the doors of the kitchen cabinets, how his eyes lit up when he went into the workshop behind the garage, with shavings on the floor and the smell of fresh timber and a piece of cherry-wood clasped in a vice on the work-top.

"Oh, it has a lot going for it, I grant you that," he said, turning at the sign for Enniskerry. "Didn't take long," he added, surprised.

She smiled. "You see, it doesn't. Told you we'd get used to it!"

He made one last attempt.

"What if we hated living up there?"

"So what if we did?" she replied. "We're young enough to sell up and start again, Rory."

"We couldn't afford it, Michelle."

"Once we're back on two salaries we'll be raking it in! And you couldn't lose on a house like this, if we did want to sell in a year or two."

"I don't know, Michelle. Gallagher doesn't seem to be having much luck. You heard him saying he'd be willing to drop the price a bit more for a quick sale?"

"I know, isn't it great! But he's only doing it because his wife is pressurising him – "

"Poor man, wonder what that feels like!" Rory said, grinning.

"Lucky you, you'll never know!"

She was quiet as they drove the last few miles to her parents' home. Helen, to her relief, had left already, and Sarah had obviously warned her parents not to say a word. Michelle could see that they were bursting to ask questions, but Una wisely held off, sensing that there was something up, and distracting Maurice the one or two times he started "What do you think –" and "When would you – "

"Go and see if the news is on," she said the third time he opened his mouth to ask something.

"But you never watch it," he said.

"See anyway!" she said, giving him a look.

Shaking his head and muttering to himself, Maurice went into the living-room to check the television.

"I suppose I can come out now?" he said a few minutes later from the living-room doorway when he heard the sounds of departure in the hall. "And, no, the news isn't on, how could it be on when it's only quarter to six, and wasn't I the fool to go and look?"

"Ah, but you're very good, all the same!" Una teased. "I'll ring you later, love." This to Michelle, with a meaningful look.

They said their good-byes and drove the short distance home where, as usual, they had trouble finding a parking spot and Rory had to drop them and all their bits and pieces off and go and park in the next street.

He made a valiant last-ditch attempt as he joined her in the kitchen.

"You have to admit, Michelle, there are loads of advantages to being near your parents. We're able to drop Katie over whenever we like and head off on our own – "

"But we don't, do we?" Michelle countered. "And most of the time we don't even want to."

"Mmm. I suppose you're right." He began taking ham and lettuce from the fridge, bread from the cupboard. "Did you see the finish on that kitchen?" he asked casually after a few minutes. "You couldn't buy craftsmanship like that at any price! None we could afford, anyway!"

"Mmm. And all that space," Michelle answered, as they fell into their well-practised routine of working round each other in the cramped little space.

"The view was something else," he said, catching sight of the bright splash of geraniums beside the rubbish bins in the little backyard. "And the workshop! It must be brilliant to have a place like that . . ."

"Great," she said, reaching past him to get at the pasta jar on the shelf above the fridge. "Though you did a fantastic job here without one." She skimmed her hand over the surface of the neat dresser in the alcove as she spoke.

"But it was a pain having to go up to Matt's whenever I needed tools or anything. Not to mention the hassle of having to load the dresser into the van every time I wanted to do a bit of work on it. What I really need is a room where I could set things up and leave them until I was ready for them."

He'd lost the battle. Michelle knew it but said nothing, concentrating on stirring Katie's pasta.

"Maybe we'll ring the auctioneer in the morning."

She turned to him with a brilliant smile and went to wrap her arms around him. "It'll work for us, Rory. I know it will."

* * *

Things moved quickly after that, though not quickly enough for Michelle. She couldn't wait to get into the house in the mountains.

"I even like the name," she told Jan when they met on the Friday for their weekly lunch. "Hunter's Moon."

Jan wrinkled her nose. "Funny name for a house."

"I suppose," Michelle agreed. "Gallagher said you get a great view of the night sky with no streetlights to distract you and that's why he called it that. Rory reckons he named it after a racehorse!"

"So when am I going to see this place?"

Michelle thought for a second. "Tomorrow, if you like. I'm going back again to measure the living-room for curtains."

Jan looked surprised. "Isn't that a bit premature?"

"Maybe," Michelle agreed. "Well, to be honest, I just want the excuse to go and have another look. I really love the place, Jan."

"And Rory is definitely on for it?" Jan asked doubtfully.

"Nearly more than I am! Once he got a look at it he knew we'd never get anything better, or even half as good, for that kind of money. We saw it again on Tuesday, and he was sold."

"And your offer has definitely been accepted?"

"Yesterday. Four hundred and seventy-five thousand euro."

"Oh? But I thought you said – "

"I know, he wanted four-eighty, down from four-ninety, but we told him four-seventy-five was as high as we could go and, luckily, he believed us."

"And was it?" Jan asked.

"Absolutely," Michelle said. "Not one cent more – we're nearly breaking ourselves as it is! But it'll be worth it."

"You're sure?" Jan said.

Michelle smiled. "Just wait 'til you see it."

* * *

Jan, to Michelle's surprise, didn't seem particularly taken with the house.

"It's very far out of town," Jan said. "And the way you were describing it I thought it was something really special."

"It *is* something special!" Michelle protested, but Jan just shrugged in response.

Michelle left her with the auctioneer and wandered upstairs again, glad that Sarah had refused the invitation to come and have a second look. Sarah rarely had a good word to say about Jan, and Michelle didn't want her to have any opportunity to add to her list of Jan's alleged imperfections.

Envious to her toenails, Sarah had said once, and Michelle wondered if it might be true. She didn't know what was up with Jan. Okay, the house mightn't be to everyone's liking, but there *was* something special about it – surely Jan could see that . . .

She was calling her now from downstairs. "D'you mind if we head back?" she asked as Michelle came to the landing.

"Oh! But I –"

"I forgot I'd arranged to meet Damien, and his mobile's powered off," she said, waving her own mobile phone. "He'll be sitting there waiting and you know how impatient he gets . . ."

"Another five minutes?" Michelle asked.

"Okay," Jan agreed with some reluctance. "But you can always come back again, can't you?"

"This is my third time," Michelle said, smiling ruefully at Gerry Quinn. "I don't know – "

"No problem," Quinn said. "I'm happy to come up any time."

Michelle had another quick look at the bathrooms before coming back downstairs to join them in the hall. She had intended to stay longer, but she could always come back in a day or two with her mother, who was dying to see the place.

"Now, let me know when you've heard from the surveyor," Quinn said as they walked through the hall door and out to the car.

"Monday, he promised," Michelle said. "I'll give you a ring."

They got into their cars and Michelle turned down the driveway, feeling almost like a local now as she navigated the roads with growing confidence.

"How soon will you have it?" Jan asked as they came through Roundwood. She was peering around her with interest as she spoke.

"Not sure," Michelle said. "Nine or ten weeks, I think, so we'll have to put our stuff into storage and stay with Mam for a few weeks. But I don't mind when it's short-term. At least it means we don't have to get a bridging loan – we'll have the full amount by the time it's due."

"You haven't had to pay it all yet?"

"That's not how it works," Michelle explained, remembering that Jan had never bought a house. "We've only paid a booking deposit so far, and we still haven't signed a contract."

"So he could still sell it to someone else?" Jan said.

"He won't do that," Michelle said quickly. "They've agreed the price, and we have Gallagher's word on it. And the auctioneer's."

"Better keep your fingers crossed all the same," Jan advised. "And sign that contract the minute you can."

"You bet I will!" Michelle said. "But don't worry, nothing can go wrong. I have a really good feeling about this house, Jan. It's *meant* to be ours."

Chapter Nine

The surveyor's report came in the post on Monday morning.

"It's great, Rory!" Michelle said when she rang him at his office in Tallaght just after ten. "Well, most of it, anyway. There are one or two small things, but I'm sure they don't matter –"

"Like what?" he asked quickly.

"Nothing much. Something about dampness on the wall of the back bedroom suggesting a slight leak in the roof valley. Oh, and we need to get the water tested."

"Why's that?" he asked, alarmed.

"No big deal. Apparently the water comes from a well – I never even thought about that – anyway, I'm sure it's nothing to worry about. I'll mention it to Gerry Quinn when I see him today."

"You're not going up again, surely?" he asked, laughing.

"'Course I am," she said. "Mam wants to see the

place, and you know I'll use any excuse! Morna will look after Katie for a few hours."

Morna cleaned for Michelle's mother once a week and doted on Katie. She was always offering to look after her, and it had worked out very well on the rare occasions Michelle took her up on it.

"Good idea," Rory said. "It'll give you a chance to concentrate without worrying about keeping her occupied. Ring me once you talk to Quinn – let me know what he says about the water."

"Sure. I wouldn't worry – Bill Gallagher looks healthy enough, doesn't he?"

Rory laughed. "Probably survives on neat whiskey! Talk to you later."

Michelle phoned Gerry Quinn and then did a quick tidy-up before getting Katie into her jacket and walking the short distance to where the car was parked.

"Soon be at Gran's, Katie," she said as she strapped the little girl into her car seat. She got in herself, started the car and joined the traffic for the short distance to her mother's house.

Morna was already there, and had Katie happily settled with some toys a few minutes later so that Una and Michelle could leave.

"It's a great treat to be going up into the mountains on a day like this!" Una said, as they took the Enniskerry road and left the suburbs behind them.

"Would you listen to her! Anyone would think you never got out!"

In fact, Una had a better social life than Michelle,

between her music society and drama group and the 'ladies' night' every Friday that she wouldn't miss, no matter what. Nevertheless, she always made time for Katie and was forever offering to baby-sit.

"We'll still see plenty of you," she said now, reassuring herself.

"Mam! Of course you will! It's not like we're moving to the far end of the country!"

"No, but all the same . . ."

"Lots of people commute to Dublin now," Michelle said cheerfully. "And I'll be dropping Katie in every day while I'm at work, don't forget!" She slowed slightly as they passed through the picturesque village of Enniskerry. "You're still sure about minding her?"

"Indeed I am! You don't think I'd let my little granddaughter be minded by a stranger, do you? Anyway, if I need to go somewhere Morna said she'll stand in for me. That's all right, isn't it?"

"But she's a stranger!" Michelle said, grinning. "You didn't even know her last year."

"Maybe not, but she's part of the family now!" Una said stoutly. "Now, where is this place you can't stop talking about?"

"Won't be long now!" Michelle said. "Just wait 'til you see it!"

Gerry Quinn pulled in just after them, greeted them as he got out of the car, and quickly went to open the front door.

Una loved every bit of it, as Michelle had known she would. The two of them examined everything, exclaimed over everything, and dragged themselves away reluctantly only when they saw Quinn glancing surreptitiously at his watch.

"I wanted to ask you about a couple of things," Michelle said quietly as Una got back into the car. "I got the surveyor's report this morning and it mentioned a leak in the roof and something about checking the water quality."

"The leak is nothing to worry about – it's been fixed," Quinn said. "You saw the stain on the back bedroom wall?"

"I looked, but there wasn't anything much," Michelle said. "A bit of a water streak, but –"

"That's all it is," Quinn assured her. "They didn't get around to re-decorating, that's all. The leak that caused it is definitely fixed – I know the man who did it."

"And what about the water?"

"I suppose it's no harm to get it tested," Quinn said. "But I wouldn't expect any problems there – after all, the Gallaghers use that water day in, day out."

"That's what I told Rory," Michelle said happily. "Now, what about the contract?"

"There was a bit of a delay getting it drawn up, but it'll be done in a day or two," Quinn said. "You can get your own man to put in a clause about water quality if you like, once he gets it. But I know it'll be okay. I've drunk it myself once or twice, and no ill effects!"

Michelle said goodbye and filled Una in on the conversation as they drove back down the hill.

"I never even *thought* about water!" Una said. "It's something you take for granted, isn't it? You turn on the tap and there it is! But I suppose with all these dumps all over Wicklow, you can't be too careful . . ."

"Nowhere near us, Mam – that was the first thing Rory checked with the County Council."

"But –"

Michelle interrupted quickly, knowing her mother was already imagining Katie in hospital with gastro-enteritis, or worse. "Now, stop worrying, you know what you're like! Tell me what you think of the living-room."

Una had already told her several times while they were there, of course, but no matter – they were off again, happily discussing every detail of Michelle's new house as they drove back down into Dundrum.

* * *

The phone call the following Friday was like a bomb dropping.

"But we agreed a price!" Michelle said finally, struggling to hold back the tears. "We *settled* it, I paid you a deposit!"

"I know, I know," Gerry Quinn said apologetically. "The thing is, with no contract in place . . ."

"That's not *my* fault! You know I've rung you twice this week asking about it!" She took a deep breath, trying to steady herself. "Anyway, what right has Mrs Gallagher to decide she wants another ten thousand? I've never even *met* the woman!"

"But it *is* her house," Quinn reminded her quietly. "So, in point of fact, she has every right. It's just not what I'd . . . she has every right," he repeated.

"Can you get her to change her mind? It's a mean, rotten thing to do, to go back on her word –"

"She didn't give her word."

"But surely to God she and her husband discussed it! You can't just sell a house without talking to your husband or wife about it! And what about *you*? Didn't you meet her when you took on the sale?"

"Well, yes –"

"And?" Michelle demanded.

Quinn cleared his throat. "She said she'd leave it in our hands, myself and Mr Gallagher."

"So?"

"So . . . well, she changed her mind. She wants to be part of the negotiations now."

Michelle thought quickly. "You told me the other day that no-one else was interested, that no-one had even been to see the house in a while."

"I probably shouldn't have said that –"

"But it's true, isn't it?"

His silence was her answer.

"So, even if she's going back on our deal, the deal I *thought* was agreed with everyone, because I had no reason to think otherwise, she might have to come back down to our price, mightn't she? If there's no-one else?"

"She *might*," he conceded. "But she wouldn't do it willingly. There's a place she's seen in Dublin and the only way she can afford it is to get a bit more for her own. So she wants us to advertise again –"

"But that'll take ages! Tell her she might lose the house she wants if she leaves it too long! Tell her the amount we're offering is all the house is worth –"

"I can't tell her that, Mrs Larkin," he protested. "My obligation is to the seller, don't forget, to get them the highest possible price for their property. That's what I'm paid to do."

"What about your obligation to the purchaser, to treat them fairly? What about acting professionally? What about –"

"I think this conversation is finished, Mrs Larkin."

"No – wait!"

Too late. There was a firm click on the line, followed by the dial tone.

* * *

"I blew it, Rory. I well and truly blew it," she said, once she'd recovered enough to ring him. Only the occasional sniff betrayed the fact that she'd given in to a twenty-minute crying bout while Katie was asleep.

"No chance this Gallagher woman will change her mind?" he asked.

"Didn't sound like it. And Quinn probably won't even *talk* to me again – I still can't believe what I said –"

"He's in a tough business, Chelle. I'm sure that's the least of what he's been called in his time!"

"But still –"

"Michelle, if you were to ring him back with an apology and an offer of a few thousand more, I don't think he'd be hanging up on you!"

"But we can't do that, can we? Where would we get it?"

"I'll think of something," Rory promised. "I'll ring you back in an hour or so."

"I'm meeting Jan for lunch," she reminded him. "But I could cancel –"

The last thing she felt like was eating. Or, come to that, talking to Jan, who was still pouring cold water on the Roundwood house.

"No need," Rory said. "No, you go on, there's no point sitting at home moping. Ring me when you get back."

Michelle took extra care with her make-up but of course Una spotted immediately that something was wrong when Michelle called to drop Katie in.

"The bloody cow!" Una exclaimed when Michelle filled her in. "She has no right to do that – "

"Seems she has, Mam. But don't worry, Rory's trying to come up with something."

Easier said than done, on both counts, Michelle thought as she got back into the car to go and meet Jan.

Jan was surprisingly sympathetic, considering her views on the house. She might not think much of it, but she knew what it meant to Michelle. "I *know* you'll get it, if it's meant for you," she said. "They're just putting you through the hoops, that's all. That auctioneer has to show he's earning his money."

"I suppose," Michelle said. "But what if they get another buyer? I know you don't like it, Jan, but it *is* a great house, and at that price . . ."

"Not everyone wants to live in the country," Jan pointed out, "And anyway, didn't you say there's a problem with the water? That's bound to put people off!"

"It looks okay. The surveyor suggested we check it, that's all, so Rory dropped a sample in to the lab and the preliminary results look fine. So I can't even rely on that to scare people away!" Michelle said, with a rueful smile.

"You're not eating at all," Jan said. It was true – Michelle's plate sat in front of her, barely touched.

"Go ahead," Michelle said, responding to the unspoken question, pushing her plate across in front of Jan.

"So, can you raise your offer a bit?" Jan asked once she'd tasted a few mouthfuls of Michelle's goat's cheese salad. "Meet them halfway or something?"

Michelle sighed. "We're at the pin of our collar now. But Rory's trying to figure something out . . ."

"What about borrowing from your parents? Or Sarah?"

"I don't think so. Sarah's already stretched and I wouldn't want to ask Mam and Dad, things are tight enough for them – "

"Rory's brothers?"

"Definitely not Stephen, they've just bought a house themselves. And Matt puts every cent back into the business."

"You'll think of something," Jan said cheerfully. "Offer them another two or three thousand euro, that might do it!"

"But what if –"

"Just do it!" Jan said. "Ring me and let me know how you get on."

"We don't *have* three thousand euro," Michelle said. "As it is, I owe Visa a fortune after buying curtains and things."

Jan grimaced. She'd already warned Michelle she was mad to be buying stuff for a house she didn't even own yet.

"No use looking at me!" she said now, making a face, and they both laughed. "You know me, money just vanishes – I never have a cent to my name!"

"I could always ask my rich sister," Michelle said, and they laughed again. Helen controlled her money as she did everything else, and Michelle could go on bended knees and get nothing for her trouble but a lecture on the benefits of sound financial planning.

"Rory will think of something," Jan reassured her. "Now, stop looking so worried. It'll all work out."

"Wish I could be certain of that," Michelle said.

"Well, *I* am," Jan said firmly. "Trust me, it'll be fine. Buying a house isn't *meant* to be easy! Now, go on home and ring Rory and see if he's come up with anything."

Michelle said good-bye, promised to ring in a few days and drove to her mother's with an uneasy feeling, as if the sky was about to come crashing down around her.

Chapter Ten

She arrived home from her mother's with Katie, settled her with her toys and rang Rory.

"Problem solved, babe!" he said, sounding jubilant.

Her spirits lifted. "Tell me!"

"The payment from Adanate Ltd. Finally! And for the full amount, after all his bitching!"

"So, how much is it?"

"Well, let me see. Something around, hmm . . ."

She could almost hear him smiling.

"Rory!"

"Eight thousand five hundred and seventy-five euro!"

"Whew! How come?"

"I paid out for the computers myself, remember? That was the deal – he was to pay me back when he was fixing up the bill, but when he stopped returning my calls I thought I was snookered!"

"So –" she took a deep breath. "Do you want to ring Quinn?"

He laughed. "And spare you the humiliation of having to apologise?"

"Come *on-n-n-n*!"

"Okay – but you owe me! What's his number?"

She gave it to him without having to consult her notebook. "Will you offer him the full amount and be done with it?"

He thought for a moment. "Better not. That way we've a fall-back if he tries to push for more."

"D'you think he will?" She thought she could hear her heart starting to pound.

"Hard to say. We thought we had an agreement already, didn't we? Seems they're capable of anything."

"Ring me the minute you talk to him."

"Sure. And stop worrying – we'll get it sorted."

She hung up, tried to concentrate on some packing – one corner of the living-room was already piled high with boxes – but it was impossible.

Instead she made some tea and curled up with it in her favourite chair, waiting for his call.

She snatched the phone the second it rang. "Well?"

"I offered five thousand five hundred more. He said he'll put it to them."

"And?"

"And he'll ring me back."

"But what else did he say?"

"That's it, Michelle. That's all he said. Nothing about you, if that's what's worrying you!" he laughed.

"No, I mean did he say they're likely to take it or anything?"

"Nothing. Just that he'll ring as soon as they get back to him."

"I suppose I'd better ring him myself and apologise," she said. "But he must know I didn't mean it, I was just so upset . . ."

"Wouldn't do any harm, I suppose," Rory said. "Though he sounded all right. Maybe a bit cool. Probably embarrassed, after accepting the deposit and giving the impression everything was all right . . ."

"It will be, won't it?"

"No guarantees, babe. All we can do is wait."

* * *

It was a long two days, made longer by phone calls from Una, Sarah, Jan and – surprisingly – Helen, all wanting to know if there was any word.

Quinn finally rang just as Rory arrived home on the Monday evening.

Michelle watched his face as he lifted the phone, saw him grimace. "I see. Right, yes. I'll have to talk to Michelle, look at our figures again, but I don't think – yes, okay. Right. 'Bye."

"What?" she demanded, the second he hung up.

"No go," he said. He was still standing in the hallway, and now he leaned against the wall, looking exhausted. "They won't even consider five and a half. It's ten thousand or nothing, he said."

"They took bloody long enough to tell us!"

Another grimace. "We still have three thousand to play with. Let's have something to eat, then look at the figures again."

They ate quickly, put Katie to bed, spread some sheets from their 'house' file on the kitchen table and got to work.

"That's it, then," Rory said finally. "You'll have to ring him, okay? I've a meeting at nine, otherwise I'd do it myself. Offer him the other three thousand, then get on to the bank – they'll surely stretch the loan by another fifteen hundred. Once they give the go-ahead you can get on to Quinn again . . ."

"But what if –"

"If the bank refuses, or if the Gallaghers want more, I'll talk to Matt. I don't see what else we can do."

They had spent a careful half-hour looking at the company's projected cash flow for the next three months to see if they could eke an extra thousand or two out of it. If it came to it, Rory was prepared to push for overdue payments and delay his own debts for a few weeks where possible, but he didn't like the idea.

"Robbing Peter to pay Paul. We'll be on our uppers for a couple of months before you go back to work . . ." He grinned at her hopeful expression. "I know, it'll be worth it. So tell that to my ulcers . . ."

"Maybe they'll settle for the extra three thousand. Should I ring him now, on his mobile?"

Rory glanced at the clock. "After nine. Better leave it – tomorrow's time enough."

* * *

"I'll put it to the Gallaghers and let you know, Mrs Larkin," Gerry Quinn said. Rory was right, definitely cool.

"Look, what I said the other day, about you not being professional – I'm really sorry. I was very upset. I know that's no excuse, but –"

"I've been called worse," he said, with a slight laugh.

"I still shouldn't have –"

"It's always a strain buying a house. People can act out of character."

"I don't know if I'd want your job," she said sympathetically.

"It has its compensations! Now, I'll ring them within the hour and get back to you."

"Will they give you an answer straight away, do you think?"

"Unlikely. They'll probably want to think it over – but I promise to ring the minute I hear from them."

Michelle hung up, started to ring Rory, remembered his meeting and put the phone down again. It rang almost immediately. Jan, wanting to know how things were going.

"We've offered our last three thousand now," Michelle said. "That's eight and a half thousand more than they agreed to in the first place!"

"It's a rotten thing to do," Jan said sympathetically. "What happened, d'you think? Just got greedy?"

"The wife, as far as I know. That's what Quinn is hinting, anyway. I could string up Gallagher *and* his wife! They *must* know how much we want the place!"

"That's the trouble, really, isn't it?" Jan said. "If you could just play it cool . . ."

"*Cool?* Jan, I didn't even sleep last night! Half our stuff is packed away and the Connollys are ringing every second day to ask if we can't hurry things up on our side because they're anxious to move in . . ."

"That's a bit unfair, isn't it? You agreed a date . . ."

"The whole bloody thing's unfair if you ask me. We seem to be the only ones sticking to an agreement. Don't *ever* buy a house, Jan! It's not worth it!"

Jan laughed. "I believe you! Ring me if you've any word before Friday."

"Sure. And thanks for letting me sound off –"

"Any time!" Jan said cheerfully. "Now, chin up. You'll get it sorted!"

Wish I could be so sure, Michelle thought as she went upstairs to start packing some of her clothes, stuff she wouldn't need in the next eight weeks or so.

Though I'll go mad living out of boxes, she thought. It reminded her too uncomfortably of the time she and Sarah had spent a summer in London in their student days, living with an accommodating cousin. Fine for a while, but not if it went on too long.

It won't, she told herself firmly as she directed her energies to keeping Katie amused in between taking clothes from the wardrobe and sorting them into piles for packing or donating to charity. It was close to the time when Quinn should be ringing, and she needed something, anything, to keep her occupied until then.

Finally satisfied that she had her wardrobe pared down to what she absolutely needed for the next month or two, she went back downstairs with Katie and tried to concentrate on making a shopping list. She had done most of her shopping at the weekend, but if Quinn didn't ring soon she'd do a quick run up to the supermarket on Sundrive Road, just to get out before she drove herself mad.

She was on the point of putting their coats on when he rang.

"Not good, I'm afraid."

Michelle waited, holding her breath.

"Is there any chance you might come up a bit more?" he asked.

"How *much* more?" Michelle asked in a tight voice.

There was a pause. "They're suggesting four hundred and ninety thousand euro. The original asking price."

"And what was all that – that *charade* about coming down to four-eighty?" Michelle asked, her voice rising out of control now.

Another pause. "They lowered the price on my advice in order to secure an early bid," he said finally.

"What do you mean, 'early bid'? You were just using us to –"

"No, nothing like that," he said quickly. "I suggested that might be an appropriate price, that's all. If they wanted an early sale."

"So why did they change their minds?"

"They – Mrs Gallagher – thinks the house is worth more."

"But it's not!"

"It depends," Quinn said. "It's worth what the market will bear."

"What's that supposed to mean? We're offering four hundred and eighty-three thousand, five hundred –"

"They'd like you to bring it up a bit."

"We already did that! They *agreed* on four hundred and seventy-five thousand –"

Steady, Michelle. You're losing it . . .

Quinn evidently thought so too. "Would it help if you talked to your husband?"

Michelle bit her lip. "Of course I'll talk to him. I'm not sure it'll make any difference, though. We simply don't have any more money."

"If you could come up to four hundred and eighty-five –"

"And after that, get dragged all the way up to four hundred and ninety?"

"I don't think it will come to that," he said.

"But you're not sure."

"No. No, I'm not sure. Particularly if someone else expresses an interest. It's still advertised in our window, and on the website."

She sighed. "How long do we have?"

"As long as you like, really. Providing, of course, that there's no competing bid."

"And there isn't."

"Not at the moment, no."

"So can we leave our offer stand? I mean, if there's nobody else –"

"Nobody at the moment," he reminded her quietly. "You can leave it stand, certainly – but I have to tell you I don't expect them to change their minds."

"What if we I talked to Mr Gallagher?" she asked as the thought hit her. "Maybe –"

"I really don't think that would be a good idea, Mrs Larkin."

* * *

"He would say that, wouldn't he?" Sarah pointed out when she called in for a few minutes on her way home. "Of *course* he doesn't want you talking to them and working out a deal that leaves him out of the loop!"

"I don't think it's like that," Michelle said. "I got the impression – I don't know, that he doesn't really like what they're doing . . ."

Sarah gave her a cynical look.

"This is his job we're talking about, Chelle! Don't forget, *they're* the ones who're paying him! So how did you leave it?"

"I'm to ring him if anything changes. Likewise."

"And d'you think it will?"

"On their side, no. Not from what he said. So I'm waiting to hear from Ed Nolan tomorrow – "

"Ed Nolan?"

"The mortgage advisor in the bank. We go back a long way – he said he'll do what he can."

"Michelle, the bank has millions! Billions! Fifteen hundred isn't going to break them!"

"No, but they have strict lending rules, even for staff. I think it'll be okay, though. As long as the Gallaghers will take four eighty-five."

* * *

She rang the auctioneer's the minute Ed Nolan gave her the news, but Gerry Quinn was out of the office and not expected back until after the weekend.

"I'll try him on his mobile."

"You might be better waiting, Mrs Larkin, if you don't mind," the secretary suggested crisply. "He doesn't actually take that many days off, and he *will* be in first thing on Monday."

"Isn't there anyone who covers for him when he's away?" Michelle asked, exasperated.

"Only in an emergency," came the reply.

"This *is* –"

"He didn't include it on his list. I'll see that he gets your message."

And Michelle had no option but to hang up.

"I've a good mind to go and see the Gallaghers myself," she said to Jan when they met for lunch on the Friday. "Imagine he just went off without a word –"

"Give it a rest, will you, Michelle?"

"I thought you were interested –"

"I am. Just not every single time we meet."

"Sorry," Michelle said, after a pause. "I suppose I'm getting carried away."

"A bit," Jan replied. "It *is* only a house, Michelle."

Michelle sighed. "I suppose. But I've bought curtains for it, I know where the piano will go, and my grandmother's writing-desk. It's *my* house, Jan. I just don't have it yet."

"You will," Jan said. "Now, let's change the subject, okay?"

* * *

He beat her to it on Monday morning.

"Mr Quinn!" she said when she heard his voice. "We've got it! Four hundred and eighty-five thousand."

He cleared his throat. "The thing is, I hate to tell you . . ."

She felt ice running down her spine. "Yes?"

"There's been another offer."

"How much?" she asked faintly, after a moment.

"Four hundred and eighty-seven."

"When did that happen?"

"Saturday, I'm told. There was a message waiting for me when I arrived this morning."

"But have they got the money? Or a surveyor's report? Maybe they're not serious, maybe – "

"I believe they're serious. I spoke to them just a few minutes ago."

"Without speaking to me first? You *promised* –"

"That I'd get back to you as soon as anything changed. Which, as you see, it has."

"That's it, then," she said, after a pause. "We're out of it." Her voice was shaking.

"I suppose there's no chance . . .?" he asked.

She almost rounded on him. Instead, she managed to sound calm as she said "I'm not into playing games, Mr Quinn. We just don't have any more money."

"Do you want to give it a day or two?"

"So we can push the price up a bit more?" This time she couldn't keep the bitterness from her voice.

"Whatever you think. I'm sorry, Mrs Larkin. I know how much you liked that house."

Everything in her was screaming '*It's not fair, it's not fair*' as she hung up the phone.

She was saying it aloud, over and over, tears streaming down her face when Rory called in on his way across the city that afternoon.

"We'll get the money somewhere, Michelle. I'll think of something."

"No, it's gone, Rory. Look at me – idiot, bawling over a house –"

"You love it, that's why. And we'll try –"

She controlled the sobs, wiped her face. "It's gone. I don't know why I'm so sure, I just know it's gone."

She was right. They managed to scrape together another six thousand between loans from Michelle's parents and Rory's brother Matt and a donation from Sarah's holiday fund – "September's *ages* away," she told them cheerfully – but it still wasn't enough, and in her heart she knew it.

"Four hundred and ninety-one is absolutely as high as we can go," she told Jan on Thursday. She was completely deflated, having just made the phone call to Quinn. "He's to get back to me, but I think I know what the answer will be."

So did Jan.

Quinn phoned Michelle as promised, late that evening.

"I'm afraid they've accepted a higher offer of four hundred and ninety-five thousand." He cleared his throat. "I think you may know the couple, Mrs Larkin. Jan and Damien Kelly."

In the split second before hurt and an overwhelming sense of loss kicked in, Michelle realised that, somehow, it was no surprise at all.

Chapter Eleven

"The bitch! The bloody *bitch*!" Sarah said when she called in on the Friday evening. "How could she *do* that to you? How could *anyone* do that?"

"With a lot of help from me," Michelle said bitterly. "I told her everything she wanted to know, I told her to the last cent how much we could afford . . ."

"But why wouldn't you?" Rory said, raging. "She was supposed to be a *friend* of yours, Michelle! Why *wouldn't* you tell her?"

"You wouldn't think of going round there . . ." Sarah began.

Michelle didn't even ask "And what?" She didn't need to; her expression said it all.

"So what happens now?" Sarah asked.

Michelle just shrugged in reply.

"We'll think of something," Rory said, dragging a

hand distractedly through his hair. "We'd better. The Connollys are moving in here in four weeks."

* * *

"You'll stay here for a while, it's the obvious thing to do," Una said when they all met for lunch the following Sunday. "You'll need every cent you have so there's no point paying out fifteen hundred euro a month for rent –"

"It wouldn't be that much," Michelle said. Her voice, drained of every spark of energy and enthusiasm, still didn't sound much like hers.

"But why pay anything at all when you can stay here?" Una asked. "We've plenty of room, haven't we, Maurice?"

Her father was quick to agree. "For as long as it takes. Six months, a year, you're welcome however long it is," he said, sending Michelle's spirits plummeting further.

"It won't be that long," Rory said quickly, noticing.

"I only meant you can stay that long, not that you'd *need* to stay that long, of course," Maurice began. "Though if it turns out that you *did* need to –"

"Maurice, bring in the apple-tart and cream, would you?" Una asked, glaring at him.

"But I'm not finished my –"

He turned to her as he spoke, caught the glare and went to the kitchen to get the apple-tart, resolving to keep his mouth closed in future and not bother trying to help people.

His resolve lasted twenty seconds.

"I've an idea," he said, arriving back with the apple-tart. "Helen was telling us there's a house just gone up for sale opposite her. If you put in a quick offer maybe they'd – what?" he asked, looking bewildered as Michelle fled to the bathroom in tears. "What did I say now?"

"Enough, Maurice. You said enough," Una told him grimly as Helen took umbrage and left abruptly with her children, saying she really didn't feel like apple-tart, thank you, *she* knew when not to make a glutton of herself . . .

"I don't know," he muttered. "Sometimes a man's better off saying nothing at all in this house."

For once, they all agreed with him.

* * *

She had no energy to do anything. It seemed that every room was full of half-packed boxes or strewn with bits and pieces wrapped in newspaper, so they could never find anything they wanted. Rory was under pressure at work with a big contract that would fall through if he didn't put in the hours, so even if anything *did* come up Michelle would have to follow it up on her own.

It hardly mattered. There was nothing that interested her, in spite of being on the mailing lists of every auctioneer on the southside of the city, and one or two outside it.

"I don't want to live in the country anyway," she told her mother one day when Una called in on her way to the drama group. "I was mad even to think about it in the first place."

"It might have worked," Una said.

"Might have," Michelle said, making circles on the kitchen table with a spoon and some spilt sugar.

"You're putting yourself under a lot of pressure, love."

Michelle looked at her mother, saying nothing. "I mean, you have to leave here in two weeks, haven't you? So why don't you just move in with us?"

Michelle felt the tears start down her face, something that happened with annoying regularity lately.

"Well!" Una said, pursing her lips. "We're not *that* bad, surely!"

"Of course not!" Michelle said quickly, grabbing a tissue. "It's just – oh, God!" The tears flowed again as she thought of giving up her home. "What if we never find anywhere else we like?"

"You will, love. Of course you will. It's only a matter of time – the right place is bound to come up."

Michelle scrunched the tissue hard, twisting it into little pieces, seemingly unaware of what she was doing. "That's the problem, isn't it, Mam. The right place *did* come up, and that – that – "

She stopped, at a loss for any word that could adequately describe Jan Kelly.

"It *was* lovely, Michelle, I'll grant you that. But it wasn't for you, love. Just you wait, you'll find something better."

Michelle wished she could believe that. Idly, she wondered if she'd ever really believe anyone again, no matter who they were or what they said.

* * *

"Time to get sorted, Michelle," Sarah said briskly when she called unannounced on Saturday morning. "Drop Katie over to Mam – she's expecting her – and then let's see if we can sort out a few more of these boxes."

"I don't think I feel up to it."

"You haven't really a choice, have you? And don't start crying on me again – I need you to see what I'm packing so it goes in the right place."

"Sarah, I really don't –"

Sarah relented, but only slightly. "Like it or not, the Connollys will be here in less than two weeks, Chelle. It's practically their house already."

Michelle nodded miserably at that. Anna Connolly had a path beaten to the door, calling every chance she got to measure the living-room for a new carpet – *'But those floorboards are great, it took us three whole weeks to sand and varnish them'*, Michelle had wanted to protest – and have another look at the little backyard and check out the bedrooms again. *Just like me with the Roundwood house,* she reminded herself, biting back her irritation at being disturbed when all she wanted was peace to enjoy her last few days in the little house she was now devastated to be leaving.

"Are you listening, Michelle?" Sarah's voice

interrupted her thoughts. "Come on, why don't you bring Katie to Mam while I get started here. And then, when we've had enough of packing, we'll check out a few auctioneers again."

The look on Michelle's face said it all. "I can't."

Sarah reached across to touch her on the arm. "You have to, Chelle," she said in a gentler voice. "You have to do something, because your choices right now are to rent a place or move in with Mam, and you don't want to do that for the rest of your life, do you? Plus, you've made it totally clear that you're not interested in being Helen's next-door neighbour, so you can't rely on *her* to look out for a place for you . . ."

There was a glimmer of a smile on Michelle's face. "God, she'll probably never talk to me again! I didn't mean it like that."

Sarah laughed and suddenly Michelle joined in.

"Yes, you did," Sarah said. "Face it, you're a city girl at heart – look what the mention of moving five or six miles out to the suburbs did to you!"

"I was happy to move to Roundwood –"

"No, Michelle. You were happy to move into that house, no matter where it was. But in no time at all you'd have got fed up trekking in and out that distance. Jan's welcome to it, if you ask me, and may she rot up there!"

"Sarah!"

"Oh, right. You want her to live happily ever after?"

"Sure. Just so long as she's snowed in first for six

months, and falls out with all the neighbours, and drops down a bog-hole and –"

"Rots?" Sarah suggested.

"Rots," Michelle agreed with a grin.

"That's more like it!" Sarah said, returning the grin. "Okay, fun's over, now let's get to work!"

It was well past two o'clock before Sarah pronounced them finished for the day.

"The packing, anyway," she said. "Let's have a quick bite and call in to a few auctioneers."

"Sare –" Michelle gave her a pleading look.

"We're on a roll, Michelle. Don't back out on me now, okay?"

"Just as long as we don't go near Quinn."

"Nowhere near him. There are plenty of other auctioneers."

And there were, but a trawl of all of them showed nothing remotely interesting. *Keep trying,* they were told again and again. *Something's bound to come up in a few weeks . . .*

"That's the problem, isn't it?" Michelle said as they left with yet another disappointing selection of properties – which came down to one or two, really – from yet another auctioneer. "I just don't have a few weeks!"

"I don't think you've much choice, Michelle," Sarah said sympathetically. "Look, we'll go through these anyway and if there's anything worthwhile we'll find it! I'll even come with you, if I can. We'll find you somewhere."

"I don't just want '*somewhere*'!" Michelle said, glaring.

"Well, if you don't look you won't find!" Sarah said, finally exasperated. "Now, come *on*, let's get home and go through these!"

They whittled it down to one or two possibilities, went to see them and even Sarah had to admit it looked hopeless. There were still plenty of houses on the market, but nowhere Michelle wanted to live in at a price she could afford.

"That's the trouble, really," Sarah said a few days later, as they returned from yet another fruitless expedition. "Anything you can afford around here needs loads of work and loads more money put into it, and we haven't seen *one* with a decent garden. There are some good houses, all right, but they cost the earth. Nothing else for it, you're going to have to lower your sights."

Michelle nodded glumly. She'd come to that conclusion herself in the course of the past few days.

"So what can you absolutely not do without?" Sarah asked. "If you could pick just one thing you had to have, what would it be?"

"A big back garden," Michelle said without hesitation. "Before I went off on that wild-goose chase up the mountains I wanted a spacious house with a big back garden, somewhere around here. And what I loved most about the Roundwood house was the sense of space up there – so if I could just pick one thing, it would be a big back garden."

"And with a big garden you could always build on later if the house was a bit small," Sarah said, relieved that Michelle could finally mention the Roundwood house without bursting into tears. "So, let's make a few more phone calls, concentrating on houses near here – doesn't matter what size, as long as they've big back gardens. Okay?"

* * *

It was Rory who answered the phone a few days later when Gerry Quinn phoned.

"I'll understand, of course, if you want nothing more to do with me," he said, "but I have a house that just might interest you. I'm not sure – and in fact I'm not even sure the owner would be willing to sell to you, but –"

"Been there, done that and we're not about to do it again!" Rory said in a voice of pure ice. "Now, if that's all –"

"Let me just give you some details," Quinn said quickly. "It's between Rathmines and Rathgar, a lovely old place set in its own grounds. Your wife did say she wanted space –"

"You know to the last cent how much we can afford, Mr Quinn. Goodbye – "

"Wait, Mr Larkin, please!" Quinn interrupted. "Look, there was nothing I could do about the house in Roundwood, but I may be able to help you now. At least hear me out and then, if you want, you can think about it."

"You have two minutes," Rory said coolly.

Quinn cleared his throat. "It's an unusual situation – the house is the family home of an elderly lady who's willing to sell at well below market value. I can guarantee it would be within your price range, because money isn't an issue. It's more a matter of who she's willing to sell to." He paused. "And there are conditions . . ."

* * *

"So go for it!" Sarah said when Michelle spoke to her later. "You'd be mad not to!"

"Mad?" Michelle exclaimed. "This is the maddest thing I ever heard! She's ninety-two, for God's sake. She *can't* be in her right mind. And I've been messed about enough already without having to deal with a doddery old woman in her dotage."

"Come off it, Michelle! What about Aunt Sadie, she could out-think and out-talk the rest of us until a week before she died!"

"Hmm. But *she* was only eighty-nine," Michelle said with the beginnings of a smile as she realised that Sarah was right.

She had nothing to lose by meeting this old woman and hearing what she had to say.

Chapter Twelve

Evelyn Lacey walked slowly and with determination towards the drawing-room, relying heavily on the silver-topped cane that had once belonged to her Uncle Hugh. With her left hand she reached for the brass rail that ran along the hallway, just above waist height, and stopped to draw breath.

"I'm perfectly fine, Annie," she told the housekeeper who stood at the drawing-room doorway, watching anxiously. "I can manage, so *please* do stop fussing, there's a good girl, and make sure you bring in the tea ten minutes after they arrive. That should give us enough time."

She gave a wry smile as she proceeded into the drawing-room and settled herself in the Queen Anne chair by the fire to await Mr Quinn and his companions. Ten minutes would be ample time for them all to see if they had anything further to discuss; it had taken the last couple precisely half that to decide that they wanted nothing to do with her or her proposition, and another thirty seconds to make their excuses and leave.

She didn't blame them. Even to herself it sounded strange, attaching such a condition to what could otherwise be the straightforward sale of Avignon, her family home. And she could make a great deal of money if it *were* a straightforward sale, according to Mr Quinn. That fair-haired man he had brought along two weeks ago, the man who told her to '*get down to business and cut the crap*' – her mouth twitched at the recollection – had offered her a frighteningly large sum of money to sell the house without any conditions. But that wasn't the point, as Evelyn had already explained to Mr Quinn. When one is over ninety years of age, money is no longer the most important consideration.

She had closed her eyes and was beginning to drift off slightly in the heat of the drawing-room when the deep peal of the front doorbell roused her. She heard Annie's hurrying steps, the slight creak as the front door opened, voices in the hall followed by a brisk knock on the drawing-room door.

The young women who responded to her invitation to come in were tall, slim and dark-haired. One, she noticed, was looking directly at her, while the other surreptitiously took in the details of the room.

"No need to get up, Miss Lacey," Gerry Quinn greeted her as he followed them in.

She stood anyway. She needed to get the measure of these women, and she would do so on her own terms, standing upright in her own drawing-room even if she *did* need the support of a cane.

She smiled and held out her free hand as Quinn introduced them. Michelle Larkin and Sarah Keogh. *Strange,* she thought as they all sat down in a circle around the fire, *I would have taken them for sisters. Unless* . . . Quickly her eyes went to their hands and noticed Michelle's wedding ring.

"Which of you is interested in buying my house?" she asked crisply.

The woman named Sarah met her gaze calmly, while Michelle seemed slightly startled. She had been continuing her quiet scrutiny of the room and was taken aback, Evelyn realised, by the direct question.

"I'm the one looking for a house, Miss Lacey," she said after a moment. "But I'm sure this isn't it. I don't know if Mr Quinn told you what my budget is." She gave a quick glance in his direction, just as his mobile phone rang.

Quickly he excused himself and went out to the front porch to take the call.

Evelyn continued to watch her steadily. "Mr Quinn explained that money is not the primary factor?"

"Well, yes, but –"

"Then all that is necessary is for us to decide if this is to be your house," Evelyn said. "And for you to agree to my conditions."

Michelle took a deep breath. "Before we say anything else, Miss Lacey, I'd better make it clear that I'm not into playing games. I've already been let down with one house and I don't want to find myself in the same position again."

"How have you been let down?" Evelyn asked quietly, and Michelle found herself telling the old lady all about Jan and the house in Roundwood. She hadn't intended to go into any detail, but gradually, prompted by one or two perceptive questions from Evelyn, she told her what had happened.

Nothing at all wrong with her *mind*, Michelle thought as she found herself warming to the older woman. "So you see, what I'm hoping for is a house I like, that I can buy without any complications and without fear of losing it to someone else. I shouldn't really have come because I know I can't afford your house, no matter how little you're asking," she concluded. "It must be worth a fortune and I'm wasting your time."

"You don't believe me, do you, my dear?" Evelyn asked with a searching, slightly amused look. "I mean it when I say money is not an issue."

"But – " Michelle was interrupted by a quick knock and the door opening as Annie came into the room and placed a tray on a mahogany side-table. At a nod from Evelyn she began pouring tea and handed them each a cup before passing the milk and sugar to them in turn. She returned the sugar and milk to the tray and left the room quietly, leaving the tray on the table.

"Have you lived here long?" Michelle asked as she took a sip from the fine china cup in her hand.

Evelyn, holding her own cup and saucer in hands that shook almost imperceptibly, looked directly at Michelle for a moment before answering. "My whole life, my dear. A very long time indeed. So you see, I must be certain it goes to the right person." She paused, took a sip of her tea.

"And why . . ." Michelle began, then hesitated.

Evelyn continued looking at her, a slight smile on her lips. "You're wondering why I'm selling now?" she asked finally, when Michelle didn't continue.

"I'm sorry, it's none of my business," Michelle said.

"But a fair question," Evelyn responded. "And one I'm quite happy to answer. My younger sister Agatha has been in a nursing home, a very good one, for the past year and at this point I would like to join her. But before I can leave this house, there's a certain matter that I wish to see settled, one way or the other. Now," she said, changing the subject abruptly, "tell me about your family. You do have children, I presume? I can't imagine anyone wanting a house this size unless they had children."

"One little girl," Michelle answered quickly. "Her name's Katie, she's just turned three."

The old lady's eyes took on a faraway look and for a second Michelle wondered whether she'd heard her.

It seemed she had. After a moment she murmured "Katie. A three-year-old named Katie. Robin would have liked that."

Instead of elaborating as Michelle expected, Evelyn Lacey put her cup down on a small round table beside her chair and reached for her cane.

"Would you like to see the rest of the house?" she asked briskly, her mood seeming to change in an instant.

"I'd love to," Michelle said.

Evelyn eased herself to her feet, aided by the cane, and led the way slowly from the room.

"There are two other reception rooms on this floor," she said as she crossed the large tiled hallway. "Not quite at their best now, as you can see," she added, turning a brass handle and giving a slight push to a heavy panelled door. "Annie does what she can, but there's a great deal of work here for one person."

She moved forward into the room, followed by Michelle and Sarah, then stood aside, allowing them space to take in all the details of the large, airy room.

"It's gorgeous," Michelle said finally. "Really gorgeous." She ran her hand lightly along the marble of the fireplace, let her eyes follow the line of the expertly-crafted cornices, the details of the elaborate ceiling-rose. "I love the high ceiling," she murmured.

"I've always liked them," Evelyn agreed. "They give a room such a sense of space, don't you think? This has always been my favourite room – cosier than the drawing-room, even if it's not quite as bright."

"It's bright enough," Sarah said. "Those tall windows are great."

"But draughty now, I'm afraid," Evelyn said wryly.

"I don't suppose I should call it cosy any more. I spend most of my time these days in the drawing-room because I can't manage to have repairs done at this stage and the windows there are in better condition. Now, the dining-room is through here."

This room was slightly smaller, but just as impressive, with windows out to the side giving a view of an ornamental rockery and some overgrown flower-beds. The colour on the walls, slightly faded, was a rich, ornate red. Michelle imagined dinner parties here, with candles on the mantelpiece and a fire blazing in the hearth. The faint musty smell suggested that nothing like that had happened here for a good many years.

A shame, she thought. *A lovely house like this and it's going to waste.*

Evelyn led them back into the hallway and, to Michelle's slight surprise, passed by a door on their right as if it wasn't there. Straight ahead were two steps, which Evelyn negotiated with some difficulty, leading down to the kitchen at the back of the house.

She mustn't have much money, Michelle thought. The three rooms they had been in were beautiful, with old, highly-polished furniture and plenty of paintings and ornaments, but everything had a jaded look, as if they had done service for a very long time. The rugs, she had noticed, were becoming threadbare, the once-rich pattern fading into obscurity in parts. *So why on earth doesn't she sell the house for what it's worth?*

"Mind your step," Evelyn warned, as they followed

her into a lower-ceilinged room with three sash windows along one side giving a view of part of the garden.

The room was basic but comfortable, with a black-and-white tiled floor, a deep old china sink and a big range set into a redbricked fireplace. An old, well-worn dresser stood against the back wall, next to a pine table and four chairs. A fifth chair, a rocking-chair, was tucked into a corner to one side of the range. The floral cushions on it bore evidence of frequent use.

Evelyn Lacey, Michelle wondered, *or the woman who brought the tea*?

More likely to be the latter. Somehow she couldn't imagine Miss Lacey, in her elegant skirt, her cream silk blouse and cashmere cardigan, spending much time in this room.

"It could probably benefit from some updating," Evelyn said as she saw Michelle's expression. "I suppose I don't really notice it any more, after all this time. Mama didn't really encourage us to come down here, and even now it's Annie's domain rather than mine."

So I was right, Michelle thought. *Talk about* 'Upstairs, Downstairs.' *If I had this house –*

She stopped the thought quickly, telling herself not to be ridiculous. No matter what Evelyn Lacey said, the house *had* to be out of her reach.

"This is the pantry, and then the scullery," Evelyn said, leading them through what Michelle had assumed to be the back door, into a series of smaller rooms and finally to a large, heavy door leading out to the back garden.

Obviously not used much, Michelle thought as Evelyn struggled with the rusting key. And then she caught her breath as the door swung open, revealing the full glory of the garden.

It was wild, no question, but it was *enormous*. Nearly *too* big, Michelle thought, smiling as she imagined Katie swinging on that tree, or running along that little pathway, though they'd have to cut back those weeds before –

Stop it! she told herself again, firmly. She was *mad* to have come here. No way could they come anywhere near owning a house like this, or a garden that looked like you could build a dozen tennis courts on it, right in the heart of Dublin 6 . . .

"Would you like to wander around for a few minutes?" Evelyn asked. "I'll wait here, if you don't mind, but do take your time. You might tell me how the rambling rose down at the back is faring . . . I never manage to get down there now, I'm afraid."

She smiled wistfully and stood watching, leaning on her cane with both hands, as they edged their way cautiously down what was left of the pathway.

Chapter Thirteen

"So, what do you think?" Sarah asked quickly as they stopped by some fruit trees halfway down the garden and stood looking back towards the warm redbrick of the kitchen wall. There was no sign of Evelyn Lacey at the door now, and Michelle assumed she had gone in to rest for a few minutes.

"I don't think she's crazy, if that's what you mean," Michelle answered. "Just maybe a bit weird."

"Seems to have all her marbles, " Sarah said.

Michelle nodded in agreement, reaching to touch some clematis that scrambled along the side wall.

"I meant the house though, not her," Sarah elaborated. "It's really something, isn't it?"

"Sare, it's way out of my reach," Michelle said. "We both know that."

"But she said –"

"It doesn't matter what she said," Michelle interrupted firmly. "I shouldn't have come. What's the point? She's not senile, so she's not about to hand over this house for less than it's worth unless there's a damn good reason – and like I told her, I'm not into playing any more games. I've had just about all the games I can handle!"

"Might as well hear what she has to say, all the same. D'you like it?"

"It's amazing! All that space, and those trees – "

"And that glasshouse, wonder what's in there?" Sarah asked, and they made their way through the overgrown grass and weeds to have a look.

There wasn't much to see, just a big greenhouse with some cold frames and gardening tools and an old straw hat hanging on a nail by the door, relic of some long-gone gardener.

They left the greenhouse, swinging the door to behind them, and continued towards the end of the long garden, through a once-ornamental hedge that surrounded what seemed to have been a vegetable patch.

At the very end there was a cherry tree, its delicate pink blossoms waving in the slight breeze that eddied round the garden. There was an old wooden bench in its shade and an elegant brass sundial set just beyond reach of its branches. On the wall behind it was a rambling rose with rich green foliage but, as yet, no blooms.

"I'd want it just for this!" Michelle exclaimed, touching the fragile petals of the cherry-blossom. "Look, isn't it beautiful?"

They sat on the bench for a few minutes, looking around. The sense of privacy was astonishing so close to the city. They could hear voices somewhere, and the muted sound of traffic, but it was difficult to see any of the surrounding houses from where they sat screened by the cherry tree and more fruit trees to the far right of them.

"It's a wonder some developer hasn't got hold of it!" Sarah said, watching as Michelle, on impulse, reached up and broke off a small branch of the cherry-blossom, holding it close to her to enjoy its sweet scent. "Think what they could do with this!"

Michelle's stomach churned. "Maybe that's just what she doesn't want?" she suggested hopefully as they stood up and began making their way back towards the house.

"Well, we'll know what she *does* want in a minute or two," Sarah murmured as they reached the back door. Evelyn was waiting for them in the kitchen.

"No roses yet, I'm afraid," Michelle told her. "But I brought you this. I hope you don't mind."

Evelyn reached out a hand to take the proffered cherry-blossom and, just as Michelle had done, breathed deeply of its scent.

"A kind thought, my dear," Evelyn said. "I can see it from my bedroom window, but I don't think I'll be going down there any more! One of the many things I miss now is the scent of my garden in bloom . . ."

The wistful look returned for a moment before she smiled at them and said briskly, "Now, let us make our way upstairs and afterwards we can have some more tea, unless you're in a great hurry."

They assured her that they had plenty of time as they followed her once more into the hall and watched as she moved slowly up the stairs with the aid of her cane.

"My doctor wants me to install one of those electric chairs," she said as she reached the first landing with Sarah and Michelle just behind her. "Silly man, it would quite ruin this beautiful staircase, and I have no intention of doing that while I can still work these legs of mine!"

She was, Michelle noticed, slightly out of breath and leaning heavily again on the cane, but her eyes were sparkling. "You have no idea the satisfaction it gives me to manage that at my age! And I hope to have left the house before I get to the point where I can no longer do so."

"And do you have any idea when you might be leaving?" Michelle ventured. "You said –"

"That there is something I would like to see settled," Evelyn added. "And I'm not sure how long that might take, my dear. We can discuss it once I've shown you the upstairs. No need to go into the attic unless you really wish to – I'm sure it's quite dusty, and heaven knows what might be up there – but there *is* a small staircase should you want to examine it later. For now I'll just show you the bedrooms, if you don't mind. I'm afraid this is one of those days when I'm feeling my age!"

Michelle was immediately contrite. "We shouldn't have dragged you up the stairs," she said quickly. "I'm sure Gerry Quinn would be happy to show us around the rest of the house."

"And I'm quite sure you're right, my dear. But I'd much rather do it myself. It won't take long to see the bedrooms, and then there's just one more room downstairs."

The door we passed, Michelle thought, wondering again why Evelyn hadn't brought them in at the time.

They examined the five bedrooms quickly. One was very small, not much more than a boxroom, but the others were very large with plenty of light and more than enough room for the elegant old furniture they contained.

Michelle would have liked to dally, drinking in every detail of the china doorknobs and hand-plates, the brass bells which presumably had once rung in the kitchen for the servants, the black fireplaces with their lovely tiled insets and the brass four-poster bed in the master bedroom, but she was conscious now that Evelyn was beginning to look strained and exhausted.

This must be hard on her emotionally as well, Michelle thought, feeling a sudden sympathy for the old lady. *It must be desperately hard leaving such a lovely place after so long. Her whole life, she said.*

She took a last quick look at the big front bedroom with the light streaming through the tall sash windows, crossed the landing at Evelyn's instruction to peer into the huge but hopelessly outdated bathroom, and finally joined Sarah to follow Evelyn slowly back down the wide staircase.

Annie appeared in the hallway as they reached the door of the drawing-room and hurried away again at a nod from Evelyn.

Gerry Quinn, waiting in the drawing room, stood up and put away his mobile phone as Evelyn led Michelle and Sarah back into the room.

"Annie is bringing more tea," she said, indicating that they should all take a seat. "I do hope you all have a few more minutes to spare?"

She smiled as they nodded, a satisfied look on her face. "It's very pleasant to have company. Annie and I are too used to each other. It makes a stimulating change to have other people here occasionally."

"Do you have many visitors?" Michelle asked without thinking.

"Do you mean since I offered my house for sale, or generally, my dear?" Evelyn asked with a broad smile.

"Both, I suppose," Michelle answered, returning the smile.

"Generally speaking, not too many," Evelyn said. "The clergy occasionally, and the doctor regularly, whether I need him or not – he's a dear, but he does fuss, as if being ninety-two years old were an illness in itself – but other than that, hardly anyone, I'm afraid. Agatha is my only remaining relative. We seem to have outlived everyone else, even my first cousin's unfortunate son, Terence. The house was to have gone to him, you see, but the silly man died following a skiing accident five or six years ago. He had already left two wives, and had no children. He never *did* manage to do anything remotely useful in his rather short life."

Michelle and Sarah sat gaping at her, not knowing what to say, while Quinn tried to hide a smile.

"Have I shocked you, my dears?" Evelyn asked quietly, watching Michelle and Sarah's expressions. "Forgive me, but it is one of the few consolations of advanced old age that one feels free to speak one's mind – assuming one is still in possession of it, of course. As I hope I am, and as indeed my doctor has assured me I am. Terence, on the other hand, was of sound mind only when he was kept from the whiskey bottle – and I'm afraid I have no sympathy at all for someone foolish enough to take to the ski slopes having consumed, by all accounts, the output of a small distillery. The only comfort we derived was that his parents had already gone to their graves, otherwise he would surely have sent them there."

She paused as Annie arrived with the tea and repeated the ritual of pouring and passing the milk and sugar.

"Am I rambling, my dears? I do that occasionally, I'm afraid, losing my train of thought, but I assure you that I know precisely what I am doing regarding the house. It is important that you be certain of that."

They waited for her to continue, but she was concentrating instead on her tea, stirring it slowly and carefully with a small silver teaspoon.

"It is important also that you know that I now have no next of kin. No-one other than my poor Agatha. I really had no idea that it would come to this."

"Miss Lacey," Michelle began when the old lady had lapsed into a silence that seemed set to continue. Gerry Quinn had begun to shift slightly in his chair and Michelle caught the quick, surreptitious glance at his watch as he downed the tea in one gulp and set the cup down on a small coffee table.

"Time is a strange thing," Evelyn said, seemingly out of nowhere, and Michelle realised with a start that she was more alert than she had seemed in the last few minutes. "When I was a child it seemed to go on forever, and now, looking back, it seems no more than the blink of an eye since I was a small child sitting at the nursery window, waiting for him."

She took a sip of tea, put the cup on the table beside her and stood up again.

"Now I must show you the remaining room. Mr Quinn hasn't seen it either, because none of the previous viewers was right for my house. And yes, my dear, that *does* mean I feel that the house should be yours. Provided, of course, that you are willing to fulfil my conditions."

Michelle forced herself to take a steady breath. "Why me? I mean, I'm delighted, of course, thrilled, but – what are the conditions? And what's the asking price? And –"

"Why you, my dear? I'm really not sure, other than I've watched your face as you went around my house; I know you could love it as I do. You have a little three-year-old named Katie – that was our cousin's name, you know. No, of course, how could you know? Katie Armitage. How she loved coming here, before they moved to Devon. She and my brother Robin were inseparable. He would have loved the idea of another little girl called Katie, here in this house. That's reason enough, my dear. *And* you were kind enough to bring some of the cherry-blossom to me – none of the others did that. I feel I can trust you. And maybe because I am finally tired of it all, who knows? I need the matter settled. If you are willing to settle it for me, then the house is yours. If you want it, that is. And if you promise that it will continue as a family home."

"Of course. I mean, that's what I'm looking for, a family home. And I'd love it, no question, and I know Rory would –" Michelle knew she was gabbling in her excitement, but didn't seem able to stop herself.

"Then come with me, my dear, because there is something I must show you."

Again she led them from the drawing-room and

they crossed the hall to the second door on the right, the one they had previously passed by.

"I wonder if you would mind, Mr Quinn?" she asked, turning to him. "The key is just up there, on that brass hook. I can't quite reach it."

He stretched slightly, grasped the key and inserted it in the lock, leaving it to her to turn it. The door opened with some difficulty and she stood outside for a moment, seeming to steel herself to enter.

Finally she pushed it open and led the way into the dim interior. They followed her through the doorway as she paused to find the light switch on the wall.

A muted light spread through the room, and Michelle found it hard to suppress a gasp.

It was like stepping back in time. The room was clean, from what she could see of it in the dim light, and there was a faint smell of polish. But other than that evidence of regular cleaning, it might not have been touched for the last fifty years. *Or a hundred,* Michelle amended quickly, taking in the heavy velvet drapes drawn across the windows, the carpet that stopped two feet short of the walls leaving a two-foot border of richly polished wood round its edges, the photographs that lined every inch of the walls. Sepia prints, most of them ancient-looking.

In the corner on a low, well-polished table there stood a gramophone and a stack of old 78's, and everywhere she looked – the large desk by the window, the deep leather sofa and armchairs, the oval mahogany table with several books and a decanter of brandy on it – there was evidence of the person, or persons, who had used this room. *A man,* Michelle thought, glancing at the sporting books, the box of cigars by the gramophone, the prints and photographs on the walls. In a small glass case on the wall behind the desk she could see an array of medals with two or three gaps along the bottom row.

It looks like a man's study. A man who'll be back any minute, she thought, taking in the general air of slight disarray, so different from all the other neat and tidy rooms.

Evelyn was watching her carefully.

"Would you like to sit down, my dears?" she said quietly, settling herself carefully on the sofa as Michelle and Sarah each took an armchair.

Gerry Quinn was about to sit down when his mobile rang again. He gave an apologetic smile.

"I'd really better go – they'll keep pestering me. Could I ring you tomorrow?"

Evelyn smiled. "Please do, Mr Quinn."

She waited until the door had closed behind him before speaking again.

"Now we come to the nub of the matter. Do you see that photograph on the mantelpiece? That one just there of two young men in uniform? Would you mind passing it to me, my dear?"

Sarah searched quickly among the dozen or so photos in ornate silver frames, picked out the faded sepia image of two young men and brought it to Evelyn.

"The First World War," Evelyn said, running her fingers lightly over the glass. "A very long time ago – ninety years, almost, and yet it might have been last year, or yesterday, so clearly do I remember it. I suppose one does remember the important things that happen when one is very young."

She looked across at Michelle and Sarah, seemed to realise that they were waiting, and handed Michelle the photograph.

"My father and my uncle," she said, as Sarah leaned closer to Michelle to see it. "Charles and Hugh Lacey. My father is on the right, with the moustache. He was twenty-seven when he went to the War, though he looks younger, doesn't he? And Hugh was twenty-four. They never should have gone, really. They didn't need to go – there was no conscription here in Ireland. But they went, like thousands of other Irishmen. Poor Hugh didn't want to go at all, my mother said, but felt he had to, to take care of my father." She gave a soft laugh. "Hugh was younger, but always the sensible one, the one you could depend on, while my father . . ."

She paused and turned her gaze directly on them.

"My father never made it home. I didn't understand then, of course, that he had died, even when Hugh came home without him. So I waited – for years I waited. And Hugh went back to France every year afterwards, searching for him, I thought."

She caught their expressions.

"I was very young. It took me a long time to realise

that he was dead – and that Hugh was searching for his grave, not for him."

She paused, reaching to take the photograph from Michelle.

"Hugh lost him, you see. They were fighting together near a place called Mericourt on the Somme, when my father was badly wounded. Hugh hid him as best he could and went to try and get help, but it was impossible – the battle had been going on for days and there were hundreds, maybe thousands, of wounded and dying men all around. In the chaos he couldn't find the place where he had left him. It haunted poor Hugh, and when the war was over he returned, year after year, to try and find some trace of him. You see, they were turning up bodies there for many years after the war ended."

She lapsed into silence, continuing to gaze at the photograph.

"Miss Lacey?" Michelle prompted eventually.

"I must apologise, my dears," Evelyn said, shifting her attention back to them with obvious difficulty. "You're wondering, of course, what all of this has to do with you."

"Well, yes," Michelle admitted.

"He found the grave, you see. Finally, he found it, a few years after Mother died, and just a month or so before his own death. He had continued to visit France over the years and his contacts there wrote to him from time to time. And then a letter came – in October, 1973, it would have been, because he died in November – and he told us that my father's grave had been found and he must go to France immediately. But he was too unwell to travel and it distressed him greatly that he could not do so. After all those years of searching, he never managed to visit the grave."

Evelyn sighed, and Michelle thought she could see the merest trace of a tear on her cheek.

"That must have been very upsetting for you all," Sarah said quietly.

"Indeed it was," Evelyn replied. "It saddened me greatly that he didn't live to finish his quest." She paused, looking directly at Michelle. "Which brings me to what I want of you, my dear. If you feel able, that is. And if you want my house."

There were needles of panic in Michelle's stomach as she waited.

"Call it the last rambling wish of a foolish old woman," Evelyn said, "but what I want is for someone to find that grave for me and bring back some of the soil so I can scatter it in the garden here. Then I can feel his spirit is at rest, and that Hugh's last wish has also been fulfilled. Would you do that for me, my dear? Would you look for his grave?"

"But, but . . ." Michelle stopped, helplessly, as a dozen questions clamoured in her brain.

"I have no idea where it actually is. It clearly isn't one of the marked ones in the war cemeteries or he would have traced it in the early days. But it's not quite as difficult as it seems. I *do* remember the name of the town the letters came from, very clearly, even after all these years."

She took in their expressions.

"An impossible task? Perhaps. But the only way, my dears, that I can deal with this – what do they call it these days, *unfinished business*?" Her eyes looked wistful again. "Can you imagine what it was like for a small child, waiting and waiting for a father who never made it home? Do this for me, Michelle," – for the first time Evelyn used her name – "and my house is yours, at whatever price you might wish to name."

Chapter Fourteen

Rory had the door open when they were still ten yards away.

"I thought you had to work?" Michelle said. Recently he had begun going in on Saturdays to try to keep on top of things.

"Couldn't concentrate," he said. "I might go in later. So, what's the story?"

"At least let us in first," Michelle said, laughing as he moved back to make way. "Why didn't you go yourself, if you're so anxious about it?"

"Because you're the one who's into looking at houses. So?"

"I don't know," Michelle said. She led the way into the kitchen and the three of them sat round the table. "I just don't know," she repeated, looking across at Sarah.

Suddenly they were both talking at once.

"Hang on a minute," Rory said, laughing. "So, you like the place, right?"

Michelle nodded and began talking again.

"Wait!" he instructed. "But the old biddy is bats, right? And you're not sure you'd get the house even if you do what she wants?"

"She's far from bats," Sarah interrupted.

Rory looked sceptical. "She'll let us have the house for whatever we'll pay, if Michelle just does this for her, and the place is worth a million or more?"

"Probably nearer two million if she sold to a developer – which she says she won't," Michelle said.

"And you think she's sane!"

"Rory, she *seems* all right. And it all makes sense, if you look at it her way."

"So look at it *our* way for a minute, Chelle. We don't need a place that size. God knows what it would cost to do it up, never mind run it. And you've no guarantee you'll get it anyway, right? A total wild-goose chase halfway across France, for nothing." He shook his head. "And who'd pay for that, anyway?" he added abruptly, looking at her.

She glanced across at Sarah, then turned back to Rory, shrugging her shoulders.

"We would, I suppose. We didn't get into that. I've to go back and see her in a day or two, once I've talked it over with you."

He made a face. "And if I say 'no'?"

"Then I don't go."

He gave a wry smile. "And you'll never let me forget it."

"Don't be silly. But Rory, I'd like you to see the place, see what you think."

He looked a bit shamefaced. "Actually, I did. Well, from the outside, anyway. I drove past while you were there."

"So why didn't you come in?"

"I was dropping something off, I hadn't much time. Besides, I couldn't know if you were nearly finished, or what. Or even if you liked it. I thought I'd better wait 'til you got home."

"So what did you think of it?" she asked.

"Incredible, what I could see of it. But I didn't take it seriously – and I don't think you should, either."

Again Michelle glanced across at Sarah, then back to Rory.

"Why not?" she demanded.

"Be reasonable, Chelle. We don't have much time, right? In just a few days we're out of here." He paused when he saw her expression. "We've got to face facts, love," he said, reaching across the table for her hand. "We've nowhere to go except your mother's, and we need every cent we have for the next house. We don't have the time, *or* the money, to go chasing off after someone who died nearly ninety years ago. I mean, for God's sake, she *must* be mad. Where would you start, even if you wanted to?"

"She has the name of a village where Hugh's contact lived. The person who found the grave for him."

"So why does she need you to go there? Why doesn't she just write to them?"

"Because she doesn't know who exactly it was. She only knows the name of the village the letters came from."

"And that's *it*?" Rory looked exasperated. "Come on, Chelle. How far d'you imagine you'd get with that? You could spend six months looking and finding nothing, and then what?"

"But I *might* find something," Michelle said, suddenly intense.

"And when is the last letter supposed to have come?"

"A long time ago, " she admitted reluctantly.

He waited.

"About thirty years ago," she said finally.

"Thirty years! Will you *listen* to yourself! Sarah, talk to her!" he appealed, turning to his sister-in-law.

Sarah looked from one to the other. "I think she should go for it."

"You're crazy. Both of you!"

"No, Rory, think about it! Evelyn Lacey picked *Michelle* to do this, not any of the others – and from what Quinn said, they all had plenty of cash to buy the place. So it's not about money. And Evelyn is serious about this, she means it. If Michelle can find that grave then the house is hers. I think it's definitely worth giving it a go."

"Well, I don't. How old did you say she is – over ninety? She could be dead next week –"

"So could we all," Sarah said dryly.

"But where would you start?" Rory asked, turning to Michelle. "And how long would it take? And who'd mind Katie? And –"

"Mam would mind her for a few days," Michelle said. "That would give me a chance to go over there, have a look around –"

"You mean it!" he interrupted.

She nodded. "I'd be mad not to. The more I think about it – come on, Rory, it's worth a try –"

"You haven't a word of French!"

"But I have," Sarah said. "God knows I should have, after all those years slaving as an au pair!"

"Huh!" Michelle laughed. "With your own little apartment and the use of a swimming pool, and you *said* the kids were adorable –"

"They were," Sarah said. "Not to mention their da –"

Michelle's eyes widened. "You never!"

"That's right, I never." Sarah said, with a wicked grin. "Unfortunately! But I *did* learn to speak French fairly well – and I'm sure I can manage a few days off work. So if you guys decide to go and you want a bit of company . . ."

"Are you serious?" Michelle asked, looking hopefully from Sarah to Rory.

"Sure! It could be fun, in an odd sort of way. And you know me, any excuse to go to France!"

"Rory?" Michelle appealed.

He ran a hand through his hair. "No way, Chelle. Even if I thought there was some chance of it working, I just can't get away right now. You know that, I'm working night and day as it is. There are times when I wish –"

He broke off abruptly.

"Say it!" she demanded.

He let out a sigh. "Look, I didn't mean . . ."

"You know you did," Michelle said, anger rising. "Go on, say it, this is all my fault, you were happy the way things were and now we haven't even got a home of our own! Say it!"

Her cheeks were flushed and she was close to tears.

Rory sighed. "I'm tired, Michelle, that's all. Worn out between work and looking at houses."

"That's not fair, Rory! You've hardly looked at three or four. I'm the one trekking in and out to auctioneers and going to see everywhere *and* trying to do the packing and mind Katie –"

"You don't have anything else to do!" he exploded. "*I'm* run off my feet trying to keep the business going while you –"

He broke off as Sarah stood up quietly.

"Where are you going?" Michelle demanded, turning to her.

"You two need a bit of space, and I don't need to be here. Ring me tonight."

"Wait!" Rory said. "Look, I'm sorry, Sarah – we're

losing it here." He stood up and moved to put his arms around Michelle. "I didn't mean it, love. It's just getting a bit much at the minute, that's all."

Michelle nodded, relaxing against him. "We have to do *something*, Rory," she said quietly. "I can't face the thought of being back living with Mam and Dad for long."

"They're not the worst," Rory soothed.

"No," Michelle agreed. "But I still don't want to be back home, it'll make me feel like a child again. And I'm afraid we'll get too used to being there – "

Rory laughed softly. "No fear of that!"

"But you know what I mean, we won't have the same pressure to find a place and – "

"And what?" Sarah interrupted. "Of course you'll want to get your own place! And personally I think you'd be mad to let this chance go. You really like the house, don't you? Even more than the one in Roundwood?"

Michelle grimaced. "Thanks for reminding me. Looks like I'll keep wanting houses I can't have!"

"So who said you can't have this one?" Sarah demanded.

"Rory's right, it's a crazy idea," Michelle said. "We've no guarantee of finding the grave, and no guarantee that even if we *did,* she'd keep her word."

"Did she look like someone who'd go back on her word?" Sarah asked.

"No," Michelle agreed slowly. "But that doesn't mean she won't. We'd have wasted our time –"

"But it's worth taking a chance!" Sarah said, exasperated. "Look, let's try and talk about this sensibly, otherwise I *am* wasting my time when I could be down at the tennis club trying to get my hands on Karl Hanlon!"

They all laughed, breaking the tension. Michelle and Sarah both knew what a waste of time *that* was. On the evidence so far, Karl Hanlon was interested only in decorative young blondes who looked good in tennis gear but were fairly useless on the court, and Sarah, as Michelle regularly reminded her, was so far failing on all counts. And while she could dye her hair and maybe throw a few matches, it was a little while – okay, quite a while – since she'd last seen twenty-two or three . . .

"Right," Sarah said when they were sitting round the table again. "So you want the house, Michelle."

"Even more than the other one," Michelle admitted. "But –"

Sarah raised a hand to silence her. "Rory?"

"I'd have to see it," he answered slowly. "From the outside it looks great, plenty of space, unbelievable location. I just can't see us getting it."

"But if you could?" Sarah prompted.

Rory and Michelle exchanged a look.

"We'd have to go for it," Rory said. "If there was any real chance we'd have to go for it. But –"

"So what have you got to lose?" Sarah asked. "The cost of a trip to France – that's not much. And a few days off work, surely *that's* possible?"

"Not at the minute," Rory said. "Really, no way. I'm pushed as it is to meet the orders I have in."

"Good complaint," Sarah commented. "So what if Michelle and I go?"

"I don't think so," Rory said as they both rounded on him. "Look, there's all the rest of the packing to do, and as Michelle pointed out she's had to do most of it herself. I haven't the time or the energy."

"Not a big deal," Sarah said. "I can help. I've helped already. It'll be done in a couple of days, then we can make a quick trip –"

"No," Rory said flatly.

"Why not?" Michelle demanded. "Sarah's making a generous offer and you're throwing it back at her. Why can't we go? And what if I go anyway!"

He shrugged. "I couldn't stop you and you know I wouldn't try. But you asked me what I thought, and I'm telling you."

"And I still don't understand why!"

He sighed. "I don't want you hurt, that's why. I saw how you were about the Roundwood house, and then afterwards . . . what if this didn't work out? If you went to France and found this blasted grave, or didn't find it, whatever, and either way she wouldn't let you have the house? Too risky, Michelle. You'd have invested too much. I just don't want to see you hurt again."

"I won't be!"

"You could be," Sarah said. "But Rory –" she added, turning to him "– you know you'll never hear the end of it if you try to stop her! And if there's any chance at all of you getting that house – "

"Then I have to try," Michelle said. "I really want it, Rory," she said, turning to him. "I want to go back to Evelyn Lacey and tell her I'll do it."

There was a bit more thrashing out, but finally it was agreed. She'd see Evelyn Lacey, finish the packing, they'd move in with her parents – and then she and Sarah would go to France and see what they could find out.

There was really no choice. She had fallen in love with the house in Rathgar and she would move heaven and earth, do whatever it took, to make it hers.

Chapter Fifteen

Michelle went alone for her second visit to Evelyn Lacey.

Sarah couldn't spare the time to go with her. "Saving my days off to go grave-digging in France!" she said cheerfully when Michelle asked her – and Rory had to pull out at the last minute when yet another rush-job came in.

"The money's too good, Chelle. I can't turn it down," he'd said apologetically.

It didn't matter. She was quite happy to go alone, having spent several days taut with anxiety that Evelyn might change her mind about the house or might ask someone else to seek out the grave for her instead. So, having arranged to call on the Thursday afternoon, Michelle wasn't about to change her plans. The sooner it was settled, the better – both for her own peace of mind and, she hoped, for Evelyn's.

Annie opened the door at the first knock. "Miss Lacey's expecting you," she said, with what Michelle felt was a disapproving look.

What will happen to her when the house is sold? Michelle wondered, as she followed Annie's stiff back into the drawing-room. *She looks ancient, but she's obviously still working and maybe she expected –*

Her reverie was interrupted by Evelyn's voice from the armchair by the drawing-room fireplace.

"Excuse my not getting up, my dear! I'm feeling quite tired today, but glad that you could come, nevertheless." She turned to give a slight nod to Annie, who left the room. "And I am hoping, of course, that you have good news for me. I understood that your husband – Rory, I think? – would be with you?"

"He couldn't come, though he wanted to," Michelle said quickly. "He's very busy at work, there was an urgent job – he hoped you might be able to arrange another time for him to come."

Evelyn looked disappointed, then smiled slightly. "I'm afraid time is one thing that may not be on my side. I take it you can't make any decision about the house until he has seen it?"

"We've decided already," Michelle said.

Evelyn raised an eyebrow.

"He saw it from the outside, the day Sarah and I were here. He thought it was too late to join us, that we'd be nearly finished the viewing, but he thought it looked amazing and said we should go for it." *Almost the truth,* she told herself, as the door opened and Annie brought in the tea-tray.

"And he agrees with the conditions? He'll go to France with you?"

Michelle paused, her heart in her mouth. Evelyn hadn't said Rory had to go.

"Oh, yes, he agrees," she said quickly, "but he mightn't be able to spare the time just now, so Sarah is coming with me instead. If we have to make a second trip he'll come then."

"I see." Turning slightly, Evelyn thanked Annie who had begun pouring the tea and who now passed her a cup. The delicate bone china clinked slightly and Michelle realised that Evelyn was nervous.

She's afraid we won't be able to do it, Michelle thought. *This is as important to her as it is to me.*

The thought gave her courage.

"We'll do the best we can," she said. "I'm sure –"

"One moment, my dear . . ." Evelyn waited as Annie poured tea for Michelle and passed her the milk and sugar.

"Thank you, Annie. I'll ring if we need anything," Evelyn said, and Michelle, murmuring a 'thank you' to Annie, wondered how much the housekeeper actually knew about the situation and Evelyn's conditions.

"Forgive me, Michelle. You were saying?" Evelyn asked as the door closed after Annie.

"That I'm sure we'll manage well enough without

Rory, if we have to. Sarah speaks French and she's been there several times before."

"On holidays, I presume? A bit different from what I'm requiring of you!"

"She lived there for a couple of years when she was younger."

"Oh?" The older woman raised an eyebrow.

"As an au pair," Michelle elaborated. "And she's been back on holidays a few times."

They sipped their tea in silence for a moment or two, taking the measure of each other.

"Miss Lacey –"

"Evelyn, please, my dear."

"Evelyn. If we don't find anything . . ." Her voice trailed away as an expression of utter sadness crossed the older woman's face.

Evelyn seemed to gather herself with a small sigh before saying, "Do go on, my dear."

"Well . . ." Michelle hesitated, not sure how to proceed. She knew – and surely Evelyn must know – that there was every possibility this would turn into the wild-goose chase Rory was afraid of. She didn't want to upset Evelyn, but suddenly she needed to be sure of where she stood, if . . .

"We'll try our best. I promise you that. It's just that, well, it's been so long . . ."

"Yes, my dear?" Evelyn's voice was subdued now, frail, almost.

"Well, we don't really have much to go on, do we?

Just the name of a village your uncle got some letters from, thirty years ago." The doubts that Rory had expressed to her suddenly seemed well-founded. She took a deep breath. "I love your house, Miss – Evelyn. I love it and I could see us living here even though it's way too big for us – well, for now, anyway – it's beautiful, it's exactly what I want – but I know we haven't a hope of affording something like this, ever."

She paused for breath, and Evelyn waited.

"I suppose I'm wondering what happens if we don't find anything, if there's nothing there to be found." A thought struck her. "Has anyone else tried since? Anyone else in the family, or, well, private detectives or –"

Evelyn gave a soft laugh, interrupting her. "I suppose I could have done that, couldn't I? Private detectives! Do you know, I never even considered it! And I suppose, even had I thought of it, there were always other calls on whatever funds were available . . ."

Her voice trailed off, leaving Michelle sorry that she'd mentioned it. It was obvious from the state of house that Evelyn didn't have much disposable income.

"As for the family – well, poor Robin, my brother, passed away some ten years ago, just a few months after his wife. No children, just a little boy who died when he was four or five months old. They never really got over that, in all that time. I suppose one doesn't. So, no, Robin wouldn't have followed it up. He never quite forgave Father, you know, for leaving him. He was the second eldest, just gone five when Father went. And for a long time, like me, he hoped he would come back; but when he gave up hoping, it was anger Robin felt, not sadness as I did, and he really had no interest in Uncle Hugh's search. My sister Poppy died of diphtheria when she was a child. And Winifred . . . well, Winifred had her own troubles. Apart from which she was the eldest, so Mother relied on her a great deal, perhaps too much, especially after Poppy's death. That took its toll, perhaps even more than Father's going. And Agatha was an infant, barely a year old when he went, so of course she had no memory of him at all and never asked about him, really, as she grew up. So, my dear, in answer to your question, there was no-one apart from myself, once Mother and Uncle Hugh had passed away, who was interested in what had happened to Father."

"And were you ever tempted to go to France yourself?"

Evelyn looked surprised at the question. Then, "Myself?" she said. "No. Not for one moment. One didn't, in those days. At least, in our family, one didn't. Mother wouldn't have encouraged it. Wouldn't have allowed it, in fact. France had done quite enough to the family as far as she was concerned, and as the years went on she became impatient with Uncle Hugh, telling him that it was time to leave my Father's ghost to rest."

Evelyn lapsed into a reverie again, leaving Michelle

wondering how to broach the question that she really wanted to ask. She put down her cup and glanced quietly around the room. More familiar with it now, she could see that it really needed a lot of attention. *But we'd have our whole lives to do it,* she thought. *It's a wonderful house and I'd be mad not to –*

"I have the impression, my dear, that something else is bothering you."

Though Evelyn spoke quietly, Michelle was startled. Once again she had the impression that not much escaped Evelyn's notice. She might seem lost in her thoughts occasionally, but she was well aware of all that was going on.

"Was there something else you wanted to say, or to ask?" Evelyn prompted. "I'm afraid I got rather carried away just now, and may have side-tracked you."

I've nothing to lose, Michelle thought. "I was wondering what will happen to the house if we don't find anything. Would you get somebody else to go? Or . . ."

She held her breath.

Evelyn didn't stir.

"What you're asking, my dear, is whether I'll sell the house to you anyway?" she said after a long pause.

"Well, yes. Though we'll try our absolute best –"

"I do know that," Evelyn said, then was silent again while Michelle sat waiting, suddenly conscious of the pounding of her heart.

"It's something I haven't thought about, because I

choose not to think about it," Evelyn said finally. "I'm not quite ready to give up my dream, Michelle. Not *just* yet, anyway. Though I know the time left to me can't be long, and I'm most anxious to join Agatha in her nursing home before –"

She broke off, leaning forward to place her empty cup on the table. "Let's just say we'll discuss it when you return from France. By then, I may be ready to make a decision," she said briskly. "Now, you're quite sure you feel able to go?" Michelle nodded and Evelyn gave a small, satisfied sigh. "Then, my dear, perhaps you would be good enough to pass me that envelope on the mantelpiece."

As Michelle stood to reach for it her attention was arrested for a moment by a very old photograph in a silver frame of a woman in her thirties or so, dressed in a white, high-necked lace blouse and long dark skirt, whose dark hair was drawn up into a lavish bun. She sat formally, one hand to her chin and the other resting on her lap, gazing directly at the photographer.

"She's beautiful," Michelle commented, as she lifted the envelope and passed it to Evelyn.

"Thank you, my dear," Evelyn said, taking the envelope. Then, "Isn't she?" she added, looking towards the photograph. "My great-grandmother, on my father's side. I never knew her, of course, but my father did – she lived with the family until he was eleven or so, when she died. He was named for her, Charles Feradot. *Feradot,*" she repeated, giving it a French inflection, "was her family name. Marie-Louise Feradot. An unusual name, even in France."

"She was French?"

"Yes, my dear," Evelyn confirmed. "I often felt, in later years, that that was the main reason my father chose to go to France. He was close to his grandmother, by all accounts, and very much influenced by her. They were forever chattering away together in French, according to Hugh. I believe my father took it very badly when she died."

She glanced down at the envelope in her hand as if she had forgotten it.

"There I go, rambling again! You must forgive me, Michelle. Now, if you're quite sure?"

"Absolutely!" Michelle said.

She took a folded sheet of writing-paper from the envelope and passed it to Michelle. There were several lines written on it in an elegant copperplate hand.

"Such information as I have, my dear," Evelyn said as Michelle studied the sheet. "My father's regiment, the Royal Dublin Fusiliers. His date of birth, 17th of February, 1889. The date and place he died – the 25th or 26th of March, 1918, somewhere between Mericourt and Eclusier, near the town of Albert on the Somme. The month the final letter arrived – it would have been October, 1973, because Hugh died in November; and the name of the village where the letters came from, Maillerain-sous-Bois, which I presume must be in the same general area as Albert."

"Maillerain-sous-Bois," Michelle repeated, reading from the page.

"That's it, my dear. I'm certain I've remembered it correctly because I saw the postmark several times. Strange, the way one remembers so clearly what happened more than thirty years ago – or, indeed, seventy or eighty years in some instances! – but one can't always quite remember what happened yesterday or the day before . . ."

She seemed to gather herself and continued more briskly, "Maillerain-sous-Bois. If there is anything to be discovered, then you will find it there, or somewhere very close to there."

She stood, with some difficulty, indicating that the conversation was at a close. Michelle watched as she grasped the cane, noticing how slowly her hands curled round its silver top.

Evelyn followed her gaze. "The scourge of arthritis, my dear. I have my good days," she gave a wry smile, "and I have, shall we say, my other days. This, unfortunately, is one of those other days."

"I'll let myself out," Michelle said. "And I'll come to see you as soon as I get back."

"Please do, my dear. And you *will* do your best, won't you? So much depends on it."

As if I didn't know! Michelle thought as she went down the driveway, got into her car and turned for one last look at the house. She wanted it. She wanted it so badly, she could hardly bear to think about the impossible, ridiculous task ahead of her in France. She only knew that, one way or the other, she would have to find out what happened to Charles Feradot Lacey if she was ever to live in his house.

Chapter Sixteen

It nearly broke Michelle's heart to wander round her little house in Harold's Cross for the last time. All the things that had annoyed her about it just a few weeks ago now seemed exactly what she wanted in a house.

No parking, but then she really didn't need a car so close to town. She could have managed the bus even with Katie in tow and there was always one passing just at the end of the road.

And no garden. But the park was only a short distance away, and their little patio was a sun-trap, with gleaming white walls and pots of geraniums, where she and Katie would often sit in peace and privacy on a summer afternoon.

You were mad to give this up, she told herself as she trailed from room to room, drinking in every detail, crossing to the little windows to look for the last time at the familiar, comforting views. She ran her hands over everything – the curve of the banister, the warmth of the worn brass doorknobs – as snatches of memory came to her unbidden.

Rory, his face alight, rushing into the house to tell her about the Morgan contract, the one that had set him up in his own business . . .

Katie taking her first tottering steps across the uneven floorboards of the living-room, stretching her arms out towards Michelle and Una . . .

Katie's first birthday, with all their family and friends crowded round the little table for a celebration they never thought they'd have . . .

Abruptly she blocked that thought and moved towards the kitchen for one final look.

The sun was streaming through the window as it only did at this time of the day, bringing life to the paintwork and the faded pattern of the floor tiles. The room was spotless, the cooker gleaming in a way she'd never seemed to manage when she was giving it a quick wipe every day. Doing it for the last time, it was a matter of pride to her to have it all looking as good as she could make it.

She envied the Connollys, whose house it was now. They'd be moving in later in the day to this warm, welcoming little place. It seemed like the biggest mistake of her life to be leaving here.

Even with the house in Roundwood to go to, it would have been difficult to leave here, she realised.

Now, with only the prospect of going home to her parents, it seemed almost beyond her.

She'd wondered a few times, over the last week or two, if it was too late to back out. You heard about people doing that all the time, she'd told herself.

But she knew she couldn't do it, not to a couple with a new baby on the way who were all set to start a life here. Not to anyone, really. She couldn't be the cause of anyone feeling as badly as she did when she lost the Roundwood house.

She had just reached the top of the stairs for one last look when her mobile rang.

Rory, wondering what was keeping her. He'd gone on ahead to her parents' house with the van carrying the last of their stuff.

"Another five minutes," she told him.

"Sure you're okay?" His voice was soft.

"Sure," she said, biting her lip. "Won't be long."

"I could come back."

"Don't do that," she said quickly. "I'm fine, I'm leaving now."

She didn't feel fine. There was a sharp pain in her throat as she crossed to Katie's room for the last time.

Katie's room. It had taken her so long to be able to call it that.

She opened the door, noticing the usual slight creak – *too late to oil it now*, she thought – and crossed to sit at the deep window seat, drawing her legs up beneath her. She wanted to stay here in this room with its bright yellow walls and its border of cartoon characters. There was too much of herself in it to leave behind.

It had taken until last night for her to realise that. No point saying it to Rory, he wouldn't understand. He never understood anything like that. And even Sarah had told her it was time to move on, that there was no point at all in going over it again and again.

None of them understood. But how could they? She hardly understood it herself, this sudden, fierce reluctance to move from the house she had brought her baby home to. The house, the room she'd prepared for Katie – and for the other babies she hadn't been able to bring home.

The phone rang again and she stirred, swinging her legs down from the seat. It was time to go, even if she knew now that a part of her would never leave here.

She took the call, chatting to her mother as if nothing at all was wrong as she moved down the stairs, through the hall and finally out the front door, her car keys already in her hand. She slammed the front door, got into the car, switched off the phone and started the engine. She drove away quickly, not looking back.

Sarah was right. There was no point at all in looking back.

* * *

When she reached her parents' house there was pandemonium. Rory and her father were struggling to move her piano into the front room – back where it used to be when she still lived there – while Helen stood in doorway of the kitchen, commenting caustically on their efforts.

Just what I need, Michelle thought. *Hellish Helen and her three little angels. Let me out of here! Please . . .*

At that moment two of the 'little angels' came tearing into the hallway, shrieking loudly. Six-year-old Oscar, taking advantage of Helen being otherwise engaged, was holding a Superman toy aloft, threatening to make it 'fly' down the stairs, and four-year-old Dylan was in hot pursuit, screaming blue murder at him.

"They're bored," Helen said sweetly, as if that explained everything. At the same time she shot them a quick glare and Oscar, catching the warning, immediately handed back the toy and turned his attention instead to the piano, now firmly lodged in the doorway with Maurice at one end and Rory at the other.

"Can I have a go?" Oscar asked, not waiting for a reply as he launched himself at the keys, fingers at the ready.

"Will you *stop* that!" Maurice said irritably as Oscar managed to reach under his arms and wallop the piano. "Just back off for a while now, will you! You can play with it later!"

"No, he can't, it's not a toy!" Michelle protested. "I've just had it tuned."

"Oh, Gawd, we're not going through all that again, are we?" Helen said viciously. "You never used to let anyone lay a finger on your precious piano – no wonder I never learned to play!"

"You never wanted to!" Michelle snapped, and Maurice set down his end of the piano, wiped his forehead with the back of his hand and scowled at the two of them.

"Would you give over, the pair of you, you're like a gang of kids! If I'd known it was going to be like this – *Now* what did I say?" he added in an aggrieved tone as Michelle burst into tears and fled up the stairs.

Helen gave a little smirk as they heard the bolt on the bathroom door shooting into place. "Some things never change. Come on, boys, time we were going!"

She called her daughter and said a chirpy goodbye to Una, who had appeared at the kitchen door with Katie in tow and a concerned expression on her face.

"Would you go up and see if she's all right?" Rory asked Una once the door had closed behind Helen and her gang. Unless he climbed over the piano, and he wasn't quite ready to do that, he was trapped in the front room for the time being.

"All I said was –" Maurice began.

Una sighed, raising her eyes to heaven. "Something you shouldn't have, obviously. Will you never learn?"

She sat Katie on the bottom step of the stairs.

"Now, you watch Grandad and make sure he doesn't drop the piano," she said, before making her way upstairs to talk to Michelle. As she went she could hear Maurice muttering something about "too many women altogether in this house".

She hoped he was wrong, as usual – and that they hadn't all made a very big mistake.

* * *

"Some start, wasn't it, Mam?" Michelle said later as they sat talking in her old bedroom, the room that would now be hers and Rory's. "I don't know what came over me."

Una reached out to brush Michelle's hair back, the way she always used to when Michelle was upset as a child.

"It's not easy, love. I know that," she said gently. "But we'll all pull together. It'll work out, you'll see. Why don't yourself and Rory go for a walk or something? You could probably do with a bit of space."

"But Katie –"

"Will be fine," said Una. "I'll get her something to eat in a few minutes and you and Rory can hop out, go for a bit of lunch or something. You've probably had nothing since breakfast, have you? It's after three now."

Michelle sighed. "I don't feel up to going out."

"All the more reason why you should. And Rory is still looking a bit upset. It'll probably do you both good to talk – "

"Mam, just leave it, will you?"

Michelle instantly regretted her sharp tone as Una's expression changed. "Sorry. Maybe we'll take you up on it later."

Of course we need to talk, she thought as Una, giving her a quick smile, went back downstairs. *But he won't. No matter how hard I try, he still won't talk about them.*

She was still lying face down on her old bed ten minutes or so later when she heard Rory, finally released from behind the piano, taking the steps two at a time.

He came in and sat beside her on the bed, reaching out to stroke her arm.

"What's wrong, Chelle? You were fine, and then – what happened?"

What happened? She suddenly found herself in a rage, wanted to scream at him.

We lost three of our children, that's what happened! We lost three children, and you try to pretend it never happened! We're on different planets, and you don't understand, you don't even try *to understand!*

"Una said you wanted to get out for a while," he said when she didn't answer.

"Oh, for God's sake, I wish she'd just leave me alone! It wasn't *my* idea!"

He shifted on the bed so that he was looking directly at her.

"Please, Chelle, what's wrong? If you won't tell me . . ."

He watched helplessly as slow tears coursed down her cheeks. "Is it that bad, being here? Because if it is –"

Still getting no answer, he gave a slight shrug, sighed and stood up to go.

"Wait, Rory," she said, as he reached for the door. "Wait, I'm sorry. It's just that I can't stand it, I can't stand any of it –"

She burst into sobs. He hesitated, an anguished expression on his face. After a moment he came and again sat beside her on the bed, smoothing her hair as she cried her heart out.

"It'll be all right, Chelle. It'll be fine, I promise," he said quietly, stroking her softly on the cheek. "It won't be for too long, and they're not the worst, are they? Your da doesn't always switch on the brain before he talks, that's all." He smiled at her, hoping for a response.

"It's not that," she said raggedly after a few minutes, pulling herself into a sitting position as he put his arm around her. "I can put up with being here. It'll drive me mad if they start treating me like a child again, but I can put up with it."

"I know how tough it is leaving the house. You put a lot of yourself into it, I know that."

"No, it's not that," she repeated.

"Then – "

"Not *just* that, anyway." Her voice was quiet now, barely above a whisper.

"Then what?" he murmured softly against her hair, prompting her.

"I never brought them home. I had the room all ready for them, three times I had the room ready, and now the house is gone and I feel – " She bit her lip, forcing herself to say it. "I feel I've lost them all over again."

"We have Katie," he said. "We're so lucky to have Katie."

She gave a bare nod. "I know that. You don't have to tell me. But I still want them." Her hand went to her mouth and the tears began again.

Like the other times, he didn't know what to say. Like the other times he could only hold her, knowing it wasn't enough, that it would never be enough, that nothing he could say or do would ever heal the pain of losing three of their children.

Chapter Seventeen

She hated flying. She really, really hated flying.

"You never used to be like this," Sarah reminded her. "Remember the time . . ."

But Michelle was in no mood for remembering anything. She was too busy concentrating on her breathing. *In, out – slowly – don't look out the window – God, why did she choose the window seat? She was never doing this again. Never . . .*

Sarah was quite right, she *had* loved flying. But that was in a different life, before she had Katie.

Katie. Suddenly it was as if her little daughter was in front of her, the image was so clear to Michelle's closed eyes. She had hated leaving her that morning. She'd be fine, of course she'd be fine with Rory and a doting Una and Maurice. That wasn't the point; it was just that she had never left her for so long before. A whole four days without her. She could hardly bear to think about it.

How could he do it? The thought came as if from nowhere. How did Charles Lacey leave a wife and five young children – one of them only a year old, for God's sake! – and go off to fight a war? Was he out of his *mind?* Why would anyone do that, if he didn't have to?

And he *didn't* have to, that much was clear. Or at least that's how it seemed to Michelle. Okay, so maybe it was true that his French grandmother had influenced him – but still, to leave a wife and family . . .

Michelle had always hated history at school, but this was different. For the past week she had devoured everything she could get her hands on about the First World War, including masses of stuff Sarah had found on the Internet. An incredible amount, really, and the sisters had watched in amazement as website after website came up, all to do with a war that had been over for eighty-five years. Every single person who had fought in it must be dead by now, and yet there was obviously still a huge amount of interest in it. Her own father, once she began talking to him about it, remembered snatches, bits and pieces, of what had been passed down by his grandfather.

"He never used to talk about it much, my father said," Maurice had told her after she persuaded him to search the attic for any mementoes he might find there. "People didn't, in those days, with one thing and another. They came back to a different world from what it was before the war . . ."

Michelle and Sarah, fascinated, had examined the

service medals their father brought down from the attic. The ribbons were still bright, the medals only slightly tarnished in their velvet boxes. "He never thought much of them," Maurice had said. "They were no use for anything in those days, he used to tell Da, except a few bob from the pawnshop every now and then. It wasn't something he used dwell on if he could help it. There wasn't much of a welcome for the lads, one way or another, when they came back home. The Easter Rising happened while they were away and when the British executed the leaders the whole mood of the place changed and no-one in a British uniform was safe."

"At least he came back," Sarah had said.

"He did," Maurice agreed. "But he was never the same, and his lungs were in tatters. That's what got him in the end, the mustard gas. But you're right, at least he came back. Not like his brother Christy. Only seventeen he was when he was killed. He didn't last six months and they never even found his body."

"I don't remember ever hearing about him before," Michelle said, tracing the inscription on his medal – Royal Dublin Fusiliers. *The same regiment as Charles and Hugh Lacey.*

"Sure why would you?" Maurice asked. "He was dead and gone long before I was born, even. The waste, when you think about it. A kid of seventeen."

Holding the medals and gazing at the faded photographs Maurice had unearthed, Michelle had finally begun to understand something of the difficulty Evelyn and her Uncle Hugh had had in letting go of Charles Lacey. This wasn't just about a vanished father and brother. This was about a whole generation of young men who went off to fight, thinking it was a great adventure, thinking they were doing 'the right thing' and that it would all be over by Christmas anyway.

The plane hit a pocket of turbulent air and Michelle drew her breath in sharply.

"Never again!" she said to Sarah as the 'fasten seatbelt' sign came on.

Never again. That's what those men were told, fighting the war to end all wars.

So much for that.

"So we're coming back by ferry, are we?" Sarah's voice interrupted Michelle's reverie.

"God!" she groaned. "I don't even want to *think* about coming back!"

The plane began its descent to the little airport of Beauvais, north of Paris, and finally, in spite of herself, Michelle began to feel excited instead of terrified. She gazed out the window, Sarah leaning across her to catch a glimpse of the forests and the huge green and yellow fields below. Somehow familiar, yet so very different from home.

The plane landed smoothly with a huge *'whoosh'* from the brakes and finally taxied to a halt. With a huge sigh of relief and butterflies still flapping around in her stomach, Michelle began to gather her bits and pieces together.

They walked quickly to the little terminal building and joined the short queue for immigration, where they were nodded through after a quick glance at their passports.

They retrieved their bags with little bother and then visited the airport shop to buy a detailed map of the area around Albert. They had so far failed to locate Maillerain-sous-Bois on the map of France they already had, or on the Internet. Then they sought directions to the car-hire office, which was just outside the airport building. Their Renault was waiting, and in just a few minutes, it seemed, they were en route to the hotel Sarah had booked over the Internet.

Michelle marvelled at Sarah's fluent, easy French and her skill and confidence in managing an unfamiliar car. She had refused point-blank herself to attempt driving in France.

"See, it was worth your while putting up with those bratty kids in your au pair days!" she said. "Your French is brilliant!"

"Wouldn't say that, but we'll get by! Now, concentrate on the navigating and let me get used to driving on the wrong side!"

Half an hour later they had checked into the hotel, which turned out to be nondescript but welcoming, and were planning a shower before dinner.

"Then down to work!" Sarah announced as she

glanced into the little en-suite bathroom and began rummaging in her bag for shampoo and toothpaste.

She was as good as her word. While Michelle took her turn in the shower Sarah gathered together the various maps and information sheets they had brought, and after a quick phone call home followed by a dinner that Michelle was too nervous to enjoy, they spread the maps on the table of the dining-room and began to firm up on their plans.

The waiter appeared and topped up their glasses from the remains of the local French wine Sarah had ordered.

"We should have drunk a toast," Sarah said, trying to help Michelle relax. Now that they were here, the task seemed more impossible than ever.

Michelle was showing the strain, but she tried to get in the mood. "To your driving!" she proposed. "You only nearly got us killed once!"

"Rubbish!" Sarah retorted. "That's how they drive here – just watch me tomorrow!" She was laughing as Michelle's expression lightened.

"Success!" She raised her glass, and Michelle responded.

"Success. Now let's have a look . . ."

Twenty minutes later they were still poring over the map.

"Where *is* this place Maillerain-sous-Bois?" Sarah was getting irritated by this stage. "Did Evelyn get the name wrong, by any chance?"

"Of course not," said Michelle, who had been thinking the same alarming thought. "It was too important to her. She was absolutely certain!"

"Well, it must be really tiny then," Sarah said doubtfully.

"Could it have been renamed?" Michelle wondered, her heart sinking further.

"Unlikely." Sarah began to fold up the map. "Look, it *has* to be somewhere around Albert. So that's where we'll start tomorrow."

Chapter Eighteen

There was a slight drizzle as they left the hotel and began to head north-east along secondary roads.

"I don't want to push my luck on the motorways," Sarah said. "Besides, this way we'll go through lots of lovely little villages."

"Including Maillerain-sous-Bois?" Michelle suggested.

"Hmm," Sarah said. "I've a feeling it won't be that easy. But maybe it'll turn up once we're near the Somme."

They were relaxed, in holiday mood, by the time they reached a little village called St Quentin, somewhere to the north-east of Beauvais.

Sarah belted out an off-key imitation of Johnny Cash. Michelle joined in and for much of the journey, in between chatting and watching out for road signs, they sang or hummed snatches of songs that came into their heads.

They were singing 'Summertime' – in spite of the drizzle the French countryside had a lovely, lush feel to it – when they crossed into the Département de la Somme. A large brown sign informed them that this was the scene of much of the fighting during World War I and brought them back, jarringly, to the purpose of their journey.

"Did it say anything else?" Michelle asked when Sarah had translated.

"That's all I saw," Sarah said as she slowed to look at a road sign. "Want me to go back?"

"No, let's keep going," Michelle said after a moment. "I'd like to get to Albert as soon as we can."

They had decided to bypass Amiens and head straight for Albert.

"Shouldn't be too far now," Sarah said. "We'll stop there for lunch and have a look around."

The mood was broken. They still hummed from time to time, but now, without planning it, the songs were the few they knew from the First World War – 'Willie McBride' and 'Waltzing Matilda' and one that Sarah had only bits and pieces of, about a soldier playing football against the Germans in the trenches on that first Christmas Eve of the war. He later heard one of the young Germans singing 'Silent Night', and next day, when everything was back to 'normal', he killed the boy who sang in no-man's land.

"Do you think all that really happened?" Michelle asked. "The Germans putting up a tree on Christmas

Eve and the two armies singing 'Silent Night' and playing football together?"

Sarah shrugged. "Maybe. I've heard it a few times. I suppose it's possible – a lot of them were only boys of eighteen or nineteen, like Dad's grand-uncle. You could imagine them doing it out of homesickness and a bit of bravado. I'm sure most of them were thinking of Christmas and home and wondering what in God's name they were doing there."

"Imagine going back to killing each other the next day. Horrible!"

"Killing *is* horrible," Sarah said, and they lapsed into silence.

Michelle broke it after a few minutes. "Are we mad?"

"Doing this? Of course we are! Though I'd do anything for a few days in France. Pity they didn't fight down south, though, where it's nice and sunny!"

"Don't mock!" Michelle said sharply, as they passed a sign indicating that they were now on what had been the Front Line in July, 1916. They both shivered, and fell silent.

"It doesn't seem real," Michelle said after a few minutes of staring at the rich, rolling, calm fields. "It just doesn't seem possible."

"It was a long time ago," Sarah reminded her.

Michelle could only nod. A long time ago, maybe, but for a moment she felt as if it was all around them, in the stillness of the fields and, suddenly, in the signs coming more and more frequently by the side of the road, pointing in this or that direction to military cemeteries.

"There are dozens of them!" she exclaimed.

"Hundreds," Sarah said. "I printed out the list from the Internet – it's in my briefcase, back there." She jerked her head towards the back seat and Michelle turned and reached for it.

"Are there really hundreds?"

"'Fraid so," Sarah said.

"You told me –"

"That I'd try to narrow it down, and I have. But we never thought it was going to be easy."

"I didn't think it would be *impossible*!"

Sarah gave a short laugh. "Maybe you should have!"

Michelle sighed. "I suppose. But maybe once we find Maillerain-sous-Bois –"

"Let's hope. Now, where are we staying tonight?"

They were pulling into the outskirts of Albert as she spoke.

It was a curious town, more like a small English town than Michelle's image of a French one.

"Looks a bit strange," she said. "Nothing like I expected."

"Bombed to bits in the war," Sarah said. "Totally destroyed, totally rebuilt."

"But not here," Michelle said. They were pulling up in a small cobbled square in front of a church with a golden statue on top. "That looks like it's been there forever."

"Don't think so," Sarah said as she maneouvred into a free space in front of it. "I saw something about it on the Internet. Seems it was destroyed as well – *whoops!"* she added as the rain suddenly began to bucket down. "Looks as if we won't be going anywhere for a while. Let's see if we can get somewhere to stay tonight."

They finally made a break for it, dashing across to a nearby hotel which fortunately had one twin room left for the night. Not the last word in luxury, but the price wasn't bad.

"Try getting somewhere at home for that kind of money!" Michelle whispered as they followed directions up the steep, winding staircase to a room at the top of the building.

It was clean and pretty basic, but more than adequate for the night.

"Lunch," Sarah suggested. "And after that we'll see if we can find Pozieres. Should be very close to here."

Michelle nodded as she put her bag in the small wardrobe. Sarah had told her about Pozieres, which she had identified as the place where many of the soldiers who died from the end of March 1918 onwards were buried, including men from the Royal Dublin Fusiliers.

"Better not hold our breath," Sarah reminded her as they went back down to the dining-room. "He's hardly buried there, otherwise his brother Hugh would have found him. But it's a start."

"Maybe Hugh didn't know about it?" Michelle suggested. She laughed. "He didn't have Internet access, did he?"

It was Sarah's turn to shoot Michelle a look. Now that they were here, it seemed almost sacrilegious to joke.

The effect of all those cemeteries, Michelle thought, suddenly dreading actually having to go into one.

They had a simple lunch in the hotel, not talking much as they ate, concentrating on what lay ahead. There was a sense of having shifted not just in place but in time; the comfortable but slightly shabby hotel, its small lobby full of First World War maps and memorabilia, had an air of being unchanged over the years.

"I wonder –" Michelle began and then stopped. She had been about to say that the soldiers might have visited this particular hotel. There was a strange sense of their presence, probably because of all the memorabilia, but if what Sarah said about the town being destroyed was true then the hotel hadn't been here, at least not in its present state. And yet there was little else on display in the lobby, and a sense of nothing at all having changed or even happened since then.

"Let's go," she said, suddenly finding it stifling and anxious to be out in the fresh air now the rain had stopped.

Sarah, in response, dragged herself away from an old wall map she had been studying of the Somme battlefields and followed Michelle across the road to the car.

"Pozieres is that way," she said, pointing as she started the engine. "Towards Bapaume."

She turned the car and they headed out of the small town.

"What's that?" Michelle asked after a while, straining to see ahead. At the left-hand side of the road, still several hundred yards away, a large grey-white structure dominated an otherwise empty landscape.

"Must be it," Sarah said.

Just then they passed a sign for Pozieres Military Cemetery.

Sarah pulled the car slightly in off the road, both of them holding their breath.

They walked back to the entrance archway which towered high above them so they had to step back slightly into the road to read the inscription far above their heads.

It reminded Michelle fleetingly of the entrance to St Stephen's Green as she craned her neck to see it.

"Pozieres British Cemetery," she read, stepping back a bit further, checking as she did so that there were no cars coming. The traffic, though light, passed at speed, seeming to make no concessions to the village just up ahead. "'*In memory of the officers and men of the fifth and fourth armies who fought on the Somme battlefields 21st March – 7th August 1918 and of those of their dead who have no known graves.*' Well, the dates are right, anyway."

"So let's do it," Sarah said, taking a deep breath as she glimpsed, through the gateway, rows and rows of neat white headstones in the walled grassy space beyond.

They stopped for a moment in the space under the archway, surrounded by grey stone walls, not yet in the cemetery proper. Two small brass doors, about eighteen inches by eighteen inches, were set into the wall just beyond the entrance gate, facing them as they walked in.

"Wonder what they're for?" Michelle asked as she opened the nearer one, drawing out a tattered A4 sized book with a red cover and the title *The War Dead of the Commonwealth*.

"Look at this, Sarah!" she said urgently, excitement mounting as she went through the list – page after page filled with the names of those buried there.

She glanced again at the front cover.

"A to C," she read aloud. "My God. A whole book just for A to C?"

"Seems so," Sarah said, rifling quickly through the other books in the brass wall-safe and handing Michelle the one for the letter L.

Michelle took the book, replacing the other one, and quickly scanned the names.

"No Lacey," she said, with a sharp stab of disappointment, beginning to go through the names again.

"Well, we didn't really expect it, did we?" Sarah

said. "That would've been too easy. We must assume Hugh knew about this place and checked it out. But come on, let's take a look anyway."

"But why?" Michelle said, suddenly reluctant to enter the cemetery. "If Hugh's already been here . . ."

"I want to see it, now that we're here," Sarah said. "Maybe we'll learn something."

She started down the steps and Michelle, with a sort of fascinated dread, followed her.

It began to drizzle again as they stood for a minute taking in the stunning sight of row after row of white headstones. Not the white crosses Michelle had expected, but headstones, all ranged neatly as if standing to attention. Yew trees guarded the central pathway leading to a tall white cross which stood sentinel over the graves.

The cemetery was big but not enormous. "Let's see if we can find the Dublin Fusiliers," Sarah said, moving away to the left of the gate.

Michelle followed, still reluctant.

"There must be a thousand graves here," she said as she looked down along the pathway.

"Nearly *three* thousand," Sarah said.

"There can't be!"

"There are. It says so on the stuff I got off the Internet."

Three thousand! Michelle thought. *Three thousand graves, in just this one cemetery . . .*

There was only one way to do it. She took a deep

breath and followed Sarah to an inscription above a neat row of graves just inside the gate.

"Canadians?" Michelle read, managing to translate that much. "But what were *they* doing here?"

"It says their bodies were recovered later and buried here. I never thought of that, that people were buried somewhere and then moved. Makes it even more complicated."

"Let's just keep looking," Michelle said. "We should be able to find the Fusiliers, if they're here . . ."

She began to move slowly down the rows, reading aloud from the gravestones as she went. Highlanders, Canadians, Australians, Royal Irish Regiment . . . and grave after grave with the heart-wrenching inscription *'Known Unto God'*.

Unidentifiable, in other words. Soldiers, or maybe – she shuddered – *bits* of soldiers, with nothing at all to say who they had been.

Little better were the graves which said *'A soldier of . . .'*, followed by the name of a regiment. Nothing at all else to say who they were, in other words, but a cap badge or maybe the tatters of a uniform.

She stopped before one grave containing, it said, the bodies of five men from the same regiment. No names, no nothing at all, but the fact that there were five of them.

So why didn't they have separate graves?

Deciding not to go there, desperate to shake off the sense of deep sadness that was settling on her, she looked around for Sarah.

This was impossible.

The ages, that was the worst part. Nineteen, twenty, here and there a seventeen-year-old like her father's grand-uncle.

Hardly one of them over the age of twenty-five or twenty-six, it seemed.

No house was worth this, to be standing in the drizzling rain in a French graveyard full of the unknown bodies of young men.

Nothing on earth was worth this. And nothing on earth, she thought, was worth what they must have suffered, what their families must have suffered.

Feeling the need, suddenly, to rise up beyond this awful sadness, she hurried across to where her sister was walking along a raised pathway just inside the walls of the cemetery.

Sarah was moving slowly, her face turned upwards to the height of the dark grey walls. And then, as she neared her, Michelle realised with a start that it wasn't the walls themselves that Sarah was looking at, but the names inscribed on them.

Hundreds – no, *thousands* – of names, ranks, serial numbers and ages – most tellingly, the ages – of men who had gone missing from the various regiments and were presumed dead. All in the space of a few short months. And this was only one cemetery out of hundreds.

Impossible. Impossible to believe that this had happened, and impossible to believe that they would ever find a trace of Charles Lacey among so many.

No wonder his brother had to return so many times.

"This is crazy," she said after a few minutes. "We'll never –"

"Shhh!" Sarah said, continuing to move slowly along, scanning the names as she went. Michelle moved with her, her own eyes drawn inexorably to the long litany of names. They were alphabetical, which made it easier, and in their regiments, but she found that that didn't stop her looking even at unfamiliar names, drawing in the sense of huge loss that hung over the cemetery, the sense that these men had lived briefly and died here, or somewhere near here, in a sheer tragic waste of young lives.

She tried to shake off the mood, to concentrate on the task in hand, but her attention was held by the names – many of them Irish, though the regiments weren't – and here and there, little crosses at the base of the lists, or little paper poppies, with a note commemorating an uncle or great-uncle.

"None for fathers," she murmured to Sarah. "I wonder why none of them –" and then she stopped, remembering the ages of the dead men, realising why not.

"This is awful," she said. "This is really horrible."

Sarah nodded, not looking at her, still intent on the long lists of names. "Look!" she said after a minute, and Michelle followed her gaze to the list of the Royal Munster Fusiliers. The names here were all familiar: *Barry, Brennan, Casey* . . . her eye ran quickly downwards, then up again to the next panel and the next. *Larkin*, but no Lacey.

"Wrong regiment anyway," Sarah said, stepping around Michelle to get to the next panel. "So where are the Royal Dublin Fusiliers?"

She came to them a few moments later and Michelle joined her as she stood silently going through the litany of names.

"No sign of him," Sarah said, as they moved along towards the last few panels listing those, from whatever regiment, whose names were added later. Finally, just inside the gateway, they examined some headstones with names along the wall above them and the moving inscription '*Believed to be buried in this cemetery*'.

There was no sign anywhere of Charles Lacey's name.

"We didn't really expect to see it, did we?" Sarah reminded Michelle as they got back into the car. "If it had been there Hugh would have found it. We'll just have to keep trying."

Michelle just nodded.

"Oh, for God's sake, come on!" Sarah burst out after a few minutes of driving in silence. "What's up with you? We've plenty of time to do some more looking around. Cheer up, okay?"

One glance at her sister told Sarah that it was absolutely the wrong thing to say. She knew Michelle well enough to realise that her thoughts had strayed far from Charles Lacey, or his house, or the graves of those who had died all those years ago.

Michelle was thinking, as she so often did, still, of her own sons, none of whom had lived for more than a few weeks.

The Thiepval Memorial, with its thousands of names of the missing, could wait.

Without a word she turned the car around and headed back in the direction of Albert and their hotel.

Chapter Nineteen

The rain was coming down in sheets when they woke the following morning.

"Look's like it's time for Plan B," Sarah said as they sat down to breakfast.

"So what's Plan B?" Michelle asked. Her mood had lifted a little during dinner the previous evening, especially once she had spoken to Rory and Katie on her mobile, and she felt ready again to tackle the task ahead of them.

"We should go to the post office and find out where Maillerain-sous-Bois is," Sarah said, "but first we could have a quick look in the church, if you're interested, and then a visit to the Somme Museum. It's just over there –" she nodded in the direction of the large plate-glass window that fronted the hotel dining-room – "next to the church."

"I don't think we've much choice," Michelle said, pulling a face as she looked through the window to rain-soaked streets beyond. "Not a great day for graveyards!"

They finished breakfast quickly and risked the dash across the street, through the puddles and up the sodden steps of the church. They stood for a moment just inside the main entrance door, shaking the rain from their hair and getting their bearings in the dim light.

"It's a basilica," Sarah whispered, as she picked up an information leaflet from the table just inside the main door. "Notre Dame de Brebières, it's called."

They wandered around for fifteen minutes or so, examining the little side altars and the memorial plaques along the wall – many of them, they noticed, giving thanks to 'Notre Dame de Brebières' for deliverance '*in time of war and peril*'.

"That looks like it's been here forever," Michelle whispered, gazing up into the vast, vaulted roof-space high above them.

"I know. But it was definitely destroyed in the war, bit by bit. The statue of the Virgin was hanging for a long time up on top, leaning out over the town holding her baby. The soldiers used to believe that Albert wouldn't fall while she was still up there."

"She still is," Michelle pointed out.

"They had to replace her," Sarah said. "When the town was shelled she was toppled off. All of the villages around were destroyed, too. They had to rebuild everything."

"Do you suppose Maillerain-sous-Bois was bombed?" Michelle said.

Sarah shrugged. "Who knows? All we know is that the letters were postmarked from there, so some of it survived, anyway."

They were moving towards the entrance, looking cautiously out to see if the rain had eased or if they'd have to make a run for it.

It was lashing. "God, worse than home!" Sarah said. "Come on, the museum's just here."

They darted across, stopping in the little foyer to shake off the rain again. They bought tickets and turned in the direction of a long, tunnel-like corridor leading downwards.

"You wouldn't want to be claustrophobic," Michelle whispered as she followed in Sarah's wake – not sure *why* exactly she was whispering, but the situation somehow seemed to call for it.

They were the only ones in the museum just then. There was a film showing in a little area off to one side, but they stayed only a minute or two to get the gist of it.

It looked strangely familiar. Black and white, grainy pictures showing columns of soldiers moving staccato-fashion, rifles over their shoulders, waving to the camera; a group of men pushing cannons along a makeshift, mud-bogged road, and, in the distance, an explosion that filled the screen with clouds of smoke. Finally, struggling out of the smoke, a group of men –

stretcher-bearers laden down, other men limping, heads roughly bandaged, supported by their companions . . .

"Come on!" Michelle said. She turned, not waiting to see if Sarah followed. She wanted nothing more than to get out of there, but instead was drawn along a still-descending passage, her eyes riveted, in spite of herself, to the displays along one side and then, as she turned a corner, both sides: weapons, small pieces of ammunition, and the more personal things that might have made life in the trenches some bit bearable. Coins, watches, photographs, postcards, pen-knives, tins of soup and 'cream custard', empty bottles, a harmonica and cigarette packets . . . and then, poignant among the guns, grenades and ancient gasmasks, a jar labelled 'anti-gas ointment'.

The innocence of it! Michelle thought, images from half-remembered stories flashing trough her head – men stumbling, coughing and choking through thick yellow clouds of mustard gas that tore the lungs out of them. Chemical warfare before the word was ever invented.

Mustard gas? Where did I hear about that? she wondered.

Dad – of course!

She'd never realised how interested he was in the First World War, but for the past few days, as herself and Sarah had prepared for their trip, he'd talked of little else.

They followed the tunnel as it curved to the left, looking at the medal display, the brigade mottoes: *'They win or die who wear the Rose of Lancaster'*, the photographs, much like the ones of Charles and Hugh and of her father's grandfather . . . bright-eyed men, young but trying to seem older with their steady gaze and their carefully-tended moustaches, sitting erect and unsmiling for the camera.

And then, as they turned another corner, a very different set of photographs.

"Before and after," Michelle whispered as she and Sarah peered through glass at rows of smiling prisoners. *Smiling prisoners*, she thought. Why would prisoners be smiling? Unless they thought that being a prisoner *had* to be better than being in the trenches . . .

And looking at the written descriptions alongside the photographs, Michelle could well believe it. The men in the trenches were, according to one little piece, *'lousy, stinking, ragged, unshaven, sleepless'*. Some, it said, even wounded themselves deliberately in the hope of being sent home, knowing they'd probably be court-martialled and executed if they were caught but preferring to take their chances that way.

It was suddenly too much, and she needed to get out. "Let's go, I've had enough," she said, almost in panic, as Sarah came up beside her.

There was only one way out, following along the tunnel, and as they turned another corner to follow its curve she found herself drawn to the newspaper cuttings and photographs that filled the glass cases along the walls. Some of them, she noticed, were Irish, and phrases began to jump out at her – *Dublin Trench, Dublin Redoubt, Casement Trench, thick black smoke covering the battle, nothing but the noise . . . casualties in their thousands . . .*

In spite of herself she began to linger, reading the newspapers, looking into the open young faces of the soldiers who smiled for the camera, and the haggard unsmiling faces of those others who were clearly wanting to be anywhere but where they were. Was Charles Lacey there among them, she wondered? Or Hugh, or anyone else she might have heard of? Christy Keogh, maybe, her father's grand-uncle, or William, his grandfather? Might they be there, somewhere among all those faces?

"Why would they do it when they didn't have to?" she whispered to Sarah – whispered, because a group had come along behind them, talking loudly, exclaiming as they examined the displays with no apparent regard for the meaning of any of it. "If there was no conscription in Ireland, or even in England at the beginning?"

"Who knows?" Sarah answered, just as quietly. "Some went for money, I suppose, or adventure – don't look at me like that! I'm just going on what I read. They were told it was about freeing small nations and were promised Home Rule after the war if they joined up. So that's probably why a lot of them went, but it backfired on them big-time because of the Rising while they were away. And maybe some of them just wanted to see a bit of the world and hadn't a clue what war would be like . . . and the English lads went even when they didn't have to, because everyone else was going. They'd have seen it as their patriotic duty, probably."

"I suppose it was the same for the Germans," Michelle said as they passed in front of several display cases containing life-sized figures of men in mocked-up 'trenches', in the uniforms of the British, French and German armies. "They probably hadn't much choice either."

"Looks like they were better set up," Sarah said, and it did. The adjoining newspaper cuttings explained how the Germans had settled in for the long haul in many areas, able to provide some level of comfort for themselves because they were in defensive positions. The Allies, on the other hand, were fighting inch by inch through the mud for very small gains and had little opportunity to build more than the most basic of shelters.

Michelle and Sarah stood in front of one sandbagged construction, peering in towards the back of it, Sarah jumping back with a shudder as she saw several rats under a makeshift bed on which a bandaged figure was lying.

"Yeuchhh!"

"They're only plastic," Michelle reassured her.

"It's what they stand for, that's what's horrible," Sarah said.

You could say the same for the whole place, Michelle thought. *What it stood for was horrible.*

Not for the first time, she wondered how Charles Lacey could have left his wife and his very young family and come to such a place, for no obvious reason.

She moved away from the displays and was looking again for the exit when she saw that Sarah had moved back along the other side and was examining some newspaper cuttings there. One, Michelle noticed, looked quite recent: an account, in an English newspaper, of how an Englishwoman had bought a French farmhouse and later discovered evidence in the cellar of soldiers having stayed there during the war.

"I thought they were deserters," she was quoted as saying, *"but then I realised it was a first-aid post."*

The tone of the article suggested to Michelle that the woman would have no sympathy for deserters, and she said as much to Sarah.

"Most people *wouldn't* be sympathetic," Sarah said. "There were hundreds of them shot, maybe thousands."

"God, you'd be mad *not* to desert, if you had the chance!" Michelle responded. "Imagine getting home for a while and then having to go back, knowing what it was like!"

"I don't suppose many of them survived to go home more than once or twice," Sarah said. "Wonder if Charles Lacey got home at all during the war?"

"Don't think so, otherwise Evelyn would have mentioned it," Michelle said.

They had been moving along the tunnel as they spoke and now came through a doorway into a darkened area that was filled, suddenly, with flashing lights and deafening noises designed to give a sense of being on the battlefield.

Except we're not wading through mud and terrified of being shot, Michelle thought, relieved nevertheless as she arrived at the final door and emerged into a large, open area with a shop at one end and a pervasive, incongruous smell of fresh coffee.

"A different world," she said to Sarah as they paid for their coffee and brought it to a nearby table.

"Makes you realise how effective all that was, down there," Sarah said, looking back towards the tunnel exit from which the loud-voiced tour group were now emerging.

"Well, after all, it was their duty!" a nasal woman with a particularly carrying voice was insisting. "I mean, what else would one expect? And they *were* given a hero's welcome when they returned home!"

"My eye!" Sarah said quietly, glancing across at Michelle. "Not the ones who came home to Ireland anyway! And what about the ones who *didn't* get home? Or the ones who came home in bits?"

Michelle said nothing, sensing, as the group began to crowd them out at the tables, that such comments would be unwelcome.

"Let's go," she suggested, finishing her coffee quickly and grimacing as she realised that the rain hadn't eased off much while they were in the museum.

They emerged into the street and found, to their

surprise, that they had travelled quite a distance underground from the little square with its basilica and museum entrance.

"It's amazing to think what's down there, under our feet," Sarah said, glancing along the street, seeing the route they must have followed underground. "Are you listening?" she asked after a minute when Michelle didn't respond.

"Mmm," Michelle said.

"What's up?" Sarah asked as they made their way back towards the square.

"Just thinking," Michelle answered, her eyes on the cobblestoned road they were walking along. "It all feels very real here, somehow, with the graveyard and the museum and everything. As if it's not that long since the war. Remember the photo of Charles and Hugh in their uniforms? You can nearly imagine them here, can't you? Frightened out of their wits and wondering would they ever get home."

For the first time she felt as if Charles Lacey had been a real person, and out of nowhere came the memory of the memorial cards and poppies at Pozieres, left mostly by grand-nieces because there was no-one else to do it.

"I'd like to put some flowers on his grave, if we find it," she said.

"*When* we find it," Sarah corrected. "Let's start thinking positively – otherwise this'll really get to us."

Too late, Michelle thought. It had already got to her,

the oppressive sense of doom in the tunnel, the thought of all those young men – Charles, Christy Keogh, all the others – who'd never made it home.

She wanted to do something, anything, to show her recognition of what they had been through. If – or *when* – she found Charles Feradot Lacey's grave, the very least she could do was put some flowers on it.

Chapter Twenty

They went for lunch in a little coffee-shop on the outskirts of Albert.

They lingered over it, ordering more coffee for Sarah and a glass of wine that Michelle didn't really want.

They looked again at the luscious pastries, the elaborate desserts, toyed with the idea of sampling them though they weren't hungry now.

Anything, just to take their minds off things, to escape the atmosphere they felt now in the square, knowing what was under their feet, knowing they still had to face the Thiepval Memorial in the afternoon.

"We'd really better try the post office now and find out where Maillerain-sous-Bois is," Sarah said, glancing at her watch.

"You're right," Michelle said, pushing aside her unfinished wine as Sarah signalled for the bill.

The post office staff were friendly but, in spite of their efforts, unable to help. The only Maillerain they could locate was over a hundred kilometres away, back over to the west of Amiens towards Rouen, and it was very unlikely to be that.

"And that wasn't even Maillerain-sous-Bois, just Maillerain," Michelle said dejectedly as they left the post office.

"Evelyn must have got the name wrong," Sarah said. "I suppose at her age –"

"She said she was certain! But . . ." Michelle broke off with a sigh. "So what do we do now? We probably won't find anything at Thiepval –"

"We'll decide *after* Thiepval," Sarah said firmly. "We didn't expect to find anything at Pozieres, remember, or even at Thiepval itself –"

"So why go there? The dates are wrong for us, aren't they? Up to the 20th March, you said, and Charles was still alive then. Besides, Hugh would have found his name if it was there, so why waste time?" Michelle asked reasonably.

"It's a starting point," Sarah said, "to get some kind of sense of what it was like –"

"We got enough of that in Pozieres and in the tunnel! And it didn't get us any nearer to finding him."

Sarah rounded on her. "So have you any better ideas?"

"It just seems like a waste of time –"

"Michelle, this whole *thing* is a waste of time! I

mean, how much chance is there that we'll really find any trace of him –"

"So we might as well go home," Michelle said despondently.

"What the hell is wrong with you, Michelle! If we're talking waste of time, what about my holidays! I was supposed to go to Greece with the girls, instead of which –"

"But you *like* France!"

"That's hardly the point, is it!" Sarah snapped. "And if you think I'm going to stand in the street arguing – Michelle, what is *wrong* with you!"

Michelle stood looking at her for a moment and then sighed. "I don't know. Sorry, Sarah. I'm disappointed about Maillerain-sous-Bois –"

"No need to take it out on me!"

"I didn't mean to. I just feel we're running out of options. And that really got to me this morning, the tunnel. I keep thinking about what it must have been like for them."

"That doesn't help anyone," Sarah pointed out. "Look, we've come for a particular reason. It's not a holiday – I know," she said as Michelle grimaced. "If work gets busy, this might be the only holiday I'll get. Well, maybe not, I might manage one week away instead of two. But –" she reached for Michelle's arm, starting to walk and drawing Michelle along with her –"whether or not we find out anything about Charles Lacey, we've got a few days away so let's just try and make the most of it!"

"At Thiepval?" Michelle said, making a face – but her mood felt lighter almost in spite of herself. Sarah could always get around her.

"*After* Thiepval, then. We'll have a nice dinner and plan what to do next – and tomorrow we'll go to Arras. I've heard the British Army was there during the war. Maybe we'll learn something."

"Don't hold your breath," Michelle said. "It seemed much more possible when I was at home, but I was just kidding myself."

"We never thought it would be easy. But if you can go back to Evelyn and say that at least you tried – well, who knows?"

The thought of the house seemed to energise Michelle. "So how far's Thiepval?"

"Not far." They had arrived back at the car and climbed in. "You'll really have to learn to read maps, Chelle."

"I've never needed to."

"Because you get Rory to do it! But fair's fair – if I'm doing all the driving you'd better learn to navigate."

She was about to say '*But you like navigating*', but one look at Sarah's face made her think better of it. She reached over and got the map.

Wish I'd paid more attention to old Brennan in Geography! she thought as she struggled to get her bearings.

"It's a straight road, we can't go wrong," Sarah reassured her, as they passed one of the heart-stopping little signs commemorating the front line.

"We turn left just here," Sarah said, as Michelle, her attention still focused on the road behind them with its poignant sign, gave up on the map and prepared herself for the emotional impact of Thiepval.

Or thought she did.

Nothing on earth could have prepared either of them for the huge stone walls covered in thousands and thousands of names.

"And they're just the ones who went missing!" Sarah said, awed. "Not even dead – *missing*!"

Michelle couldn't even answer. She stood under the vast immensity of the walls, looking up and up, knowing that Charles Lacey's name couldn't be there but driven by some compulsion to look anyway.

Heart in mouth, she climbed the steps with Sarah just behind her, and they began looking through the books containing lists of names and regiments.

"Royal Dublin Fusiliers!" Sarah said. "Pier 16C." She glanced towards the huge stone pillars that formed the central core of the monument. "They must mean those."

They moved quickly to the big vaulted archway and began scanning the pier numbers.

8D and 7D, immediately to their left, listed the Coldstream Guards. To their right were 9B and 10B, showing the names of the Royal Warwickshire Regiment.

"How does this work, anyway?" Michelle's impatience was mounting. "There must be *some* kind of order to it!"

"Mmm," Sarah answered, her attention taken as she

turned the corner of Pier 10 to find 15 just in behind it.

"So 16 must be that one," she said, checking the pier to her left which turned out to be 14A, "or that," she added, moving across to the base of another. "Here!"

Michelle went quickly to her side.

"16B," she read. "So C must be –"

"This side," Sarah said. "There it is, Royal Dublin Fusiliers!" she finished triumphantly.

Quickly they scanned the list.

And then they saw it.

All the more shocking because they never expected it to be there. Unbelieving, they stared at the name etched into the white stone of the panel.

"Look!" Michelle said, turning.

"I wonder if –" Sarah said at the same moment, glancing at Michelle, then back at the name on the panel above them, the name they never even thought of finding.

Pvte. Christopher Keogh, aged 17, died 30 July, 1916.

"It can't be him," Michelle said. "Can it?" Unexpected tears filled her eyes.

"Why not?" Sarah said. Turning to her, Michelle saw the glint of tears in her sister's eyes as well. "The name's right, and the age, as well as the year he died. The Regiment, too."

"There could have been more than one," Michelle said.

"So, what difference?" Sarah asked. "The name is

his, and he *did* go missing in July 1916. It's as likely to be him as any other Christy Keogh."

"God, this is ridiculous!" Michelle said, swiping at her eyes. "We never even *heard* of him until a month ago! And it's not like we'd ever have met him, even if he hadn't died in the war. He was – what was he? Dad's grand-uncle. What does that make him?"

Sarah stood looking at the name for a minute or two before replying.

"Family," she said finally. "It makes him family."

They quickly finished scanning the list, but found no trace of Charles Lacey. It hardly seemed to matter. They were too stunned by the discovery of Christopher Keogh's name.

"It makes it very real, doesn't it?" Michelle said as they finally turned away and made their way on to the terrace at the back to look out over the rows of white crosses on the left, and headstones on the right, marking six hundred symbolic French and British graves.

Sarah didn't answer and they both stood in silence, their thoughts on all those thousands of names, all those thousands of families like Evelyn's and like their own who had spent a lifetime waiting for, remembering, mourning young men who never made it home.

Chapter Twenty-one

The plan next morning was to head for Arras straight after breakfast and see if they could find out anything useful.

"Not very likely, is it?" Michelle said glumly as they pulled away from the hotel. "We've no reason to believe he ever even went there!"

Her mood was still very low. They had spent hours the previous evening poring over information Sarah had got from the Internet and talking about the tunnel, the cemeteries, their discovery of Christy Keogh's name . . .

Especially that, Christy Keogh's name.

Michelle couldn't believe it would have such an impact, the finding of someone's name so long after he died, someone she hadn't even known existed.

"It's because he's family," said Sarah over dinner. "I

feel it too, a kind of sense of loss. You know, wondering what might have happened if he'd lived."

"We'd probably never have heard of him," Michelle had said. "I mean, Dad's grand-uncle! We might never even have met him."

"But we might," Sarah had answered. "We see Auntie Maura every few weeks and she's our grand-aunt. If she'd ever married and had children we'd know them too. Same thing. Dad would've known his grand-uncle if he had lived."

If he had lived.

Michelle had gone to bed with those words circling in her brain and three names threading in and out of her thoughts.

Peter... Tim... Christopher...

Christopher!

She had sat bolt upright in the bed, then glanced across to make sure she hadn't disturbed Sarah, who was sleeping.

Christopher.

She settled slowly back down in the bed, unable to believe that it hadn't struck her at the time. Probably because she had been caught up in the shock of finding Christopher Keogh's name, and the surname was different anyway. But of course, of *course,* she had been reminded of her own Christopher, named not for a distant relation she'd never heard of, but for Rory's own father.

If he had lived...

Only he hadn't.

Like his brothers Peter and Tim before him, he had died without ever leaving the hospital he'd been born in. A rare congenital disorder, they'd explained.

And Katie, absolutely wonderful little treasure that she was, didn't make up – how could she? – for the big brothers who had died before she was born.

There wasn't much sleep for Michelle after that as she lay thinking about her lost boys, all the lost young men . . .

I'm mad to be doing this, she thought, *completely mad . . .*

Followed by the giddying thought, just before she finally fell asleep . . .

Maybe we should try again.

That thought was still in her mind the following morning as they drove into the main square of Arras.

"Isn't it gorgeous!" Sarah exclaimed, pulling into a convenient parking spot in the centre of the square.

They were surrounded by tall, terraced buildings, similar but not identical, with their timbered fronts and pastel colours, towering three or four stories above a series of arches at pavement level.

"They don't look French either, do they?" Michelle said. "They look like something out of a Dutch painting."

Sarah laughed. "Since when are you an expert on Dutch paintings?"

"You know what I mean! It's nearly too perfect, like

someone's idea of what a town square should look like."

"This was all destroyed during the war, too, so maybe when they rebuilt it –"

"Rubbish! Looks like it's been here forever!"

"No, really! It was all rebuilt, so maybe they did try to make it look perfect. *And* as if it'd always been here. I suppose that's what you'd try to do, make it the same as before. Or better, even."

They were crossing the road towards the tourist office as they spoke.

"And speaking of Dutch paintings," Sarah continued, "there's one of Breughel's here. Remember him? He did all those lovely pictures of plump little men and women wearing funny hats and clogs –"

"Sounds charming!" Michelle said, making a face.

"Oh, come on, you *know* them!" Sarah said impatiently. "There're some copies in that pub in Ranelagh, the one you used always go to with – whoops," she added as she saw the look on Michelle's face. "Sorry. Won't mention *that* war. But I'm sure you know Breughel. His stuff is everywhere, on Christmas cards and that kind of thing. I'd like to see the painting while we're here. Come on, it's worth a look."

Michelle shrugged. "Okay, if you want to."

It didn't really interest her, but at least it wasn't anything to do with tunnels, or battlefields. She hoped.

They found a small hotel for the night and then walked the short distance to the Musée des Beaux-Arts.

The Breughel was in a long room just inside the entrance hall, and to Michelle's surprise it *did* interest her.

It was strangely familiar, as Sarah had predicted, and yet she'd swear she had never seen it before.

But she had seen many like it, on Christmas cards and once, vaguely remembered, on a chocolate box her granny used to keep jewellery in. Colourful figures in a village setting, with animals roaming around and children playing chase.

The painting enchanted her, and she stood in front of it drinking in every detail until a party of tourists gathered around her and she had to move.

"Want to go?" Sarah asked.

Michelle shook her head, her attention taken by another painting, this one a religious scene by an artist unknown to her. Then a carving, over six hundred years old.

"Look at this," she said to Sarah. "Amazing!"

It was – and there was more, much more. Old, old paintings, woodcuts, coins, a huge stone fireplace rescued from an ancient house . . .

"So the war can't have had much of an impact here," Michelle said. "Otherwise there'd be none of this stuff here."

"I don't think that's true," Sarah said slowly. "You've a point, but maybe they hid it away or something . . ."

Michelle raised an eyebrow and smiled. "That?" she

said, nodding her head towards the elaborate, ancient fireplace on display behind her.

"Know-all!" Sarah said. "Okay, so I'm not sure. But definitely the stuff I read said that Arras was wrecked. The fighting was just out the road from here."

Michelle didn't want to think about it. Her mood had lifted while she wandered round the art gallery, and just for an hour or two she wanted to relax and forget all about the war.

But there was no escaping it. They turned a corner that brought them into another wing of the gallery and an exhibition by *Matheurin Méheut – un artiste combattant – 1914-1918*.

"Does it mean what I think it means?" Michelle asked.

"Probably," Sarah answered. "We could give it a miss."

But she couldn't, Michelle realised.

Drawn by an awful compulsion, she entered the exhibition room and went slowly round, looking at the sketches and paintings that Méheut, and other artists she'd never heard of, had done during the Great War.

There was one in particular that stood out for her. Later she couldn't remember the name of the German artist who had painted it, but she knew that the painting itself would continue to haunt her. A sentry, dressed in grey, stood still as death under a bright moon, looking out towards the front line.

"A German," she said quietly to Sarah. "You don't

think about that, do you? That thousands of Germans died too. *Hundreds* of thousands, I suppose."

"I never thought about any of it before, and neither did you!" Sarah replied. "It happened a hell of a long time ago, Michelle."

True. And yet it seemed no time ago, and no distance away, as they stood looking at the paintings.

"Imagine being able to do that, in the middle of a war," Michelle said as they moved away finally from the painting and went to look again at one or two more on the far side of the narrow room. "How could you concentrate on drawing? Wouldn't you be terrified?"

"It wasn't all fighting," Sarah reminded her. "Seems they spent a lot of time hanging around in between battles, waiting for something to happen. I suppose he did it then."

"But still – you'd think he'd find something else to do."

"Like what?"

Michelle shrugged. "Like helping the wounded, or something."

"Maybe he thought he could help more by doing this. A bit like TV cameramen in the middle of fighting. They don't stop to help, they keep on filming because that's what they're there for. He painted because it's what he did best. And to make a record of it."

Michelle was about to protest but stopped, remembering the photographs from the trenches, the haunting quality of the German artist's painting.

"You're right. If we hadn't seen the photos or the paintings we wouldn't have a clue what it was like."

"We *still* haven't a clue," Sarah said quietly as she paused in front of the large white poster just inside the exhibition room door, with an explanatory text on it.

"What's it say?" Michelle asked.

"Wait a minute. Something about – it's a bit hard to understand – something about an artist shooting a German soldier and then finding paints and brushes in the man's stuff, and a sketchpad with the names of some artists written on the back cover. He went away and cried."

"God, that's awful!" Michelle said. "Was it Méheut or some other artist that shot him?"

"I'm not sure," Sarah answered. "Whoever it was, he must have felt horrible. Imagine killing another artist!"

"Imagine killing *anyone*," Michelle said as they left the exhibition. "And imagine doing it again and again. How could they *do* that?"

"Because they had to," Sarah said simply as they came out to the front hall. "It was their duty. And besides, they would have been shot themselves if they didn't."

They were about to leave the building when Sarah noticed an advertising poster in the foyer for another exhibition, of photography this time.

"The British Army in Arras, 1916-1918," she read. "So they were definitely here. Want to go? It's on in the Town Hall."

"I don't think I could face it," Michelle said after a pause. "Really. I think I've seen enough."

"I think we should –"

"I couldn't, really," Michelle repeated, looking at the photograph on the poster of a British soldier sitting on sandbags, wearing a helmet and greatcoat, writing a letter home.

She couldn't know that, of course. He could have been writing anything. But she felt sure it was a letter home.

All those men, in all those paintings and photographs, were becoming real to her. No longer just faces, but someone's family. Someone's son, brother, father . . .

She turned away from the poster, thinking of Charles Lacey and of young Christopher Keogh.

"What's the point, anyway?" she asked Sarah as they left the Art Gallery and walked out through the front courtyard to the tree-lined street outside. "We've no proof that he was ever here, so why look at more photos? It's not as if we're going to find him that way."

"Have you any better ideas?" Sarah snapped. "Honestly, Chelle, you're leaving it all up to me. This is ridiculous!"

"So maybe we should go home," Michelle said. "Just leave it, and go home because we're never going to find out anything about him, or this Maillerain-sous-whatsit, and I'm fed up with it. We've done nothing since we came but look at cemeteries and photographs of dead soldiers and talk about the war. I'm sick of it!

All I wanted was a bloody house, I didn't need all this! I'm starting to wish I'd never even *seen* Charles Lacey's house!"

Sarah took a long look at her. "Do you mean that? Or do you just need a bit of a break from it?"

Michelle sighed. "Sorry, Sare. I'm not in great form since last night. It's really getting to me, all this stuff about soldiers and dying." She attempted a little laugh. "Plus, I'm starving, and you know how scraggy I get then."

Sarah glanced at her watch. "Well past lunch-time. Come on, we'll find somewhere to eat."

They had passed a lovely little coffee-shop in the square, and made their way back to it. It was quiet at this time of day, with just one or two people finishing a late lunch.

They ordered baguettes and coffee, which arrived quickly.

"So, what's really up?" Sarah asked, taking a grateful sip of the rich coffee.

"Nothing. Just fed up, like I said. Beginning to feel we're getting nowhere."

"We'll definitely get nowhere if you don't snap out of this!" Sarah said. "Sure there's nothing *really* wrong?" She looked at Michelle shrewdly, knowing her too well.

Michelle stalled for time, nibbling on the baguette, then finally, with tears in her eyes, told Sarah about the thoughts that had gone round and round in her head last night.

Sarah listened, then said quietly, "You'll have to move past it, Michelle. It's been, what? Five years since Christopher died, six or seven for Tim and Peter? You'll have to –"

"What?" Michelle interrupted angrily. "I'll have to what? Forget about them?"

Sarah touched her gently on the arm. "You know I wasn't going to say that! I just meant that for all of you, for Rory and Katie as well as yourself, maybe it's time to think about – God, I shouldn't have started this, it's none of my business, I just hate to see you so upset, that's all. Sorry . . ."

"It's okay," Michelle said. She hesitated. "I thought about it myself last night, that maybe we should –" she broke off impatiently. "Oh, what's the point?"

"Have you talked to Rory?"

"What do you think? Look, let's leave it, okay? Concentrate on what we'll do next."

"So," Sarah said carefully. Michelle really was rattled, in a way Sarah hadn't seen her for a long time. "What do you want to do? Do you really want to go home?"

Michelle thought about it as the waitress, at Sarah's signal, brought more coffee.

"No, I suppose not. We really should have another try at finding Maillerain-sous-Bois. Maybe the tourist office can help. And if not, what about going to the Maillerain they suggested in the post office?"

She said it without much hope – but if there was a better plan right now, she couldn't think of it.

Chapter Twenty-two

They finished lunch and crossed the square to the vast grey building that was the tourist office, where they spent half an hour with the staff checking out all the possible options within a hundred-kilometre radius of Arras.

"And you are certain, Mesdames, that it is not Maillerain that you seek? There," the helpful young man pointed to the map which was open on the counter in front of him, "towards Rouen, near Neufchatêl?"

"We don't think so," Sarah answered. "The place we're looking for is somewhere near the Somme, we're fairly sure of that."

"But not certain?" he pressed.

"No, not certain," Michelle agreed.

They went through the litany of possibilities again. Mirrail-sous-bois, Marain, Milleran, Alerrain-sous-bois . . .

"Not that one?" the assistant asked hopefully, but they shook their heads. It was too far away, and in the wrong direction. And besides, Evelyn had been quite certain of the name. Maillerain-sous-Bois, nothing else.

"That Maillerain over there," Sarah said finally, pointing to the map. "The one we think is too far away. Could that ever have been called Maillerain-sous-Bois instead of just Maillerain?"

The assistant gave an expressive Gallic shrug. "Who knows? I have only the information I have here, nothing more."

"And there's nowhere else you can check?"

The man's patience was holding, but only just. He'd spent half an hour checking already and his colleague had gone for a break; there was a queue beginning to build and, attractive as Sarah and Michelle were, he couldn't afford any more time for them.

"Désolé, Mesdames. Perhaps if you tried at Maillerain itself?"

There was nothing else for it.

"Pity we didn't think of trying it first!" Michelle said as they left the tourist office. "It's not too far from Beauvais. Should we go now, d'you think?"

"First thing tomorrow might be better, " Sarah said. "If we leave early enough we can have a quick look at Amiens on the way."

They went back to the hotel for a while before wandering out again in the late afternoon.

"Wish I'd brought my shorts!" Michelle exclaimed

as they made their way to the square again. As if in apology for its absence of the past few days, the late afternoon sun was dancing off the cobbles in the middle of the square.

"No time for that!" Sarah laughed. "We're not here for the sun!"

"But we'll make the most of it!" Michelle said, and they spent a pleasant few hours wandering around the streets and investigating the shops.

After an early dinner in a candlelit cellar ("How romantic is that!" Sarah had said. "You really should come here with Rory sometime.") they got back to the hotel around ten. To Michelle's great relief, and thanks in part to the local wine, she fell quickly and soundly asleep.

They left after an early breakfast next morning and stopped briefly at Amiens, wandering round the enormous old cathedral with its commemorative plaques to various regiments which fought in the First World War.

"Strange when you think of it," Sarah said. "I'm sure lots of them must have come here to pray before going to the Front."

They were in a sombre mood again when they reached Maillerain just after midday.

They saw it immediately as they drove into the little village – an ornate old iron sign indicating that this was Maillerain-sous-Bois.

"It's it!" they shrieked simultaneously, as Sarah pulled sharply into the kerb.

Quickly they made plans. The tourist office first – if there was one – to find out where the military cemeteries were. Then the post office, to find out –

"What?" Sarah asked as she sat looking at Michelle. "What exactly are we trying to find out? I mean, it wasn't Charles Lacey who was writing, so how do we know who was? Could've been anybody!"

Again the impossibility of the task struck Michelle, but buoyed up now by the excitement of finding the right village, she felt ready for anything.

"We'll worry about that *after* we look at the military cemeteries," she decided. "First things first – the grave could be there!"

They found the little tourist office and discovered, to their surprise, that there were no military cemeteries anywhere near Maillerain-sous-Bois.

"None?" Michelle asked, perplexed. "None at all?"

"None at all," said the woman behind the desk, who had also explained that the "sous-Bois" had been dropped more than twenty years ago, for reasons that weren't entirely clear to her. "There was no need of them, you see. There was no fighting near here, so, no military cemeteries. The new cemetery on the road toward Beauregard, yes, and the old one in the churchyard, but military cemeteries, there are none."

Michelle and Sarah looked at each other in dismay.

"So what do we do now?" Sarah asked as they left the tourist office.

Michelle sighed. "Give up?" She attempted a smile.

"Go home and convert Mam's garage into something we can live in?"

Sarah laughed. "Wrong answer!"

Michelle shrugged. "Look for Hugh's contact? If he was getting letters from here, the chances are that this is where he kept visiting so *somebody* here must remember him."

"After thirty years? Wouldn't bet on finding anyone!"

"But we don't know 'til we try, do we?" Michelle said.

"So what do you suggest? Chat up all the oul' lads we can find?"

"If that's what it takes! Come on, let's try the post office and see if they know anything."

They didn't. The old man behind the counter made short shrift of Sarah's enquiries about an Irishman named Hugh Lacey, before turning to speak sharply in rapid French to a younger man who joined him, trying to help.

"What was that all about?" Michelle asked Sarah as they moved away from the counter and the young man, with an apologetic glance at them, went back to his work.

"I only got the gist of it, he spoke too fast," Sarah said. "Something about wasting their time. A wonder he gets any business at all," she added as she glanced back and caught him scowling. "We were only asking!"

"So we'll ask somewhere else," Michelle said as they stopped in the quiet street outside the post office. "Any ideas?"

"The bars might be our best bet," Sarah suggested.

"Though if all the old men around here are like that fella . . ."

"They can't all be," Michelle said reasonably.

It seemed they were.

"They're obviously not up for the Friendliest Village in France Award," Sarah commented after they were rebuffed, yet again, in the third bar they tried. "They know nothing about any war, and they never even heard of Ireland, let alone anyone called Hugh Lacey!"

"Maybe the war's still a sore subject?"

"It wasn't in Albert or Arras, so why should it be here?"

"Must be your French then, maybe you'd better brush up!" Michelle teased.

"Smart-ass! So, d'you want to stay here tonight or head back towards Beauvais? The flight's at noon tomorrow, that doesn't leave us much time."

Michelle looked around the gloomy little bar they were sitting in.

"Stay here, I suppose. Beauvais's close enough, and now that we're here I'd like to look around a bit more, see if we can get any ideas. And we can try again tonight."

"We can," Sarah said, not relishing the prospect. "I suppose there's no point in ringing Evelyn?"

"Wouldn't think so," Michelle said. "I'm sure she's told us all she knows."

"So we're stuck," Sarah said.

"We'll think of something. Feel like driving around a bit?"

Sarah laughed. "Good job I'm on Orangina!"

"Don't know how you drink that stuff! Come on, let's see if we can find a hotel."

There was nothing in the little village square apart from the bars they had visited, a row of ancient-looking houses on either side of a little church, and a few haphazard shops, among them the post office and tourist office. Back behind it, though, they could see from the rooftops that the village had grown in every direction.

"Let's head that way," Sarah suggested, seeing the sign for Beauregard. "Seems as good a direction as any."

They drove for a kilometre or two, past a hotchpotch of houses and garages and cafés alight with neon signs until they finally found a hotel out near the new cemetery on the Beauregard road.

"Doesn't look great," Michelle said.

"It's only one night. It'll do!" Sarah replied.

"Suppose there's no point looking there?" Michelle added, glancing towards the cemetery at the far side of the busy road.

"None," Sarah said. "That's the municipal cemetery, look, there's the sign. We'd be wasting our time."

They checked in, went to their room and found that it looked out towards the cemetery.

"Lovely view!" Michelle said. "As if we haven't had enough of cemeteries!"

They unpacked their clothes quickly and drove round the outskirts of the little town, really not much more than a village. It was a sprawl of a place that seemed to have grown in a haphazard way with nothing much to distinguish it. Beyond the cemetery they found factories, a school, more houses with small shops dotted among them and a nondescript little park with a sluggish river that seemed defeated by its surroundings.

"Nothing much to see," Sarah said as they finished their circuit of the outskirts. "This seems to be about it, besides what we saw earlier."

They were pulling into a square with a small fountain and some monuments standing in front of a dilapidated Hôtel de Ville. At the far end of a street leading from the square they could see the spire of the dusty reddish church across from the post office.

They left the car and crossed the square to the front of the Hôtel de Ville.

"The town hall," Sarah explained.

"Any point asking there?" Michelle wondered. "What for?" Sarah asked, moving towards the door of the building anyway as she spoke.

"Closed," she said, giving the doorknob a twist. "Until tomorrow," she added, glancing at the notice on the stand to her right. "I suppose they don't have much to do around here – it's fairly quiet."

She was right. There was no-one at all in the square apart from two old women sitting on a bench at the far side, watching them.

"Any ideas?" Michelle asked as they wandered over

towards the stone statue of three soldiers on a pedestal above the inscription *"Mort pour la France."*

"Died for France," Sarah translated. They glanced, from habit, at the list of names from two world wars, finding none familiar but not expecting to. "Two hundred and twenty from this village alone," Sarah said, still translating.

"My God! And the war didn't even reach here!"

"The whole of France was occupied for the second one, remember," Sarah said. "But I suppose, even for the first, everyone was affected one way or another. I don't suppose Frenchmen had a choice about going."

"No wonder the men in the pubs didn't want to talk about it," Michelle mused.

"People have long memories," Sarah said. "No different than at home, really. And some of the men we tried to talk to probably fought in the Second World War – I didn't think of that. I'm sure they don't want reminding."

"So where does that leave us?"

Sarah shrugged. "The bars again? Unless we want to go around knocking on doors!"

Michelle laughed. "It might come to that!"

"You'd think *somebody* would remember him," she added seriously as they reached the car. "Thirty years isn't so long ago, is it?"

Sarah raised an eyebrow as she started the engine.

"It's not!" Michelle insisted. "And if he came here lots of times –"

Michelle sighed. "Okay, so I'm clutching at straws. But it's not as if we've any better ideas."

"Well. . ."

"Come on, *what*?"

"I don't suppose you'd, you know, bring back a little bit of earth and tell her you found the grave?"

"What!"

"Well, why not?" Sarah asked, turning now to face her as she warmed to the theme. "Look, she said she can't leave the house until she finds out what happened to Charles, right? And we've done our damnedest to find out and I don't know what else we can do. Hugh found something here, or we think he did. So why not bring her back some soil and say we –"

"I don't *believe* this!" Michelle burst out. "You don't seriously mean to cheat her like that!"

"It's not cheating, it's –"

"It's lying, and cheating! How could you, Sarah!"

"She'll never know."

"And that makes it okay, does it?"

"I didn't say that. But it might make her happier –"

"If that's what it takes, I'm not doing it! I wouldn't do that to her, Sarah, no matter what the consequences!"

I'll lose the house, she thought, her heart pounding. But she had no alternative. What Sarah was suggesting just wasn't an option.

"Would you really do that to her? Would you go back and tell her lies about something like that?"

"You've been known to tell a few lies in your time,

Michelle Larkin! So you can stop the holier-than-thou act!"

"Never about anything serious."

"Oh no?"

"No," Michelle said firmly. "Not about something like this. And I still can't believe you're suggesting it. It would be like betraying her."

"It was just a thought, Michelle," Sarah said. "I'd never have suggested it only I know how much you want the house."

"Not that much, Sarah!"

They got out of the car and crossed the road to the nearest bar in an uneasy truce.

They ordered some wine and sat toying with it.

"Look, I didn't –"

"Just leave it, okay?" Michelle said. "Just forget it!"

Sarah looked around, trying to gauge who they might strike up a conversation with. There was a crowd of young men gathered around a pool table and three older men sitting at the bar, who had looked around to stare as the two women came in, before turning their backs pointedly and concentrating on their drinks, muttering to each other.

"I'd say they don't miss much!" Sarah said, trying to lighten the atmosphere.

But Michelle wasn't in a mood to be appeased. She sat in silence, thinking about what Sarah had suggested.

There was no way she could do it.

Absolutely no way.

It wasn't in her to pull a stunt like that – any more than she would have thought Sarah could – and besides, the hurt of Jan and her betrayal was still too raw.

She wasn't about to betray someone else. Not for a house, not for anything.

"I'm going for a walk," she said as she finished her drink.

"I'll –"

"You stay here. I won't be long."

"No, I'll –"

"Sarah, I just need a bit of space, okay? I won't be long."

Sarah didn't look thrilled but didn't object either, and Michelle wandered out across the road into the sunshine of the late afternoon.

She stood outside the church looking up and down the street.

Now what? she wondered.

They had seen what there was to see, and there was nowhere to go but back to the remaining two bars. Unless . . .

Turning, she glanced towards the little church behind her, noticed the door was slightly open and went in.

It was a small, dark place, slightly musty, but obviously still in use. The prayer books scattered here and there on the wooden chairs looked new, and there were fresh flowers on the altar.

Not much to see here either, Michelle decided, as she examined the carved Stations of the Cross and the one glimmering stained-glass window set high above the back door of the church, facing in the wrong direction for the afternoon sun.

She left as an old woman with a small child came in and gave her a sharply suspicious look.

They'd eat you for breakfast around here, she thought, moving down the little pathway towards the village street. As she reached the gate she noticed an overgrown graveyard, half-hidden by the ubiquitous yew-trees, off to her right.

Why not? she thought. She was still raging at Sarah and in no rush to get back to her.

It was very, very different from the other cemeteries, the military cemeteries. Different, even, from the cemeteries at home.

She began, with growing fascination, to examine the gravestones.

Old, carved stones, some of them dating back more than two hundred years.

They seemed to live a long time around here. At least, those who weren't killed in wars did.

She followed the little path back through the graveyard, absorbed by the names and the ages.

Edith Leboyer, 1878-1961, 83 ans . . .

Philippe Martin, 1876-1972, 96 ans.

My God, she thought as she passed two little stone buildings that were like shrines and were, she realised as she peered inside, elaborate family tombs containing photographs and other mementoes of those who were buried there. *Philippe Martin, whoever he was, died when I was two years old . . . and* he *was born in 1876. What must that have been like, to live through two world wars? How did he manage* that?

She had been moving towards the crumbling stone wall at the back of the cemetery and now followed it back towards the gate, passing some newer-looking graves off to her right.

They looked different again, with modern little plaques and colour photographs on some of the graves.

Some, not very many, had flowers on them; the memorial plaques with their poignant inscriptions *Pour mon frère . . . pour Mathilde, nos petite ange . . .* were more in evidence.

She blinked back tears, having enough school French to translate.

Enough of this, she thought, stepping off the path to take a shortcut back to the gate.

And then she saw it. Nearly fell over it, half-hidden as it was in the shade of a yew-tree.

Charles Feradot. 1889-1973. 84 ans.

1889.

My God, she thought. *1889. That's when Charles Lacey, Charles Feradot Lacey, was born . . .*

She was sure of it.

He was twenty-seven when he went to the war, early in 1916, so he was born in 1889. That's what Evelyn had said, 1889. He was born in 1889 . . .

Her row with Sarah forgotten, she ran back to tell her what she'd found.

Sarah was not in good form, and was quick to dismiss any possible connection.

"That proves nothing, Michelle. There must be dozens of Charles Feradots –"

"Evelyn said it was a very unusual name. Even in France."

"It's still coincidence. The first two names are the same, that's all."

"And the year he was born." Michelle was animated, and one or two of the men at the bar glanced at them, then at the barman, who shrugged and continued polishing glasses.

"Well, okay. But not the year he died, that's way out."

"But it's here, in Maillerain! It's in the right place, Sarah!" Michelle persisted.

"Michelle, we're wasting our time! This lot will tell us nothing anyway. God knows, I've tried! They never heard of anyone called Hugh or Charles Lacey and – "

"But what about Charles *Feradot*? Charles Feradot Lacey!"

It took a moment for the light to dawn – and then Sarah went back to the bar, more willingly this time. For a moment she wondered if buying them a drink would help, then decided that nothing would soften these guys.

She began, without much hope, to ask about Charles Feradot who was buried across the road.

The shutters came down.

"Told you," she said, making her escape back to Michelle who had sat watching. "They don't know, or else they're not saying."

"Not saying what?"

"Michelle, they hardly admitted to knowing the graveyard, let alone anyone buried there! You saw them yourself, they only glared at me!"

"But that man in the black jacket, the one looking at us now – no, don't turn! He said something!"

"Only that Charles Feradot didn't live here long and his family moved away. No-one knew them well, and no-one knows where they are now. They don't ever visit here."

"Not even the grave?"

"No, seems not."

"But was he Irish?" Michelle asked.

"French. Your man looked at me as if I'd two heads when I asked him that. He was French, Michelle. Forget it."

But she couldn't. She tossed and turned through another restless night.

"Just look at it with me, that's all!" she begged as they were preparing to leave next morning. "It'll only take a minute!"

"Michelle –" Sarah began. "Well, all right. We're going past it anyway."

She thought she saw a movement at the post office window as they parked the car behind a red Peugeot outside the graveyard.

"Nosey beggar," she said. "You think he'd have something better to do at this hour of the morning!"

It was early, not quite nine, and they didn't expect to see anyone in the graveyard.

To their surprise a tall man with longish black hair was just leaving. He nodded, holding the gate for them as they went in.

"Not bad. Not bad at all!" Sarah said, glancing back in his direction.

"We're not here for sightseeing, remember?" Michelle said, laughing softly. "Now come on, it's just over here, behind these trees."

She looked back to make sure Sarah was following, brushed aside a branch . . .

And her heart almost stopped.

Because there, right in the centre of it, almost obscuring Charles Feradot's name, was a large bouquet of creamy fresh lilies and red carnations.

Chapter Twenty-three

"For the last time, Michelle, no! You're obsessed with this! It's not as if we can just drop everything and go to France – and besides, even if we did, what have you got? A grave that's the wrong one, with a bunch of flowers on it, and a black-haired man disappearing off in a red Peugeot – and no-one in the village knowing anything about anything! Just forget it, Michelle. Okay? We need to –"

"Rory –"

"No, Michelle! Just *no*! Okay?"

"It is *not* okay! And *don't* you –"

With an impatient noise he brushed past her and clattered down the stairs.

Miserably she watched from the bedroom window as he ran down the front path of her mother's house and got into his van.

She was on her own.

In every sense of the word.

She wandered listlessly down the stairs in the empty house, wondering what the hell was going wrong between them.

From the time Rory had picked her up at the airport they'd been at each other's throats. Michelle, full of excitement, couldn't stop talking about what she'd found, and fully expected Rory to feel the same.

Rory, however, was distracted, focusing on a rush-job he had to get finished. He bristled as they were held up at yet another set of roadworks on the M50. "I'll just drop you at your mother's and go," he'd told them. "I don't really have time for this, I should be over in Donnybrook by now . . ."

Michelle had wanted to scream, but not in front of Sarah.

There would be plenty of time later to sort things out with Rory.

Or so she'd thought.

Now, three days on and the situation hadn't improved.

If anything it was worse, because now they couldn't even talk to each other without it escalating into a huge argument.

It had started the night she came home from France.

She had spent a delightful day playing with Katie and talking to her parents. Maurice, in particular, was cock-a-hoop, sitting at the kitchen table polishing his grandfather's and great-uncle's war medals.

"Heroes, that's what they were, bloody heroes!"

"Not everyone would agree," Una had said mildly, but there was no stopping Maurice.

"It'd take a small-minded person not to," he asserted. "Imagine, his name carved there, given pride of place –"

"Dad, there were thousands of names. I didn't exactly say –"

"Well, what of it? What if there were millions of them? His name was there, he was a hero, that's all that counts! That's worth a lot more than any of them fellas that pretended they were in the GPO for the Rising when –"

"Maurice!" Una had warned him, and he had given her a reproachful look and gone back to polishing the medals, whistling an off-key version of 'Tipperary' as he worked.

"We should go across, you know," he said. "Go over there and see the graves and the monuments for ourselves."

Una had agreed readily, knowing that it would take an act of God to get Maurice Keogh into a boat or plane to go anywhere 'off the island', as he referred to going abroad.

She and Michelle were sharing a quick smile behind Maurice's back when Rory arrived, clearly not in the best of form.

"I missed the meeting," he announced, glaring at Michelle. "I should have let you get a taxi back from the airport."

"We did suggest that, but you insisted. Remember?" Michelle said quietly.

"I don't know how you make that out!"

"When I phoned to see how Katie was. You said you'd be there, it was no bother."

She continued speaking quietly, unwilling to get into a row in front of her parents. Rory was the best in the world most of the time, but when things went against him work-wise he was inclined to take the hump. Michelle usually left him to cool off, or managed to cajole him, but here, with her parents as an unwilling audience, she felt there wasn't much she could do.

And besides, they hadn't parted on totally the best of terms when she went to France.

Una had summed up the situation in about two seconds flat.

"Time for our walk, Maurice!"

"But we don't –"

"It's a lovely night, it's a shame to be stuck in!"

"What are you talking about, Una? We never –"

"Yes, we do, Maurice. Starting now. Get your coat and we'll –"

"Ah, Una, for God's sake! Can't you see I'm busy." He had finished polishing the medals and was putting them up on the mantelpiece. "Could we not just –"

"*Now,* Maurice!" There was steel behind the smile, and Maurice finally picked up on it, grumbling as he went for his coat.

"Now look what you've done!" Michelle had said, rounding on Rory the minute they were gone.

"What *I've* done? *I've* done nothing but work all day

and collect you and your sister from the airport and look after Katie and put up with *your* mother and father while you –"

That was it. She had gone straight to bed, staying as far over on her own side as was possible without actually falling out. And when, sometime in the night, he had reached for her – their time-honoured way of making up when all else failed – she had rebuffed him in a sharp whisper, reminding him that her parents were just next door.

He had left the following morning without saying a word.

And now, after just one day of an uneasy truce, they were back to square one and he had left again without so much as saying good-bye. Worse; he had never walked out on her in quite that way before. It just wasn't like him.

Thank God Dad's at work, she thought, *and Mam's gone to the shops with Katie.*

She'd have hated any of them to see this.

It just wasn't like him. He'd never kept a row up for so long before.

It was the pressure of living with her parents. It *had* to be.

They had gone out for a drink last night, just the two of them, to get a bit of space. Her mother had been all for it, sensing their tension, offering to put Katie to bed and telling them not to worry, it didn't matter what time they came back.

"Makes me feel like a bloody kid again," Rory had muttered as they pulled the door after them.

He had begun to relax after half an hour or so in The Orchard and was on his second pint when Michelle broached the subject of France again.

And met with his flat refusal to even discuss it.

"But why?" she had asked in what she hoped was a reasonable tone. "*Why* won't you talk about it? And why did you let me go over there if you hadn't any intention of backing me up? Why did you do that, Rory? It's not fair to –"

"Fair?" he had said sharply, so unlike his usual tone that it startled her. "Let me tell you what's not fair, Michelle! It's not fair that you go traipsing off on a holiday with –"

"It was not a holiday! My God, Rory, if you think –"

"On a holiday," he repeated, "on a whim, leaving me trying to manage Katie while I'm stuck in your parents' house – which was *your* idea, let me remind you!"

She took a sip of her drink and looked at him, really looked at him as if she'd never seen him before. As, right now, she felt she hadn't.

"I don't know what's wrong with you, Rory," she said finally. "Really I don't. I thought we were in this together."

"We *are* in this together. I'm doing the best I can, Michelle. I just didn't expect it to be this bloody hard."

"And *I* don't know what you're talking about. We agreed about the house, Rory. Come on, be fair. You know we agreed. So what exactly is so hard? You have to tell me! We're getting nowhere arguing like this."

He sipped his pint and sat watching the creamy head as if he could find answers there.

"It's not just about the house, Michelle. Is it? There's much more going on than just the house."

"What's *that* supposed to mean?"

"I mean we don't want the same things. I mean we were fine where we were, and we should have left it at that. But you couldn't, could you? You couldn't just leave it, and be happy. You had to change everything."

"That's a rotten thing to say, Rory! We were in it together! And what do you mean, anyway, that there's more going on than the house?"

He sipped the pint again. "I mean the way you like to be in charge of things. The way you make all the decisions. We'll do this, we'll do that, why don't we move, we need a bigger house . . ."

"You *agreed* on that, Rory!" She was near tears now. "We talked about it and you agreed! The house was too small and we decided, we *both* decided –"

"Oh, so I had a choice?"

"Of course you had a choice. There was always a choice, Rory. You could have said no."

"And put up with the consequences? No, Michelle. I don't think so."

She considered walking out, but realised there was nowhere to go. Certainly not back to her parents' house until this was sorted out.

"And what's *that* supposed to mean?"

"It means you're never satisfied, Michelle. You always want more, nothing is ever enough for you. Remember the flat we had in Rathmines? I loved that place. I really did. Remember all the time we spent doing it up?"

"Rory, it was freezing cold, and up four flights of stairs!"

"We could have put in heating, and the stairs were never a problem. We could have bought the landlord out that time when he was anxious to sell the flats off. Shay Duggan bought his and took a lease on the other two, and now he owns the whole place. Must be worth a fortune!"

"It took him ten years!" Michelle protested. "He had to deal with squatters and bad tenants and hadn't a cent until the last year or two! You know he told us that! And if you're suggesting –"

"We could have done it, Michelle. If you had backed me up, we could have done it!"

"This is *ridiculous*! You know we couldn't have, Rory! We'd never have managed it. Not with everything that was happening, not with –"

His eyes flashed a warning. *Don't go there. I'm not ready to go there.*

She doubted that he would ever be ready to go there, to talk about the babies they had lost. He was re-writing history. How in God's name could they have managed to buy the house Shay Duggan had now, the house where they all used to live in their various flats and get together a couple of times a week just to celebrate using any excuse at all . . .

And then the *real* celebration.

It was crystal-clear in her mind, the night she discovered she was pregnant for the first time.

They had all got together, the whole gang of them, celebrating Rory and Michelle's great news, breaking out the Chilean wine Shay had been hoarding, and Michelle, laughing, had refused to touch a drop, determined to do everything right.

She and Rory had sat up all night making plans, doing sums, deciding – *together* – that with a baby on the way they should try for one of the little houses at Harold's Cross and forget the semi-student existence of living week to week in a crumbling redbrick in Rathmines.

She had done everything right, all the way through that first pregnancy and the ones that followed . . .

And it still hadn't been enough.

Quietly she gathered her bag and her jacket. She had finished her drink and there was no point sitting any longer with Rory who was gazing into his pint as if she didn't exist.

"I'm going home," she announced. "Are you coming or staying?"

He looked at her sulkily.

"Remind me," he said. "Home. Where's that?"

She wanted to scream at him, to shake him.

"I've had enough of this, Rory. I don't know *what* happened while I was in France, but –"

"What happened? You want to know what happened? Your precious bloody father, that's what '*happened*'! Only being 'helpful' taking phone calls that were none of his business, and then forgetting to tell me so I missed a deadline I'd been waiting three months for! *That's* what happened, Michelle!"

Her heart sank. "The Gilmurray contract?" she asked tentatively.

He nodded miserably.

"Oh, Rory!" Then, after a moment, "I'm sure he didn't mean to. He was only trying –"

"Trying to help!" Rory added bitterly. "As if I didn't know, Michelle! As if he wasn't blue in the face listening to him with that wheedling voice of his –"

"Stop it! Rory, he *was* only trying to help! You don't think he'd do something like that deliberately!"

"No," Rory said after a pause. "No, I don't. Because if I did, my God, if I thought that, I'd have planted him."

That was it. She grabbed her bag and stood up.

"Michelle, wait. Please. Look, I'm sorry. I *do* know he was trying to help." He clenched his teeth without realising. "It was my own fault for leaving the number with the Gilmurray people. I left it as a fall-back in case they couldn't get me on the mobile, but it seems they never tried the mobile. So really, I can't blame him. It just wrecks everything, that's all."

"How does it?" she asked, slowly sitting down again.

"Because the Clifford contract's in danger too. That

new guy on the Stillorgan Road is hell-bent on undercutting everyone while he builds up a trade. Things are going to be tighter than you'd believe. Everyone's taking a hit now, the way things are. Everything's slowing down all of a sudden."

"Except house prices," she ventured.

"Except house prices," he said, sighing. "You know something? We probably couldn't even buy our old place back now. The house across the road, you remember, the Geraghtys? It sold while you were away for twenty thousand more than we got. Add stamp duty and we wouldn't have a hope."

She reached out a hand to him, trying to think of something, anything, that might help.

'*Sorry*' seemed a good place to start.

"I'm sorry, Rory . . ."

He smiled at her, his arm going around her. "And so am I." He kissed her gently on the lips. "I know I'm acting the complete bastard," he said, moving back, reaching for her hand. "It's just that I don't know where we go from here. And don't say France! It was a wild-goose chase. No, shhh, hear me out. I shouldn't have encouraged you. It was crazy, love. A crazy waste of time, when we could have been looking for somewhere else. And now I don't see how we'll even be able to *afford* anywhere else."

"Which makes Evelyn's house our only option," she suggested.

He looked at her and sighed. "Maybe. I don't know.

Let's just leave it, Chelle. I'm exhausted. We'll talk about it tomorrow, okay, love?"

She was happy to agree, relieved to be back on good ground with him and reassured that when they spoke the following day she'd be able to convince him.

And it might have worked. Very probably it would have.

Except that when they got back to her parents' house, Maurice was sitting with Rory's mobile phone in his hand.

"I pressed the wrong button," he said miserably as they came in. "There was a fella looking for you urgently and I was trying to find a pen to take down his name and I pressed the wrong button. I forget his name now – Cliff something I think it was. Rory, what's the matter? I was only trying to help. Rory –"

He was still sitting there muttering "I meant no harm" in an aggrieved tone as Rory, grabbing his mobile, stalked out to the van and Michelle made her way miserably to bed.

Chapter Twenty-four

It was her third time calling to Evelyn's house with no reply.

Puzzled, she went back out towards the front gate and stood for a moment looking up at the windows trying to gauge if there was anyone there.

Might they not have heard the bell?

Or might they have gone away for a few days?

It didn't seem very likely.

Still puzzling over it, she turned back to go through the gate and nearly bumped into Annie who was just coming in, carrying a shopping-bag.

The normally distant housekeeper looked pleased to see her for once.

"So you've heard?" she asked. "I wasn't sure whether I should let you know."

"Know what?" Michelle asked, her heart giving a sudden lurch. "Is Evelyn –"

"Miss Lacey is in hospital, she was admitted on Saturday night. Would you like to come in for a minute? I'm sure she wouldn't mind."

Michelle followed her round the side of the house and in through the back door to the scullery and then the kitchen.

"I don't like to use the front door," Annie said, catching Michelle's expression. "Not since –"

"Since what?" Michelle prompted, sitting on one of the pine chairs in response to Annie's nod.

"Since the accident," Annie responded. She turned quickly to put away a few things from her shopping bag, and when she turned back Michelle noticed, for the first time, the strained look on her face, the slight, tell-tale redness around her eyes.

"What happened?" she asked gently as Annie, having folded away the bag, sat down herself in the old rocking-chair by the range.

"The stairs," she said finally. "I was forever warning her, and so was Dr Moore. She wouldn't listen. Well, she'll have to now, won't she? She'll have to now."

To Michelle's dismay the older woman started weeping silently, her face contorted in an effort to hold back the tears.

Michelle sat saying nothing, dismissing all the empty phrases that sprang to mind, like *I'm sure she'll be all right*. She couldn't be sure of any such thing. Why did people say things like that, anyway, when they couldn't be sure?

"Can you tell me what happened?" she prompted gently when Annie seemed to have the tears under control. "She fell down the stairs? Is she badly hurt?"

"Bad enough," Annie said. "She broke her hip, it'll be in plaster for months. But that's the least of it! She gave her arm a bang, they think she caught it on the corner of one of the brass fittings, there's a bit sticking out. I never saw so much blood, a right wallop she gave it. And her head . . ."

"Her head was bleeding?" Michelle asked, thoroughly alarmed.

"No, not her head. It was her arm that was bleeding. But she banged her head as well, and now she's making no sense at all."

"What do you mean?"

"Confused. They say she's confused, that's why she doesn't know me. They say she might have to go into a home. For a while or for good, I don't know, and they won't tell me a thing. I'm not the next-of-kin, they say. But amn't I all she has?"

"What hospital is she in?" Michelle asked.

"St Vincent's. She'll be there a while yet."

"Could I go to see her, do you think?"

"She won't know you. She knows no-one, she doesn't even know who she is herself half of the time. She doesn't even recognise me." The silent tears started again and the housekeeper began hunting in her sleeve for a tissue. "She doesn't know me, and they can't even tell me when she might know me," she said, sniffling now to try and hold back the tears. "And if she has to go in somewhere the house will have to be sold and then what'll become of me?"

"But –"

The housekeeper seemed not to have heard. "Can you tell me what will become of me then? Can you tell me that? She used to talk to you, didn't she? Can you tell me that?"

Numbly Michelle shook her head and stood up. The housekeeper started to her feet, reaching for Michelle's arm.

"Well, can you find out? Can you do that for me?"

"Did you ever talk to her?" Michelle asked. "I mean, about what would happen if she ever *did* have to go into a home?" She'd have preferred not to become involved, but it seemed that Annie saw her as some sort of confidante and was relying on her for information.

"She said I'd be provided for," Annie answered. "When she had that man Quinn showing it off to everyone she told me I'd be provided for if the house had to be sold. And then you came yourself," Annie added, her face taking on a pinched look, "and I thought to myself, *well, that's it,* but then Miss Lacey said not to be worrying about anything, she wasn't going to let the house go for a long time yet. And now, look what's after happening! After all she promised me!"

Not to mention what she promised me, Michelle thought, taking her leave of the still-weeping Annie, promising to get in touch again once she'd been to see Evelyn.

"You'll get no sense out of her, mind," were Annie's parting words. "None at all. She doesn't even know me!"

And at this she buried her eyes in her tissue as Michelle let herself out through the scullery door.

She rang Sarah on her mobile as she got back into the car, arranging to meet in Coman's on Sarah's way home from work.

"It's a total mess," she said, filling Sarah in quickly as they sat down with their drinks. "God only knows what I'll tell Rory."

It doesn't matter what I tell him, she realised. He'd made it quite clear that they'd reached the end of the road anyway where Evelyn's house was concerned.

"Any point in going to see her?" Sarah asked. "You never know, she *might* recognise you."

"Not from what Annie said. But I want to see her anyway, to see for myself how she is. And she might be glad of a visit if she hasn't many others coming."

"Only if she knows you," Sarah pointed out.

"Only if she knows me," Michelle agreed. "I'm going to go tonight. Will you come with me?"

"Tonight's the tennis tournament, I can't."

"What about afterwards?"

"Too late. I'll go with you tomorrow after work."

But Michelle couldn't wait that long, suddenly anxious to see for herself how Evelyn was.

Briefly she toyed with the idea of asking Rory, then

dismissed it just as quickly. Rory had been adamant about the house and he was still in foul form about what he regarded as Maurice's interference. No, there was no point in asking Rory.

Una. She'd ask Una to go with her. It wasn't the kind of thing she fancied doing on her own.

"Is everything all right, Michelle?" Sarah's voice broke into her thoughts. "I know you said it was when I dropped in last night, but Rory hardly said a word and then he just vanished. That's not like him. And he was like a bear the other day when he met us at the airport."

"He's fine," Michelle said. "Just under a bit of pressure at work."

She felt herself colouring as she said it. Normally she didn't lie to Sarah, not even white lies usually in spite of what Sarah had said in France, but she still hadn't quite forgiven her for suggesting that she should cheat Evelyn. She still wasn't quite ready to trust her fully again. And besides, this was something she and Rory would have to work out between them.

"I'll ring Mam," she changed the subject, finishing her drink quickly and reaching for her mobile. "Maybe she'll come with me tonight. I don't want to go on my own if I can help it."

"Who'll mind Katie?"

"She has a father," Michelle said so sharply that Sarah raised an eyebrow. She had sense enough, though, to say nothing.

Una, when Michelle rang, was only too happy to

join her. "Don't worry about Katie, your dad'll manage her fine until we get back, or until Rory gets home. I've made a bit of stew and Rory can help himself when he gets in."

"You're the best!" Michelle said, wishing that Rory realised it too instead of taking them so much for granted. "I'll meet you at the front door of the hospital, okay? I'd never make it across to pick you up at this hour."

"I'll be there at about five, depending on traffic," Una promised.

It was crazy trying to get out to St. Vincent's at that time, but Michelle managed to make it by ten past five.

Una was already there.

"I checked at the desk, love. She's in St Peter's ward, on the fourth floor."

"Thanks for coming, Mam," Michelle said as they crossed the hall and got into the lift. "God, I hate these places. I didn't want to come on my own unless I really had to."

"I haven't much time for them myself!" Una replied. "Now, St Peter's . . . there we are."

They reached the ward and stood back to make way for a tea trolley that was being pushed out onto the corridor.

"Hope we haven't timed it badly," Una said. "I never thought of asking about visiting hours." "Just as long as they don't throw us out!"

She looked around for a nurse as she spoke.

"Excuse me, we're looking for Evelyn Lacey," she said to a nurse who was passing.

"Evelyn?" the nurse answered. "Yes, she's at the far end of the ward. I'm not sure if she's finished her tea yet. Are you relatives?"

"Friends."

"Have you been in to see her before?"

"No, we only heard today that she was here. Does it matter?"

"No, no. Just, she mightn't recognise you. She's a little bit confused."

"What does that mean?" Una asked as they followed the nurse up the corridor. "Does she know where she is?"

"Not really," the nurse said, leading them into the room. "She's rambling a bit, it's hard to make sense of it," she said quietly to them.

Michelle was shaken by Evelyn's appearance. She seemed shrunken in the bed, and her hair was falling in wisps across her forehead. A tray lay on the bed-table in front of her, the food on it barely touched.

She had a lost look about her.

"Now, Evelyn," the nurse said in a louder tone, touching her on the arm, "I have some visitors for you. I have some people here to see you, Evelyn. Can you hear me?" She turned to them. "See how you get on. But don't stay too long – she should really be resting."

She left the room and Michelle moved across to take her place.

"Evelyn?" She wasn't sure how to continue and looked to Una for support.

"We came to say hello, Evelyn," said Una. "To see how you're getting on. I'm Michelle's mother."

Evelyn turned distant eyes on them.

"Mother?" she said, her voice wavering. She tried to focus, settled on a place to the left of them. "Mother? Is that you? Mother? Mother, is that you?"

Chapter Twenty-five

Mother was cross.

She didn't like it when Mother was cross.

Evelyn concentrated on eating her jelly.

She'd pretend it wasn't happening.

She'd pretend it was just a game like the one she played with Winifed and Robin and Jula.

Winifred, she reminded herself silently. And Jul-ya.

Because Father got cross too. Father got very cross when Evelyn didn't speak properly.

Father was cross a lot of the time.

He was cross now. He and Mother were shouting. And Uncle Hugh was there too.

But Uncle Hugh wasn't shouting.

Uncle Hugh never shouted.

She liked Uncle Hugh. He was nice. Whenever he came he'd lift her high up above his head and spin her round like a sycamore leaf.

Evelyn knew all about sycamore leaves. Uncle Hugh had told her. He told her the names of all the trees in the garden.

Sycamore, oak, alder, elderberry, mountain ash . . .

She said the names out loud to hide the noise of the shouting.

Mountain ash. She rolled it round on her tongue, liking the sound of it. Mountain ash. It had another name too, but she couldn't remember.

She'd ask Uncle Hugh. She'd ask him when the shouting stopped.

"Are you finished, Tuppence?"

Tuppence was Jula's special name for her.

Their secret.

Nobody knew. Especially not Robin. Because Robin would laugh.

He wasn't unkind, but he'd laugh at her.

Boys were like that.

"Time for our walk," Julia said. "The baby is ready. We just have to get your coat on."

Julia was crossing to the nursery cupboard as she spoke, taking out the red coat with the fur collar. Evelyn's favourite.

"We need to wrap you up well," she was saying. "November's a chilly month. You can't trust it."

November. Remember, remember. Guy Fawkes.

Guy Fawkes was November.

Evelyn was afraid of Guy Fawkes and Robin scoffed at her. Robin wasn't afraid. He called her silly.

But Robin was a boy.

And boys weren't afraid of anything.

Robin had told her so.

"Good, that's you all wrapped up!" Julia announced, fastening the last button on Evelyn's coat. "Now, let's get you downstairs."

Evelyn walked carefully down the stairs, holding on tight to Jula's hand.

She could see Agatha's big black baby carriage waiting in the hall, with the baby all wrapped up inside.

And she could hear the voices, louder now, coming from the drawing-room.

She hoped she and Jula were going for a long walk.

A very long, long walk.

* * *

"It's intolerable, Charles! Absolutely intolerable! You're being completely unreasonable. You cannot do this!" Isabel said, her voice shaking.

She was sitting on the edge of the drawing-room sofa, an untouched pot of tea in front of her.

Charles, sitting opposite with his long legs stretched out towards the fire and his hands joined lazily on his stomach, regarded her with a half-smile.

"You surely don't expect me not to go, Isabel. Not now that everything's arranged. And as for its being intolerable, imagine how I would find it here with you and the children, knowing that there were other men taking my place."

"It is *not* your place!" She struggled to keep her

voice under control. "It's not your place, Charles! You do *not* have to do this!"

She turned to appeal to Hugh who was sitting in the window seat, fiddling with his pipe, an expression of utter misery on his face.

"Tell him, Hugh. Please! Make him see sense!"

There was a pause before her brother-in-law met her eyes.

"Isabel . . . I'm going as well."

She thought she would faint. The dress with its close-fitting bodice and its high frilled neck seemed suddenly far too tight. There was no air in the room.

"Why?" she managed finally.

The word hung heavy in the air between them.

"To do my duty, like Charles. And . . . to keep an eye on him."

Charles guffawed, the noise seeming to echo round the room.

"Marvellous. That's marvellous. I have nothing to fear, in that case. And tell me, little brother, who will be keeping an eye on you?" He laughed again. "Tell me that!"

"Don't scoff!" Hugh said sharply. "Isabel is absolutely right, Charles. You're under no obligation to go. You have a family to consider. And Father needs you now more than ever to help in the business."

"In that case why don't you stay, Hugh, and help Father? Lord knows he can do without my help, he tells me so often enough."

"But Isabel can't. She can't do without you."

"What? With Lily and Julia to help? Isabel will manage splendidly. I've never doubted Isabel's capacity to manage. In point of fact, it's Isabel we should be sending, and a dozen more like her. She'd show them all a thing or two over there!"

And again he guffawed. A harsh sound. Isabel tried to remember the time, not so long ago, when she had found his loud, explosive laughter exciting, a rich expression, so it had seemed, of his very maleness.

Now she could remember nothing beyond three days ago, when he had told her he intended to take up a captaincy in the Fusiliers and go and fight in this war that, so little time ago, had seemed to have nothing at all to do with them.

She tried one more time.

"Charles, please!"

He stood up and crossed to her, taking her chin delicately between his thumb and forefinger as he did from time to time with his daughters.

"I'll be home before you know it, Isabel. I promise you that. You'll barely have time to worry at all!"

He kissed her lightly on the forehead and left the room, humming as he went.

They both sat looking after him for a moment, heard his footsteps running lightly up the stairs, knew that the discussion, as far as he was concerned, was over.

"Are you really going?" Isabel asked, turning to look directly at Hugh.

He refused to meet her gaze, fiddling with the pipe again instead.

"Yes."

"But, Hugh, why? Why would you do that? You detest any sort of violence. You've never even *held* one of your father's hunting rifles! I don't see how –"

"I think it's for the best," he interrupted gently. "It's what I should do."

"How can it possibly be for the best? I thought you, of all people, could make him see sense, and you're not being any more reasonable than he is. Surely . . ."

Her voice trailed away, impotent. She took a short impatient breath to gather back the tears. There was no point in crying. It would change nothing.

"I don't understand," she said quietly. "I don't understand why either of you would do this."

Hugh sighed. "Charles is doing it because – well, because he's Charles. You know Charles. He'll come home with a pocketful of medals and stories of heroic deeds, all of them true. Whereas I . . ."

"Whereas you don't want to go at all," she said, when he didn't continue.

"No. No, I don't," he agreed.

"You don't have to."

"But I do. Who else will keep him out of trouble?"

"You would do that for him? Even though you don't want to, even though you know the dangers?"

"He doesn't see the dangers," Hugh said. "But I will. And I'll be there to look out for him."

"You'd really take that risk?"

"He's my brother," Hugh said quietly. "I'll take that risk for him. And for the children, because they need a father."

And for you, he added silently.

But he didn't say it.

He didn't dare say it.

* * *

They weren't being cross any more.

But that was because Father had gone away.

Father and Uncle Hugh. Both of them. And Mother was very sad.

And Evelyn was trying not to be sad, because Father would be home soon.

"I'll be back before you know it, Evie," he had said, swinging her high up above his head, the way Uncle Hugh did.

Then he had given Robin a little punch on the shoulder, playing with him, the way Robin hated. But Father didn't know that. Only Evelyn knew that.

He had hugged Winifred and Poppy, kissed baby Agatha and Mother, and then turned again to where Evelyn was sitting at the bottom of the stairs and winked at her.

She loved it when he did that, just as she loved it when he kissed her cheek, his big moustache tickling her and making her laugh.

"Just you wait right there, you hear, Evelyn? Wait right there and I'll be home before you know it."

Evelyn had nodded, watching from the bottom step as the door closed behind them.

She was going to do exactly what Father had told her.

She would wait and wait, right there where he said.

Wait and wait and wait.

Until he came back home.

Chapter Twenty-six

They were going nowhere fast.

Actually, they were going nowhere, full stop.

It was six weeks since they had moved into her parents' house, three since she and Sarah had returned from France, and nothing at all had changed. She was beginning to doubt that they would ever move out of her mother's or that they would ever have their own place again.

And if she was finding it hard, Rory was fit to strangle someone. Probably her, the way things were going.

He had started on at her again this morning.

When she came down with Katie he was already having breakfast, the Sunday paper open in front of him at the list of show houses on view that day.

"We really should have a look," he'd said, and she'd

noticed that several advertisements were ringed in blue biro.

"But why?" she had asked, her heart in her mouth as she set about getting Katie's breakfast, concentrating on the routine tasks – get the Frosties, pour the milk, move Katie's chair well in, get the spoon – to numb herself to what Rory was really saying. "What's the point?"

"What's the point?" he had asked, his voice dangerously quiet. "The point, Michelle, is that *one* of us had better stop living in cloud-cuckoo-land and sort out a place to live. And since it seems it's not going to be you –"

"Rory, that's not fair –" she began, and stopped herself. Too many of their conversations these days seemed to start with *That's not fair*.

"I'm only asking you to come and look, Michelle. That's all. And it's not as if we have any other options, is it?"

She bit back a reply and sat down beside him, grateful that her parents were out at Mass. There was no privacy at all here, no chance to talk, to argue, even to . . .

Even to make love. And that was part of the tension between them, she realised. It had to be. The only other times they had gone six whole weeks and more without making love was after the babies were born.

Don't go there, she reminded herself. *Just don't.*

Instead she said, "It's early days. That's what the doctor said last night, that Evelyn might begin to remember things any day now, it's just a matter of –"

"Michelle!"

Her stomach clenched at the sharpness of his voice. She looked quickly towards Katie, in time to see the little girl's stricken face.

"Now look what you've done!" she said, the sharpness in her own voice making it all too much for Katie who began crying. It wasn't like her at all, but she was easily upset these days.

The tension is getting to all of us, Michelle thought as Rory stood abruptly, leaving the paper and the remains of his breakfast scattered on the table.

Halfway to the kitchen door he relented, turning back to lift Katie from her chair and give her a cuddle.

"Come on, kitten," he said gently. "Sorry. Daddy was cross. Silly me. I'm sorry."

Katie curled into his shoulder, her thumb in her mouth, a habit she had almost outgrown except when she was very distressed.

Like now, Michelle thought. *God. Wonderful.*

"Look, I'm sorry," Rory said quietly to Michelle as he sat down again, Katie on his lap. "I'm worried, that's all. What if it doesn't work out with Evelyn's place? I mean, look!" He gestured to an article at the top of the property page. "Prices are still going up, even with all that's happening. Jobs are being lost all over the place, but house prices are still flying up. And they say it looks set to continue."

"Couldn't we just wait a bit longer? Please? If Evelyn is okay in a week or two . . ."

Her voice trailed off. In spite of trying to convince herself, she could see for herself that Evelyn hadn't looked anything like okay last night. It was, as the doctor had said, a matter of time. But there were no guarantees.

"And even if she is okay, love?" Rory asked, his voice gentle now as Katie, cuddled against his chest, began visibly to relax. "What then? We're still no nearer to finding the grave and doing what she wanted."

We, Michelle thought, with a fleeting sense of hope. He said '*we*'.

"But we'd still be in with a chance. We could go back and look. We could try to find out more about the grave we *did* find, Charles Feradot's grave."

"And then what? Where does that get us? You said no-one in the village even knew him and the family had moved. Chelle, all you've got is the grave of some old man who happens to have the same name. *Part* of the same name. That's all! It's like someone coming to Ireland from the States and finding the grave of an eighty-year-old called – let's say Sean Duffy, in Dublin and arguing it *has* to be the grave of their great-grandfather Sean Duffy O'Brien who lived in Cork and was born the same year and was supposed to have died when he was in his twenties. Don't you see? It's ridiculous to think there's a connection."

"But there's much more to it than that!" she protested.

"God, you're stubborn!" he said, but at least he was smiling.

"Rory, just listen a minute, okay? Feradot is an unusual name, not a common one like Duffy or O'Brien. And it's the right village. That's where all those letters came from. They didn't just come out of nowhere."

"So what are you saying?" For the first time since she had told him about the grave she had his full attention.

"That there *has* to be a connection!"

He grimaced. "There doesn't, you know. You find bits of what you're looking for and read too much into it. It happens all the time, everyone does it. Coincidence, that's all it is. What else can it be?"

She looked straight at him, her eyes holding his.

"It could be Charles Lacey's grave."

Rory made a scornful sound, his patience snapping. "Come *on*, Michelle! How d'you figure that? Charles Lacey died in, what, 1918? And in the Somme. How could –"

"He *fought* in the Somme," Michelle corrected. "We know he was wounded that day, that he was dying and that Hugh left him there and went to try and get help, and when he came back he couldn't find him."

"Which just means he went back to the wrong place," Rory pointed out. "Look, from what you've said, and from what I've heard, the whole thing was crazy, a battle in a sea of mud with noise and smoke and bombs going off all over the place and thousands of men being slaughtered like animals. Who could find anyone? Hugh just went back to the wrong place."

"Maybe."

He shrugged. "Has to be. Hugh went to the wrong place, Charles was dead already anyway, probably, and his body was taken away with all the others and buried."

"So why is there no grave for him in the Somme?"

"Why should there be?" he asked a bit impatiently. "You said yourself you saw lists of thousands and thousands of men who went missing and no-one knows where they're buried, or whether they're in some field somewhere or maybe just blown to pieces –"

"Shhh!" she said, with a quick look towards Katie. But Katie had picked up a picture book from the table and was looking through it, seeming to pay no attention to them now that they sounded back to normal.

"It's true, isn't it, Michelle?" he asked quietly. "He could have been made bits of, which is why there's no grave."

"So why is his name not on any of the lists?"

He shrugged again. "Who knows? He wasn't on the lists you found, that's all –"

"Or on any of the websites Sarah checked out."

"That still doesn't mean anything, Chelle. You said yourself people were added in later, which means they were overlooked first time round."

"So why wasn't he added in, then? Why didn't Hugh get his name added, if they'd forgotten to include him?"

"We're not going to know that, are we? Maybe that's why he kept going to France, checking out lists in different graveyards –"

"Until his friend in Maillerain found the right one for him?" she suggested.

"We don't know that he did –"

"Well, *somebody* did!" Michelle said. "Evelyn said the last letter from Maillerain came just before he died, telling him the grave had been found."

"But not saying where it was?" Rory frowned slightly, thinking.

Michelle shrugged. "Apparently not. He didn't say – and Evelyn said the letters weren't among his effects after he died."

"But – when did you say the last one came?"

"In 1973," she said without hesitation.

"You're sure?"

"Certain. He died in November '73 and he got the letter a month before that. That's why he was so upset," she reminded him. "He really wanted to go, but he just wasn't well enough."

"And when did Charles Feradot die?"

"1973." She waited, willing him to reach the same conclusion that she already had, a week or so ago. Rory looked startled. "What month?"

"I don't know, it didn't say on the gravestone.."

"Because if – just suppose for a second you're right – *if* it was Charles Lacey's grave, if somehow he didn't die until then – no, it still doesn't make sense. If it *was* him, why didn't he come back home as soon as the war was over? Or even contact them –"

He broke off as he saw her expression.

"You think he did!"

She nodded, waited.

"And *that's* who was writing to Hugh from Maillerain? Charles was still *alive?*"

Michelle looked steadily at Rory and took a deep breath. "Charles Feradot died in 1973," she reminded him.

"But wouldn't his family have recognised his handwriting?"

"Not if he got a friend to address the letters!"

He held her gaze for a moment. "You're right, Michelle. You have to go back."

They were still thinking about the implications when her parents' car pulled up outside.

Rory put Katie back on her own chair and gathered up the newspaper.

"But promise me one thing," he continued quickly, reaching out to touch her arm. "Suppose you *did* find something, Michelle. If somehow that *was* his grave. You'd be opening God-knows-what sort of a can of worms and there's no guarantee what would come of it, even if Evelyn gets better. So we need to have a fall-back, to look at other houses, just in case. Because I can't stay here much longer," he added quietly as they heard her father's voice in the hall. "Promise you'll look at other places?"

"I promise," she answered.

She was happy to promise him anything, as long as she was still in with a chance of getting the Lacey house.

Chapter Twenty-seven

"What about having a look after lunch?" Rory asked as they set the dining-room table. "I could do with an excuse to get out."

"Shhh!" she said, laughing at him. "They'll hear you."

But for once she didn't really care. She and Rory were on good terms for the first time in weeks, and that was all that mattered. *That, and getting a house,* she reminded herself.

He had paused in the act of putting out the placemats and was waiting for her answer.

"I'll look, that's all," she said. "I won't promise anything else."

"I'm not asking for anything else. Except – well, if we find somewhere half-decent –"

Her heart sank. "I thought we were just looking. You said ten minutes ago that I should go back to France –"

"And you should. But there's no harm in putting a

deposit on a place in the meantime, is there? We wouldn't have to follow through – we could just put on a booking deposit."

"You mean on *any* house, just for the sake of it? Rory, if we go that far, we're committed!"

"Not with a booking deposit," he said quickly. "We'd lose little or nothing if we decided to pull out. And the way things are going, even if we did end up buying, we'd probably sell it at a profit after a few weeks!" He looked anxious as he waited for her reply. "Michelle –"

They heard a car pulling up outside, followed by doors slamming and Helen's strident tones organising the children.

"*No,* Dylan! Don't go *near* that tricycle – you don't know who's been on it!"

Michelle made a face at Rory. "Cheek of her! Who does she think's been on it except Katie? It's inside the gate – it's not as if it's in the street!"

"You really want to stay and make small talk with her?" Rory asked wryly.

"You win," Michelle said, laughing as they finished setting the table. "Anything to get away from her. Pity Sarah's away, she's the only one able to handle her! But Rory, about looking at houses –"

He leaned across and gave her a quick kiss on the lips. "Talk later, okay?"

"Okay," Michelle said, kissing him again before going out to face the hordes.

Brilliant, she thought as she reached the door of the

living-room and peeped inside. *Helen and kids* and *Graham. Aren't we honoured*?

She never had much to do with her brother-in-law if she could help it, finding him even worse than Helen. Helen was bad enough, but Graham was intolerable. She was only jealous, of course, because Graham knew everything and Rory knew so little about anything. At least, that was how Helen saw it, and lost no opportunity to let them know it.

"Oh, you're here!" she said now, catching sight of Michelle. "I thought you'd be out house-hunting! From what I heard, you're going to need to!"

"What do you mean?" Michelle asked, her voice icily calm.

"Well, Mummy was saying that that senile old woman is practically at death's door – so you've no choice, have you? I mean, you can hardly go on living *here*! I know you're saving a fortune, but it's not very fair, is it? Mummy and Daddy are the best in the world, but *really*!"

Michelle took a sharp breath and realised that she was digging her nails into the palms of her hands in an effort to control herself.

"It's none of your business, Helen!" she said, just as Maurice came up behind her.

"Now, what's this, what's this?" He gave a false, hearty laugh. "Come on now, girls, no fighting! Let's all enjoy ourselves!"

"Oh, we are, Daddy! Nothing to worry about, we're just talking!" Helen said with a bright smile.

Two-faced cow! Michelle thought. Helen had the 'sweetness and light' act down to a fine art.

"That's what I like to see!" Maurice said. "Everyone getting along. Now, let's get the kids into the kitchen and we can –"

"The kitchen?" Helen asked as if she'd never heard of it before.

"Well, yes," Maurice began, looking confused.

"You want them to eat in the *kitchen*?"

Maurice rubbed the back of his neck, a habit he had when he was nervous.

"But don't they usually –" he began, looking around for support. "Ah, there you are, love," he said, relief written all over him as Una came to the living-room door. "Una, don't the kids usually eat in the kitchen?" He glanced back at Helen then back towards his wife. "I was just saying –"

"That they should eat in the kitchen," Helen interrupted. "And, tell me, Daddy," she continued sweetly, "will Katie be eating in the kitchen?"

"Well, no. No, she won't," Maurice said. "You know she doesn't, you know she'll be in the dining-room with us. That's what she always does."

"Yes, and my children always eat in the kitchen. Well, that's about to stop right now. Graham and I have discussed it and we feel that if our children are not considered good enough for your dining-room, then maybe we shouldn't bring them. I don't see why they should be treated as second-class citizens."

"But –" Maurice looked at Una again, appealing

for help. Rory and Michelle exchanged a quick glance.

"But –" Maurice began again, as Una stood silently at the living-room door, her face a vision of disbelief. "Merciful God, Helen, what brought this on!" Maurice continued, suddenly exasperated. "God Almighty, it was yourself that said they should eat in the kitchen in the first place – they always do it, they did it every other week and don't they do it at home?"

"We don't see why they should be treated differently when they're guests here like everyone else, that's all." She looked pointedly at Katie who had come into the hall and was standing, half-hidden, beside Una. Her thumb, Michelle noticed, was in her mouth again and she had slipped her hand into Una's for reassurance. She may not have understood what was being said but she was clearly upset by the tone.

"We don't treat them differently, Helen," Una said brightly. "You've always said you don't like children eating in the dining-room with the adults so we were going along with that."

"Up to a point," Helen said, with another look at Katie. "But if there are going to be other children here anyway then I don't see why mine should be excluded. Do you, darling?"

She glanced towards her husband who was, as usual, looking bored.

"Hardly seems fair," he said. "It's not as if they're going to wreck the place. Are you, kids?" he added with a smirk in their direction. "What do you think, should we wreck the place?"

Graham thought he was very funny. So, obviously, did his children – except for Joanne, who glanced disdainfully at him. The two boys began rolling about on the sofa in exaggerated amusement.

Spare me, Michelle thought with another glance in Rory's direction.

She'd lost her appetite, but she knew she'd upset her parents if she invented a 'forgotten' lunch arrangement. Better to just get through it and escape as quickly as possible.

She took her cue from Una. Ignoring the smirking Graham and speaking in a falsely bright voice, she said "Okay, we'll bring in the other table! Give me a hand, Rory!"

With much rearrangement of furniture, they finally got everyone seated around an extended table and Maurice carried in the joint of beef.

"Now, look at that!" he said heartily as he set it down. "The picture of perfection. You girls could learn a thing or two from your mother!"

"Michelle already did!" Rory said lightly. "Look at me, I'm not exactly fading away!"

"Meaning?" Helen challenged him.

"Meaning nothing," Rory said quickly, glancing at Michelle. "I'm just joking, Helen."

"Graham has lost weight because his doctor advised him to, not because I don't cook for him. Actually, I changed all my recipes to suit him and the doctor is very impressed."

"I didn't mean – "

"Helen, we didn't even notice that Graham had lost weight!" Michelle began. *Whoops,* she thought as she stopped talking and concentrated on the food Una was passing round. *That won't go down well.*

It didn't.

"Well, of course you didn't notice!" Helen said. "You two don't notice anything these days, you're so totally wrapped up in yourselves!"

"Helen!" Una warned.

"Well, it's true, Mummy. You must see it! All they can talk about is houses. They're not interested in anything or anyone else. Joanne was in her first school play and they weren't even there to see her!"

Maurice, with the air of a man bewildered by life, asked "What school play?" He looked from one to the other of them as if he had missed several beats.

"We didn't know about it!" Michelle protested.

"You wouldn't have come anyway, so there wasn't much point in telling you. And you were wonderful, weren't you, darling?" she added, glancing at her daughter.

Unfortunately for Dylan, she saw him from the corner of her eye as he tried to slide some carrots – his least favourite food – onto Oscar's plate.

"Dylan, if you won't behave you'll have to eat in the –" She stopped herself just in time and glanced at Michelle and Rory, silently challenging them to comment.

Michelle knew better. And anyway, he was only four. What did Helen expect?

"So what was the play?" she asked Joanne.

"I don't think you'd know it," Joanne said smugly, with the barest of glances in Michelle's direction.

"Try me," she said, keeping her tone light. *God, the child was a pain!*

She was reminding herself that she *was* only a child when Helen launched another attack.

"Would you mind leaving her alone?" she demanded icily. "It's not fair to keep on at her. I wouldn't do that to Katie."

"I was just making conversation," Michelle protested.

"I could see that, I knew you weren't really interested. And yet you expect everyone else to listen while you go on and on about houses!"

Michelle glanced at Katie's plate. The little girl hadn't eaten a thing and was staring transfixed at her Aunt Helen. Rory had cleared his plate, having decided to concentrate on that and get out of there as soon as possible.

Michelle glanced at her own half-finished lunch and spoke in Una's direction. "We'd better go, we've something to do this afternoon. You don't mind, Mam, do you?"

"Ah, now, Michelle!" Maurice protested. "After your mother going to all that trouble!"

"Actually, I helped, Dad," she said. "And I'd stay only we've got something to do."

"And what could be more important than spending time with your family?" His chin was up, a rare but certain sign that he was spoiling for a fight.

"We've to look at some houses," Rory said.

"There!" Helen said triumphantly. "What did I tell you? They can think of nothing but themselves and their houses!"

"You can't have it both ways, Helen," Rory said calmly. "You obviously feel we've outstayed our welcome here. We're doing the best we can to sort out a house."

"Yes, well, you might have done better to have sorted it out before you sold the one you had. Jan says –"

"*What!*" Michelle no longer cared what her parents thought – she'd had just about enough of Helen for one day. Or maybe one lifetime. "What do you mean, Jan says! When were you talking to her! How *could* you, Helen!"

"I have a perfect right to talk to whoever I want!" Helen said, with a look at Graham for encouragement.

"Yes, but –" Michelle began. But it was useless. What was the point of talking to Helen about loyalty? She didn't know the meaning of the word. Michelle had heard her often enough criticising 'friends' behind their backs when they were barely out the door. Helen's only loyalty was to herself, her children and that stupid husband of hers.

One look at his expression and Michelle's stomach turned. He was sitting back in his chair, arms folded, enjoying the spectacle and silently egging Helen on.

"We have to go," Michelle said, standing up. "Sorry, Mam. Keep us some apple-tart, will you?"

"Wouldn't you think you could sit and have a civil conversation!" Maurice said, pushing away his unfinished meal. "I don't know what's got into you, Michelle!"

Too many years of putting up with Helen, that's what! Michelle thought.

She hated to see him looking upset, though. "We won't be long," she said, touching him lightly on the arm. "Helen will still be here when we get back and we can chat then."

"About houses?" Helen said, her eyebrows raised. "I don't think so!"

"My God, there's a pair of you in it!" said Maurice.

"Maurice . . ." Una said warningly. "You go ahead, love. Leave Katie with us – she won't want to be dragged around looking at houses."

"Actually, I was going to drop her off at Matt's," Rory said, with a quick look at Michelle. "Stephen will be there with his gang and it's a while since they've seen her."

"You don't trust us to mind the child for a few hours, is that it?" Maurice demanded.

"Dad, come on," Michelle said, finally showing her exasperation. "Don't be ridiculous. She hasn't seen her cousins for weeks."

"And I suppose my children aren't her cousins?" Helen began, but was silenced by a sharp look from Una.

"That's a great idea, love," Una said, turning to Michelle. "She'll get fed up being with us all the time."

"I didn't say that!"

"No, but I did!" Una said. "Now, if you're going, go, because there are bound to be long queues."

There were.

Michelle became increasingly depressed as they joined hordes of others looking at houses that seemed small, overpriced and featureless compared with the Lacey house.

"That last one wasn't bad," Rory said cajolingly as they got back into the car. He started the engine, glancing at her when she didn't reply. "I could fit a decent enough shed in the garden and – Chelle, come on! It's worth thinking about, at least. What's wrong with it?"

"Everything!"

He switched off the engine and turned to face her, his expression closed. "You're making this impossible. We're running out of options here. And that house is the best of what we've seen. It's a good size and near the shops and the school. And we can afford it. We won't get better than that."

"And what about Evelyn's house?" she asked tightly. "What about going back to France?"

"You can still do that," he said. "I'm talking about a booking deposit, that's all. You saw the way they were being snapped up – if we don't grab one now, we've no chance. Michelle, come *on*! We can always let it go again, or sell it. This way, we've lost nothing."

She sat staring out the window towards the brand new house.

Lost nothing? Only her lovely little house that she knew in her heart she'd never have sold for this one. Only her dream of somehow, against all the odds, owning somewhere as amazing as the Lacey house.

For the first time she allowed herself to think that perhaps that was all it was and ever had been, a futile dream.

Slowly, reluctantly, she got out of the car and went back across the road, stepping carefully past a heap of building rubble, to have another look at the Glenberry Manor show house.

Chapter Twenty-eight

"We need to get away, Michelle!"

"So why don't you come with me to France?"

"But isn't Sarah's going?"

"Only because I don't want to go on my own. Really, it should be you, Rory – you know she wants to keep her holidays for Greece. It's only for a few days, can't you –"

"You know I can't," he said, exasperated. "I can't get away for that long. But we could go somewhere overnight, just the two of us."

He was taut beside her in the bed, keeping his voice low even though they knew, from the faint sound of snoring, that Una and Maurice were asleep. Well, Maurice, anyway.

She knew he was right. They had arrived back to glum silence from Maurice who was still put out that

Michelle had "put a damper on things" and upset Helen.

It was all Michelle could do to hold back her tears and her anger.

The whole thing seemed so unfair, so bloody unfair. Just because Helen had taken the hump again and left early was no fault of hers – in fact, it had probably been planned in advance to allow precious Graham an excuse to get away from his in-laws. There was no love lost, though Maurice refused to see it and Una pretended not to.

What might have been a reasonably happy occasion had been spoilt for her.

By the time they reached home she had finally begun to see some of the better points of the new house and was looking forward to telling Una about it, but the minute she spoke Maurice butted in with, "I can see now what Helen means – all you talk about is houses, houses, houses!"

Una was quick to defend Michelle and within minutes it had escalated into a rare but full-blown row that finished with Maurice grabbing the Sunday paper and muttering about "no peace at all in this house" as he went out the front door in the direction of the pub.

Una had tried to make light of it, saying he'd get over it soon enough and they all knew what he was like, the best in the world if he'd only learn when to keep his mouth closed.

But Michelle knew it was different this time. The strain really was beginning to show in all of them.

And the new house wasn't much help because it wouldn't be ready for five months. She wasn't sure she could last that long and Rory definitely couldn't.

He'd hardly said a word all evening, even when Una made encouraging noises about the new house and Maurice came back from the pub with a hangdog expression and an apology that started with "losing the run of himself" and went on and on until all three of them felt like screaming at him.

"Where do you want to go?" Michelle asked now, whispering back to Rory.

They had gone to bed early, anxious to make their escape but nowhere near sleep. And anything else was out of the question, Michelle just couldn't relax enough with Una and Maurice right next door to them.

"I don't know," Rory said. "Somewhere. Anywhere. Some fancy hotel. I really don't care as long as we get away from here. Your mother would mind Katie, or we could leave her with Stephen and Liz."

"But we've never gone away without her before. Not both of us."

"Exactly."

"She'd miss us."

"She'd manage for one night."

"Okay," Michelle said finally.

"You mean it?"

She could see his smile in the light from the street-lamp outside the window.

"As long as it's only one night. I'll miss her like mad."

He moved towards her to kiss, her but when he kissed her again, more passionately, she pulled away. "You know we can't."

It was then that he turned his back on her and, hurt though she was, she knew he was right.

They needed to get away.

* * *

The sun was shining as they left Dublin early on the following Saturday.

She wouldn't have cared even if it had been lashing rain, but the sunshine was a bonus, making her feel she was going on holidays rather than just an overnight trip to Kilkenny.

She rolled down the car window, turned up the music, smiled across at him.

"We should do this more often!"

"We will, once everything's settled," he promised.

The journey down passed quickly and they pulled into the gravel drive of Killonan Country House just before noon.

"Looks okay," Rory said, getting their bags from the boot.

It looked much more than okay. A flight of balustraded granite steps led to a massive front door, on either side of which were tall urns overflowing with a rich tangle of fuchsia. The grey stone of the three-storey building was softened by clusters of green that crept upwards and around the mullioned windows, and it was set at an angle to the driveway, giving a view out over fields and down to the river.

And it was even better inside.

Michelle's breath caught for a second as she entered the hall.

It was enormous, with a Kilkenny marble fireplace to one side and a Red Setter making himself at home in front of it. And there was something about it – the curving staircase, perhaps, or the way the light was slanting through the landing window – that reminded her of the Lacey house.

She banished the thought quickly, looking around at the various pieces that were scattered here and there – two tall, ancient-looking oak chairs, a mahogany table with a bowl of deep pink roses on it and, over by the little reception desk, a harp.

"Can't wait to see the rest of it!" she said as a young woman came through the far door to greet them and show them to their room.

They followed her up the ornate staircase to a high-ceilinged room at the front of the house. She opened the door, ushered them into the room, told them to ring if they needed anything and left.

"A bit much?" Michelle laughed, raising an eyebrow when she saw the four-poster bed, complete with canopy.

He smiled at her. "Thought we'd do it in style."

They hung up some clothes quickly, stowed the bags and headed for the city. After lunch in Kilkenny Design and a ramble round the craft shop they crossed the road, went in through the imposing castle gates, paid their entrance fee and hurried to join a tour group on the far side of the courtyard.

Leaving the castle a few hours later, they wandered down into the centre of the city and found a lively pub by the river.

"What do you want to do tonight?" Rory asked as they sat by the window, drinks in hand, looking out at the stream of people passing in the street. "Looks like there's plenty going on. We could check out a few places, maybe have dinner in one of those restaurants we passed."

"I thought you'd already booked in Killonan."

"I could probably cancel if you want to. Looked a bit quiet."

She laughed. "Isn't that what we came for? No, I'm happy with Killonan. The dining-room looked lovely."

They spent another hour or so wandering the streets in the warm evening before going back out to the country house. After a quick shower and a change of clothes they went down to the hall to be greeted by Mrs Loughery, who owned the house.

"You've settled in? Good. Now, we've a fairly large party tonight, celebrating a birthday, so I've put you in the conservatory instead with a few other couples. Is that all right?"

Michelle's heart sank. She'd been looking forward to eating in the elegant room. The thought of having to eat in the conservatory with other people, maybe sharing a table and making polite conversation, left her cold. Fine at any other time – maybe – but not when she and Rory really needed space.

She needn't have worried. Beyond a nod in their direction from each of the other three couples, nobody but Mrs Loughery and the young waitress who served them paid them the slightest bit of attention as they settled into a quiet corner, surrounded by exotic-looking plants and, to Michelle's relief, far enough away from the others to allow them all some privacy.

There was nothing she hated more than the feeling of having her conversation overheard. Except, maybe, having to make stilted conversation with strangers.

The waitress handed them menus and took their wine order.

"Looks interesting," Michelle said, still skimming through the menu as the waitress poured the wine. "What's Lamb Cariverra ?"

The young woman launched into an explanation that left Michelle none the wiser.

"Your mother's roast lamb by another name," Rory suggested with a smile as the waitress moved to another table.

She pulled a face.

"Not criticising your mother's cooking, are you?" he teased.

She laughed. "Would I dare? I just remembered she's got lamb for tomorrow."

"Lamb *and* Helen. Pity we're missing it!"

"At least I won't be blamed if she storms out," Michelle said.

"Of course you will. She'll be upset that you weren't there to see her and it'll be all your fault if she decides to go early!"

"Thanks a lot! How do they put up with her?" she wondered. It was a constant refrain when she thought of Helen.

"Because they love her," Rory said. "She's their daughter."

"But –"

"People see what they want to see, Chelle. You know that. Besides," he added after a moment's thought, "she's not all bad."

He paused and quickly chose from the menu as the waitress arrived to take their order.

"You don't mean that! About Helen?" Michelle was aghast.

"I do, you know. Really, she could be worse. She has her moments, but –"

"Rory, she's a bitch! Look how she treats me! And not only me – she can't keep friends for more than two minutes and she walks all over Mam and Dad –"

"But she has her good points."

"Name one!"

"Her sense of humour. Acid, but funny as long as you're not on the receiving end. And she does her best for those kids of hers."

Michelle thought of the designer clothes, the 'good' school and the self-possessed Joanne's ballet, drama lessons, piano . . .

"If you call that doing her best!"

"A lot of people would."

The food arrived and they focused their attention on it.

"Do you ever see things getting better between you and Helen?" Rory asked. He had finished his Cajun chicken starter and was watching Michelle carefully as she toyed with her pasta.

"Why do you ask?" she said, playing for time.

He shrugged. "Just wondered. It'd be easier all round if you could get on with her."

"Put up with her, you mean!"

"No, I suppose really I mean ignore her. Smile and nod at everything she says and then forget about her until you have to see her again. Could you do that?"

It was Michelle's turn to shrug. "Anything's possible. But why should I let her get away with things?"

"Because she's not worth it. She's not worth having rows with. Better just to ignore her."

"But I don't have rows with her," Michelle insisted. "I just can't stand her bossiness and her superior attitude. Sometimes I *have* to say something or I'd explode!"

"Was she always like that? Bossy, superior, knowing everything?"

"God, yes! She took every chance she got to stir up

trouble. She was always trying to set Sarah and me against each other. I think she resented it that we were so close."

"And did you never resent her for anything? Being the eldest, the first to be let out late, that kind of thing? I remember –"

He stopped talking as the waitress brought their main courses to a side table, cleared away their empty plates and put their food in front of them, the Lamb Cariverra for Michelle and Duck Provençal for Rory.

"What do you remember?" she prompted.

"That when I first met you, the three of you used to get on fine a lot of the time – most of the time, really. You looked out for each other. Sarah and Helen gave me a really hard time making sure I was up to scratch! She was okay then, wasn't she? But since then I sometimes feel . . ."

Michelle tasted the Lamb Cariverra as she waited for him to continue. He was right – exactly like her mother's roast lamb.

"What?" she said when he didn't go on.

"Like I said, that maybe you resent her. Do you?"

"Why would I do that?" she asked sharply.

He shrugged. "People resent others for all kinds of reasons. Or maybe for no reason. Do you?" he added gently.

She opened her mouth to say 'no' and found, on the tip of her tongue, a very definite 'yes'. Yes, she did resent her. She resented the hell out of her sometimes.

"Why?" Rory asked. She hadn't answered, but he could read her face.

"Oh, her perfect house," she said lightly. "Her snazzy new car, her lovely clothes . . ." She laughed, not meaning a word of it.

"Her marvellous husband?" he teased.

"Of course, and her amazing children."

Something clenched in her stomach.

Because *that* bit she meant.

It had been there all the time, half-recognised, suppressed, hidden in the don't-go-there space in her mind that she tried to pretend didn't exist.

She resented Helen for nothing else . . . but she resented her for her children. For having them so easily, for taking it so much for granted . . . and most of all for her attitude when Michelle lost her own children. The boys would have been just about Oscar and Dylan's age, if they had lived.

But they hadn't lived. And while Michelle felt as if her life had ended, Helen had gone breezily on with her *own* life, her only word of 'comfort' when Peter died being that 'these things' happened for a reason, and 'maybe it was meant to be'.

Yes, Michelle resented Helen. She resented her – hated her – as she had never resented or hated anyone else.

"Are you okay?" Rory's concerned voice interrupted her thoughts. "Michelle, are you okay?"

"I'm fine," she said, fastening on a smile, pushing all thoughts of her children back into the hidden space.

"What's the matter?" he asked.

"Nothing. Really, I'm fine!" she insisted. "Too much talk about Helen, that's all. Let's change the subject, okay?"

"Sure. How's the food?"

"Lovely," she said, hardly tasting it.

"Better than your mother's?"

She forced a laugh. "Maybe not. But the surroundings are better. I like the conservatory."

"It's good," he agreed. "We could add something like this to the new house, you know. There's enough space in the back garden. We'd use it for eating, make the dining-room a playroom for Katie . . ." He laughed, misunderstanding her horrified expression. "I don't mean right away. When we can afford it. And obviously I don't mean anything like this – a much smaller one but with proper heating and air conditioning –"

He was leaning back in his chair as he spoke, beginning to relax as he took another sip of wine and watched the late sun slanting on the river.

"You're joking!" she said sharply, startling him into turning abruptly from the view.

"Hmm? No. But not right away," he repeated.

"Not at all!" she said. "Rory –" she stopped, not sure how to go on.

His look of puzzlement was turning to irritation.

"You *said* just a booking deposit!" she said. "We're not committed, you said – it's just in case Evelyn's house doesn't work out. Rory, we're *not* making plans for it! We're *not* going to live in Glenberry! And even if we had to –"

"Michelle, it could be okay. Really."

"It's not big enough, you know that! So even if we have to move in for a while, we won't be staying long enough to start changing it and building conservatories!"

The waitress came to check if they'd finished, took one look at their faces and moved quickly to another table.

"I don't see the problem. Three rooms downstairs, four bedrooms – plenty of space."

"You wanted room for an office," she persisted. "The dining-room's tiny, you saw the size of the table they had in it –"

"So? I'll use a bedroom. Two bedrooms," he added, remembering that they, too, were as small as the builders could get away with.

"You can't," she said. The room seemed suddenly chilly, the food sour in her stomach.

"Why not?" He ran his fingers back through his hair, pushed his unfinished dinner aside. "Michelle, what *is* the problem? This was supposed to be time away, time to relax . . . what the hell's the matter with you?"

"Nothing," she said in a muffled voice. "I've a headache, that's all. Maybe I'll skip dessert."

She felt guilty at the sight of his anxious face, but couldn't help herself. "I think I'd better go to bed. You stay and have coffee."

"No, I'll come with you. I'll have it in our room. Got any headache tablets?"

She shook her head. "Doesn't matter. You know me, it won't last."

She stood up and he signalled the waitress, ordered the coffee and followed her upstairs.

She was standing at the window when he came into the room, her back to him, looking out over the darkening view.

He crossed the room and stood just behind her.

"What's wrong, Chelle?" he asked quietly. "This isn't like you. What's the matter?"

"I'm tired, that's all."

He reached to touch her shoulder, ran his hand lightly down her back.

"You're very tense."

"A bit," she admitted.

There was a light knock at the door and the waitress appeared with coffee.

Rory answered, took the tray and placed it on the table by the window.

"Actually, I don't think I'll bother," he said to Michelle. "An early night might be good for both of us."

In bed he reached for her, meaning merely to hold her, and felt her rigid body tense even more.

"No, Rory!"

"I only meant –"

"Please, I'm exhausted. I really need to sleep."

He was tired too, and he needed sleep.

But more than that he needed the comfort of her arms, the comfort of knowing that everything would be all right again between them, and soon.

Chapter Twenty-nine

It was still dark outside when she woke again, just before dawn.

Neither of them had slept much. She had woken from time to time, still tense, claustrophobic in the big, curtained four-poster, knowing from the way Rory held himself beside her, very quiet, very still, that he too was awake.

She heard him sigh now as she tried to stop the thoughts racing in her head.

"Michelle?" he whispered.

"Mmm."

"What's wrong, Chelle?" He reached out a tentative hand. "Was it something I said? What's the matter?"

Her heart was pounding, seeming to miss a beat every few seconds. There was a tightness in her chest that scared her.

"Chelle?" he prompted when she didn't answer. "Talk to me. Please."

Talk to him? She looked for words, but couldn't find them.

"Okay, forget it," he said finally, sharply, and turned his back to her.

She felt tears stinging the back of her eyes. "Sorry," she said, reaching to touch his arm.

At once he turned and gathered her in his arms, his cheek against hers in the darkness.

"What is it? What's wrong?"

She was afraid to start, afraid she'd cry, afraid she'd never be able to stop.

"The boys," she said finally, swallowing against the lump in her throat.

"Oh, love," he said, helpless as ever in the face of so much pain.

He began slowly to stroke her shoulder, feeling her unyielding tension. He knew she was holding back the tears.

"Did you sleep at all?" he asked after a few minutes.

"No. On and off. I'm too wound up."

"I know. You'll be exhausted." He lay like that, holding her, stroking her gently, then said "Wait a minute," and got out of bed, going to the wardrobe to get his bag. She could hear him rummaging in the dark, made out the lean shape of him against the window as he stood and came back to the bed.

"This might help you sleep," he said. She heard

the faint sound of a cap being unscrewed as the heady scent of massage oil filled the air. He rubbed his hands together gently and reached out to touch her shoulder. She turned on her stomach, almost too tense to be touched, aching, at the same time, for him to touch her.

He spread the oil across her shoulders in long, firm strokes, kneading gently at the knot of muscles there. With his thumbs he began slowly to circle the base of her neck, moving gradually downwards, tracing the curve of her spine.

She felt him move closer, adjusting his position to reach her shoulders again, then along her arms, finally resting his hands briefly on the backs of hers. The scent of ylang ylang surrounded her, heady, deeply relaxing . . .

She could feel her body easing, melting almost as he worked his hands along her back in a sure, familiar movement and then suddenly, without warning, she was sobbing and he could only say "Chelle, oh Chelle," and hold her until finally it ceased.

"It never gets better," she said, her voice jagged. "It really doesn't ever get better. I think I'm moving on and then something happens . . ."

"What was it? Talking about Helen?" he asked quietly.

She moved away from him, raising herself on her forearms to look down at him.

"She was rotten, Rory. Really she was. When Oscar was born she went on and on about how lovely it was to have a son *and* a daughter, how really lucky she was

– and then she'd look at me in this really pitying way until I wanted to hit her . . ."

"She just didn't think," he said. He turned slightly sideways to face her, trying to catch her expression in the first faint rays of light filtering through the window.

"But she should have! She should have known what it was like for me, for us, and instead she just expected us to get on with it, to act as if nothing had happened – my God, we had to go to Oscar's christening on Tim's first birthday –"

"I didn't know it was – "

"Of course you didn't! You didn't know because you didn't *let* yourself know! You didn't let yourself think! You didn't even miss me when I went to the graveyard with Mam, because it would have been his birthday. Everyone else was celebrating and you were celebrating with them and I was standing at a grave with Peter and Tim in it."

The tears and the quiet rage were barely under control.

"You can't blame Helen for that, Chelle," he said in a ragged voice. "You can blame me, but not Helen. It was her day, her child's day, but I should have been with you."

"So why weren't you? Why weren't you there, and why do you never talk about them, and why did you try to pretend it wasn't happening all over again when Christopher died? Why did you do that?"

"I didn't –"

"Yes, you did! Yes, you bloody well did! Every day in the hospital you told me he was looking better, every day until I nearly believed you because I *wanted* to believe you. And then he died and you wouldn't talk to me about him, just like Peter and Tim! Why did you do that?" she said again. "Why did you make it harder for me?"

"Chelle! Oh God, Chelle, I didn't mean to." His voice was rough with unshed tears as he turned on his back, staring at the darkness, no longer seeing her. "I just thought . . . I don't know what I thought. That it was a way of getting through it. Don't think about it, get on with life, try to act as if –"

"As if they never existed?"

"No! God, no!" He brought his face level with hers. "How could we do that?"

"So why won't you talk about them!"

He moved again to lie silently in the half-dark, and she could feel the tension in him now.

"Because it hurts too much," he said finally.

"It hurts just as much not to!"

"I know that. I know it now. Michelle, there's never a day I don't think of them. I look at Katie and I think –" his voice caught. "I think they should be there teasing her and chasing her, hiding her dolls, all the things Steve and Matt and I did with Siobhan. Teasing her and playing with her and loving her to bits. And instead there's . . . silence. Empty spaces." His voice was so quiet she had to strain to hear. "Every time I look at

Katie I see them too. We're so lucky to have her, I know that. But I see them too."

"I didn't know."

"I didn't know myself. I wouldn't let myself feel it."

"I thought . . ." Michelle said.

"What?"

"That . . . I don't know . . . that it didn't matter to you –"

"How could you think that?" His voice was sharp.

"I don't. Not now."

"But you did?" he persisted.

"Yes." Almost a whisper.

He gathered her in his arms. "I'm sorry, Michelle. I'm so sorry."

She could feel the tears on his cheeks and on her own.

"Remember how terrified we were when we had Katie?" he asked. "We used to stand by her cot, willing her to breathe, when there was no need, when she was perfectly healthy. Remember that?"

"I remember. Weeks with no sleep." She gave a soft little laugh and felt him begin to relax.

"I'd forgotten that," he said. "All I remember is how she felt when I was holding her, how she'd open her eyes and I'd think she was smiling."

"Rory –"

"Mmm?"

"I want to try again."

Immediately he was tight as a coiled spring.

"No."

"Why? At least talk about it, Rory! Don't shut me out!"

"You know we agreed –"

"We didn't agree. You decided."

"We can't, Michelle. We just can't go through all that again. I can't."

"Katie is fine. Another child could be –"

"We were lucky with Katie."

"We could be lucky again."

"I just can't, Michelle. Don't ask me to."

She understood. It went against all she wanted, but she understood his fear, because she felt it too. And, surprising both of them, she turned to him and they found comfort in each other as the first rays of the sun began filtering into the room.

Later, she lay in his arms, tracing her finger along his shoulder.

"I don't want to go back today. If it wasn't for Katie, I wouldn't go back."

"What would you do?" he asked, amused.

"Oh, fly off with you somewhere. To the Caribbean, the south of France, somewhere we've never been before. Somewhere we could relax and get away from everything."

"Hmm. We could use a holiday."

"You definitely can't get away?"

He sighed.

"No chance."

"Not even –"

"No," he said quietly. "I didn't mean to tell you – I don't want to spoil this –"

She had a sudden gripping pain in her stomach.

"What?"

"I've hardly any orders in. I've worked my back off to get the ones I've got and I can't let up now. You know what it's like, everything's folding, everyone's under pressure. I meant it about working from home, I can't afford to keep the office on much longer and that's part of the reason I'm anxious to get the house. If we moved into Glenberry, at least for a while, I could work from there. I know you don't want me cluttering up the bedrooms, but –"

"It's not that," she said quickly.

"Then what is it?"

"Nothing," she said. "It doesn't matter." And she moved to distract him, knowing how to distract him – and wanting to distract herself from the sudden sharp realisation that her hopes for the future had been not so much for the house she would have, as for the children who might one day fill it.

Chapter Thirty

Michelle was in two minds about going back to Maillerain. She remembered the unfriendly feel of the place, the way everyone had seemed to look sideways at the two strangers.

And yet it was the only way to find out anything more about Charles Feradot.

"Is there any point, love?" Una had finally dared to ask the night before after a week of holding back. "Michelle, I don't want to upset you, but she's not getting any better, is she?"

They had been to visit Evelyn and it was true that she still wasn't herself, or anything like herself. But she *had* smiled at them with a hint of recognition, which had raised Michelle's spirits slightly.

"The nurse thought she saw a change in her. So, maybe. And it's the only hope I have, Mam."

"It's not as bad as that, is it? I mean, if this does fall through, if it doesn't work out, you still have the house in Glenberry, love. It's a lovely-looking place – I told you that last week when your father and I drove past. It's . . ." Her voice trailed off as she registered Michelle's expression.

"A house, Mam. That's all it is, just a house."

"Which is what most people live in!" Una said sharply. She sat down beside Michelle, reaching for her hand. "I don't want to make it harder for you," she said a bit more gently, "but you must be reasonable, love. Maybe you were never meant to have the Lacey house. A place like that is beyond most people's reach. You wouldn't normally ever have a chance of something like that. And you know that, love, don't you? If you think about it? You always knew it was a very long shot."

Michelle nodded.

"And I see yourself and Rory looking more and more miserable every day," Una said. "I know you must hate it here – no, wait, maybe 'hate' is the wrong word – but it's hard on you, all the uncertainty. It's hard on everyone."

"Mam, if you want us to leave –" Michelle said miserably, but Una interrupted her.

"No! No, not at all! Don't imagine that for one minute! But it's true that we're all tiptoe-ing round each other a bit, and you have to admit that Sundays can be difficult when yourself and Helen are both around, if Sarah isn't here to help things along. What I really mean, though, is that it's hard for your father and myself to see you looking so anxious and so unhappy, and not be able to do anything to help."

"You are helping! You're letting us stay while we get sorted, that's a lot – I know how hard it is for you and Dad –"

"Listen, love, there's something I need to say to you. It's that there's a value, sometimes, in being happy with what you've got. It's what a lot of people have to do, Michelle. What most people do. And really, when you think about it, you have a lot."

"I know," Michelle said quietly, with the beginnings of a smile.

"But you want more."

"Doesn't everyone?"

"Not always," Una said. "Your father and I are happy. Helen is –"

Michelle made a wry face. "Is Helen!"

Una laughed quietly. "Is Helen!" she agreed. "But I think she's happy. And Sarah would be too if only she'd –"

"Don't say it!" A laugh behind them startled them.

"We didn't hear you come in," Una said as Sarah bent to kiss her on the cheek.

"That's because you were too busy gossiping about my love-life!"

"We were doing no such thing!" Una said, pretending to be shocked.

"No – but you were about to! And before you ask,

Michelle," she said, turning with a smile, "yes, I went out with Noel Curtis last night, no, he's not married, yes, he is gorgeous and no, I'm not interested! Happy?" She sat down across from them, laughing.

"Ecstatic," Michelle said.

"Or will be, if by some miracle we find out tomorrow that Charles Feradot and the long-lost Charles Feradot Lacey are one and the same?"

"That would help!" Michelle laughed.

"How's Evelyn?" Sarah asked more seriously. "Any word?"

"Maybe a slight improvement," Michelle said.

"Or maybe not," Una added with a glance at Michelle.

"You still want to go tomorrow," Sarah said. A statement, not a question.

"Sure. But if you don't want to . . .?"

"I'm all packed," Sarah said. "But, Michelle, if Evelyn's not well . . ."

"I know. It makes no difference whether or not it's his grave."

"Why not wait 'til she's better? To be sure?"

"Because she might not get better," Michelle finally admitted.

"But then –" Una grappled with the logic of it. "Michelle, if she doesn't get better . . ."

"I know," she said again. "There's no point. And even if she does get better, she mightn't remember our agreement, or she might change her mind. But I want to do it for her."

"Even though it mightn't work out for you?" Sarah asked.

"I promised her," Michelle said. "She trusted me, and I promised her. And, yes, I want the house. I really, really want it. But one way or the other I made her a promise and I'm going to try to keep it."

"Even if she doesn't realise it?" Una said.

"She might. But if she doesn't I'll have kept my promise, I won't have let her down. And besides, we've done most of the work, we've found the grave –"

"Maybe," Sarah said.

"Maybe. And in a day or two we'll know whether or not it's his, or whether we can find out anything else while we're there."

"And after that?" Una asked. "Suppose it's not his?

"If it isn't, we've no more leads. And if we find out it *is*, we've done what we set out to do. One way or the other we're home in a few days and one way or the other we're finished."

"You've put a lot of effort into this," Una said.

"Worth every minute of it, Mam. Besides, didn't we find Christopher Keogh's name? We'd never have thought –"

Maurice came in as she was speaking. "Wasn't that a surprising thing?" he said. "Wasn't that worth going to France for in itself? Though why you're going back now I don't know. Haven't you enough on your plate and don't you need every last cent you have for when you start paying a mortgage? You probably forget how dear everything is now when you don't have a mortgage or rent to worry – oh, Merciful God, what have I said now!"

The three women, glaring as one, had stood up and gone out the back door into the garden.

"He didn't mean it," Una said. "I'll kill him, but he didn't mean it."

"I know," Michelle said, sighing all the same.

Una was right. They were all feeling the strain.

* * *

The drive from the airport had the virtue of being familiar.

And Maillerain, when they reached it, was depressingly familiar.

The square with its ancient timbered houses and few scattered shops was silent in the muggy noonday heat. They parked outside the church, looked across towards the post office and Michelle could have sworn she saw the curtain twitching.

"Your imagination!" Sarah said.

Michelle wasn't convinced. "Maybe. Come on."

She was halfway up the churchyard path, fuelled by an urgency to see the grave, by the time Sarah had locked the car and caught up with her.

"There it is," Michelle said, pushing aside a branch of the shading yew-tree and stepping off the dusty pathway.

She had a moment of sharp disappointment as she saw that the grave was empty of flowers. It looked just as it had when she first saw it, as if no-one had been there in years.

They stood looking at it, taking in the inscription on the headstone again.

Charles Feradot. 1889-1973. 84 ans.

"What now?" Sarah asked after a few minutes.

They had spent time over the last few days discussing various possibilities, but Michelle realised now that she had really been hoping to find more fresh flowers on the grave, and preferably someone – the dark-haired man, maybe? – in the act of placing them there.

"Go with Plan A," she said. "A place to stay, and then the town hall."

"A place to stay, and then lunch!" Sarah said firmly. "We won't find the town hall or anything else open for at least two hours."

"Back to the *Belle Vue*?" Michelle asked, pulling a face. They hadn't bothered booking in advance although it was the height of the tourist season; they didn't for a minute believe that Maillerain, or the *Belle Vue*, was likely to be overrun.

They were wrong.

"Twenty-two rooms, and all of them full!" Sarah said in exasperation as she got back into the car in the *Belle Vue's* car park. "A wedding, apparently. And no suggestions as to where we might try."

"The tourist office?"

"Closed for lunch, I'll bet," Sarah said. "Let's try and find somewhere to eat."

They drove back into Maillerain, passing no likely eating-place until they were back in the main square.

"The bars, or nothing," Sarah said.

"God. I'm not sure I'm up to eating in there with all of them sneaking looks and glaring at us!"

Sarah laughed. "Mightn't have much choice! But if you like, we'll try somewhere out the road a bit."

She pulled back out of the square, heading in a different direction, and drove through open countryside until they came to a tiny village some five or six kilometres away.

"Don't get your hopes up!" Sarah said as she parked in front of a little bakery. It was, of course, closed for lunch, but a woman was just locking up and Sarah got out to talk to her.

"There's an auberge out the road," she said, getting back into the car. "She suggested trying there."

Le Petit Canard was off the beaten track and un-signposted. They'd never have found it without the woman's directions.

"Looks a bit quiet?" Michelle said as they pulled up in front of a long cream-coloured building with fading jade shutters and wisteria growing up the walls.

As they got out of the car a dog lying in the porch got lazily to his feet and barked, and a middle-aged woman with grey-streaked black hair came to the door, shushing him.

"*Bonjour*!" she said brightly.

"*Bonjour*!" Sarah answered, crossing the front yard and continuing the conversation in French.

"She doesn't normally do lunch, but she'll cook us something," she explained to Michelle. "*And* we've got a bed for the night!"

"Brilliant!" Michelle went to get the bags from the boot and followed Sarah into the dark, cool reception area of the auberge.

The woman reached to take one of the bags.

"*Venez avec moi*!" she said, indicating that they should follow her up the narrow, curved staircase.

Two flights later she led them into a dream of a room.

It was long and low-ceilinged with three small shuttered windows through which the sun was streaming, picking out the rich pattern on the quilts covering the two double beds.

The woman opened another door to show them the little en-suite bathroom, said something quickly to Sarah and left the room.

"She's doing some soup and an omelette," Sarah said.

"Sounds great," Michelle answered. "Beats the *Belle Vue* hands down!"

It certainly did. They had a lovely lunch, followed by some very French-tasting coffee, and afterwards felt able for anything.

Even Maillerain.

Chapter Thirty-one

The square was a bit more lively now.

Michelle resisted the temptation to ask Sarah to stop at the graveyard again. Instead they continued out the Beauregard road until they came to the second, larger square containing the Hôtel de Ville and the memorial to the French war dead.

"Seems we've timed it well," Sarah said as they left the car. The big wooden doors of the Town Hall were open and there were several people going through.

Michelle and Sarah followed, stopping for a moment to get their bearings as they reached the large, airy room that seemed to be the main hub of activity.

Sarah had a quick look around the room and indicated a desk with a '*Renseignements*' sign. "Information. Let's try there."

The man behind the desk met them with a smile.

Mustn't be from around here, Michelle decided.

After a few words with Sarah he pointed them towards a stairs in the far corner and Michelle followed Sarah up to an office where a small queue of people was waiting.

"We could have tried the church, you know," she said as they took their turn in the queue. "The priest might have known something."

"We can always try that if this doesn't work out," Sarah said, keeping her voice down, conscious of a few glances in their direction. The people around here clearly didn't like visitors – or else they didn't get that many, and were curious.

"Talk about nosey!" Michelle whispered as an elderly woman glanced towards them for the third time. "You'd think Hugh Lacey's visit would've gone down in history. They could probably tell us what he had for breakfast!"

Sarah laughed, drawing more glances. "Coffee and baguette," she said. "What else?"

The queue moved quickly and Sarah took her place at the counter, speaking to the young woman who sat at a computer behind it, an expression of polite inquisitiveness on her face. Michelle recognised the words *Charles Feradot,* and then the woman's fingers were flying over the keyboard. She glanced at the screen in concentration, tapped again on a few keys and said something to Sarah, pointing towards another counter.

"So what was that all about?" Michelle asked as they moved to the counter she had indicated.

"The computer records for births, deaths and marriages only go back to 1992. Anything before that is entered in ledgers. They'll get them for us over here."

"Has she nothing at all on computer?" Michelle asked.

"Nothing. She said she'd have a record if the Feradots were still living in the area."

Sarah stepped up to the counter and began talking to the middle-aged man behind it. He shrugged, gesturing over his shoulder through the half-open door of a room filled with shelves of red-, brown- and grey-covered ledgers. He passed a form across the counter to Sarah and she began completing it, leaving lots of blanks where she didn't have information.

"It could take a while," she said, joining Michelle in the row of seats against the side wall.

Thirty minutes later the man returned, carrying two heavy ledgers.

He came from behind the counter, telling them to follow him as he placed the books on one of the two small tables in the centre of the room. He gestured to the chairs, said a few words to Sarah and went back behind his counter.

"We've to go through them," said Sarah. "The grey one's births in 1899, the brown one's deaths in 1973."

"It'll take forever!"

"Shouldn't be too bad," Sarah said. "They're done alphabetically as well as by year."

The man returned, placing two smaller books in front of her. She thanked him, turning to Michelle. "The indexes," she said. One, a tattered book, bore the dates 1875-1900 on the front cover, and the word *Naissances*. The other, with the inscription *Morts*, was for 1950-1975.

She picked up the first one and looked through it quickly, under F for Feradot. "Nothing," she said, looking at Michelle with a puzzled expression. "No Feradots."

Michelle's heart sank – and then immediately began beating faster. "So he wasn't born here!" she said in an excited voice which caused heads to turn.

Sarah shrugged. "Or he just wasn't registered."

"Could that happen?"

"I suppose. I think I've heard of it happening at home. I'll check in a few minutes. Let's have a look at the 1973 index."

And there it was, *Feradot, Charles. 15 Octobre, 1973.*

Quickly Sarah opened the ledger with the brown cover and turned to October, running her finger down along the list of dates and names until she found the relevant entry.

15 Octobre. Feradot, Charles. Mari de Dominique Feradot, née Delavert.

"It's there, look!"

"What does it say?" Michelle asked, peering over her shoulder.

"That he was married to this woman, Dominique."

"When? And where?"

"Doesn't say."

"Can we look it up?" Michelle persisted.

"I'm not sure how," Sarah said. "Maybe. But where would that get us?"

"Names of other family members?" Michelle suggested. "Bridesmaid, best man?"

"If they had them," Sarah said. The thought struck her. "And if they were married here. We don't know that."

"So where does that leave us?" Michelle asked.

"We know he was married, and we know what her name was. We could ask around and see if that family is still living here."

"If they ever were," Michelle said. "If they were still around, surely someone would've said. All we were told is that the Feradots moved away, not that – what's her name?"

"Dominique Delavert."

"Nobody mentioned that the Delaverts were still here," she said, her voice taking on a despondent note.

"Well, *somebody's* still around," Sarah pointed out. "Whoever put those flowers there is still around." An image of the dark-haired man flashed into her mind.

"It could have been anybody," Michelle said. "An old friend passing through, anybody. It doesn't really get us anywhere."

"At least now we know he was married," Sarah said. "And if he had a family –"

"Then they've moved away, or they were daughters

who married, because there was no computer record, remember? No mention of Feradots."

"So let's try Delavert," Sarah suggested.

They returned the ledgers, took their place again in the queue downstairs and enquired for information on any Delaverts living in Maillerain.

Again the woman tapped the keys rapidly, nodding several times as she spoke to Sarah, then shrugging expressively as Sarah asked her a further question.

"What did she say?" Michelle asked, nearly beside herself with impatience as Sarah returned from the counter.

"There are dozens of them."

"Brilliant!" Michelle said.

Sarah made a face. "Not really. Without specific information we can't get any further. She said it's okay to look up dates of births and deaths when you already know the year, but for anything else you'd need permission, or if the person was dead you'd need full details. The only way to find Dominique Delavert is to go through all the ledgers. And there's no point, anyway, because we still wouldn't have an address for her."

"But if we get an address for the Delaverts who still live here, then maybe –"

"She's not allowed to give that information," Sarah said. "She suggested we look up –"

"The phone books!"

"Exactly!" Sarah said, making a face.

"Oh, God. Mr Nosey Parker in the post office!"

Sarah laughed. "We haven't much choice. Let's go."

They left the car where it was and made their way to the post office.

To their delight the older man was nowhere to be seen and the young man who'd tried to be helpful on their last visit came to the counter with a smile.

When Sarah explained what she wanted he said "No problem" in heavily accented English, pointing to a shelf along the far wall where there was a stack of local directories.

She smiled her thanks and went with Michelle to check the directories.

"That woman was right," she said after a moment. "Loads of them. Only one or two in Maillerain itself, though."

"Maybe that guy could help. He was very friendly," Michelle said.

Too late. The postmaster came through the door and glared at them, extremely put out, apparently, to see them there.

"Relax," Sarah said. "It's a public building, he can't throw us out."

But he could, and did, make things uncomfortable for them, tidying up the shelf around them, bringing a broom to sweep the spotless floor and all but hanging on their shoulders to see what they were looking up.

"Cheeky beggar," Michelle said as he finally moved

away from them with a disgruntled expression. "We can't ask the young guy now, not while he's here. We'd better jot down a few addresses."

They made a list of seven names that were either in Maillerain or in local hamlets they remembered passing, and Sarah began calling them one by one.

"So much for that," she said after twenty minutes, crossing off the final name as one last caller hung up after a brief and fruitless conversation. "That only leaves the second name, the one we got no answer from – Yolande Delavert. We'll try later."

In the meantime, with no better ideas in mind, they went back to the Hôtel de Ville to see if they could find out anything more.

"Electoral registers," the man at the *Renseignements* desk suggested, speaking English now. "You will find them on the first floor. But you will have a big search, Mesdames – they are not alphabetical, they are, what is the word, *geographical*," he finished, looking pleased with himself.

It was, as he had warned them, a long process.

They spent the next two hours going through lists of names and getting nowhere, before deciding to try telephoning Mme Yolande Delavert, the last person on their phone list, again.

When there was still no reply they looked at each other for inspiration.

Deciding they were thirsty enough to brave the unfriendly bars, they went for coffee in the one with the pool table, trying to ignore the gazes of the other customers.

"God, you'd think we were a travelling exhibition or something!" Michelle said, exasperated. "Have they never seen women in here before?"

"There's a couple over there," Sarah said, nodding discreetly in their direction. "And they're looking daggers at us too."

"Wonderful," Michelle said. "It seems to be all the older ones who are ignorant as hell. The younger ones are friendly."

"Mmm!" Sarah said. "That guy in the post office is gorgeous –"

"And about ten years too young for you!" Michelle said. "Keep your mind on the task in hand . . ."

"But if I chatted him up, maybe he'd know something?"

"Huh, any excuse. If you're going to do any chatting up, you might try those old guys at the bar. The one at the end looks about a hundred – he'll surely know something!"

"So chat him up yourself!"

"Can't. Language barrier. He's all yours!"

"I might have to yet!" Sarah said as they ordered a second coffee which was brought by a begrudging barman. "I'm not sure what else we can do if the last phone number's a bummer."

"Back to the electoral registers. And then back home."

"At least we've given it a good shot," Sarah said.

Michelle nodded, but her expression suggested that that wasn't enough.

They finished their coffee and tried telephoning once more. Still no reply.

"Seven o'clock. You'd expect an answer now, wouldn't you?" Michelle said.

Sarah shrugged. "No way of knowing. She could be on holidays or anything. And it's only a name. Chances are she never heard of Dominique Delavert."

They wandered around for a short while, decided it was too early to go back to the auberge for dinner, and went into one of the other bars.

"I think I prefer the first one," Michelle said. "At least in there, after they glare at you, they turn their backs on you. I know now how the monkeys must feel in the zoo."

"I'll call their bluff," Sarah decided suddenly, standing up and approaching a group of four older men sitting at one of the red formica tables.

She might have saved her breath. The shutters came down, and if they had ever heard the names Delavert or Feradot they weren't saying.

"This is ridiculous!" Sarah said crossly as she returned to Michelle. "The way they're acting, you'd swear they were hiding something!"

The sisters looked at each other as the thought struck them.

"You don't think –"

"But why would they –"

"No," Sarah declared after a second. "It makes no sense."

"It makes no sense either that no-one knows anything," Michelle said. "God knows they're nosey enough. "

"Well, if they know, they sure ain't tellin'!" Sarah said, affecting an American accent. "Come on, let's go. I'm getting very fed up of this."

The woman in the auberge was as friendly as earlier, but unable to help when they told her what they were trying to find out.

She hadn't been here long, she explained. The auberge had been in her late husband's family for well over a century, but she'd been living there herself for only fifteen years or so. Not a long time in these parts, she explained. And she'd never heard of any Delaverts or Feradots. But she'd ask Papin, who had a room in the auberge and did odd jobs for her. He was well over seventy and knew everyone in the locality and far beyond.

Sarah thanked her and translated for Michelle as they finished their meal.

"Let's hope he's not one of the guys from the bars!" Sarah said.

To their dismay he was. They recognised him from the first bar. But at least this time, in the company of the auberge owner, he was civil. Nonetheless he knew nothing, and doubted that his friends would know anything either, saying it was hard to keep track of people these days.

"There's a reward for information," Sarah said on the spur of the moment.

His eyes were shrewd. *"S'il n'ya pas des renseignements, il n'ya pas des renseignements, Madame,"* he said with a shrug. *If there is no information, there is no information, Madame.*

She had a sense, all the same, that he was holding something back. And it was heightened a short time later when, on her way to spend a few minutes in the garden after Michelle had gone to bed, she passed the little telephone booth in the lobby and saw him huddled over the phone in urgent conversation.

She was sitting in the garden, listening to the sound of crickets and enjoying the scents in the cooling air, when a man she had never seen before came quietly up to her.

"You are the woman who is looking for Charles Feradot and Dominique Delavert?" he asked abruptly, in French.

"Yes!" she said, sitting up straighter, trying to make out his features in the light from the auberge window. "Do you know something about them?"

He paused, seeming to weigh up something.

"That depends. Why do you want to know?"

"It's a bit complicated," she said. "I'm Irish and Charles Feradot might have relatives there. I don't know – that's what I'm trying to find out."

"And would it make them happy, these relatives, if you did find out?"

"I don't know. Maybe."

"Ah." He was quiet for a few minutes, his eyes shaded in the darkness.

Sarah waited.

"Quel dommage," he said then. *What a pity*.

Chapter Thirty-two

"Michelle! Michelle, wake up! Mich-elle!"

Sarah shook her roughly in her urgency, afraid that the strange man in the garden, who refused to give his name, wouldn't wait. She cursed the fact that she'd let Michelle come to bed before her. At this rate –

"What? What's wrong?" Michelle said, sitting up suddenly.

"Get dressed. Hurry up. There's someone with some information. Come on, *hurry*, before he goes!"

Michelle pulled on some clothes and, heart pounding, followed Sarah downstairs and out into the garden.

The man was still there, waiting in the shadow of a tree. Soundlessly he moved towards the gateway, gesturing to them to follow.

"No way!" Michelle said as he stopped beside a battered Citroen in the lane outside. "I'm not getting into that. Tell him to forget it."

"He says he has information!"

Michelle raised her eyebrows and Sarah went to exchange a few words with the man. She returned saying, "We'll follow in our own car."

They rushed back upstairs to grab the car keys and their purses.

"Come *on,*" Sarah said impatiently as Michelle, in her anxiety, struggled to lock the door behind them.

He was still there waiting as they breathlessly scrambled into the car.

"What are you doing?" Sarah asked as she drove. Michelle was rummaging in her bag.

"Ringing Rory."

"At this hour? Are you mad? What for?"

"We're an hour ahead, it's not too late," Michelle said. "And yes, I'm mad. This is insane. We've no idea who this guy is or where he's taking us."

"And you're ringing Rory – *why,* exactly?"

"So someone knows where we were last seen. And don't think I'm joking."

"Isn't that a bit dramatic?" Sarah laughed. They were rattling along the country road in the wake of the Citroen, which pulled in off the road after a few kilometres to follow a winding track. They followed the Citroen steadily uphill until the driver turned into an open gateway. In front of them was a ramshackle farmhouse, all in darkness except for one small window.

The sisters turned to face each other.

"God, maybe you're right," Sarah said as the man emerged from his car and came back towards them. "What do you think?"

Michelle was jabbing buttons on the mobile. "Damn! Still no signal."

"Michelle?" Sarah said urgently. The man was at their car door now. "Should we go?"

Michelle looked at him through the window, trying to make out his features in the dim light.

"No, hold on," she said. She jabbed at the phone again, put it to her ear and began talking quickly, then switched off and put it back in her bag.

"Let's do it," Michelle said, reaching for the door. "So far he's the only lead we've got."

"Yes, but – maybe we should ring the auberge and tell them where we are. Rory won't be much help to us back in Dublin."

"None at all – I couldn't get through. I just put that on for your man's sake. Still no signal."

She got out and Sarah, alarmed, followed her.

The man gave a soft laugh when he saw her face, as if he knew exactly what she was thinking.

"You have nothing to fear," he said in French, leading the way towards the house.

"So why couldn't we talk at the auberge?" Sarah asked as he rattled the key in the lock and gave the door a push.

"Jacques Berthol does not tell the world his business," he said as he led them into a low-ceilinged room with flagstone floors. It was part kitchen, part living-room, and was simply furnished. "Not unless he wishes to do so."

He gestured them towards the table and went across to the kitchen area, returning with an open bottle of red wine and some glasses.

They sat down at the table and he put glasses in front of them.

"Now," he said, when he had poured the wine. "What do you know of Charles Feradot and Dominique Delavert? And what of the reward for information?"

"Do you have information?" Sarah asked quickly.

He eyed her for a moment and swallowed some wine before saying, "Perhaps. And you, Madame – do you have money?"

Michelle watched anxiously, understanding, without the need for translation, that they were doing more than making small talk.

"Not much," Sarah said. "It depends."

"For me, also, it depends." He sat silently, looking at her.

She did a quick estimate of his age. Seventy or so. Old enough to have known Charles Feradot? Yes – but did that mean he *did*?

She voiced the question. "Did you know them?"

His face clouded. "No. Fortunately, I did not."

Michelle looked at her, puzzled at the change in Sarah's expression. Quickly Sarah translated.

"So why did he bring us here?" Michelle asked,

watching his face as she spoke, trying to read something from it.

Sarah asked him.

"To find out what you know, who you are. To see also if I might gain by telling you about Charles Feradot. Because I should gain, Madame. He destroyed my father. I *should* gain."

"What's he saying?" Michelle asked.

"Shhh!" Sarah said. She waited, but he said nothing more, just sat there continuing to look at them steadily.

"How much money, Madame?" he asked finally. "How much is it worth to you, this information?"

She did a quick calculation. If they paid the auberge by Visa . . .

"Five hundred euro," she said.

He laughed, a bitter sound.

"Or perhaps six."

"Six hundred euro." He laughed again. "Six hundred euro!"

He emptied his glass and poured himself some more wine.

"We're wasting your time, Monsieur," Sarah said finally into the silence. "We should go. Come on, Michelle," she added in English.

"But –" Michelle began.

The man cut across her.

"Stay!" he said. "You have not told me your names."

"I'm Sarah Keogh and my sister is Michelle Larkin. You are Monsieur Berthol?"

"Who else?" he said. "As my father was Monsieur Berthol."

"You said –" Sarah prompted, then stopped, not sure if she should continue.

"That Charles Feradot destroyed him. It is true. That is a name I never dreamed to speak in this house. And now . . . tell me, Madame, these relatives of his, why do they seek information? And how much would *they* pay?"

"I have no idea," Sarah said truthfully, thinking *Loads, probably,* before remembering that Evelyn had an extremely valuable house but, apparently, no money.

He sat thinking.

"Two thousand euro," he said finally. "For two thousand euro, Madame, I will tell you what I know."

"We don't have that kind of money," Sarah said. "Besides, we're not even sure if he's the right Charles Feradot."

"My information might help."

"But I can't afford it. Thank you for your time, Monsieur, but –"

"You have come a long way to go back with nothing."

"We expected that. Besides, we might find out from someone else without having to make a payment."

He gave them a look that was half-amused, half-warning,

"They will not talk."

"You can't know that!" Sarah said.

"They will not talk!" he repeated. "Those who know, will not talk. And those who will talk know nothing."

"We're getting nowhere," she said quickly to Michelle. "He wants two thousand euro."

"God. Well, offer him a thousand."

"Are you mad? We don't have a thousand!"

"We'll get it! Go on, offer it to him!"

"We will pay a thousand euro, Monsieur Berthol. But only if he is the correct Charles Feradot."

"And how would you know, Madame, that he is the correct Charles Feradot?"

"The man we're looking for was Charles Feradot *Lacey*," Sarah said. "He was Irish, a soldier in the British Army in the First World War. His brother Hugh came here about thirty years ago, looking for him, we think."

She was watching his face intently as she spoke. It clouded over at the mention of 'First World War' and he swore quickly under his breath.

"Was it him?" Sarah pressed.

"The man I know of was a soldier in the First World War. A British soldier."

"What can you tell us about him?"

The man's eyes had a bitter look.

"As I said, that he destroyed my father. He was a traitor, Madame. A traitor to his country – and to my father."

"But how?" she asked urgently, ignoring Michelle's appeal for a translation.

"My father rescued him, he saved his life. In return he married the woman my father loved."

"Then he's not the man we're looking for," Sarah

said, disappointed. "Charles Lacey was already married."

His glance pitied her.

"And that would have stopped him, Madame? You think that would have stopped a man who was already a traitor?"

Chapter Thirty-three

Thirst. Head aches. Thirsty.

Try to move.

Darkness.

Can't move leg.

Try . . .

Murmur of voices . . .

"Maman! Maman, vite! Il bouge!"

A hand on his forehead. Cool, cool hand.

Another voice. Older . . . familiar?

Grand-mère?

Concentrate. Concentrate on the voice . . .

"Monsieur! Monsieur, écoutez! Monsieur, est-ce que tu m'entends? Que-est ce que tu t'appelle, Monsieur? Monsieur?"

Tu t'appelle . . .

Je m'appelle . . .

He struggles to open his eyes, tries to focus.

His voice is a rasping sound. "Je m'appelle Charles Feradot."

How many weeks? Hard to say.

May, now, he thinks. Perhaps early June.

No calendars here.

And no point in asking. What difference?

He hears footsteps coming up the stairs and sits up with an effort. Getting easier now. The leg is healing well.

The door opens quietly. Dominique peers in, sees he is awake and crosses to the makeshift bed carrying a bowl of soup.

"Eat!" she commands, smiling at him.

"Thank you."

He takes the bowl and begins supping ravenously. Appetite coming back. A good sign.

"No headache today?"

"No."

No headache today, or yesterday. Another good sign.

"We must leave soon. Marc says it is not safe."

His guts clench, turning the soup sour.

"Who is Marc?"

"My brother. You remember? He brought you here."

He struggles. Does he remember?

Not sure.

Hard to be sure of anything.

His name is Charles Feradot.

He is wounded. *Was* wounded, he reminds himself. Almost better now.

He is a British soldier.

He *thinks* he is a British soldier. He was wearing a British uniform.

But he is speaking French, he is thinking in French.

Why is that?

"Do you understand?" Dominique says urgently. "We must leave soon."

Again the sense of a knife in his belly.

"To go where?"

"Away from here."

He tries to imagine where they might go. Tries, as he always tries, to find faces in a mind that is clouded.

There is a war and he is in France. He knows that much.

And he is a soldier.

"Back to my men?" he asks, gripped with fear. Why is that?

"No," she says. "No. Away from here."

She takes the soup bowl and goes back downstairs.

Where am I? he wonders. *And who am I?*

I am Charles Feradot.

Who is Charles Feradot?

The village is quiet as they approach it.

They have left the truck hidden in the woods and will go the rest of the way on foot.

They must skirt the village and go some kilometres beyond, but to drive would be too risky.

Yves will go back for it in a day or two. If they are still alive.

He is leading the way now, signalling them to be silent. Dominique follows close behind, then Charles and finally Marc. He is fifteen, but already has the bearing of a man.

And he carries the rifle like a man.

Charles feels for the revolver at this belt. A Webster, familiar to him.

The uniform, though, is strange. French, slightly tattered, slightly too big for him.

"My brother's," Dominique had said, without further explanation. "Quickly, put it on."

He put it on, noticed the bullet hole. Did not need to ask what happened to her brother.

They climb steadily uphill under cover of the trees. Charles feels the pull on his leg, thinks he can go no further without resting and then Yves signals and they halt in the shadow of the trees.

The farmhouse is all in darkness as they stand looking down on it. In the light of the moon as it comes from behind a cloud they see that part of the roof is missing.

The barn, also, has suffered damage. One door is hanging on a hinge, the other is gone completely. It is, as far as they can tell, empty.

"Wait here," Yves says. "I'll go alone."

"No!" Dominique answers. "We'll come with you."

Yves faces her, his eyes dark and commanding. "Stay."

He leans towards her, kisses her briefly and is gone down the slope in a slantwise fashion, working his way round to the side of the house.

Minutes pass. There is a brief flicker of light as a match is struck, then the sound of a cricket – once, twice. The signal.

Cautiously Marc leads the way to the house.

Yves is at the door and they follow him into the room. An elderly woman sits in a rocking-chair by an unlit range. At the far end of the room a woman of fifty or so is busy at the kitchen table. She comes forward quickly to kiss Dominique and Marc, then looks uncertainly at Charles.

"You are welcome, Monsieur."

Perhaps, he thinks. Or perhaps not.

They eat, not talking much, while the woman sits looking at Yves, touching him occasionally for no reason, reaching to stroke his hair as she passes on her way to the cupboard where she stores the food.

"Maman!" he laughs.

"Women!" he says to Charles. "Do you have a mother?"

"I don't know."

"Ah. Still you remember nothing?"

"Nothing," Charles says. And then, because that is no longer quite true, he amends it. "Very little."

The old woman is brought to the table and sits, playing

with some bread, apparently lost in her own world as her daughter Claudette, Yves' mother, encourages her to eat.

"Enough. Enough!" she says finally, brushing her daughter's hand away.

"You. Pierre!"

Her daughter draws a sharp breath.

Yves regards her steadily. "I am not Pierre, Grand-mère. I am Yves. Remember?"

"You are Pierre."

"No," he says patiently. "Pierre was my father. He is . . . I am Yves."

"Bah!" she says dismissively. "And you!" She turns her gaze on Charles. "Why are you not fighting?"

"I fought, Madame. I was wounded."

That clenching of the belly again, and a sudden roaring sound. The noise, the infernal clamour in his head. *Can't escape it. Noise and sheer bloody terror, sitting there waiting for –*

"Charles? Charles, are you all right?"

He blinks, tries to focus. Dominique's concerned face looking at him.

"Are you all right?"

"Yes. Yes, I'm all right."

He smiles apologetically round the table.

"Where did you fight, Monsieur?" Yves's mother asks. "Were you with my son?"

Charles looks uncertainly in his direction.

"Was I?"

Yves shakes his head. "No."

"Then how – ?" Charles begins.

"I found you," Marc says. "You know this."

Does he?

He thinks he remembers. Is not sure.

"You were alone," Marc prompts. "And you were wounded. There were some Germans close by. I was afraid for you."

"But –"

A hundred questions clamour in Charles's head, but the grandmother interrupts.

"You should be fighting!" she says sharply. "You should all be fighting! It is the act of a coward not to fight when France is in danger!"

"We *are* fighting, Grandmother," Yves reassures her. "We are going now, to fight."

He winks at his mother, beckoning Charles and Marc to follow him.

The grandmother is led back to her seat by the fireplace while Dominique helps to clear the table.

It is dark in the yard outside the house. Charles stands for a moment, his back to the door, trying to gauge if there is danger in the lane beyond or in the trees that surround the house. Impossible to say.

Quickly he follows Yves and Marc who have already disappeared into the barn.

With difficulty he climbs the ladder to the darkness of the loft.

"You will sleep here," Yves says. "Both of you."

He turns to make his way back to the ladder.

"Yves. Wait!" Charles says.

Yves pauses.

"Is it safe here?"

An eloquent shrug, a soft laugh in the darkness. "Safe? Where is safe?" he says.

"It is as safe as anywhere," he relents, turning to go. "There has been no fighting in this area for almost a year now."

He moves nimbly down the ladder as Charles and Marc make pillows of their jackets and try to find a comfortable position on the floor of the loft. Marc, Charles notices, is turned towards the door below, one arm cradling his rifle.

He takes his revolver from its holster, checks once again that it is loaded and lies awake as the moon climbs high in the sky, listening to every small sound.

Two days later Yves and Marc are gone.

They leave suddenly and without warning.

Claudette is resigned, Dominique distraught.

"They should have stayed!" she says, time and again. "They were safe here!"

"They had no choice," Claudette reminds her. "Five days, that is what he said he had. He had no choice but to go back."

"But to take Marc! He's only a boy, a child!"

"He is fifteen!" Claudette says gently. "Could you have stopped him? Would you have wished to?"

"Yes, I would have wished to!"

"And he would have listened?"

"No," Dominique admits finally. "He would not have listened."

The days settle into a pattern.

In the morning he washes, has breakfast, exercises as well as he can in the barn.

At noon he eats and afterwards he rests.

At night he lies awake, listening.

And when he sleeps the nightmares come.

For three weeks now he has been waking in the quiet of the night, bathed in sweat, his heart pounding and his hand already reaching for the revolver.

He is afraid to keep it too close now.

Two nights ago he woke abruptly, sitting up with the revolver already aimed and heard just in time Dominique's soft, anxious voice.

"You were calling out. I heard you from my room. Charles?"

Wild-eyed he looked towards the trapdoor of the loft, strained to make out her form in the darkness, eased finally into sleep with her sitting by his head, talking softly, touching his forehead occasionally with a cool hand.

Now he does not trust himself. He keeps the revolver loaded but at a distance. And he cannot trust the night sounds, he cannot trust the dreams and images that come to him.

Nightmare, or real?

If real, then they are worse than any nightmare.

Sandbags. He dreams of sandbags. Filling them, hauling them to the dugout entrance, packing them tight to shore up the crumbling walls of the trench. Ignoring the sounds, trying deliberately not to think of the rats.

Some of the men kill them. Quiet discussions in the death-watch time before dawn, the dangerous time. To kill them, or not to kill them? Let them live and they grow big as cats and fearless as you might have been, once. Kill them and the stench is added to all the other unbearable stenches.

He lets them live.

"Charles? Charles, wake up!" An urgent whisper, a tug at his shoulder. "Charles, what is the matter?"

Slowly he becomes aware of her.

"What? What's wrong?"

"You were crying out. I heard you scream. Please, Charles, you must be quiet. Please!"

Frightened, he tries to settle again into a half-sleep.

He hears her go quietly down the stairs, feels himself begin to drift . . .

And then it comes again, the face he has seen for three nights now. Young, younger than he is. Black hair.

Blue eyes. A white face, a trickle of red blood at the corner of the mouth as the staring eyes continue to stare and Charles, with a tug, removes the bayonet and watches as the boy drops dead at his feet.

He screams again.

But this time silently.

"I am afraid, Charles."

Dominique has come to him with bread and some cheese. He nods as he takes it.

"No word of Yves still. Or Marc." He can feel her trembling as she says the names.

"You're cold."

"No. No," she says. She cannot be cold. It is August and the air is warm.

But still she trembles.

He is crossing the yard in the dark of the evening two nights later when he hears it.

A faint clink as a stone drops away on the hillside, the merest rustle as the branch of a tree is disturbed.

Instantly he is on his belly, revolver drawn, taking what shelter he can behind an old oak rain-barrel.

The face of the young German is before him again and he blinks to banish it, concentrates on the flesh-and-blood figure making his way between the barn and the dwelling-house.

His surefooted way.

Yves?

No, not tall enough.

A cloud shifts and the moon throws light across Marc's uneasy face.

Charles follows slowly to the house, careful not to startle him until he has knocked and the door is opening.

A moment later they are both inside and Claudette is embracing Marc, bombarding him with anxious questions.

"I don't know, I don't know," he replies, again and again. And then "I saw him fall. That's all I can be sure of. They were running and there was an explosion and I saw him fall."

"But did you not go to him? Was he alive? Marc, you did not help him? Tell me!" In her anxiety Claudette is squeezing his arm so hard his face turns white.

"Leave him," Dominique says, moving her gently aside. She kneels to face him where he sits, exhausted, in the chair. "Marc, is there nothing you can tell us?" she pleads in a voice full of fear.

He opens his mouth to speak but no words come, only wrenching sobs that go on and on, long into the night.

He is almost asleep when he hears her come quietly up the ladder.

"Charles?"

He stirs, begins to sit up.

"No. Shhh! Stay there."

"What's the matter? Is Marc all right?"

"For now, he is all right," she says. He has slept all

through the day and into the night again, waking only to eat before turning exhausted eyes on his sister and collapsing into sleep again.

"And you?"

"I am afraid," she says. "They say in the village that the Germans are coming."

"They said that last week and the week before," he reminds her. "And none came."

"Charles, what if he is dead?" Her voice holds infinite sadness and fear but she does not cry. "What if he does not come back?"

For answer he reaches out a tentative hand and gathers her against him. He moves to make space on the straw pallet that is his bed and holds her as, together, they lie in the darkness and wait for dawn to break.

Chapter Thirty-four

Jacques Berthol sipped his wine, pretending indifference, as Sarah translated for Michelle.

"You will pay for information?" he asked quickly when Sarah and Michelle had finished their brief conversation.

"We're not sure he's the right person," Sarah said.

They were very sure. There couldn't be two British soldiers named Charles Feradot who had ended up in Maillerain. But they didn't trust Jacques Berthol. It was hard to know how much to tell him – and harder still to decide whether to pay him for information that might be worth nothing at all.

"I don't fully understand," Sarah said as Berthol took another sip of wine, watching her carefully. "I can see that Charles Feradot betrayed your father – but why do you say he was already a traitor?"

He made an impatient sound.

"Is it not obvious? He was here, so far from any battlefield, where he had no business to be. He should have been fighting with his regiment."

"But how did he get here?"

"As I said, Madame. My father rescued him. He brought him here. Marc Delavert found the man wandering near his home, close to the river Somme. He had left the battlefield. There was much confusion, the army was in retreat, but still the men attempted to fight. But not Charles Feradot. He was walking away when Marc found him. A deserter!" He almost spat the word.

"But – what was Marc doing so near a battlefield? Surely if –"

"You are right, he should not have been there, he should have stayed under cover like any sane man. But he was a boy, a young fool – and besides, the battle was moving, the soldiers, as I said, in retreat. Marc was close to home when he met Feradot and he was afraid for him. He brought him to his home, to hide him." He laughed bitterly. "To make trouble for his family – and for my father."

"And your father brought him here?"

"My father, and the Delaverts. It seemed safer."

"But how does that make him a deserter? How can you say that, if the soldiers were retreating? And besides, surely if Marc and your father *brought* him here –"

"Pah!" he was impatient now. "Enough! I say what I say. And if you want to know more, then you pay, Madame. Two thousand euro, that is my price."

"Do you know anything else about them?" A thought struck her suddenly. "Did they have children? The records don't –"

But he was already standing. He moved to the door and opened it.

"Follow the road to the right, Madame, and left at the bridge. That will take you to Maillerain."

"Can we call again, if we get the money?"

He regarded her coldly. "I will contact you."

"We'll be here for two more days."

He shrugged, impassive.

They had no option but to get back into the car.

"It had to be Charles Lacey," Michelle said as they left the lane and turned onto the main road. "*Had* to be! But where do we go from here? There's no way I'm paying Berthol two thousand euro, even if I had it. He gives me the creeps!"

"He might be our only chance," Sarah said. "Wonder if he was right when he said no-one else would talk to us?"

Michelle shrugged. "It might explain a lot. Those old guys weren't exactly rolling out the red carpet."

"We could try them again," Sarah suggested without much hope. "Or maybe advertise locally?"

"If he's right, we'll have no takers."

"Maybe you should just pay him?"

Michelle gave a little laugh. "You're joking, right?"

"You were all set to give him a thousand."

"I've changed my mind. Like I said, he gives me the

creeps. He's just out to make trouble for someone. Besides," she added, "even if I had the money – which I don't – we still don't know if he knows anything else. We don't even know if Feradot had a family or anything."

"*Someone* left those flowers."

"Someone did. And I'd give anything right now to know who."

Sarah laughed as they pulled into the courtyard of the auberge. "Two thousand euro?"

They got out of the car, noticing a movement in the shadows as they neared the door of the auberge.

Papin, Michelle thought. *Wonder what else he knows*?

They went quietly up to their room and sat on the bed making plans.

"So what do we have?" Sarah recapped, pen and notebook at the ready as she sat cross-legged on her bed. "One," she said, saying it aloud for Michelle's benefit as she jotted down some notes. "We've found the grave of Charles Feradot, who was born the same year as Charles Feradot Lacey."

"Right," Michelle said. "And it's in Maillerain."

"And we found flowers on his grave, but we've no idea who put them there," Sarah said, continuing to make notes. "And – let's see – he was married to Dominique Delavert."

"And we've tried nearly all the Delaverts on our list, and none of them ever heard of Dominique," Michelle added.

"Or of the Feradots," Sarah said. "And there's no record of them locally."

"And the only one who seems to know anything is Berthol, and we don't trust him," Michelle finished.

"So – where does that leave us?" Sarah asked, looking up as she finished scribbling in the notebook.

"We try ringing Yolande Delavert again," Michelle suggested. "Or . . ."

"Hmm?" Sarah prompted.

"We could leave a message on the grave?"

"Would that work?"

"Why not?" Michelle asked. "If someone is visiting they'll see it and maybe contact us."

"Mmm," Sarah said. "We could try it – and I suppose it's all we've got, besides Yolande."

"And Berthol and his two thousand euro! We'll do it in the morning."

Immediately after breakfast they tried phoning Yolande Delavert again.

"No go," Sarah said, "but at least the answering machine's on now. I've left the number of the auberge as well as the mobile."

"Should we try the town hall again, see if they have any ideas? It's open on Mondays, isn't it?"

"Until lunch-time anyway, probably," Sarah said. "What about the graveyard?"

"We could try, I suppose. I can't think what else to do."

She phoned Rory on the mobile as they drove towards Maillerain.

"Katie's fine and Mam and Dad are okay," she reported as Sarah parked in front of the church. "But I think Rory's had a stroke – he made a *very* funny noise when I mentioned the two thousand euro . . ."

Sarah laughed. "Wonder why? Okay, let's write a message –"

"No, wait!" Michelle said. "I wanted to get some flowers, remember? To put on Charles Lacey's grave if I found it?"

"But we're not sure –"

"It's as close as we'll get. Either this is it, or we'll never find it. Come on, we'll try over there!" She nodded towards one of the little shops across the road, with a sign outside saying '*Fleurs*'.

Leaving the car, she crossed the road with Sarah following.

To her delight there was quite a display inside.

"Some lilies," she said as Sarah joined her. "And some of those white chrysanthemums, I like those. Oh, and poppies!" she added as she saw the blood-red flowers in a container beside some ferns.

"Would red chrysanthemums not look better?" Sarah suggested.

"Maybe. But poppies are what I want, they seem right. Remember the little bouquets of poppies at Pozieres?"

Quickly Sarah placed the order and the florist made

the bouquet up carefully, casting occasional glances at them when she thought they weren't looking.

"*Pour les fleurs,*" she said as she attached a little packet of powder to the cellophane wrapping. "*Vous le mettez dans l'eau avec les fleurs –* "

"*Merci, mais ce n'est pas nécessaire,*" Sarah answered. "*C'est pour la cimetière.*"

"*Ah, bon,*" the woman said, her expression questioning as she removed the little packet of plant food.

"What was that all about?" Michelle asked as they left the shop with the bouquet.

"I told her we didn't need the plant food because they were for the cemetery," Sarah said.

"Why? Now the whole village will know!"

"And you think they don't anyway?" Sarah laughed, with a glance towards the post office where she had the impression of someone moving quickly away from the window.

As they passed the car Michelle handed the bouquet to Sarah, then opened the car door to reach in for an empty glass Perrier bottle and Sarah's notebook.

"What'll I write?" Sarah asked as they made their way up the gravel pathway.

"Just that we're trying to find anyone who knows Charles Feradot," Michelle said. "Put your mobile number, and the address at home just in case. Though they'll hardly bother writing to us!"

"And we can hardly stay around waiting for them to

phone!" Sarah said reasonably. "We have the rest of today, and tomorrow, but that's it!"

Michelle sighed. Put like that, it seemed unlikely that anyone would contact them at all.

"Maybe if you mentioned a reward?" she suggested.

"I don't think so. You could do that in an ad in a shop window, or in the paper – but not on the grave. You could insult someone."

"Maybe we should forget the note and just advertise?"

They had reached the grave while they were speaking.

"We're here now, so let's do it," Sarah said. "You've got to leave the flowers, anyway."

Michelle stood in silence for a moment, looking at the bouquet.

"Strange, isn't it?" she said quietly, her gaze still on the flowers. "Lilies have always reminded me of death, but now poppies do, too. You wouldn't think something so beautiful would be the symbol of a war."

She lapsed again into a reverie, looking now at the grave and its inscription. Then she bent down and arranged the flowers on the grassy plot. Clearly no-one had visited for some time, or else hadn't brought flowers with them.

She took the note from Sarah, rolled it up and placed it just inside the mouth of the bottle before screwing the cap back on. Then she tucked the bottle in under the flowers, leaving just the top of it showing, and stood back to survey the grave one last time.

"It's likely to be his, isn't it?" Sarah said quietly.

"It has to be," Michelle said. "It all fits. He was married to Dominique Delavert. And the Charles Feradot who married Dominique Delavert was a British soldier, that's what Berthol said. It has to be him. I wonder why he didn't go home? Why didn't he go back to his wife and children?"

"We'll never know," Sarah said. "And we don't need to know, anyway. But I think it's his grave. I think you've done what Evelyn asked. You found the grave."

Michelle looked at her, eyes wide. "I did, didn't I? I found his grave! Which means –"

"That the house is yours!" Sarah said, hugging her. "You did it!"

If Evelyn ever remembers anything about it, thought Michelle. "*We* did it, Sare."

They kept their voices low, reining in their excitement, conscious of their surroundings.

"So all you have to do is take some soil and –"

"What if we're wrong?" Michelle interrupted.

Sarah stifled her impatience. She'd already had one row with Michelle for suggesting that Evelyn wouldn't know the difference, and she wasn't about to risk a second.

Instead she asked, "We've gone through this again and again, Michelle! You said *yourself* that he had to be the same person! What more proof do we *need*?"

Michelle frowned. "I suppose I'd like to find someone who could tell us definitely that they were one and the same. Maybe someone who remembered Hugh coming and visiting him. If he *was* the same person."

Sarah sighed. "You're being too picky, Michelle! It's the right place. This is the place the letters came from. Otherwise we wouldn't be here!"

"True. But," she paused, considering. "Let's give it one last try, to see if we can find someone who knows anything, and who'll talk to us."

"And if we can't?"

"Then we take some of the soil and go back home and give it to Evelyn."

Who won't know the difference anyway, Michelle thought sadly. Rory had told her that Evelyn was still showing only slight signs of improving.

"We'll see if Yolande rings us, and maybe put some notices in the shops," Sarah said as they left the grave. "But that's it, okay? You're running out of time, and so am I. We really can't afford to come back again, Chelle – we need to sort it now."

They were nearing the gate to the churchyard as she finished speaking, and stood back to make way for a dark-haired man carrying some flowers, who smiled his thanks as he passed.

"It's him!" Sarah hissed. "The guy who was here last time!"

"Are you sure?" Michelle asked.

"Yes, positive! And look – " as she went through the gate she indicated the red car parked in front of theirs. "The same Peugeot, too!"

Michelle was suddenly breathless. "Sarah, you don't think –"

"*Damn*!" Sarah interrupted.

"What?" Michelle, puzzled, followed Sarah's gaze.

"A flat! How're you at fixing tyres? No, don't answer that!" she finished glumly.

They looked in dismay at the flat-as-a-pancake wheel.

"Must've picked up a nail on the way in," Sarah said. "It was fine this morning."

"What do we do now?" Michelle mused. "Can't see the locals rushing to help. Can we ring the AA or something? Is it included in the car insurance?"

The look Sarah gave her told her not to go there.

Michelle gave a quick glance back over her shoulder towards the gate of the graveyard, then began helping Sarah to clear away some bits and pieces in the boot so they could get at the spare tyre.

Together they struggled to heft it out, then Michelle looked back at the gate again as Sarah reached in for the jack and a spanner.

"Sare, d'you think we should –" Michelle began urgently.

"Hmm?" Sarah looked up, a perplexed expression on her face as she battled with the jack.

"I'm going back in there. I *have* to talk to him! Come on!"

"Yes, but –"

There were urgent footsteps just behind them.

The man! Michelle's heart was in her mouth.

He seemed preoccupied as he glanced in their

direction. Then, after hesitating for the merest fraction of a second, he came over to them.

"Je peut vous aider?"

Sarah's acceptance of help was heartfelt, while Michelle stood watching, waiting impatiently for him to finish.

Within a few moments he'd replaced the tyre and was putting the flat one back in the boot of the car. As he turned towards them, wiping his hands on some paper towel Sarah had given him, there was a 'clunk' and he turned in surprise, glancing back towards the car boot, which he'd just closed.

"Ah, c'est ça," he said, removing a bottle from the pocket of his jacket.

"Where did you get that?" Sarah asked, speaking English in her excitement.

He looked at her, raising his eyebrows. "You are English, Madame?" His accent was charming. "Your French is excellent!"

"We're Irish," Sarah said quickly. "The bottle –"

"Yes, it is very strange! You don't, I suppose, know anything of it? There is a note inside – and I have found it just now on the grave of my great-grandfather!"

Chapter Thirty-five

"Oh Lord Above, send down a dove,
With wings as sharp as a razor,
To cut the throat
Of the bloody old goat
They call the Sergeant-Major!"

Charles almost cuts himself in shock.

Where the devil did that come from?

He is standing by an old wash-table above which a speckled mirror hangs on a rusty nail.

He is wearing his navy uniform trousers, the braces of which are looped down by his sides, and he is bare-chested.

In front of him there is a bowl of warm water, in his hand there is an open razor . . .

And in his head, again, there are those words. In English.

He knows it to be English, and he knows the verse.

Oh Lord Above . . .

He has heard his men recite it time and again.

His men.

Sharp as the razor a face comes to him. He can almost touch it. Young, younger than he, with the same dark, curly hair and the same clipped moustache.

He looks in the mirror. No moustache now – but in his image of himself there is a moustache.

He is staring at the mirror, the razor-blade still aloft, when her voice calls softly to him and in an instant he is by the bed, the razor abandoned, his still-wet face seeking comfort against the softness of her skin.

"What is the matter, chéri? You looked startled."

For a moment he has to translate in his head, so strong is the impulse to answer her in English.

"Nothing," he says finally. "There is nothing the matter."

"Come back to bed," she urges.

He gives a quiet laugh. "It's morning. Eight o'clock, almost!"

"So?" she says teasingly. "One more hour will not matter! Besides, who is to know but us?"

It is true. They are staying in a remote little farmhouse some four or five kilometres from Maillerain, and no-one, as far as they are aware, takes much notice of them.

It is a strange time, this month since the war has ended. There is too much happening for anyone to take much notice of them. People are beginning to drift around the countryside again, some returning home, others in search of family members they have lost. Soon it will be time to –

To what?

Because Charles has no idea what he must do next.

He knows he does not belong here.

But where *does* he belong?

He belongs in Dominique's arms.

He is certain of nothing else, but he is certain of this.

He removes his clothing and returns to the shelter of the bed and the protection of her yielding body.

The dream comes again.

Not dream, nightmare.

The face of the young German soldier, blood trickling from his mouth.

And, this time, the face of another German – older, with deep-set brown eyes. Kind eyes, gazing wearily at him.

The German speaks again. Charles strains to hear the words he can't understand – but the intent is clear. Charles must help him to lift the wounded man from the shell-hole they are sharing.

He cannot see the face of the man.

He has dreamed this part of the dream before, never seeing the face.

Then –

Conroy!

Out of nowhere the name comes to him.

Conroy, the young corporal, the reckless lad who put them all to shame in the midst of their retreat.

It was Conroy who had insisted on manning the Lewis until the last possible minute, Conroy who crawled to the fire-step to find the Verey flares and fire them in an effort to draw air cover for their straggling retreat.

Conroy who is lying in a shell-hole now with half his arm torn off and blood leaking through the crude bandage covering his skull.

Conroy closes his eyes.

Charles opens his in a wild-eyed stare, sweat pouring from him.

Quietly he leaves the bed and gets dressed. Dominique is dozing, she will be awake in a few minutes. He must get out of here, he must be on his own.

He leaves the house by the back door and climbs into the woods behind to sit on a rock, looking towards the house.

He needs to think.

He must decide what to do.

They cannot stay here forever.

He wants to, of course.

He wants nothing more than to stay here with Dominique in the sweetness of the love they have discovered.

But that is not possible.

He doubts that Yves will return. There has been no word.

But soon, he will have to leave here.

Almost Christmas. *The war will be over by Christmas.*

And so it is. He gives a hollow laugh.

"Charles?" she asks, alarmed. "What is the matter?"

"Nothing," he says. "Just thinking."

"Thinking of what?"

Christmas. A tree in the drawing-room, chosen by himself and Hugh, chopped down by the wood-cutter in a place they know, up in the mountains near Killakee. It gives a festive air to the room, adorned as it is with baubles and trinkets. The children's faces are shining and Isabel sits at the piano playing a Christmas carol and then Thomas Moore's 'Love's Own Sweet Song' and Hugh joins in, in his rich baritone voice . . .

"Charles? Charles, what are you singing? Charles, speak to me!"

"Hmm?" He turns to her and with an effort focuses on her worried face.

"Charles, are you well? What is the matter?"

"Fine. I'm fine," he says, folding her into his arms, telling her not to worry so much.

He doesn't tell her that he is worried enough for both of them.

It is only a matter of time until they find him.

It will be better, far better, if he finds them first.

The problem is that he doesn't quite know where to start.

"They're shooting deserters!"

The word has been all around the village for days now.

It seems that every building is yielding up young men, frightened and injured men, who come sheepishly into the daylight, reluctant to look anyone in the eye.

He doesn't belong with them. Does he?

The discussion rages up and down the village. Seventeen men have been found so far.

Within a twenty-kilometre radius, that doesn't seem so many. Not when you consider the numbers who went, the numbers who returned home wounded, and those who died.

Seventeen is nothing at all, almost.

The authorities will not know where to look for these men who have managed somehow to make their lone way to isolated farms and distant relatives, to remain hidden until the worst is over and the rest of the men begin to make their way home.

They will blend in with them and will not be found, will not be shot.

Unless they are betrayed.

The village is divided.

Gustave Paschal, who has lost two sons and a nephew, is adamant. They are cowards, they must be handed over.

René Aubertin, still mourning his youngest, is eloquent in his despair. The villagers listen as he demands to know who among them would turn out any man who had suffered for France? Who among them would not give everything he had to see a son of his emerge from hiding – shamed, perhaps, but still alive. Who among them would deny that to anyone?

None, it seems. The villagers close ranks and the men vanish again.

He cannot vanish with them, he has nowhere to hide.

He does not wish to hide.

He wants, more than anything, to know who he really is.

More than he wants Dominique?

The question is a constant companion, it will not let him be.

And neither will the memories.

They come more frequently now, during the hours of daylight as well as in the dead of night.

The curly-haired man of his dream is Hugh. He knows that now. Hugh who sits with his wife Isabel and their children in a drawing-room with a tall Christmas tree, singing round a piano.

Hugh's wife Isabel? How can he be sure?

He is sure. He is absolutely sure.

He feels no connection with Isabel beyond a certain fondness.

And he sees, again and again, the look that passes between Hugh and Isabel when they are unaware of his glance, the same look that he knows he and Dominique share.

He must go back, he must tell them that he is alive, and then he can be free to be here with Dominique.

But back to where?

"You are insane," Dominique insists. "They will shoot you. Please, Charles!"

"They won't shoot me," he tells her. "I didn't desert. I was wounded and I was brought here. They'll understand."

"And if they don't?" She is sobbing now.

"I have to take that chance. I have to find my brother and tell him I'm still alive."

"*Forget you have a brother*!" The sergeant-major's voice is loud in his ears. "*You're in the Army now and you're here to fight and, by God, you'll fight when I tell you to fight*! *When you get the order to advance then you advance and you keep on advancing and if your brother falls down dead in front of you then you bloody well jump over him and you keep on GOING*! *Do you UNDERSTAND*? *I said*, DO YOU UNDERSTAND!"

The parade-ground resounds with the roar of a thousand men answering.

They understand. Oh, yes, they understand.

Until two years later when the bullet hits him and the explosion stuns him and then suddenly Hugh is there, not understanding at all, forgetting to jump over him, instead pulling Charles into the spurious shelter of a shell-hole where he leaves him while he goes to get help.

Is Hugh alive?

He didn't return.

What if he's not alive?

He has to find out.

Finally he has persuaded Dominique.

She is not happy, but she lets him go.

She knows there is no choice.

The journey takes longer than he expects.

Ten days, heading east towards Amiens. Stopping at farmhouses along the way, begging food where he can when his is gone.

Walking, and the occasional lift on a peasant cart.

Walking again.

And then, finally, the field ambulance. Familiar sight with its tarpaulin cover and its big red cross on the top.

"Fancy a lift?" A corporal, cigarette clamped firmly in his lips as he speaks, calls out as they pull in ahead of him. The driver, in a hurry, barely glances at Charles as the corporal gets out to wait for him.

"Here, hop in the back, mate, you'll be all right there. Where you headed?"

A Cockney. *London Rifles*, Charles thinks, noticing the cap badge.

"Thank you," Charles answers, climbing stiffly into the back of the ambulance.

He is not alone.

In the dimness he can see three other men, one lying on a stretcher and the others, both with bandages on their heads, staring vacantly in front of them.

In his dismay he glances back towards the corporal, still positioned by the tail-gate, who shrugs.

"Should have left them where they were – we can't do nothing for them up ahead. Where you going, did you say?"

"Headquarters."

The corporal glances at him uncertainly, taking in the French uniform.

"Don't know where your headquarters are, mate. Better off getting yourself home, most likely."

Home . . .

"That's exactly what I'm trying to do," Charles says, and this time the corporal notices the accent.

"You're no Frenchie! Where you from?"

A shout from the driver interrupts, and the corporal makes to rejoin him in the cab.

"Amiens do you?" he calls back over his shoulder.

"Amiens will be fine."

Amiens, when they reach it, is a hive of activity.

"Company HQ's that way," the corporal indicates as

the ambulance stops briefly in a cobbled square. "Good luck, mate!"

He finds it without too much difficulty, following the lines of men scurrying to and fro.

What are they doing here with the war finished almost six weeks?

He feels an urge for home so strong that it twists his stomach and he almost gags.

The private on guard at the door looks him up and down.

"British soldiers only. Sorry."

"I *am* British."

Again the look, more measured this time in response to Charles's educated tones.

"Name, rank, serial number?"

"I don't know."

"No name?"

"Charles Feradot." It comes out with a French inflection, *Charle,* and he repeats it.

"My name is Charles Feradot."

"Wait here."

The private returns a minute later, accompanied by a captain.

"You're British, I'm told?"

"Yes, sir."

"Well, come in then, there's a good man, no point standing about out here!"

Charles follows him gratefully. The French uniform

cape is no match for the bitter wind, no match for the lost greatcoat he yearns for.

"Charles Feradot, you say?" the captain asks as they sit at his desk drinking tea from chipped white china cups. "What regiment, Feradot?"

"I don't know. I was wounded, I don't remember."

"Do you remember where you fought?"

"No."

"Not at all?"

"Not at all."

"When did this happen? Do you know?"

"Nine months ago, I'm told."

The captain lowers his teacup and looks steadily across the desk.

"I see. And where have you been in the meantime?"

Charles sips the tea and it turns to ice in his mouth.

"Answer me, man! Where have you been?"

"I was wounded," Charles says. "A French family found me and took me in –"

"Found you where?"

"Near the battlefield."

"*Near* the battlefield?" A raised eyebrow.

Fear turns to impatience. "Look, can you help me or not, do you think? From what I can remember – it only comes to me in snatches – I was taken prisoner by some Germans when I was already wounded. My brother left me in a shell-hole – he said he'd come back, but they found me there. They were taking me away in a cart when a bomb exploded and they were both killed. They were kind to me," he adds, almost to himself, remembering the staring, deep-set brown eyes of the German who had used his own field dressing for Charles's head wound.

"What happened then?" The captain's expression is still sceptical.

"There was a boy, a French boy. Marc. He led me away."

"I see. And you are certain that you are British?"

"Yes," Charles says, startled.

"You're wearing a French uniform."

"They burned mine. They were afraid to keep it."

"And your cap badge, your identification tag?"

"Gone."

"How very convenient."

Charles is angry now. "What are you implying?"

"Oh, nothing. Nothing at all."

"And how do I find out who I am?"

The man gives him a last, cool look. "Wait here."

The second man who comes is a major, the fatherly type, though hardly older than Charles himself. He introduces himself before seating himself in the captain's chair.

"They tell me you have a problem, old chap."

Charles relaxes slightly. "I need to find out who I am."

"No information at all, I hear."

"Only my name, Charles Feradot."

"Hmm." The major regards him across the desk. "Could be a bit tricky."

"What do you mean?" Again the sensation of ice as Charles realises that the 'hail fellow well met' act may not be all it seems.

"Lots of chaps turning up in places they shouldn't be. No names, no proper identification. Difficult."

"Surely it's just a question of . . ." His voice trails off.

"Of what, old chap? Of dusting them down and sending them off home on the next boat? 'Fraid it's not quite as simple as that! There are certain things we need to be sure of first."

"Such as?" Charles asks.

The major steeples his hands on the desk and leans forward.

"Such as, my dear fellow," he says carefully, continuing to look steadily at Charles, "that those we send home *deserve* to be sent home."

It takes several seconds for the implication to sink in.

"You think I'm a deserter?"

The major shrugs. "I can only go on facts. And so far there are precious few, either way. Don't worry yourself, though – you can stay here while we try to establish a few more details. Captain Hendron will look after you –"

He is interrupted by a shout from beyond the doorway to the back.

"Blast. Stay there one moment, would you? Wilson,"

he calls to the private at the door. "Keep an eye on our visitor."

"Sir!" Wilson responds.

He positions himself further inside the doorway, rifle at the ready, his gaze never wavering from Charles.

How long they are there Charles is not sure. Ten minutes, fifteen, perhaps.

Then, "Open up!" Loud voices and banging on the front door. "Open the bloody door!"

With a glance at Charles, the private moves to the big wooden door and opens it slightly.

"Major Ellsworth here?" a voice demands.

From where he is seated Charles, with a sideways glance, can see several figures in uniform outside. Three – no, four . . .

"Open the bloody door, man, and let us in! The major's expecting us. Tell him the Orders have come."

"Wait there. I'll speak to the major."

Charles hears the protest. "Bloody freezing – c'mon, mate, give us a –"

The door is closed firmly. With a swift glance at Charles as he passes, the private goes through the door at the back of the room.

Charles moves swiftly. The men are just outside the front door as he opens it.

"You'd better wait inside," he says as he steps out, leaving the door ajar. "But not a sound, mind." He jerks his head towards the door. "Our friend wouldn't like it."

"Bigger fool him, then," one of the men answers.

"What we've got is Orders for home. Should have the bloody welcome mat out, he should!"

One of the men mutters a warning.

"Bugger that!" the other responds. "Don't matter who knows now, does it? War's over, mate. Don't matter who the hell knows we're going home. Besides, he's one of us, ain't you, sir? If he's not a British officer then I'm a bloody Uhlan!"

Charles smiles at them by way of reply. He has slipped away before they are in through the door.

Orders for home.

He wonders how that would feel. Wonders how long it will take him to get home.

At least now he knows where home is.

Luck is with him this time.

In six days, exhausted, he arrives in Maillerain.

"Charles!" Laughing and with tears streaming down her face, she hugs him to her. "You have returned to us!"

"Us?" he asks, confused, because they are alone in the little farmhouse.

For answer she takes his hand and places it on her belly. "Us," she repeats softly, her eyes shining as carefully she watches his face.

"What did you discover?" she asks later as they lie entangled on the straw mattress. "Did you find out who you are?" Her voice is fearful.

"I know who I am," he says, reaching to touch her cheek. "I am Charles Feradot." He smiles at her. "And you will be Dominique Feradot, and our child . . ."

The rest of the sentence is lost in the hunger of their kiss.

Chapter Thirty-six

"Robin?" she asks. "That is a name, Charles?"

Yes, it is a name.

It is the name that comes to him as he gazes at his baby son for the first time.

Robin. He didn't realise he had said it aloud. *Robin Feradot*.

She looks exhausted and he can see that she is not convinced.

"You don't like it?" he asks. "Robin Feradot?"

Robin Feradot Lacey.

The name comes from nowhere.

Robin Feradot Lacey. A child's voice. *Robin Feradot Lacey*.

She interrupts his thoughts. "Gilbert. Gilbert Feradot. What do you think, Charles? Shall we call him Gilbert? It is a name I like very much."

And because he loves her, because he can deny her nothing, he agrees.

But for days and days, weeks, afterwards, he hears the insistent voice of a very young child in his mind, stumbling over the words.

Robin Feradot Lacey. My name is Robin Feradot Lacey.

Two days after the christening the news comes to them.

They are still living in the little farmhouse. Dominique is beginning, slowly, to feel safe there.

She had talked of moving, of feeling easier at a remove from curious neighbours and from Yves's mother and grandmother.

But Claudette has been kind to them, kinder than Dominique feels they deserve.

It is she who found the farmhouse for them, she who persuaded the owner to let them use it in return for some work on the land, now that Charles is well again and there are few enough to do it.

Still in mourning for her son, she has helped them to face down the gossip of the village and has been with them all through the preparations, and for the birth itself.

A child, she insists, is a blessing at a time such as this.

Even in the circumstances – and they do not dwell too much on the circumstances – a child is a gift from God. With so many lost, as her own son was lost, this new life should be made welcome among them.

Slowly she convinces them. Slowly the women of the village, in ones and twos, begin to bring small gifts to Claudette, to pass on for the child.

There are few newborn children in the village.

There have been few enough men to father them.

Anna Paschal, with a furtive glance over her shoulder, knocks on Claudette's door late one night.

Her husband would not approve of this.

But he does not know she is here.

He is sitting in the kitchen of his house, as he has done every night since their second son died, drinking a bottle of cheap red wine to help him sleep.

Claudette's door opens and Anna darts quickly in, a small parcel under her arm.

She thrusts it at Claudette.

"Pour le bébé," she announces. *For the baby.*

And then she bursts into tears.

Together they undo the package and take out the christening clothes she has been saving, the clothes she has no use for now.

And then they hold each other for a long, long time, weeping together for the sons they have lost.

And now the word has come to the village, and from there to the small hamlet where Charles and Dominique Feradot live with their infant son Gilbert.

Yves Berthol has returned.

A full year with no word, and now he has returned.

It is Marc who tells them, Marc who has been living with them from time to time since there is nothing left now of the farm near the Somme and their mother, Marie, is living with relatives near Nantes.

"What do you want to do?" he asks her that night. For the first time since the birth of his son he is feeling fear again. "Do you want to be with Yves?"

For answer she clutches him tightly to her.

"No! Charles, no!"

"I should go to see him."

"He will kill you, Charles!"

"He'll be angry, yes. Hurt, probably. But surely –"

"When I was young," she begins quickly, and he almost smiles. She is barely twenty years old. "When I was young, when Yves and I first met, there was a boy who liked me. Yves said that I was his, that he would kill this boy if necessary, to keep me."

"How old was Yves?" he asks gently.

"Sixteen. Almost seventeen."

"That is how young men talk at that age," he says. "They talk of killing and dying as if it were a game."

Do they? he wonders.

He knows they did. He knows *he* did.

But do they now, those who are left?

"I will go to see him," he repeats. "Don't worry. It will be all right."

"Charles, how can you be sure?"

"I'll make it all right," he says, hoping it is true. "I'll

speak to Yves. And afterwards, if you want, we will move from here, away from Maillerain."

There is no reply. He knows that she is considering what he has said.

"Would you like to do that?" he asks.

"I don't know," she says. "Perhaps." And then quickly, a moment later, "We should do it, Charles. We will move from here and make a new life where people do not know us."

The fear is there in her voice, the fear that is almost always in his heart and in his belly.

They know that they are living on borrowed time, that sooner or later the Army will come looking for him.

They may not find him, but they will come looking for him.

"Perhaps you should not see him," she says. "Perhaps we should just go quietly from here and say nothing."

"I can't," he answers her.

"Why not?"

"It wouldn't be –" the word eludes him and then it comes to him in English and he has to translate it in his head.

"Decent," he says. "It wouldn't be decent."

"Promise me something," he says as they begin to drift towards sleep.

"Anything."

"When I die –"

She sits bolt upright.

"Charles!"

There is a wail from the crib in the corner.

"Now look what you've done! You've frightened him!"

Furiously she gets out of bed and goes swiftly to the crib in the corner of the bedroom. She is already suckling Gilbert as she comes back to the bed.

Charles watches her in the bright moonlight streaming through the small window of the room.

He loves the sight of her like this, loves the way she cradles the baby to her and feeds him as if it were the most natural thing in the world.

As it is.

There is an almost primitive sense about it, this nurturing of an infant, oblivious of all else in the room, oblivious of Charles's eyes on her.

He feels as if he could lie here forever simply watching her.

Isabel never used to –

Isabel!

What is he doing, thinking of Isabel at such a time? *And in such a way*!

He shakes his head, closes his eyes tightly, tries closing his mind against it, but the image persists.

Isabel.

Isabel with an infant.

Robin Feradot Lacey.

A child's voice again in his head.

"My name is Robin Feradot Lacey."

Isabel, holding by the hand a small child whose name is Robin Feradot Lacey.

And Isabel, in his bedroom.

In his bed.

He is breathing fast.

The baby is sleeping now and Dominique, calm again, notices.

"What is the matter, Charles?"

"Nothing."

In the half-dark he can see her expression of alarm.

She knows that the nightmares still come, but less often now.

And never when he is awake.

"You are certain?"

"I am certain," he manages.

And he *is* certain.

Certain that he is losing his mind.

"Charles?" she whispers.

The child is back in his crib and she has crept quietly back into bed.

Charles moves a little to make room for her.

"You wanted me to promise you something," she says as she snuggles against him.

She is relaxed now, ready to forgive him those terrible words.

When I die.

He means, of course, when he is a very old man.

She realises that now.

He has survived the war. He will live to be a very old man.

He *must*, because she needs him. She and Gilbert need him.

"Charles?" she prompts. "What must I promise?"

Her voice comes to him through a long dark tunnel.

"Hmm?"

"What do you want me to promise?"

"Oh. Nothing," he says. "It doesn't matter."

Nothing matters, but that he is losing his mind.

Chapter Thirty-seven

"You're sure you want to do this?" Sarah asked as they sat in the car outside the house on the outskirts of the village of St Guillaume, thirty kilometres from Maillerain. "If Charles Feradot really *was* Charles Feradot Lacey, it changes everything."

Michelle nodded glumly. She was only too well aware of that.

They had already gone over it again and again since their meeting that morning with Laurent Feradot.

He had been in a great hurry – especially after helping with the tyre – and although intrigued to find that *they* had left the message, he didn't have time to do more than invite them to dinner that evening with himself and his father.

"Michelle, we're opening up a whole can of worms here."

"I know."

"All the stuff Hugh obviously wanted to keep hidden. You're sure you want to do this?" Sarah persisted.

Michelle sat brooding as she stared through the windscreen at the Feradots' house.

What if Laurent wanted information as badly as they did? Even if they left now, he had their address in Dublin. What if he somehow found out about Evelyn and . . .

Evelyn.

It all came back to Evelyn.

She had a right to know the truth, hadn't she?

"We have to talk to them," she said finally. "I don't know what other choice I have."

"There's always a choice," Sarah said briskly. "*Lots* of choices. We can drive away, and you can tell Evelyn you found the grave. Or that you found a grave, but you're not sure it's the right one. Or we can go in and talk to the Feradots and see what they say and then decide afterwards."

"What should we tell them?"

Sarah sighed. "What we decided. We tell them we're looking for the grave of someone our grandfather knew – a Charles Feradot Lacey."

"Or we tell them the truth."

"Right. And then what happens? They're on a plane before we are, claiming their inheritance from a confused old woman who doesn't even know they exist. And you live unhappily ever after in a house you hate."

Michelle was close to tears. "I wish I'd never bloody started this!"

She was exhausted from all of this, she was missing Katie so much it hurt – and her conversations with Rory were becoming more difficult each time she rang him.

The house was only a house, she realised. A wonderful, amazing house, and a house that maybe, *maybe* could be hers. The house of her dreams . . . but only a house, nevertheless.

And a house is only a house. A home is what you make with someone.

"What's up?" Sarah asked.

"Thinking," Michelle said.

"Well, I'd never have guessed!" Then she noticed the tears in Michelle's eyes. "What's wrong, Michelle?"

"Nothing," Michelle said, wiping her eyes. She gave a little laugh. "Well, everything, really. Rory, mainly."

"Not happy?" Sarah said, a question that was more of a statement. She'd caught the tail-end of a conversation Michelle was having just before they left the auberge. When Michelle said nothing about it, neither did Sarah.

"Hopping mad," Michelle said now. "He can't understand why I don't just grab a bit of earth from the grave – or any grave, he says he really doesn't care which – and get the next plane home."

"Well, to be honest –" Sarah began slowly.

"I know. Neither do you. But I can't betray Evelyn, you know that. I can't lie to her."

"You might have to."

"Why?" Michelle asked, startled.

"It depends on what we find out, doesn't it? If we find out it's Lacey's grave, either you lie to her, betray her – whatever you want to call it – or you tell her that her father lied and betrayed her. *And* her uncle did," she added as an afterthought.

Michelle sighed. "Brilliant." She shook her head as if to clear it. "Let's do it," she said after a moment.

"What, go in?"

"No, leave. You're right. It's all too complicated. We'll get a bit of earth from the grave and tell her it's Charles Feradot's and he could have been her father. That's all we have to say. She'll probably be too confused anyway to –"

"Oh, God," Sarah said.

"What?" Michelle asked, following her gaze towards the house.

"He's seen us. We can't just leave now, we'll have to go in."

It seemed they had no alternative. Laurent Feradot was already making his way down the path towards the gate, smiling warmly at them.

"So," he asked, as he reached the open window of the car, "you are not sure if this is a good idea, yes?"

"No," Sarah said quickly. "We were just – em – "

"Considering?" he suggested, still smiling at them.

"Considering," Sarah agreed, laughing. He really was gorgeous. Almost before she realised it she was getting out of the car, leaving Michelle no option but to follow her.

The house was cool and bright inside. The large windows looked out over a garden and the view was stunning. They stood for a moment taking it in.

"It is very charming, is it not?" Laurent said, his gaze following the slope of the garden to the stream at the far end, just beyond a grove of ancient-looking trees.

He's very charming himself, Michelle thought, watching Sarah's reaction to him.

Her thoughts were interrupted as a man appeared around the corner of the house, coming towards the open door. Laurent's father. A lean, compact man, older and slighter than Laurent but obviously related, with the same wavy, flowing hair and the same startling blue eyes.

Laurent, laughing, said something in rapid French as the older man brushed at his clothing.

With an apologetic smile and a shrug the man disappeared again into the garden.

"I have told him that he must change his clothing for our guests!" Laurent explained, laughing again as took a bottle of chilled white wine from a side-table and expertly opened it.

He stilled their protests with a wave of his hand.

"It is no matter. I prefer him to change his clothing because I do not wish wood-dust in the food! Now, you would like some white wine? Or some red, perhaps, or maybe something else?"

"White wine, please. For both of us," Michelle said with a quick, confirming look at Sarah.

"Your father works with wood?" asked Sarah as he handed her a glass.

"He works at the – how do you say? – the turning of the wood. It is his hobby, and now it is his business also. He makes beautiful pieces, but the dust, it is everywhere if he is not careful! Ah, Papa!" His father came through the far door, now looking far cleaner, but just as relaxed, in different clothes.

There was a flurry of introductions, in English and in French.

Jules Feradot was as charming as his son, and Michelle found herself looking at him intently. She was, she realised, trying to find some trace of a likeness to the half-remembered sepia photographs of Charles and Hugh Lacey. She thought there was something in the chin, the tilt of the head, the dark wavy hair – but she couldn't be sure.

She glanced towards Sarah, aware that they were both staring, and then Laurent said, "We eat!" and led them towards the kitchen at the back of the house. He gestured towards the long wooden table and chairs in the centre of it.

"You do not mind if we eat here?" he asked as they sat at the table, which was already set. "We have a *salle-a-manger*, a – what is it? Dining-room? But unfortunately it has been taken over by my father's work, which is everywhere." He turned to Jules and they laughed together as he translated.

The father and son clearly got on well together. Michelle wondered if anyone else lived there. It seemed not, since the table was only set for four and there was no sign of anyone else around.

Where's Laurent's mother? Or brothers and sisters, if he has any? she wondered. Well, she'd probably find that out soon enough. Among other things.

"Laurent says you work with wood, Monsieur Feradot?" Sarah asked in French as Laurent began bringing food to the table – a fresh, simple salad, some baguette, plates of pâte and *saucisson.*

"It is my hobby," he answered. "My preoccupation, if one is to believe Laurent."

"What kind of things do you do?" Sarah asked. "Furniture?"

"Some small pieces, yes. But mainly, now, I concentrate on my bowls and on – how should I put it? – objects which are beautiful for themselves. They are nothing, they are pieces of wood only, but they are beautiful. I will show you later, if you like."

"We'd like to see them," Sarah said, translating quickly for Michelle. "My sister's husband loves to work with wood."

"Oh? He is a carpenter? Or –"

"An information technology consultant," Sarah said, laughing. "He'd prefer to be a carpenter – or a wood-turner."

Jules smiled wryly. "There is more money to be made in information technology, I am sure."

"It depends," Sarah said. "The market's a bit strange at the moment."

Jules shrugged. "No matter," he said, passing the *charcuterie*, waiting as they helped themselves before speaking again. "I do not think you have come tonight to discuss the economic situation, am I correct?"

He smiled, raising an eyebrow.

"You're correct," Sarah said, translating rapidly for Michelle.

"We will continue in English," Laurent suggested, "and I will translate for my father. That will perhaps be easier for you, and Papa understands some English and may follow what we are saying. *D'accord, Papa?"*

Jules nodded his assent. *"D'accord."*

Sarah hesitated, uncertain where to begin, and Michelle took over, speaking slowly for Jules's benefit.

"We're trying to find a grave, the grave of a man named Charles Feradot Lacey," she said.

She saw the quick look that flashed between the men.

"Continue," Jules said in English, watching her carefully.

"We think – I wouldn't want to upset anyone," she said, trying to gauge their reaction, "but we think – we wondered might Charles Feradot and Charles Feradot Lacey be the same person."

Again a look passed between the Feradots.

"And why would you think so, Michelle?" Laurent asked softly.

"Because the name is nearly the same," Sarah said, seeing Michelle hesitate now. "And he was born in the same year, and we understand that Charles Lacey's brother, Hugh, used to get letters from Maillerain, perhaps even visited there – "

"His brother!" Jules interrupted with a startled expression. "*Son frère*?" he confirmed with a glance at his son.

"Oui, son frère." Turning to Michelle, Laurent switched back to English. "And why are you interested in this man's grave?"

"Because we think –" Michelle began, and Sarah saw her lick her lips quickly, the sign that always gave her away in a lie – "that he might have been a friend of our grand-uncle."

"And your grand-uncle is –" Laurent asked.

"Christopher Keogh," Michelle said, sending a silent prayer to him to forgive the use of his name. *So much for being honest,* she thought. But until she had the measure of these men she really wasn't sure how much to give away. "He was a soldier during the First World War."

"So . . . but surely he is not still alive?"

"No, he died during the war," Michelle said, then mentally kicked herself.

So much for a connection, she thought.

"So why do you think he might have been a friend of my great-grandfather?" Laurent persisted.

"They were in the same regiment," Michelle said. "Well, Charles Lacey was."

"Charles Lacey," Laurent said, seeming to mull over the name. "Charles Lacey," he repeated, looking towards his father. "And he was in what regiment, Charles Lacey?"

"The Royal Dublin Fusiliers," Sarah said.

"Dublin? He was Irish, Charles Lacey?"

"Yes," Michelle said.

"In the *Irish* Army? I have not heard that Ireland was –"

"The British Army," Sarah said. "Ireland was under British rule then."

"So he was British?" Laurent asked, raising his eyebrows.

"Yes," Sarah said, as Michelle said "No."

"It depends," Sarah said.

Laurent shrugged. "My great-grandfather was French. I do not see that he can have been the friend of your grand-uncle."

He intercepted a glance from Jules.

"Forgive me, I am forgetting my manners. I will bring the meat to the table."

He busied himself at the oven for a few minutes while Sarah made small talk with Jules and Michelle sat silent and disappointed.

"It is important to you to find this grave?" Laurent asked as he finished serving the main course.

"Yes," Michelle answered.

"And why?" Laurent asked.

"Because . . ." Michelle began, floundering.

"Because his name isn't on any of the lists showing men who were killed or missing in action, and my father is interested in compiling a complete list," Sarah said in a sudden burst of inspiration.

"And why would he wish to do this?" Laurent asked.

"Because Christopher Keogh was his uncle and fought in the War," Sarah said. "It's – kind of like a hobby."

Whoops, Michelle thought, seeing the look that passed between the men.

"Une marotte?" Jules asked softly.

Laurent nodded.

"War is not a hobby," Jules said, his voice sharper as he turned back to Michelle and Sarah. "In France we do not regard war as a hobby."

Could've fooled me, Michelle thought. Whatever about a hobby, it was a full-blown part of the tourist industry.

"Maybe hobby isn't exactly the word," Sarah hastened to explain. "But people in Ireland have been showing an interest in the war for the last few years now. They're beginning to realise that there was no shame in fighting –"

She broke off, seeing their expressions.

"Shame?" Jules asked. "War is a terrible thing, yes – but *shame*? Why should there be shame?"

"It's a bit complicated," Sarah said, looking to Michelle for help.

You're on your own, Michelle's glance told her, because the one thing Michelle was certain of was that it was more than a bit complicated.

"It's to do with politics," Sarah said finally.

Laurent gave a short laugh. "Isn't everything?"

"I suppose. But this was actually *very* complicated. Ireland was ruled by Britain, but there was no conscription. No Irishman had to go to war. But they went anyway, in their hundreds of thousands, for all kinds of reasons."

"Brave men," Laurent said, again with that look at Jules.

"And those who made it home when the war was over were hated by some people. As if they hadn't been through enough."

"And why was that?" Laurent asked, interested now, translating quickly for Jules and then leaning forward to hear Sarah's reply. "Why were they hated?"

"Things had changed in the meantime," Sarah said. "While they were away there was a rebellion at home against the British. The leaders were shot and by the time the soldiers came back from France everyone hated the sight of a British uniform. It wasn't a good time to be in the British Army."

"And how do you know this, Sarah?" Jules asked. "It is your hobby, also?"

"Well, no. But my father talks a lot about it."

That and nothing else, ever since we found Christy Keogh's name, Michelle thought.

"Fathers are like that, with their hobbies," Laurent said, with a smile that didn't quite reach his eyes. "Would you like to see *my* father's hobby, if you have finished eating?" he asked, with a glance at their almost-empty plates. "We can have coffee later, if you wish."

Almost without waiting for a response he began clearing the plates and then led them, with Jules, towards a large workshop at the back of the house.

Rory would give his eye-teeth for this! Michelle thought, taking in the lathe, the array of tools hanging on the wall, the various pieces of wood lying around.

She recognised oak, cherry, beech, knowing them from pieces Rory had made himself or had worked on with Matt.

He'd love it here. Or anywhere with room for a workshop like this.

And if we have to settle for the house in Glenberry he can forget it, because there'd never be enough space.

But in a garden the size of Evelyn's . . .

Sarah's voice interrupted Michelle's train of thought.

She was speaking to Laurent, watching intently as he ran his hands over the burl of the wood in a chestnut bowl.

Glancing at her, Michelle recognised Sarah's tone – and her expression.

She'd seen that expression often enough before, heard that tone of voice and knew just what they meant – and right now it was a complication Michelle didn't need.

She'd kill Sarah, absolutely *kill* her, if she fell for Laurent Feradot.

Chapter Thirty-eight

His hands move carefully over the walnut cradle, smoothing the wood.

He knows that it is a beautiful piece of work.

Dominique will be pleased.

This birth has been harder than the others.

He wants to please her.

He stands upright, stretches and looks out through the outhouse door. The boys are playing in the sunshine outside.

Gilbert, at four, is tall and confident, with Charles's own curly black hair.

Antoine, barely two, breaks into a stumbling run after one of the hens, laughing as he trips, still laughing as he struggles to get up and begin the game again.

A cheerful little boy, Antoine.

And now, this exquisite child, this infant daughter, just two weeks old.

Their happiness is complete.

Nothing can touch them now.

And then it happens.

Through the small window of the shed, as he turns back to his work, the field behind the house is framed for an instant.

A field full of poppies.

And out of nowhere, as clear as the field of poppies, there is a voice calling.

"Poppy! Poppy! Penelope!"

The child hesitates, looks back over her shoulder.

Isabel only uses her full name when she is very angry.

At three-and-a-bit the child already knows that.

She hesitates, halfway down the long garden, looking to Charles for guidance.

He smiles encouragement at her and she runs towards him and he lifts her up, swinging her around, both of them laughing now.

"Poppy, I told you to leave your father be – oh, really, *Charles!" Isabel, coming into view, looks crossly at him. "I wish you wouldn't do that! You asked me to keep the children away while you finished your work, and now, look at you!"*

He feigns apology.

"She's hard to resist," he says with a smile.

But smiles no longer work with Isabel.

"It's not fair, Charles. It's I who must discipline them while you do nothing but spoil them! You undermine me all the time. You have no sense of responsibility, Charles, none! It's time you learned to be a father to them instead of acting like a favourite uncle. Hugh cares more deeply for them than you do!"

He puts the child down and looks more closely at Isabel. She is a stranger to him.

A stranger who looks exhausted, worn and older than he knows her to be – but a stranger.

He knows she does not mean what she is saying. It is a well-worn refrain with her, but she knows it is not true. His children mean the world to him.

And to her, of course. If only they didn't exhaust her so much.

She brushes back some hair that has escaped its combs. Something in the gesture tugs at him and he feels a fleeting sympathy for her. Her pregnancy is clearly visible now in spite of the heavy clothing she wears.

He looks at her kindly, as one might look at a stranger.

"Try to get some rest, dear," he suggests. "Tell Lily to keep an eye on the children for you."

He smiles at her before returning his attention to the books on the garden table in front of him.

It is an act.

He cannot concentrate while he knows that she is still standing there looking at him with something close to hatred.

Charles clutches the workbench for support, has to sit down.

What was *that*?

He is breathing heavily, sweating though the day is not particularly warm.

Isabel.

Isabel and her children.

Their children.

God in Heaven . . .

Their children.

"Are you sure that you are well, *chéri*?" Dominique asks, again and again, as the weeks go by. "You do not look well. Should you not perhaps visit the doctor?"

Sometimes he answers.

Sometimes not.

When he answers it is to say only that he does not need a doctor.

Alarmed, she goes to see her friend Sophie Delavert who is living nearby.

They share a name but no blood relationship.

Like them, Sophie has moved from Maillerain to St Guillaume.

She is one of the few people Dominique trusts.

He has changed, Dominique confides.

He sits every day for a long time staring at nothing or watching the children with a strange expression on his face. Do you think he is ill?

And then, very quietly because she cannot bear the thought of it, *Or that he has tired of me*?

Sophie hastens to reassure her.

He cannot have tired of her, Sophie says. All the world knows how he looks at her, how much he cherishes her.

But it is true that he has changed.

More and more often now the memories come to him, sleeping and waking.

Isabel.

Their children.

Their five children.

Over and over again he recites their names and their ages in his mind.

Winifred Eleanor Lacey, six years.

Robin Feradot Lacey, five years.

Penelope Abigail Lacey, four years.

Evelyn Constance Lacey, three years.

Agatha Ursula Lacey, one year old.

One year old. Agatha Ursula Lacey, one year old.

Is that possible? he asks himself.

Is it possible that he left a wife and five young children behind when he went to fight?

He cannot believe it of himself.

Watching Gilbert and Antoine as they play, watching Dominique as she rocks the infant Amélie in the new cradle, he cannot believe it of anyone.

But he cannot pass a poppy-field without a deep wrenching in his gut, and in his heart.

Chapter Thirty-nine

Yolande Delavert was a bird-like little woman with a darting manner.

She had left a message at the auberge the previous evening and they had arranged to see her at her home.

Late sixties or so, maybe a bit older, Michelle judged as Yolande led them into a sunny little courtyard at the back of her house in the middle of Maillerain.

She beamed at them as she offered them tea. "It is so pleasant to have someone come to visit me. I have just returned from my daughter who lives near Paris now. I may move to be near her, she has suggested it and it may be a very good idea. What do you think?"

Without pausing for breath, and certainly without giving them the chance to reply, she darted into the house, still talking over her shoulder.

"We're getting tea?" Michelle asked.

Sarah grinned. "A photograph, I think."

"Of Dominique?" Michelle asked in sudden anticipation. They knew what Charles Lacey looked like. Could Yolande possibly have a photograph of –

Sarah was laughing now.

"Of her new granddaughter in Paris."

"Oh."

Yolande was back again, polishing the framed photograph on her apron, still beaming and talking non-stop as she passed it to them.

"Is she not beautiful?" she demanded. "Her name is Alysse. Is not that a very beautiful name?"

They began to reply but she was off again, returning the photograph to its place in the *salle de séjour*, fussing about with the tea and still talking nineteen to the dozen, occasionally darting back into the doorway to fix them with a bright look and ask questions they never got a chance to answer.

Sarah translated as rapidly as she could.

Who are we? – *Where are we from*? – *Do we have any children*? – *Do we like Maillerain*? – *Have we ever been here before*? – *Were we ever in Paris*?

"God," Michelle whispered. "We'll never get a word in!"

"Shhh!" Sarah said as Yolande came back into the courtyard, put the tea in front of them and said, laughing at herself, "You would think I had spoken to no-one for a year! You must forgive me, I am always like this when I return from Paris to my quiet little house!"

She was still smiling as she poured the tea and handed them the cups.

"And now, Sarah," she said with a more serious expression, "You must tell me what you and your sister wish to know of Dominique Delavert."

Michelle caught the name. "What's she saying?" she asked urgently. "Did she know Dominique and Charles?"

A quick exchange in French and then Sarah said "She knew them both. She was in her late thirties when Charles died. Dominique died a few years before him."

For some reason she didn't understand, this saddened Michelle. She had expected somehow, for no particular reason, that Dominique would outlive him.

"Why were they not buried together?" she began, but Sarah was already asking that question.

"Because Dominique was buried with their daughter Amélie who died as a child," Sarah explained. "And by the time Charles died the cemetery was closed – they had no more burials there."

"The Feradots must have found that very hard!" Michelle said. "Was Yolande related to them? To Dominique?"

"No. It was just coincidence that the name was the same," Sarah said, "but Dominique and Yolande's mother Sophie became good friends because of it. And Yolande and Sophie lived in St Guillaume for years – Yolande only moved back here after her mother died."

They sipped their tea, wondering how to proceed.

They could hardly ask outright if she had any reason to believe Charles Feradot was really an Irishman called Charles Lacey.

Could they?

Michelle thought for a moment. No vague story like last night's would satisfy this woman. She could tell that much, in spite of knowing no French, from the careful way Yolande was watching them.

"Tell her we've seen the Feradots," Michelle said. "See what happens. And Berthol," she added.

At the mention of his name Yolande's face darkened. She turned to Sarah quickly, eager for the translation.

"We had dinner with Jules and Laurent Feradot last night," Sarah said.

"*Ah, bon.*" Yolande's comment was noncommittal; she was waiting for something.

"We explained that we're trying to trace the grave of someone called Charles Feradot Lacey. We wondered if Charles Feradot might be the same person."

"And Jules said no," Yolande said.

Sarah nodded.

"So, that is that, no?"

"*I* think so," Sarah said.

"But there is a reason that you are here, with me," Yolande suggested. "You are not convinced, perhaps?"

"*I* am," Sarah said. "My sister isn't, though."

"And it matters to you, to know if they are the same? You are perhaps related to this other man?"

"No," Sarah said.

Yolande waited, the sharp eyes missing nothing in their expressions.

Sarah spoke quickly to Michelle. Then, in French,

"There is someone to whom it *does* matter. An old lady we know who's very ill."

Yolande spread out her hands, seeming to examine the backs of them intently.

"I am afraid I cannot help you," she said finally.

Sarah translated.

Michelle shrugged. "So where does that leave us? The only other thing we can do is see Berthol again, and I don't –"

"What does she say?" Yolande interrupted urgently. "Why does she speak of Berthol?"

"Because he offered us information," Sarah said. "For money."

Yolande made a dismissive sound. "Berthol! Berthol is an idiot! His grandfather would be ashamed –"

She stopped suddenly, like someone who has said too much.

"I am sorry that I cannot help," she said. "But it has been a pleasure meeting you. Now, how will you spend the rest of your time in France? Do you think –" and she was off again in her flurry of questions, talking all the time as she ushered them to the front door.

As they reached the pavement Michelle couldn't escape the sense that they had been very deftly handled.

"I think it's time to call quits, Michelle. That's what I think," Sarah said as they walked back to the car.

Michelle gave one quick glance back towards the house. There was no sign of Yolande and no way of knowing that she was already upstairs, searching in the deep recesses of her mother's old wardrobe to assure herself that something was still well-hidden there.

They walked back to the square in the late afternoon sun.

"Sure you won't come with us?" Sarah asked as they reached the car which they had left parked near the graveyard. She had arranged to meet Laurent for dinner.

"And cramp your style?" Michelle laughed. "Don't worry about me – I'll eat in the auberge."

"Better go, then," Sarah said, opening the car door.

"Just give me a minute," Michelle replied.

While Sarah waited, she went back into the cemetery one last time and scooped, with infinite care, a little of the soil from the grave of the man she was certain had been Charles Feradot Lacey.

Chapter Forty

Charles Feradot Lacey.

He can no longer deny it.

His name is Charles Feradot Lacey. His brother is Hugh Oliver Lacey . . .

And his wife's name, his *other* wife's name, is Isabel Beatrice Lacey.

He has no idea where she lives, but he could find her.

The British Army could find her, now that he knows who he is.

They could find her . . .

And tell her that her husband has been shot as a deserter?

His biggest threat is no longer Yves Berthol.

Yves made a promise and kept it.

"I will not forgive you," he had said on that long-ago day when Charles went to visit him.

"But neither will I betray you. For Dominique's sake I will not betray you."

Berthol has kept his word, Berthol who is now married with a family of his own.

Berthol is not a threat.

And neither are the neighbours in St Guillaume, who have accepted the Feradots into their community and who are wise enough to ask no questions unless about the weather, or the children, or the cost of the carpentry work for which Charles is well-regarded and which brings in just enough money to sustain his family.

No, the neighbours are not the biggest threat.

He himself, Charles Feradot Lacey, is the biggest threat to his family's peace of mind, and to their future.

What to do?

How to tell Dominique, whom he loves – how he loves her! – that there is a wife somewhere, and children, *his* children, of whom she knows nothing.

Waking and sleeping he recites their names . . .

Winifred . . . Robin . . . Poppy . . . Evie . . . Agatha.

Baby Agatha.

But no longer a baby. Seven years old now, she must be.

And Robin, Robin who was so angry he refused to say goodbye . . . Robin is eleven.

Eleven years old.

No longer the little boy who stood scowling as his father and his uncle left.

As Evie is no longer the little girl watching with infinite sadness from the bottom of the stairs.

"Charles. *Charles*!"

Dominique's voice, urgent.

He drags himself into wakefulness, into thinking in French.

It is becoming more and more difficult, these days, to think in French.

"Wake up, chéri. It is happening again, the nightmare."

She is wrong. It is not happening *again* –

It is happening still. It happens all the time, all the time.

It never stops, this nightmare.

And then . . .

The address, when it comes, comes suddenly.

He is delivering a carved rocking-chair to a house some ten kilometres away, a house where there is still great wealth.

A house with a piano, and a small boy playing that piano.

Through the open door of the *salle de séjour* Charles can hear the notes as they are picked out one by one, one by one, and as he leaves the house he is humming softly to himself . . .

Sur le pont
D'Avignon
On y danse,
On y danse . . .

And the image is there.

A small boy playing the piano.

A small boy whose name is Charles Feradot Lacey playing the piano, helped by his grandmother, Marie-Louise Feradot, in a house named for the part of France she was born in, Avignon.

Avignon.

The house is called Avignon, and it is in the village of Rathgar, in Dublin.

And he is Charles Feradot Lacey of Avignon, Rathgar, Dublin – and of the Royal Dublin Fusiliers.

For three long days he cannot decide what to do.

But he knows he has no choice, he must decide.

And then, finally, he knows exactly what it is he should do.

He kisses Dominique and holds her tightly to him, bids the children to be good for their mother and sets out for Maillerain and one of the very few men he trusts completely: his friend Jean-Paul Delavert, uncle of Sophie, who is schoolmaster there.

Chapter Forty-one

He wonders what Hugh looks like now.

Whether, indeed, he will come.

Nonsense. Why would he not come?

He will surely come.

If he is still alive, then he will come.

Four weeks have passed since Jean-Paul sent the letter for him.

Four weeks, and still no word.

It is hard to concentrate on anything, hard to lose himself as he usually does in the pleasure of crafting the wood, fashioning it into furniture, bowls, useful and necessary things, like the sabots he has just finished carving for Dominique.

Dominique.

How can he tell her?

What can he tell her?

She knows, of course, that all is not well with him, knows him better almost than he knows himself.

Better, certainly, than Isabel ever did.

Isabel.

He wonders if Hugh will tell her.

Probably not, since he will ask him not to.

The shock would be too great, as it has been for him.

And as it will be for Hugh.

If he is still alive.

No way of knowing, of course, other than to write.

He and Jean-Paul had discussed it all that long night.

If they write to the Army enquiring whether Hugh has survived the war, might not the Army, in turn, ask questions of an unknown Frenchman, Jean-Paul Delavert, living in an obscure French village nowhere near the site of any battle?

Can they be sure, in writing to the Army, that there will be no untoward consequences?

Or would it be safer to write to Hugh at the address in Rathgar and take the risk that he, like Charles, might not have returned from the war?

They decide that Jean-Paul will write to Hugh at the Rathgar address – Jean-Paul, of course, because his handwriting would not be recognised.

A brief letter, asking that Hugh tell no-one of its

contents and contact Jean-Paul to discuss a matter of importance to the Lacey family.

The Lacey family.

On his journey home Charles sees their faces.

Not Isabel and the children now, but his own parents, Richard and Margaret.

He wonders if they have forgiven him, remembers the bitter words exchanged before he left with Hugh.

They did not want him to go, did not understand why he would go.

Even his father, half-French, did not understand.

As he had never understood Charles.

Hugh they forgave.

Hugh, they saw, was going not because he wanted to, but because he felt he had to watch out for Charles.

Hugh, who always did what was right.

Who even now – assuming he has survived – will have taken over Charles's expected role in the family's business.

Assuming that it, also, has survived.

Assume nothing, Charles reminds himself.

He can assume nothing.

He has almost given up hope of a response when word comes from Jean-Paul.

Hugh Lacey is coming in person to Maillerain and expects to arrive in three days' time.

For two days Charles hardly speaks.

Nor does he sleep for two nights.

Dominique is distraught.

"You must tell me!" she begs. "You must tell me what is the matter! Never before have I seen you like this!"

He holds her, comforts her, but can tell her nothing other than that he will go to Maillerain on Thursday, and that he is not certain when he will return. Two days, perhaps three, he assures her, but no longer.

She wants to go with him.

Much as she hates Maillerain, she is frightened by Charles's distracted manner and does not want him to go alone.

Sophie will take care of the children, she pleads. There is nothing to stop her going with him.

But Charles, for once, is deaf to her.

"You are afraid?" Jean-Paul asks quietly as he opens the door to Charles.

Charles barely nods, doesn't speak.

Yes, he is afraid.

Of what, he cannot be sure. Only that he is very afraid.

The knock at the door startles them both.

They have been expecting it, waiting for it, and yet it startles them.

A moment later and Jean-Paul opens the door, ushers in the man who is clearly the brother of Charles, and quietly leaves the room.

Charles and Hugh stand facing each other, neither for the moment knowing what to say.

And then it is as if the floodgates open and these men who have gone through a war and a lifetime and have not cried, not since the age of four or five – they move to clasp each other, each saying his brother's name over and over again, while unashamed tears come spilling down their cheeks.

Chapter Forty-two

They were sitting in a nondescript little restaurant by the river some ten kilometres or so from St Guillaume. It was in the middle of nowhere but, to Sarah's surprise, it was full.

"The food is superb here," Laurent explained. "Even if the decor needs a little – what is the word? – updating."

Sarah was surprised. There weren't many men she knew who took much interest in decor.

And then she remembered the Feradot family home. The decor there had been amazing.

She wondered again whether Laurent and his father lived there alone.

"My remark is so interesting?" he asked, smiling. "You are lost in thought, Sarah."

She loved the way he said her name, loved his voice . . .

"Sorry," she laughed. "I do that sometimes."

"As we all do! Have you decided what you will have to eat?"

She glanced over and noticed the waiter hovering at a discreet distance.

With a quick look at the menu she chose duck. He signalled the waiter, who took the order and then topped up their glasses from the bottle of *Fleurie* that was already open on their table.

"Good job I'm not driving to Beauvais tonight!" she said, raising her glass.

"It is tomorrow that you return?" he asked.

"Yes. Unfortunately."

"Why *unfortunately*?"

"Because I like it here and I wouldn't mind staying a few more days. Instead I'll be back at work and up to my eyes the day after tomorrow."

"What is it that you work at?"

"Graphic design," she said. "I run my own small company – well, with my partner, Lainey – so it's interesting, but we're always really busy. I was lucky to get the time off."

He began asking questions, surprisingly knowledgeable, about her work. Almost before she realised it they had finished their main courses and were being offered the menu again.

"Your turn," she said when they had helped themselves from the cheeseboard. "Do you work with your father, or – ?"

He laughed. "No, I do not work with my father. I love him very much, my father, but if I worked with him we would not agree. It is enough that I am living with him at present. But to work with him – *pfft!*" He spread his hands as he made an explosive sound, an amused expression on his face.

"You're living there?" she asked.

"For the moment. I have sold my apartment and have not yet found the house I am looking for."

"Like Michelle," she said. "It's a tricky time."

"Oh? Michelle has sold an apartment?"

"A little house. Was your apartment near here?" She changed the subject swiftly. "Will you still be close enough to your work?"

"That is not a problem. Like you, I work for myself. I am an architect."

"I nearly did architecture," she said. "Right up until my last year in school that's what I wanted to do."

"Oh? And you changed your mind because – ?"

Because of David.

She laughed, was about to shrug it off and then thought, *What the hell, I'll never see this man again.*

"I had a boyfriend. I wanted to go to the college he was going to, do the same course he was doing. So I put that down as my preference instead of architecture, and was offered a place. Stupid of me."

"You regret it?" he asked gently.

"Not the course, no. I love what I'm doing."

"So why do you say stupid?"

"Because it *was* stupid, to change what I'd wanted all my life just to be with him. The relationship was over six months after we started college."

"Maybe that is what you wanted most at that time. To be with him."

"Well, yes. But I still shouldn't have given up my whole life –"

"But did you do that? Or did you simply choose a different life?"

"What do you mean?"

"That if you had truly wanted your other life, your other choices, then surely you would not have let him persuade you –"

"He didn't. I persuaded myself, because I wanted to be with him."

"Then it was right for you, to be with him. If we love someone enough then we will give up our world, because they *become* our world."

"Have you ever loved anyone that much?" she asked, intrigued.

He laughed softly. "Alas, no. I have thought that I did, perhaps, but –" he shrugged. "No."

"Then how can you say that?"

"That we will give up our world?"

She nodded.

"Because I have seen it. And because I have heard of it."

She waited.

"My father had such a love for my mother," he said.

"It was for her that he gave up his plan to live in Paris, because she loved it here."

"And is she –" she began softly.

"She is dead," he said quietly, meeting her eyes. "She died two years ago, we are becoming used to it now. Almost."

"And will your father stay here? Or might he –?"

"Go to Paris?" he finished. "No, not now. He will not live there now. He believed always that what matters most is not where you are living, but with whom you are living. His grandfather told him –"

He broke off, quickly reaching for the wine bottle to replenish their glasses.

"Told him what?"

He laughed, not quite looking at her. "It does not matter. I talk too much if I drink wine when I am tired. I should have learned that by now."

An excuse, she knew. His glass was still half full, which meant he had drunk barely a glass and a half in all.

"Could I ask you something?"

He shrugged. "Why not?"

"Michelle thought . . ." having started, she wasn't sure how to continue.

He sat with one hand supporting his chin, smiling slightly at her as he waited.

"What is it that she thought?" he prompted after a moment.

"That you are not telling us the whole truth," she said finally.

"Ah . . ." The smile was gone now, his expression serious again. "And you, Sarah?" he asked quietly. "What do you think?"

"That it's none of our business and that I shouldn't have said it. Sorry," she said, meaning it. "Let's talk about something else." It was a lovely evening, he was a lovely man and she was mentally kicking herself for spoiling the mood.

"You are sure?" he asked.

"Yes."

He sat looking steadily at her until she began to feel slightly uncomfortable.

"And if Michelle was correct?" he asked finally. "What then?"

"Then . . ." *I wouldn't want to know,* she thought. *It would complicate everything. Far better to just –*

"Then . . .?" he prompted.

"It would change nothing," she said quickly.

"Even if I have lied to you?" he asked quietly.

"And did you?" she asked, almost in spite of herself.

"No. Not exactly. But Michelle is right in saying that I have not told the full truth."

"And – if you didn't, why are you saying this now?"

He shrugged. "I do not know. I only know that you are someone I do not wish to lie to."

"Then maybe we should just change the subject," she suggested.

He shrugged slightly, looking thoughtful. "Would you like some coffee? Or a *digestif*, perhaps?"

She hesitated. She couldn't manage another mouthful.

On the other hand, she was in no rush to end the evening.

"You are not sure?" he asked, watching her, amused.

She smiled. "I'll just finish the wine. Coffee would keep me awake all night."

He smiled broadly now, raising his eyebrows. "And that would be a bad thing?"

She was lifting the glass to her lips and paused, startled.

"I have offended you," he said quickly. "I am sorry, Sarah. I did not mean –"

Oh yes, you did! she thought. He *had* meant to flirt with her. He was interested in her.

She felt like singing.

"You didn't offend me," she said, smiling warmly at him.

"I would not wish to," he said quietly, his expression serious.

"Are you having coffee?" she asked, lightening the mood.

"I don't want coffee," he said, "but I do want the excuse to spend some more time with you. I wish you did not have to go back home tomorrow."

"Me, too," she said regretfully.

"So, no coffee," he said, smiling again as he signalled the waiter and passed over his credit card. "Do you wish to go home early, in preparation for tomorrow? Or would you perhaps like to go for a walk?

It is a beautiful night." He indicated the nearby window.

While they had been eating and talking the moon had come up, casting a silvery light over the river and the little bridge leading to a small island in the centre of it.

"It really is a beautiful night," he repeated and, glancing at the sleeveless dress she was wearing, added, "You will be warm enough, I promise." He turned as the waiter placed the bill on the table. "Ah. *Voilà– merci !*" He signed it with a flourish and stood up.

"Here, take my jacket," he said, as they left the restaurant.

The night was warm, she didn't really need it. But he urged her again and she took it, loving the feel of it against her bare arms and the slight scent of him that lingered on it.

There were several other people walking along the pathway by the river, making the most of the warm, starry night.

"It has been a good holiday for you?" he asked.

"Oh, yes," she said.

"But unusual?" he added. "No beaches, no sightseeing?"

She laughed. "No. That's what I planned to do, in Greece. But Michelle needed –"

She caught herself and he waited to see if she'd continue.

"She needed you to come here?" he prompted gently.

"Yes. To translate."

"Sarah –" They had reached the little bridge leading

to the island and he stopped, leaning on the parapet with one hand.

"Yes?" she said, puzzled by the intensity of the look he was giving her.

"You are very lovely, Sarah. I am sorry that you are going home tomorrow, because I would like very much to see you again. But –"

He hesitated and she waited, heart thumping.

"There is something I must tell you, Sarah. You have said that it will change nothing, and I cannot lie to you anyway."

As he was speaking he had moved towards her, his right hand going to her face, caressing her cheek, brushing back her hair.

"You really are *very* lovely, do you know that, Sarah?" he said quietly, the last few words spoken in a whisper as he moved closer, bringing his lips to hers.

Later, hours later it seemed, as they reluctantly stopped for breath, still holding tightly to each other, she whispered, "What were you going to tell me?"

"Hmm?" he asked, still nuzzling her cheek, her ear, the back of her neck.

"You were saying . . ."

"Oh, yes," he said, as if from a long way off. "That I have something to tell you. That we believe, my father and I, that my great-grandfather and the man whom you and Michelle seek, Charles Feradot Lacey, are one and the same."

Chapter Forty-three

"And doesn't that put the cat rightly among the pigeons!"

"Maurice!" Una said warningly.

"I was only saying –"

"Well, don't," she said in a quiet, steely voice.

"But –"

"Well, *I* think Dad's right!" Helen said loudly. "One way or the other it will end badly."

"That's rubbish, Helen!" Sarah flared up. "You don't know what you're –"

Michelle wanted nothing more than to get up and leave. So much for the 'homecoming' celebration Una had planned.

* * *

And it *should* have been a celebration. Rory was jubilant to say the least, delighted with her for having found the right grave, delighted anyway that she was back home. And Katie hadn't let go of her since they met at the airport a few hours earlier.

"Never go away again, Mammy," she'd pleaded.

"Not for a while, anyway," Michelle had promised. "I was only gone five days, you know."

"Five days is *very* long, Mammy."

Michelle had shot a look at Rory over Katie's head. The little girl was right. Five days had felt like a lifetime, not helped by the fact that she and Rory weren't on good terms when she left.

At least that seemed to be resolved now.

"Miss me?" he'd asked quietly as he kissed her.

"Every minute. But it was worth it," she'd added, smiling at him. "Is Evelyn really better?"

"Back home and all!" Rory had said. "She'll be hobbling on the ankle for a while, but she'll manage."

"But she was confused as well."

"The shock of the fall, the doctor said. And the knock on her head didn't help. But she's fine. She'll need to take it easy, but she's back to herself."

"Rory, what if –"

"Shhh," he'd said, kissing her again. "Try not to worry."

* * *

He was smiling at her now across the dinner table as Maurice tried to get to grips with what they were telling him.

"But what I don't understand is –" he was saying, ignoring the look he got from Una. He glared around the table as if they were hiding something from him. "What I don't understand is any of it!" he lamented, looking so mournful that they all burst out laughing with the exception of Helen, who tutted at no-one in particular and raised her eyes to heaven.

He tried again. "So would you mind explaining, once you all stop laughing at nothing at all, why you can't just give her the bit of earth and pretend nothing? You got her what she wanted. I thought you were mad to be going off on your wild-goose chase, but you did it and all credit to you for doing it, so why can't you just say nothing and –"

"Because, Dad, it wouldn't be fair," Michelle explained patiently for what seemed like the third or fourth time. "We think she has a right to know."

"To know what? That her father ran out on her, you mean? And what'll that do to her, d'you think, at her age? Tell me that!"

"We still have to tell her," Michelle said.

"And did you tell them, these French lads?"

"No," Michelle admitted with a glance at Sarah. It had been a bone of contention between them. Sarah had wanted to tell Jules and Laurent the truth there and then, while Michelle felt that Evelyn should know first.

"And why didn't you, if it's that important?" Maurice persisted.

"Because she's hoping Evelyn won't want anything

to do with them," Helen said. "At least that way she has *some* chance of getting the house."

Michelle, Rory and Sarah rounded on her at once in loud protest.

"Will you all be quiet," Maurice said, roaring. "I forgot how peaceful this house was with the two of you gone!"

"Maurice!" Una said sharply.

"Well, isn't it true?" he protested.

"And if it is, do you need to upset everyone by saying it?" Una reminded him.

They missed the smirk Helen cast in Michelle's direction. "Of course, if all else fails, you could always buy Jan's house," she said. "She told me she's willing to give you first refusal."

"She *what*!" Michelle said.

"She's selling up. She'll make a tidy profit, of course, prices being what they are now, but she's said she'll do what she can for you, Michelle," she said sweetly.

Michelle and Rory glared at Helen, speechless, as Sarah launched an attack.

"The cow! And you're worse, Helen, to have anything to do with her! I thought you had more sense, but I obviously got it wrong. You're well suited!"

"Sarah –" Una warned.

"Mam, it's true! She should have nothing to do with that –" She bit back the word, turning again to Helen. "Why is she selling, anyway? I hope she hates the place and hates every minute she spends there. *And* I hope she never gets a buyer."

"She'll have to," Helen said, glumly now. "Herself and Damian have split up."

"Good enough for them!" Sarah snapped.

"Oh, an unhappy house!" Maurice said. "Weren't you well out of that, now! Who knows but that yourself and Rory –"

"Don't, Dad!" Michelle said.

"But I was only saying –" Maurice began. "Tell me about these French fellas anyway," he said, quickly changing the subject as he was met by glares from all around the table. "How do you know they won't come after Evelyn's house themselves when they find out about it?"

"They're not like that," Sarah said.

"Now, *that's* ridiculous!" Helen mocked. "*Everyone's* like that where money and property are concerned."

"They aren't," Sarah persisted.

"How can you be sure of that?" Helen asked, echoing what Michelle felt herself. "Anyway, I think they'd be mad not to – and you'd be mad to even think of telling them! But it's up to yourselves, I suppose," she finished in a disparaging tone.

"Actually, it's up to Evelyn," Rory said, looking at her levelly.

Helen shrugged, knowing from experience that it was better not to get into an argument with him.

Michelle felt as warm as if he were holding her. It was great to be back in tune with each other again, or at least getting there. She couldn't believe how much she'd missed him, couldn't believe how lovely it was just to be back with him again.

"That's right," she agreed as they all looked in her direction. "It's up to Evelyn. And first thing tomorrow I'll go and see her."

Chapter Forty-four

Evelyn looked fragile, much more frail than Michelle had expected.

Her bandaged ankle was resting on a footstool and she looked exhausted, but her voice, when she spoke, had something of her usual air of authority and she had no difficulty at all in recognising Michelle.

"I *will* call if I need you, Annie. I promise," she said as the housekeeper hovered and then reluctantly left the room.

"She's making rather a fuss," she said to Michelle in a confidential tone when Annie had gone, leaving the door slightly ajar. "They all are, since my little mishap. You'd imagine no-one had ever had a fall before."

"She probably got a fright," Michelle suggested.

"No doubt she did." She gave a little laugh. "As I did myself. I was in hospital for two weeks, you know!"

"I know. Actually, I went to visit you, but . . ."

"And I don't remember. I *do* know you came, my dear, because your mother told me. A lovely woman, your mother. But I don't remember your coming. Isn't that dreadful?"

"You seem better now. Much better than when I saw you last."

Evelyn chuckled. "By which you mean, I recognise you. I'm told I had trouble recognising anyone at all and talked a great deal of rubbish! But gradually it all came back to me, very clearly in the finish, I'm happy to say. Though I confess that it's left me shaken, and more anxious than ever to move to the nursing home with my sister Agatha. And poor Annie, although she's naturally concerned for her own future, thinks she'll never get me there fast enough!"

She sat watching Michelle for a moment.

"I'm glad you've come to see me, my dear. I was going to contact you anyway, to tell you that I'm ready to sell my house."

Michelle's heart leapt into her mouth.

"We agreed that you could name your price, so that's what I would like you to do."

Michelle looked at Evelyn, desperately trying to gauge how much to tell her, how much she was well enough to hear.

She took a breath, but Evelyn was already speaking.

"I realise now how impossible a task I set you, and that you will have tried your very best." Evelyn said brightly. "So the house is yours, my dear," she said, smiling. "In spite of –"

Michelle took another breath, deeper this time.

"Evelyn," she began, almost in a whisper. "There's something I must tell you . . ."

* * *

Evelyn sat staring into space for a long time after Michelle had finished.

"Extraordinary," she said, just as Michelle was beginning to regret having told her. "Quite extraordinary. And upsetting, of course. That must have been what the last letter said. Not that my father's grave had been found, but that he had just died. Imagine that. For most of my life, he was alive."

"I wasn't sure . . ."

"Whether you should tell me?"

Michelle nodded.

"I have always preferred the truth, my dear. No matter how difficult. I would have wanted to know – even if it means learning that my father was not quite the man I believed him to be. "

"Are you angry?" Michelle asked quietly.

"Angry?" Evelyn said, as if it had never occurred to her. "I was angry, very angry, as a little girl. He had left us promising to return, and he didn't, so I was angry then, and sad. But now? I don't know. It was a very, very long time ago."

She lapsed into her own thoughts again and

Michelle glanced around the room. It was just as she remembered it: the elegant fireplace, the grand piano, the beautiful, tall, sash windows. It was all she could do to stop the tears. She had come so close, so very close, to it being hers . . .

"What are they like, these Feradots?" Evelyn asked. "Do you have an opinion of them?"

"I liked them," Michelle said honestly.

"And what do they look like?" Evelyn asked. It seemed to Michelle that she was holding her breath.

"Dark wavy hair. Well, Laurent has. Jules is almost grey. And deep blue eyes, both of them."

Evelyn nodded. Her father's colouring.

"And do they look like –?"

"Your father? I think so, but maybe I'm looking for a resemblance. You know the way that happens . . ."

"But you feel that they are related – that they are Laceys?"

"Yes," Michelle said. *Wish I didn't, but I do.* "Hugh visited him for years. Not in Charles's own house, in a friend's, but it was definitely Hugh."

"And when you told them, what did they say?"

"We didn't tell them," Michelle said quickly. "Sarah wanted to, but I felt you should know first."

Another pause, then "I'd like to meet them." The sparkle was back in her eyes. "Do you think they might come to see me?"

"I think so," Michelle said. "Laurent is planning to come to Dublin anyway." *Probably on his way already*, she thought, remembering the look he and Sarah had shared as they said goodbye.

"Will it be a shock to them, do you think? That my father already had a family?"

"They've already guessed," Michelle said. "The older people in Maillerain always knew he had been a British soldier during the Great War and found it a bit strange that he had never wanted to go home, even for a visit. At first they thought it was to do with the Army, because he shouldn't really have been there. But as time went on they thought there must be more to it than that."

"They never asked him?"

"They were protective of him. Laurent says he was *honourable* – that's how Jules and everyone in the village remembered him. So if there was something he wanted to keep a secret, they were happy to go along with that."

"As Hugh went along with it," Evelyn said. "But I doubt very much that he was happy about it."

"He never said anything?"

"He wouldn't. Not Hugh. He kept my father's secret to the grave, though it must have broken his heart."

She paused to move her leg slightly on the footstool.

"They were in love, you see. My mother and Hugh. That much was obvious to everyone. Of course, they wouldn't have done anything about it, not in those days. Not while my father was alive. When he was missing for five years or so there was talk of marriage, my brother Robin remembered. But then Hugh went to France, and that was the end of it." She sighed deeply. "That must have been when he found Father again. With Dominique, I presume."

"And do you think your mother knew?" Michelle asked, suddenly feeling sorry for the woman.

"Almost certainly not. Hugh would never have told her, because it would have broken her heart and he loved her too much to do that."

"He couldn't just have married her? If everyone else thought your father was dead?"

Evelyn fixed her with a look that held all her old air of authority. "Absolutely not. Not when he knew otherwise. It would have gone against everything he believed in."

Michelle moved slightly in the chair to find a more comfortable position.

Evelyn noticed. "Forgive me, my dear. I haven't even offered you tea and I'm sure you're getting quite tired listening to the ramblings of an old woman. But could I ask you to do one more thing for me?"

Michelle's heart sank. Evelyn saw her expression and laughed.

"It's not too difficult. I promise! I thought perhaps, if you would be good enough to help me into the garden, we could do something with this."

She indicated the little container of soil that now rested on the coffee table in front of them.

"I could ask Annie, but she'd have a fit. And,

anyway, it seems appropriate that you should be the one to help me do it." She glanced towards the door. "If we move quickly, we might manage to avoid her," she said conspiratorially.

Michelle laughed. There wasn't a hope of them moving quickly. But they moved as well as they could and eventually, in spite of Annie flapping like a mother hen, they reached the seat under the cherry tree at the end of the garden.

The tree itself was well past its springtime glory, but everywhere else the garden looked wonderful – lush foliage, all kinds of flowers and plants and trees Michelle didn't know the names of but loved the look of.

Katie would have loved it here, she thought sadly. *We'll just have to do the best we can in Glenberry . . . Rory will put up a swing and –*

"What do you think, my dear?" Evelyn was asking as she lifted the little pot of soil. "Do I scatter it, or bury it?"

"I'm not sure," Michelle said. "I'll get a little shovel, if you –"

"No, don't bother," Evelyn said suddenly. "I'll just scatter it because, you know, it hardly seems to matter now. I imagined this would be an ending of sorts and, really, it's more of a beginning, isn't it?"

She stood shakily, with Michelle's help, and gathered the soil into the palm of her hand. Then moving slowly she scattered it all around the base of the cherry tree.

When she looked at Michelle again her eyes were shining. "Do you really think they'll come?" she asked. "These other Laceys?"

Michelle nodded. "I think so."

They made their way slowly back up the garden in the bright afternoon sunshine, chatting as they went, and, much as Michelle had wanted the house, she felt it was worth the loss of it to see the happiness that lit up Evelyn's face.

Chapter Forty-five

"Charles?"

He moves quickly to her bedside. "*Chérie*?"

"I am frightened, Charles."

He reaches for her hand, stroking it gently.

He, too, is frightened.

They have overcome everything else together.

They cannot overcome this.

"Charles?"

"*Chérie*?" he repeats, still rubbing the back of her hand.

"Do you have any regrets?"

"None," he says, without hesitation.

"None at all?" she asks, her voice almost a whisper now.

He thinks in a flash of that other family, grown to adulthood now.

Of Hugh, loyal even now, in spite of his abiding belief that Charles should have returned to his family. And Isabel, poor Isabel whom he had never truly loved.

Of his sons Antoine, killed in the next war, and Gilbert who survived but was never well afterwards.

Of his beloved Amélie, barely two when she died.

And of Dominique, his rock, his other self, through all the times of heartache and of joy.

Her voice has barely trailed away when he answers her.

"None at all," he says, smiling at her.

Her eyes flicker, a smile touches her lips and he kisses her one last time.

He struggles to hold back the tears. There will be time, plenty of time, later for tears.

For now it is enough to hold her, stroking her grey hair, telling her again and again how much he has always loved her.

Chapter Forty-six

"Rory?" she said softly, not sure if he was awake.

"Mmm?" He turned lazily, smiling as he reached for her, remembering their lovemaking of last night.

She nestled against him. "This was a good idea."

He laughed quietly, beginning to caress her again. "A great idea, I think!"

She smiled as she kissed his cheek. "That too. But I meant coming away for the night. I couldn't have stood meeting them at the airport."

"I thought you liked them."

"I do. I just wish –" she sighed.

"Shhh! We promised, remember? No meeting trouble halfway."

"Like we have a choice!"

"We do. We'll get through it, Michelle. Whatever happens. I learned something while you were away."

"Mmm?"

He kissed the top of her head. "How much I love you."

"You didn't know?" she said, half-teasing.

"Oh, I knew." His expression changed, serious now. "Sometimes it's easy to forget, that's all, in the middle of everything."

"Should I remind you?" she asked, smiling as she trailed the tip of her finger along his early-morning stubble.

* * *

They were dozing in each other's arms when the alarm went off.

"No!" he groaned, turning to pull the pillow over his head. "It's Sunday, for God's sake!"

She laughed. "Which is why we have to get up and go back for Katie, so my parents can get to Mass."

"Just five minutes more," he pleaded, flicking on the radio, and immediately the hotel bedroom filled with the rich huskiness that was unmistakeably Marlene Dietrich.

"'Lili Marlene'," Michelle murmured as they lay in each other's arms, listening as the mesmerising, insistent rhythm of the song drew to a close. "It was written by a German soldier during the First World War."

"So now you're an expert?" he asked, laughing softly. "Anyway, I thought it was –"

"Shhh!" she said, turning the radio up slightly to hear the presenter who was saying "– *and it became an anthem for both the Germans and the Americans in the Second World War.*"

"Strange, isn't it, when you think about it?" she said after a few minutes. They had switched the radio off but were finding it hard to leave the intimacy of the bed.

"What?" he asked, tracing a finger down along her arm.

"All those soldiers on different sides, all ready to kill each other and all singing the same song. What was that all about? I wonder how many of them were even sure why they were fighting?"

"Who's ever really sure of anything? War or no war, you just get on with whatever life throws at you and do the best you can."

"I suppose," she said.

"What else is there? In the end it all comes down to love, and luck, and getting on with things."

"Rory –"

He saw in her eyes what she was about to ask.

"I know," he said softly. "I did a lot of thinking while you were away and you're right, we should take the chance, even if it means – " his voice caught and he took a deep breath and went on. "I want to try again, Chelle. If you still want another baby, so do I."

Chapter Forty-seven

She would meet them standing in her drawing-room.

It was important to her that she stand, even if she needed the support of two canes rather than her usual one.

Something to do, she thought, with meeting them on her own terms. And with showing respect to them and to her father's memory.

She was nervous, of course. But also – a sensation unfamiliar for many years – excited.

She was looking forward more than she would have believed to meeting these unknown men who were related to her.

Not strangers.

Somehow she felt that they would not be strangers to her.

A tap at the door and Annie's flustered face appeared.

"They're here!"

Her heart missed a beat. It was time.

Steady! Steady! she told herself silently as she rose slowly to her feet, hearing their quiet voices in the hallway.

At a nod from Evelyn, Annie disappeared back into the hall, returning with them a moment later.

Evelyn wanted to stand looking at them all day, these unknown men who were strangely, utterly familiar to her. She wanted to reach out and touch them, these men with hair so like her father's, the same firm chins, the mouths that were his mouth curving in broad smiles that reached the depths of heart-stopping blue eyes.

She could not trust herself to speak.

Instead she nodded to Annie, a signal to bring tea.

And then, finally, she was able to return their smiles, take their hands and hold back the tears as they kissed her once, twice on the cheeks.

"You are very, very welcome," she managed as she struggled to keep her voice from shaking.

* * *

The last of the evening sun flickered in the room, picking out family photographs and glancing off her father's cap badge which Jules held in his hand, the badge Yolande's mother had kept carefully hidden on her uncle's instructions.

They had talked the afternoon away.

Once over their initial caution they had rushed to put together the jigsaw, eventually seeing a picture that was almost complete and strangely satisfying.

"I'm glad she loved him," Evelyn said finally.

"You do not mind?" Laurent asked, adding softly, "It should have been your mother."

"It should, but it wasn't. It was Hugh she really loved all along. Robin saw that, though I couldn't. So I'm glad my father found someone who could love him. And I'm glad, after all these years, that you have come."

'Glad' was far too small a word. It was, she felt, as if something of her father had returned, finally, in the form of Jules and Laurent.

Her heart filled as she watched them sitting there, relaxed and at ease in the armchairs that had been her father's favourites, and Hugh's.

No, more than relaxed, she corrected herself.

Jules and Laurent Feradot looked completely and utterly at home.

Chapter Forty-eight

Michelle hesitated outside the house.

A really bad idea, she thought. *Why did Evelyn have to do it this way, telling them in front of everyone? As if it wasn't bad enough losing Avignon, without the whole family there to see it happen . . .*

For a moment she considered not going in, but Maurice was already leading the way, talking loudly and shepherding them all along. He couldn't wait to get inside the door. It seemed to him that they'd talked about nothing else for months and he couldn't wait to see the place.

She felt Rory's hand slip into hers and squeeze tightly. Warmth spread though her.

"Nervous?" he asked softly.

"A bit. Sad, mainly. And I wish Helen wasn't coming."

His eyes flashed agreement. "I still don't see why she has to."

"You think she'd miss it?" Helen had made no secret of her belief that Michelle and Sarah would be at each other's throats before the night was out. And if they didn't do it themselves, she'd probably do what she could to help things along.

"What's keeping Helen?" Maurice asked, as if on cue. "She said she'd be here on the dot."

"Maybe she changed her mind," Sarah said acidly, knowing there was no chance.

She was right. Helen and Graham arrived just as Annie was opening the door to Maurice's knock.

As Annie ushered them into the drawing-room Rory lingered for a moment in the hall, taking in the high ceiling, the ornately carved wood of the banisters, the fine detail of the plasterwork.

Michelle, turning, met his eyes. She knew what he was thinking, because they had talked about it long into the night. Charles Lacey had left this wonderful house and had been happy anyway, because he was with the woman he loved. And they would be happy too, no matter where they ended up. Glenberry would be fine and they'd do what they could to make it a home.

A house, no matter how amazing, was still only a house. A home was what they'd make together, for themselves and Katie.

They had talked about it and they believed it. One way or the other it would be all right, because together they'd *make* it all right.

But, just for a moment, as their eyes met, they let

themselves think of how it might have been if *Avignon* was theirs.

* * *

The faded old dining-room was coming to life under the warm glow of flickering candles and animated conversation.

"This is how it should be!" Evelyn said, smiling around the table. "It's far, far too long since this room saw a dinner party."

"Well, here's to many more!" Maurice said.

He was in his element, having just finished telling them all about Christy Keogh and the great coincidence it was and how he and Charles Lacey must surely have known each other.

The whole evening had been an unexpected success, with Laurent translating willingly though it was clear to everyone that he and Sarah would much rather be on their own tonight, as they had been every other night since his arrival.

"Isn't it a pity, all the same, the way it happened," Maurice said, relaxed by the wine and forgetting Una's strict instructions to think twice before opening his mouth, and then think again. "I mean, wouldn't it have been better in a way if Michelle never met Jules and Laurent at all because –"

He stopped abruptly as he saw Sarah's expression.

"All I mean is it's a shame that –"

"Rory, why don't you tell Jules about the cabinet

you're working on?" Una said brightly. "Your father's interested in woodwork, isn't he, Laurent?"

"I know exactly what you mean, Daddy," Helen said in a honeyed, conspiratorial tone that cut right through Una's attempt to change the subject. "It's a lovely house and it's a shame Michelle won't be getting it after all her hard work."

She was sweetness itself as she beamed round the table. Una and Sarah looked livid, Rory and Maurice miserable, while Michelle was concentrated on keeping her jaw tight to hold back the angry words . . .

And Evelyn and the Feradots looked puzzled.

"Whatever do you mean, my dear?" Evelyn asked quietly.

"Just that Graham and I feel so sorry for poor Michelle. She's set her heart on this house and she'll never be satisfied anywhere else now. It's a shame, like Daddy says. Though of course we're delighted for you that you found your relatives."

"I'm afraid I still don't quite understand," Evelyn said.

"That it's a shame that Michelle won't be getting your house after all," Helen said patiently, her eyes bright as she glanced at Michelle to see how she was taking it. "But she's put a deposit on a new one, so you needn't worry."

Laurent was translating quietly for Jules as Evelyn turned towards Michelle.

"You've changed your mind, my dear?" She still looked puzzled.

It took Michelle a moment to answer. "No," she said softly. She didn't dare look at Rory, didn't dare let herself feel the beginnings of hope.

Evelyn glanced back at Helen. "So why –" She turned sharply back to Michelle. "You think I've changed mine?"

Michelle nodded, holding her breath.

"We had an agreement, my dear!" Evelyn said crisply. "Nothing changes that, unless you choose to."

"But Michelle wouldn't think of holding you to it –" Helen began, a bit less sweetly now.

"And I wouldn't dream of reneging on it!" Evelyn said, holding Helen's gaze. "Is that what you thought, my dears?" she asked in a softer tone, looking from Michelle to Rory.

"Well, yes," Michelle said, glancing at Rory. "Everything's different now."

"Because of us?" Laurent asked softly. "But no. This changes nothing, that we have found Evelyn at last. My father and I are aware of her arrangement and we are delighted for you."

"But that's ridiculous!" Helen burst in. "It's worth a fortune!" Graham, sitting beside her, looked as if there was a vile smell in the room.

"It's worth whatever Michelle and Rory are willing to pay for it," Evelyn said, smiling at them. "That was our agreement and I fully intend to honour it."

"And isn't that very decent of you!" Maurice said energetically. "It must be worth at least a million and a half. More, probably, the way things are going. Though it needs a lot of work and you have to admit the carpets have seen better days and the windows are fit to be –"

"Maurice!" Una said, but she was smiling. She could do nothing else, looking at Michelle and Rory's faces.

"All I'm saying is it's a very decent thing to do," Maurice persisted. "An *honourable* thing."

"As Michelle has been honourable," Laurent said. "We would not have met if she had not been honourable." He smiled across the table at Evelyn, then at Sarah.

"My great-grandfather chose not to return to this house," he continued. "He found happiness elsewhere and that happiness has been his legacy to us. My father and I hope very much that Michelle and Rory will find happiness here."

"I'll drink to that!" Maurice said, then looked in surprise at his empty glass.

"You'll drink to anything!" Helen said crossly. "Come on, Graham, before he makes a complete disgrace of himself!"

Poor Maurice, who rarely drank more than one or two pints and hardly ever drank wine at all, sat stunned and instantly sober as Helen left, dragging Graham in her wake.

Una, Michelle and Sarah sat looking at each other, mortified and furious.

"Evelyn, I'm terribly sorry –" Una began.

"But not, I suspect, as sorry as Helen will be!" Evelyn said, laughing lightly as she reached for the wine to pass it to Maurice.

Laurent reached quickly for the other bottles and replenished their glasses.

"The toast was 'happiness', I believe?" He was smiling as he raised his glass to Evelyn.

"Happiness," she replied, as all round the table glasses were raised and warm smiles lit up their faces in the soft glow of the candles.

Happiness.

Elusive, indefinable . . .

But just at that moment, theirs.

Chapter Forty-nine

"How do I look?" Maurice asked anxiously, examining himself in the bedroom mirror.

"I've seen you better," Una teased. "But don't worry, it's not you they'll be looking at."

"Una!" He whirled round, his face a mixture of hurt and alarm.

She smiled innocently at him. "On our own wedding day – gorgeous, you were." Leaning forward, she kissed him lightly on the lips. "And you're gorgeous now," she added, still smiling as she flicked imaginary dust from the shoulders of his dress suit. "No wonder your daughters are so beautiful, Maurice Keogh."

And they were. None more than Sarah today, of course, in the simple ivory sheath that Una had chosen with her – but Michelle and Helen both looked wonderful, and as for the children . . .

She hoped they'd behave. Joanne had spent the morning preening herself, and Oscar was capable of anything and they'd have to keep a close eye on him. Being a page-boy didn't come naturally to him.

But Katie looked adorable and Dylan, for once, was good as gold.

And no matter how they behaved she was going to enjoy every minute.

She turned to the mirror, adjusted her Mother-of-the-Bride hat and smiled at their reflections.

The day was going to be perfect. She just knew it.

* * *

"Michelle, remind me again – why wasn't Charles Lacey buried with his wife?"

Michelle was distracted, busy securing gypsophila in Katie's hair. "Because the cemetery was already full and – what?" She turned to look at Maurice. "Dad, *what* are you talking about?"

"My speech. I want to tell them all about how Sarah and Laurent met and –"

"And this is what you'll tell them," Una said crisply, coming up behind him and handing him a sheet of paper. "Say one word that's not on that page and I'll kill you in front of the lot of them!"

"That's what I like, a vote of confidence!" he began, but stopped at the sight of Sarah coming down the stairs.

She had never been lovelier, or looked happier.

He moved forward, offering his arm.

"Sixty-eight steps," he said, smiling at her.

"What?" she laughed.

"Sixty-eight steps from the porch of the church to the altar rails. I counted them again last night. We'll just take it slowly and we'll be fine."

"You managed it before!" Michelle laughed.

"Ah, but I was young then," he said, smiling.

"Cheeky!"

"And anyway, I never expected to be doing it again."

"Really?" Sarah raised an eyebrow, pretending annoyance.

"Really," he said softly as he took her hands. "And I'm delighted, because you couldn't get a better man anywhere than Laurent Feradot. Seeing that Rory's already spoken for," he added quickly.

Una raised her eyes to heaven. "I'm warning you. Not a word that's not on that page. Not a single word!"

* * *

The day had lived up to all their expectations. Maurice only strayed from his script once or twice, and with such great effect that Una was delighted with him.

And everyone agreed that Avignon had been the perfect venue for the reception.

The lovely old house seemed made for this, with the marquee in the garden, candles everywhere and music drifting out into the warm June night where the last of the guests were lingering beneath the huge, gleaming moon that hung low in the sky.

Sarah and Laurent were already gone, staying in a hotel overnight en route to France and a celebration with their friends from Maillerain and St Guillaume.

The band had finally packed away their instruments and the music filtering into the garden came from the drawing-room where Jules played evocative French melodies on the grand piano.

"You can't imagine what this means to me," Evelyn said brightly as Michelle sat down beside her. "Seeing the house so full of life again, knowing that Annie still has a home here . . . it's more, *much* more, than I would have dared to hope for, my dear."

"You don't miss living here?" Michelle asked softly.

Evelyn didn't hesitate. "Strangely, not at all. I know it's in excellent hands!"

"It's that, all right," Maurice said, joining them. "And she's given me a list as long as your arm of things she wants done before the baby . . . whoops!"

One look at his face and they both started laughing.

"Did I miss something?" Rory asked, sitting beside Michelle and taking her hand. "Let me guess!"

"For God's sake, don't tell Una I let it slip," Maurice said.

"Tell Una what?" They hadn't heard her approaching.

"Don't worry, Mam," Michelle said. "I decided I'd tell everyone anyway, after today."

"That's right," Maurice said enthusiastically. "Share the happiness. I've a feeling this will be a very happy home."

And he sneaked a look at the glowing moon to see if there was the tiniest hint of blue in it.

Because they were all agreeing with him.

The End